THE
PERFECT
HOSTS

THE PERFECT HOSTS

HEATHER GUDENKAUF

PARK
ROW
BOOKS

PARK
ROW ™
BOOKS™

Recycling programs
for this product may
not exist in your area.

ISBN-13: 978-0-7783-6004-9
ISBN-13: 978-0-7783-0566-8 (Hardcover)
ISBN-13: 978-0-7783-0597-2 (Canadian Exclusive)

The Perfect Hosts

Park Row Books
22 Adelaide St. West, 41st Floor
Toronto, Ontario M5H 4E3, Canada
ParkRowBooks.com

Printed in U.S.A.

In memory of my mother,
Patricia A. Schmida

THE
PERFECT
HOSTS

CHAPTER 1

MADELINE

MADELINE DRAKE LOOKS out her bedroom window, one hand resting on her belly, one hand shielding her eyes. The hard disk of sun sits like a crown atop what Wes calls their own personal stretch of the Tetons. In the long shadow of the mountain, beneath snowcapped peaks now blazing orange from the early evening sun, sits Lone Tree Ranch and their home. All fourteen thousand square feet of it designed from the ground up with its copper roof, charred cypress siding, and walls of windows.

Madeline knows it is presumptuous, calling the mountain and the three thousand acres at her feet theirs. She knows the mountain belongs only to itself, a stoic deity looking down at her with neither benevolence nor disdain, only indifference. The thought makes Madeline shiver despite the surprisingly warm May evening, and she cups the swell of her stomach protectively.

Below, the back lawn, as green and manicured as a golf course, ends abruptly and gives way to the horse paddocks and barns. A row of hay bales forms a barrier between the yard and a bald patch of earth where the horses chewed the alfalfa down to nubs. A hundred yards from the bales sits a champagne-colored '55 Dodge pickup truck with a black *X* painted on the side and stuffed with explosives. Because what gender reveal would be complete without a mushroom cloud of pink or blue smoke to announce whether their baby is going to be a boy or a girl?

And then there is the rodeo. A goddamn rodeo where guests can take part in events like saddle bronc riding, bull riding, barrel racing, and team roping by local talent. There's even a mechanical bull set up in a corner of the party barn. And to top it all off, Wes has somehow managed to get Reba McEntire to fly in to provide the entertainment.

This isn't only about learning the gender of their baby, it's an opportunity for her husband to network, to show off their horses, the property.

Madeline knows that everything Wes does is for her and now the baby. And while the land that comprises Lone Tree Ranch was left to Wes and his brother Dix by their father, they aren't free and clear. There are taxes and the mortgage on the house, and the cost of raising and training world-class horses and riders is exorbitant. In short, the Drakes have to work hard to keep what they have.

Beyond the truck are miles and miles of tall, windswept native grasses that creep up to the base of mountain. Leggy lodgepole pines look down upon the narrow trout stream that meanders through the property, where gray wolves lower their shaggy heads to drink.

Most of the horses are in a paddock well away from the impending cacophony. Still, Madeline worries for them as she does for the animals who will take part in the rodeo. Any loud noises can be traumatic, especially for the young, skittish colts and fillies on the ranch. But Wes thinks it won't be much different than the target skeet shooting he and the guys do. It will be better, he said. One loud boom and it will all be over.

"Hey, beautiful!" comes Wes's voice from below. Madeline pulls her eyes from the snow-tinged mountains to see her husband, head thrown back, holding a bouquet of ivory-colored balloons in one hand and a high-powered shotgun in the other. At his side is their big shaggy lug of a dog, a Great Pyrenees named Pip.

"Hey," Madeline calls back, feeling anything but beautiful. Not today, anyway. The fabric of her white sundress strains against her midsection. It's been expanding at an alarming rate over the past several days, and the cloth bites uncomfortably into her skin. But she knows her husband thinks she's beautiful, and that's enough.

"You coming down?" Wes asks, pulling his fawn Stetson from his head and pressing it to his chest. "The guests are arriving."

Wes is right. The steady parade of friends and neighbors is making their way into the yard, where a photographer is waiting to snap their pictures as if they are strutting down a red carpet. Everyone looks as if they stepped from the set of a glam '80s soap opera based in Wyoming dressed to match the baby's gender reveal party theme: Pearls or Pistols. The women who normally wear yoga pants and ponytails are dressed in Western-chic cocktail dresses and pearls while the men wear stiff jeans, cowboy boots, hats, and holsters at their hips. Madeline is certain that many of those holsters hold loaded guns. Wes's friends, rivals, business associates, area ranchers, horse brokers, and bankers certainly do like their guns. Madeline was ambivalent about the idea when the party planner, Alyssa, suggested it. Was it sexist? Definitely, but Alyssa was so convincing, and frankly, Madeline was tired of looking at swatches, menus, and balloons.

"I'm coming," Madeline assures him. "I have to put my shoes on."

"Well, hurry up," Wes says good-naturedly. "I have no idea what to do with these balloons."

Madeline watches as Wes moves toward the meadow and the truck, stopping periodically to greet guests, the balloons bouncing lazily above him, his million-dollar smile at the ready. Ten years earlier Madeline fell hard for that smile when her sister introduced her to Wes. She was twenty-five and still on the competitive equestrian circuit. Despite the age difference, they were engaged within three months and then married less than a year later.

One of the waitresses approaches Wes, and Madeline sees him stiffen. Even from this distance Madeline can see she's pretty with a heart-shaped face framed by short burgundy-dyed hair. She lays a hand on Wes's arm, and he lowers his head as if trying to hear what the young woman is saying. He frowns, shakes his head, and hands the bouquet of balloons to her before walking away. The young woman stands there for a moment, holding the balloons, a defeated expression on her face, then rushes back toward the catering tent.

Though Wes is known for being a tough businessman and even tougher boss, his curt dismissal of the young woman is unusual even for him. Madeline chalks it up to the chaos of the day. It's not every day that Reba is flown to the ranch for a private concert.

Madeline bends over, retrieving her handmade alligator boots from the floor, and sits down on the king-size bed. She looks down, barely able to see the tips of her toes, lifts one leg, and tries to slide her foot into the boot but is met with a hard stop by her swollen ankles. Tears prick at Madeline's eyes, and she lies back on the bed and considers skipping the spectacle about to take place on their land. The party to reveal the gender of their baby has been scheduled for months, the planning has finally come together, and now she is too tired to enjoy it.

Besides, she doesn't care if the baby is a boy or a girl. It doesn't matter one bit, just as long as the child is healthy, which Johanna, her midwife and best friend of nine years, insists is the case.

"Sweetie," comes a voice from the doorway. Madeline opens her eyes to find Johanna, dressed in a denim shirt and a long fringed suede skirt, standing over her. "Why are you hiding up here?"

"My boots don't fit," Madeline says tearfully. "I think the baby has migrated down to my ankles."

"Not in all my years of being a midwife have I attended an ankle birth," Johanna says, tossing her long black braid over her shoulder and sinking down on the bed next to Madeline.

"Well, that's something," Madeline says wearily, sliding over to make room for her.

"Everything is going to be okay," Johanna assures her. "There are going to be no ankle-birthed babies, I promise. And even if there are, it will be okay. In approximately six weeks, your baby will be here, safe and sound. I'm going to make sure of it. And then you can start riding those dreadful creatures again."

"Ha," Madeline says. "You know you love them. Otherwise, you wouldn't offer to ride Maize every time you come to check on me." The horses on Lone Tree are, for the most part, docile, but Maize is Johanna's favorite.

"I'm kidding. Now, come on," Johanna says, throwing her legs over the side of the bed and getting to her feet. She holds out her hand. "Trust me?"

"You know I do," Madeline says, grabbing Johanna's hand and pulling herself up to a sitting position.

"Wait," Johanna says, disappearing into Madeline's walk-in closet. "Wear these," she says, reemerging a few seconds later with a pair of white flip-flops. "Much more comfortable than cowboy boots." Johanna bends over and gently slides the sandals onto Madeline's feet.

"If you say so," Madeline says glumly.

"I do say so. You look beautiful. Now, come on, put on your pearls, and let's go meet your public."

"You mean Wes's public," Madeline clarifies, getting awkwardly to her feet. In fact, few of the people on the guest list are truly her friends or even Wes's. Ranching and raising world-class equestrian horses and training the riders is a cut-throat business, and Madeline has no illusions that any one of the people who are going to raise their glass to toast the upcoming birth of their baby wouldn't hesitate to stab them in the back if it's a good business decision. Madeline wiggles her toes. Johanna is right. The flip-flops are much better.

"True," Johanna concedes, "but you know they love you much more than Wes. You raise his likability factor by a thousand percent."

"Yeah, right!" Madeline smiles, slipping a triple strand of pearls over her neck. "Everyone loves Wes. But you feel free to tell him he owes it all to me."

"Oh, I do. Every chance I get," Johanna says as she threads her arm into Madeline's and guides her from the bedroom and to the landing that looks over the living room with its hand-scraped oak floors perfectly aligned with the concrete walls, earthy and austere at the same time. The space is softened by plush sofas and chairs in the shades of green found in the trees and flora seen through the expansive window walls. Outside, the Wyoming sky is periwinkle blue. It is the perfect evening for a party, though the forecast calls for a chance of rain.

"You know," Johanna begins in a conspiratorial voice, "I can tell you if you're having a boy or a girl. No one else has to know. It can be our little secret." As always Johanna seems to be able to read her mind. It would be nice to know before everyone else, to have a little piece of this day just for herself. But no, Wes wants to be surprised right along with their guests. Wants their friends and colleagues to share in one of the happiest days of their lives. Wes does love a grand gesture—the bigger the audience, the better.

"Well?" Johanna says, raising her eyebrows. "Do you want to know? It's almost time."

"No," Madeline says, shaking her head. "If you tell me, it will be written all over my face. Everyone will know."

"True," Johanna agrees, sliding her arm through Madeline's. "You're a terrible liar."

If only she knew, Madeline thinks.

Together they make their way down the steps, through the great room, and out the glass doors that lead to the terrace where they are greeted by the smoky scent of barbecue. The same waitress that Madeline saw talking to Wes earlier approaches, holding out a tray of steak tartare bites.

"No, thank you," Madeline says, now too nervous to eat. This was the night. The night they will learn if they are having a boy or a girl. Although Madeline doesn't care either way, she knows this one little tidbit of information will make it all the more real. The waitress turns to Johanna.

"Oh, no. I don't eat meat," Johanna says giving a little shudder.

The waitress lingers, and Madeline examines her face. She is beautiful, with large cat eyes that are a startling green against her pale skin. And she is young. Younger than Madeline initially thought. Twenty-one if she's a day.

"You look familiar," Madeline says. "Have we met before?"

"Probably at another event," the girl says. "I've worked for this caterer for about a year. Were you at the Whitneys' anniversary party in March?"

"Yes!" Madeline says, making the connection. "You were the bartender at that one." She is about to ask her what she was talking to Wes about earlier when the waitress turns to Johanna. "You're a doula, right?" she asks shyly.

"Actually, I'm a midwife," Johanna says.

"There's a difference?" the young woman asks. Madeline reads her nametag. Mellie. She then zones out as Johanna goes into detail about how midwives can provide medical care during pregnancy, birth, and after, while doulas stick to information and emotional and physical support.

The back lawn has taken on the festive air of a carnival. The ceiling of the clear-top tent is festooned with pampas grass, wildflowers, and Edison bulbs of various lengths. Dozens of linen-covered tables are set for the barbecue dinner that will be served later. *Picnic glam,* the party planner called it.

The evening would begin with games that Alyssa has insisted will be a hoot: Name That Baby Song, Guess That Celebrity Baby, Pacifier Hunt, and more. Madeline immediately nixed the How Big Is the Bump? game. There is no way in hell that she is letting people guess the circumference of her belly. Still, Madeline knows a ridiculous amount of money is at stake in the pool that includes the sex, length, weight, hair color, and God knows what else. Madeline also knows Alyssa has overplanned, that this crowd will spend most of their time drinking the expensive alcohol and gossiping about the person just out of earshot.

After the fun and games, there will be the dinner consisting of shaved fennel and celery salad, ribs, barbecue-spiced hot-smoked salmon, and grown-ups' s'mores made with cinnamon graham crackers, milk chocolate ganache, candied pecans, sweet coconut, and a topping of almond-scented toasted meringue. Madeline would have been happy with a plain old s'more, but Alyssa said the guests would swoon over these, so she agreed.

Just before dusk, the guests will gather behind the long row of hay bales to watch the big reveal. Waiters and waitresses will be standing by with flutes of champagne topped with either pink or blue cotton candy depending on whether the explosion shows they are having a boy or a girl. Madeline, of course, will have sparkling cider. Then comes the rodeo where some of Madeline's students will show off their equestrian skills, and young men and women new to the rodeo circuit will try and catch eyes in hopes of landing a sponsor. Then the guests will get their chance. Men and some of the women will drunkenly ride one of the more docile broncos while the crowd whoops and hollers. Finally, Reba will take the outdoor stage that was erected for the event.

"I may have a new client," Johanna says, pulling Madeline from her thoughts.

"She's pregnant?" Madeline asks, looking at the young woman with new eyes. "No way."

"Apparently she's four months along," Johanna says. "I'm going to meet with her later, get more info."

"We hate her, right?" Madeline says. "I swear when I was at four months, none of my clothes fit me anymore." A niggle of something tugs at her. Why was a young, pregnant waitress talking to her husband? How does she even know who he is?

"You're gorgeous," Johanna assures her. "Hey, do you see Dalton?" she asks.

Madeline searches the crowd for Johanna's husband in the sea of cowboy hats. "Not yet," she says. "Didn't you two drive over together?"

"No, separate. He's coming in from a job, and he's pissed at me again."

"Why?" Madeline asks, though she can guess why. Johanna and Dalton haven't been getting along for a while now, and though Johanna hasn't come right out and said it, Madeline is beginning to wonder if there is someone else in the picture.

"Who knows?" Johanna says, rolling her eyes. "It's always something. Hopefully I can avoid him for most of the night. I'm not going to let him ruin your party. Hold on," she says, pulling her phone from her pocket and glancing at the screen.

Just then, Alyssa comes bouncing up to them, clipboard in hand, a slightly harried expression on her face. "Madeline," she says, tucking a wayward strand of blond hair behind her ear. "I can't seem to find Wes. Any idea where he might be?"

"Oh, I'm not sure," Madeline says, scanning the yard. It's hard to tell who's who with the dozens of cowboy hats obscuring faces. "He has to be around here somewhere."

Alyssa bites her lip. "I really don't want to bother you with logistics. This is supposed to be your special night."

"Excuse me, but I have to take this," Johanna says abruptly, holding up her phone.

"Another mother-to-be?" Madeline asks.

"Always," Johanna said with a little sigh. "I'm sure it's nothing, only Braxton-Hicks. If I see Wes, I'll tell him to come find you."

Madeline nods, well familiar with the pesky false contractions that she, too, has been experiencing. As Johanna rushes off in search of a quiet spot for her phone call, Madeline turns back to Alyssa, who is intently studying the sky.

"Does it look like rain to you?" Alyssa asks. "The forecast now says we could get some rain right around sunset."

Madeline follows Alyssa's gaze. The sky is still cloudless and blue, though the sun is quickly losing its earlier ferocity. "It looks fine to me," Madeline says, her eyes trailing back to the waitress.

"I'll keep an eye on it," Alyssa says before scurrying away.

Madeline feels a sharp tug on her elbow, and she turns to find Dalton Monaghan. "Where's Johanna?" he asks, bluntly.

"She had a phone call," Madeline says, looking up at Johanna's husband. Sweat beads from beneath his cowboy hat and rolls down his temple. His shirt is damp with perspiration.

"With who?" Dalton demands, squeezing her arm more tightly.

"A client," Madeline says. He stares down, scanning her face as if trying to figure out if she's telling him the truth. "Dalton, you're hurting me," Madeline says, trying to extract herself from his grip.

He quickly releases his grasp. "I'm sorry," he says, not looking the least bit apologetic. "If you see her, tell her she needs to find me. It's important."

"I will," Madeline says, rubbing her elbow as Dalton disappears into the crowd. There is something much more going on with Johanna and her husband than her friend is letting on. The first chance she gets, Madeline is determined to get to the bottom of it.

She continues to make the rounds, greeting guests and pausing to watch a group whooping and hollering around a woman dressed in Levi's and a bandeau handkerchief top riding the mechanical bull Wes arranged for.

"I think we should move things up and do the reveal now," Alyssa says, coming toward her with a frown. "Then we can serve dinner. If it starts to rain, we can move the concert to the barn."

It seems like a lot of shuffling around to do, but nothing will dampen spirits like two hundred partygoers getting caught in a downpour. "Sounds okay to me," Madeline says. "I'll find Wes while you corral everyone over to the meadow." Before she can change her mind, Madeline asks, "Do you know who that waitress is?" She nods in Mellie's direction.

Alyssa peers through the crowd. "No idea. The caterer would know. Probably a college student trying to earn a few bucks. I'll meet you over by the hay bales in a few."

Madeline nods as Alyssa rushes away. The waitress had to have been talking to Wes about something to do with the catering arrangements. She is being silly. Overthinking things, like she usually does.

Butterflies swirl in Madeline's stomach. This is it—they are about to learn the gender of this little creature inside her. Will they have a little girl who has Madeline's love for horses? Or will it be a little boy who has Wes's dimpled cheeks and stubborn streak?

Madeline wades through the crowd in hopes of finding

her husband, but all she sees is a sea of cowboy hats and Gucci purses. A property developer who has been sniffing around their land reaches out a hand to touch her belly just as the photographer they hired snaps a picture. Madeline recoils, turns, and comes face-to-face with Mia and Sully Preston, their neighbors to the west. If the Drake family is a Wyoming institution, the Preston family is a downright dynasty. Sully Preston brokered horse sales for Madeline and Wes's ranch and equestrian business, but that didn't last long. Sully was more interested in making money than the health and safety of the horses and their riders. The dissolution of the partnership was swift but ugly. And now the Prestons have shown up, uninvited.

Mia, dressed in cowboy boots, a short denim skirt, and a bustier studded with pearls, places both hands upon Madeline's stomach. "You are absolutely glowing," Mia says, her long red nails garish against the white cotton of Madeline's dress. Beside her is Sully, wearing a black shirt with a flying eagle embroidered on each side of his chest. He's carrying a large package gift-wrapped in Tiffany blue and topped with a black satin bow. Madeline suddenly finds it hard to catch her breath. These people, thinking that they have the right to touch her. Where is Wes? And why hasn't Johanna come back? She would step between Madeline and anyone who dared to try to caress her stomach, and with her narrowed-eye stare the offender would back away.

"Look at all this," Mia says, her overly made-up eyes wide with mock admiration. "I have to say, you've really outdone yourselves. I mean, a rodeo? Reba? You two are the perfect hosts, now, aren't you?"

The Prestons have made their lives miserable for the better part of a year, and Madeline wants to tell Mia to take her husband and leave but is aware of all the eyes on them eager to see what will happen next.

"Why are you here?" Madeline whispers, stepping back, away from Mia's touch, but making sure to keep a smile on her face.

"We wanted to congratulate you," Sully says, pressing the gift into her hands. "A little peace offering. Where's Wes? I'd like a word."

"This isn't the time or place," Madeline says, trying to keep her voice low. "Please leave."

"Come on, now," Mia says, pulling her face into a pout. "We're just trying to mend fences, Madeline. Let's not get ugly."

Madeline pulls her phone from her pocket and begins typing an SOS message to Wes. Over the buzz of the crowd, she hears her brother-in-law's booming laugh. Three years older than Wes, Dix Drake is a hulking bull of a man with a quick sense of humor and two ex-wives who are still a little in love with him. Madeline gets it: he's fun and laid-back. The life of the party. But Dix always seems to disappear when it's time to go to work and goes through money hand over fist. They argue over everything from the kind of hay to feed the horses to how much they should sell a prized gelding for, but before their father died he insisted that the family business stay in the family. Wes and Dix Drake may have an even more complicated relationship than Madeline and her sister, who she hasn't spoken to since their father's funeral.

"Why don't you go talk to Dix?" Madeline says. "I'm sure he'd love to catch up with you both." She hands the wrapped package to Mia. "He'll know what to do with this." Madeline turns her back to the Prestons and begins to say hello to other party guests with what must sound like false cheerfulness. Out of the corner of her eye she watches as the Prestons approach Dix. With a tight smile, he leans in and whispers something in Sully's ear. The two stare at one another, faces stony, until Dix claps Sully on the back and turns away.

Package in hand, the Prestons move toward the gift table but are stopped by Johanna, who greets them with her hands on her hips. Johanna knows the history Madeline and Wes have with Sully and Mia. They appear to exchange a few words before Sully hands the package to Johanna and moves toward a waiter carrying a tray of champagne. From across the yard, Johanna catches Madeline watching, and Madeline smiles and waves, but Johanna only lifts her hand half-heartedly and then rushes away, gift in hand.

Madeline spends the next fifteen minutes making small talk with a former congresswoman and her husband until she finally sees Wes coming toward her, rifle in hand. Alyssa must have found him and told him about the forecast. He holds up the rifle. "It's showtime."

"Wes, the Prestons are here," Madeline says, as he grabs her by the hand and leads her toward the hay bales.

"Ignore them," Wes says. "Don't let them ruin our night." Madeline wants to tell him that they already have, but he's right—this is their day, their special moment.

The crowd that has formed behind the row of bales parts, and two hundred pairs of eyes stare back at them, smiles wide, eyes bright. A man wearing Johnny Cash–black and a Stetson pulls a handgun from its holster, lifts it in the air, and shouts, "Pistol!" Madeline, for a second believing that the man is going to fire the weapon, nearly stumbles. Wes steadies her, and a woman wearing a turquoise jumpsuit cries out, "Pearls!" A dueling chant follows.

"Pearls, pearls, pearls!" the women shout.

"Pistols, pistols, pistols!" the men counter.

I don't care! Madeline wants to cry out. Why does it matter? And why did they invite these people, strangers really, to their home?

From the crowd, Alyssa reappears, clipboard in one hand and a wireless microphone in the other. She hands the microphone to Wes, but Dix steps in and grabs it from his fingers. Wes gives a little laugh, shakes his head in resignation, and gives a sweep of his arm, as if inviting Dix to speak.

Dix waits until the chants quiet before speaking. "Welcome, everyone!" he begins. "Thank you for joining us in this momentous event. I know that Wes and Madeline are so happy that you're here with them tonight to find out who's going to be taking over their lives in a few short weeks!" His comments are met with knowing laughter. "Rain may be heading our way, so there's been a change in plans."

Madeline glances over at Wes, expecting to see him simmering with irritation. Instead, he is smiling broadly and laughing along with the crowd.

Someone from the back of the group lets out a big whoop and shouts, "Pistols forever!"

Dix hands the microphone to Wes who in turn holds it out to Madeline. Madeline shakes her head. The last thing she wants to do is speak in front of a large group—and where is Johanna? It doesn't feel right to find out the sex of the baby without her.

Again, Wes pushes the mic toward her, forcing it into Madeline's hands, and gives her an encouraging smile. A challenge. Reluctantly, she takes the microphone and scrambles for something—anything—to say. Finally, she speaks. "Thank you, everyone, for being here and for joining us on this very special day. And whether we have a boy or a girl or anything in between, we'll be happy." Madeline hands the microphone to Wes and takes a little step backward to let him know that she is done. When she was competing in dressage, Madeline didn't mind all the eyes on her. She knew that spectators were really watching the horse, and that Madeline was just an accessory, an extension of the beautiful beast she was riding.

"All right, then!" Wes says, "Are you ready for the big boom?" It's followed by a cry of "Yes!" and another round of chants. *Pistols . . . Pearls . . . Pistols . . . Pearls . . . Pistols . . . Pearls . . .*

"Okay," Wes says, "simmer down and make sure everyone stays behind the hay bales and plug your ears if you don't like loud noises."

Madeline takes a step back, but Wes reaches for her hand. "Where are you going? Let's do the honors together." He holds out the high-powered rifle toward her.

Does she want to be the one to send a bullet flying eighteen hundred miles per hour toward a vintage truck holding an explosive device filled with blue or pink powder? No, she does not. Madeline doesn't like the feel of guns, doesn't like the heft of them in her hands or the cold metal against her fingers. She doesn't like the idea of how its simple mechanism can send a tiny piece of metal through the air with such force that it can shatter bone, pierce a spinal cord, or eviscerate organs.

"You do it," Madeline says, pushing the rifle back toward him. "I'm fine watching."

Wes sets the rifle on the top the stack of hay bales, bends his knees, and presses his eye against the rifle's sight. Then he straightens and snakes an arm around Madeline's waist. "Everyone is watching, Madeline," he says through clenched teeth. "Just do it." Reluctantly, Madeline nods, and Wes slides behind her so that his chest rests against her back. He settles his chin onto her shoulder and gently bends her over the bales in a way that feels slightly erotic. The partygoers must think so too, because there comes a cascade of knowing laughs and whistles.

Wes repositions the rifle so that both their fingers rest upon the trigger. Madeline feels his warm breath on her neck, smells his cologne. She doesn't like the idea of a firearm so close to the baby. Madeline thinks she can feel its tiny heart slamming into its birdcage chest in fear. Or maybe that's her own heartbeat. "Ready?" Wes asks.

"I was hoping to wait for Johanna," Madeline says, trying to stand up straight, but Wes's weight keeps her pinned in place.

"Come on, Madeline," Wes says, impatiently. "This isn't about Johanna. It's about us and our baby. Let's go, already."

Off to the side, someone starts a countdown. "Ten, nine, eight, seven." The rest of the guests join in. Madeline closes one eye, and the black painted X on the truck comes into crisp focus. "Six, five . . ."

"Here we go," Wes says, smiling against her cheek. He increases the pressure atop the finger that is crooked around the trigger. "No going back now."

Madeline feels a surge of excitement shoot through her. This is it. "Two, one!" the crowd shouts. Wes presses his finger sharply against hers, and Madeline feels the bullet rip smoothly through the chamber. The kickback is immediate, and the butt of the rifle slams into the soft skin just below her collarbone. The truck explodes into a fiery ball, and she hears a chorus of *oohs* and *aahs* and excited laughter. Madeline looks to the sky, eager to see the plume of blue or pink smoke, but from behind her comes another eardrum-crushing boom that ricochets against her skull.

Madeline is lifted from her feet. The reassuring nearness of Wes's body disappears, and the rifle flies from her fingers. For one panicked second, Madeline imagines the gun discharging a rogue bullet into the unsuspecting crowd or, worse, into her womb. A blast of heat envelops her, and Madeline can feel the fabric of her dress curdle against her skin. She closes her eyes, and for a moment she remains suspended in air. The world around her falls silent: she feels no pain, no sensations of any sort. It's a pleasant, floaty feeling, reminding Madeline of when she and her sister were young, lying together in a big black inner tube, legs intertwined, floating languidly down Prairie Creek.

Then Madeline hits the ground hard, her breath lodging in her chest like thick sludge, blocking any air from reaching or leaving her lungs. Her eyes pop open. Around her people are screaming, stumbling, clutching at one another's arms, clambering to get away. Cowboy hats and wineglasses litter the ground. Where is Wes? Johanna? Unable get up, Madeline looks into the sky. Black clouds hang heavily in the air. Has the storm arrived? No, it isn't that.

Pain floods her limbs, her back, her head. Madeline's hands fly to her midsection. The baby. Is the baby okay? She tries to cry out, but a charred, burnt taste clings to the back of her throat. Snowflakes float lazily down. But that doesn't make sense. It doesn't snow at this elevation this late in May. Besides, Madeline thinks, giving way to the irresistible urge to close her eyes, snowflakes aren't pink.

CHAPTER 2

MADELINE

"MADELINE," COMES WES'S voice, tinny and faraway-sounding. "Are you okay?"

She is lying flat on her back, the air still hazy with smoke. Is she? Is she okay? The ringing in her ears is fading, and she can hear again. In the distance she can hear sirens. Help is coming. Madeline does a mental scan of her body. Nothing seems broken, but her head is pounding. She touches her hairline, expecting her fingers to come back with blood, but instead they find an egg-sized lump. She tries to remember exactly what happened. Wes pulled the trigger, and the truck exploded. An explosion, that's what it was. Something had gone wrong with the reveal. The baby. Oh God, is the baby okay? She presses her palms against her belly.

"Madeline, Madeline," comes Wes's voice again, this time more insistent. His frantic face comes into view.

"Shhh," Madeline orders. "Please be quiet." She needs to lie completely still, has to concentrate so she can feel the baby move. She. The baby is a girl, Madeline thinks, remembering the wisps of pink smoke she saw among the fiery black cloud. Her little girl will kick her in the bladder, one of her favorite moves, any second now. There is nothing. No cartwheels or wiggles. Nothing.

Wes kneels beside her and slips his hand into hers. "Help is coming. Stay put. Don't move."

Madeline nods as hot tears roll down her cheeks. "What happened?"

"It must have been the truck," Wes says. "It must have triggered a bigger explosion."

"But how?" Madeline asks. "You said it was safe . . . Is anyone hurt?"

"It was. It was supposed to be." He shakes his head, bewildered. "I don't know what happened."

Madeline struggles into a sitting position and looks around. Charred lumber litters the lawn. The canopy over the dining tables has collapsed and is covered in dancing flames that a handful of guests and waitstaff are trying to smother with whatever is handy: cowboy hats, table linens, an old horse blanket. Other guests are gathered in small, tight clusters, holding on to one another. Some sit in the grass crying, others stand slack-faced, as if in shock. Through the smoke a rodeo clown appears, his brightly colored clothing now blackened with soot and his makeup running down his sweaty face. The clown is helping the photographer, who is bleeding from the head. But it is the old storage barn that Madeline finds herself fixated on. Huge flames shoot from the hayloft window and the roof. Someone pulls a hose from one of the horse barns, and suddenly buckets and containers of all sizes appear. Others, including Johanna's husband, Dalton, are running toward the burning barn and tossing water onto the structure. They know that one wayward spark could ignite the house or, worse, the barns filled with her beloved horses.

"Can you walk?" Wes asks. "We have to get you away from here."

Madeline nods, and Wes helps her to her feet. She is barefoot. The blast had lifted her in the air and knocked her flip-flops clear off her feet. Madeline, leaning against Wes, winces with each step, the rough ground pricking at the soles of her feet. He leads her to the meadow, a safe distance from the burning barn, but still close enough for her to see what's happening. Some of Madeline's earlier numbness is beginning to wear away, and the enormity of what has happened begins to descend.

"Go," Madeline says, knowing they need as many hands as possible.

Wes shakes his head. "No," he says. "I'm not leaving you."

"I'm fine," she says, but is she? She fell hard, and still the baby hasn't moved.

Madeline scans the crowd. "Where's Johanna?" she asks. "Have you seen her?"

"I haven't," Wes says. "But I'm sure she's around here somewhere. Have you seen Dix?"

"No," Madeline says. The last she saw Dix was just before he handed the microphone to Wes. "Go," Madeline repeats. "Really, I'm fine. I just have to get my bearings," she assures him when he turns his gaze to her doubtfully. "Go help, find your brother. And check on the horses."

"You wait here," Wes says. "Don't move from this spot, and I'll come back and find you." He squeezes her hand and kisses her cheek before darting away and disappearing into a cloud of black smoke.

Madeline continues to eye the property for any sign of Johanna's long dark braid, her suede skirt. In the distance the wail of sirens grows closer. Help is coming. The meadow to the left of the house was being used as a makeshift parking lot for the guests' vehicles. One wayward spark from the fire landing on the stubbled field could set off a chain reaction where upward of a hundred cars and trucks, tanks filled with gasoline and diesel, sit idly.

The air is filled with inky smoke blotting out the face of the mountain and the setting sun. A fire truck pulls through the side yard, crushing Madeline's lavender and Russian sage, its massive tires carving deep ruts in the soil. Madeline barely notices—it's what she sees as a group of guests part to let the truck through that causes her breath to lodge in her throat. A woman lies on the ground, her arm thrown over her face, while someone presses a blood-soaked cloth to her abdomen. One by one, Madeline registers the carnage. Someone is doing CPR on Gary Wilson, the president of the bank that holds their mortgage. One of her equestrian students is wandering aimlessly through the smoke, tears running down her face. A fifteen-hundred-pound bull has escaped the rodeo paddock and is trotting toward the mountains. She sees Mellie, the young waitress, running and screaming, fire dancing up the front of her legs. A partygoer tackles her, smothering the flames with his body.

This is bad. So very bad. Madeline fights the urge to vomit. She wants to help. But how? Water, Madeline thinks. She can pass out bottles of water, try and keep the guests calm and reassure them that help is here, that everything is going to be okay. On unsteady feet she moves toward the party barn, where she knows there is plenty of bottled water, but someone grabs her arm. Mia. "Have you seen Sully?" she asks tearfully, her arm hanging at an odd angle. "I can't find him."

Madeline shakes her head. "I'll help look for him," she promises. "You're hurt. Sit down."

Mia shakes her head. "I need Sully," she says thickly and stumbles away. There are too many injured and not enough emergency personnel.

The fire truck has come to an abrupt stop. Two firefighters are urging those guests who jumped in to try to put out the fire to move away from the blaze. With machinelike efficiency, they unroll the hoses.

Madeline is mesmerized by the flames that roll across the roof of the barn, the dense cloud of smoke, the roar of lumber being eaten by the flames. She moves closer, unnoticed by the firefighters, her face growing pink from the heat. Madeline vaguely becomes aware of more sirens and shouts of "Over here" and "Please help!" More help has arrived. The spray of water hisses and snarls as it strikes flames and wood. The barn turns into a living thing then, twisting and groaning until it collapses in on itself, turning to a big heap of charred lumber with sooty farm equipment peeking out here and there.

"Ma'am, ma'am," comes a voice. "Stay put. We're going to take care of you." Madeline pulls her eyes from the barn. A woman wearing a collared shirt in robin's-egg blue with the words *Woodson County EMT* stitched above her heart is standing next to her, forehead furrowed with concern.

"There was a girl," Madeline says, "over there. She was on fire. Did someone help her yet?"

"Yes, ma'am," the EMT says. "But you're the one I'm worried about. You're bleeding."

Madeline looks down. Her white dress is smudged with soot and something pink. Madeline smiles with relief as realization flows through her. "Oh, that's not blood. It's pink powder. I guess that means I'm having a girl."

"Congratulations," the EMT says waving a hand frantically in the air. Suddenly, three more blue shirts are around her, and arms are guiding her to a stretcher that seems to have materialized out of nowhere.

Madeline strains to see around them to watch the firefighters who are now moving cautiously forward with their pickaxes, tentatively poking at the barn carcass.

"Ma'am, you're bleeding," the woman says, this time speaking with more urgency. "We need to get you and your baby to the nearest hospital," the EMT says more insistently.

"I have a midwife," Madeline says, finally registering an uncomfortable wetness below her waist, a rising panic flooding her chest. She tentatively touches the soaked fabric of her dress, and her fingers return covered with blood. "Can you find her? She's here somewhere, but I don't know where she is."

Her baby. Is she in labor? It's too soon, Madeline thinks. She still has six weeks to go. She allows the EMTs to ease her down on to the stretcher, arranging her on her left side. Using his stethoscope, one of the EMTs presses the cold disk to her abdomen, while another runs her hand up and down Madeline's arms and legs in search of—what?—broken bones?

"You've got some old bruises here," an EMT says. "Have you had a fall lately?"

Madeline shakes her head. "I have horses," she explains. "They get restless when they see me."

"You've got a nasty cut on your back. Are you in any pain?" she asks.

Was she? Madeline scans her body, searching for any discomfort. She only feels numb. "No," Madeline says. "Please, where's my husband?"

"We have to go," the EMT with the stethoscope says. Madeline examines his face for clues. It's unreadable.

"Go where?" Madeline asks with alarm. "Where are we going?"

"To Jackson. They have the nearest trauma center," he says. "But don't you worry about a thing. We'll take good care of you and your baby."

Jackson? Trauma center? This can't be happening.

"Hey!" one of the firefighters shouts, raising one hand in the air. "I got something here. We gotta back up."

Madeline flinches, as if expecting another explosion, but nothing happens. The EMTs begin to roll the gurney over the bumpy ground. A spasm of pain roils through her abdomen and lower back. She lets out a guttural cry of surprise. The EMTs pick up their pace and move more quickly toward the waiting ambulance.

In contrast, there is no more urgency in the firefighters' movements. They simply lift their axes to their shoulders and step from the wreckage, moving to just beyond the burnt edges of the grass surrounding what's left of the barn. Their heads are lowered as if in prayer.

Where is Wes? Johanna? Understanding begins to buzz through Madeline. Have they found someone? A body? She has to find out what the firefighters are looking at. "Stop!" Madeline screams, and the EMTs come to an abrupt halt. Before they can start moving again, Madeline slides from the gurney, her bare feet striking hard ground. She limps over to the wall of first responders and elbows her way past them.

"Hey," a firefighter says, snagging her by the elbow, but she shakes him off and takes another step forward. Lying on the ground in front of her are the charred, blistered remains of something that at one time must have been human. Madeline's eyes travel the length of the blackened body to a swath of singed dark hair. Bile, thick and bitter, gathers in her throat, but she sidesteps a pile of debris to get a better look. She has to see who it is.

"Ma'am," another rescue worker says, "we have to get you medical attention."

She ignores him and continues forward. "Johanna?" she says in a small voice, but she knows that it is. Johanna's eyes are wide open and unseeing, her face remarkably untouched by the fire. How can that be? "Is she dead?" Madeline asks, unable to pull her eyes away from Johanna's face. No one answers her, but she already knows the answer. A scream begins to bubble up her throat, but another current of pain shoots through her back, and she doubles over in pain. She is guided back onto the stretcher and whisked toward the ambulance, then lifted smoothly into the back.

"Hold up," someone calls out. "Have room for one more?" Another EMT pokes his head inside. "We've got one with burns and shock. I already gave her Demerol."

"Load 'em up," the first responder says as she shifts Madeline's gurney to make more room.

A caustic odor fills the space. A mix of kerosene and burnt flesh. Madeline fights back the urge to gag as another stretcher slides in beside her. It's Mellie, the waitress. She is writhing in pain, the carefully placed straps on the gurney the only thing keeping her in place.

Up close, the burns on Mellie's leg are a horrific mess of melted polyester and angry red blisters. "It hurts!" Mellie cries. "Please, make it stop!"

"We've got you," the EMT says soothingly.

One of Mellie's arms flails, striking her in the cheek. Poor girl, Madeline thinks, she must be terrified and in unimaginable pain. "It's going to be okay," Madeline says as she reaches for Mellie's hand. Her fingers are cold and trembling. "Here, squeeze my hand," Madeline urges. "The pain medication should kick in soon, and you'll start feeling better." Madeline has no idea if this is true, but this potential lie seems like the kindest thing to say. To the EMT, Madeline says, "Please hurry. She's pregnant too."

Mellie turns her head, making eye contact with Madeline for the first time. Her gaze is cloudy, unfocused. "It's going to be okay," Madeline says again. "Just breathe."

Mellie nods, closes her eyes, takes a deep breath, and exhales but is overtaken by the pain and lets out another cry.

"Go!" the EMT shouts to the driver, and the ambulance begins to move and the siren wails.

"Mom!" Mellie cries. "Oh, please. I want my mom." Her grip on Madeline's hand tightens.

"They'll call her," Madeline assures her. "We'll get to the hospital, and someone will call her for you."

Mellie shakes her head, finds Madeline's eyes again. They are filled with despair. "They can't." Mellie licks her dry lips.

"Your mom died?" Madeline asks, and the girl nods.

"When I was little," she says.

Something they have in common. They are both motherless, Madeline having lost hers when she was sixteen. She knows this kind of hurt.

Another contraction roils through Madeline and she grimaces, but her pain is nothing compared to the girl next to her, so she stifles her cry. Something she's perfected over the years. "Look at me," Madeline manages to say once the contraction passes. "Your name is Mellie, right?" The young woman nods, her frightened eyes pinned on Madeline. "It's going to be okay. You're going to be fine," Madeline says, knowing that she has no business making these kinds of promises. Johanna is dead. Her best friend is dead.

CHAPTER 3

LUCY

LUCY QUAID SILENCES her phone, tosses it on the seat next to her, and turns on the radio. Her ex has been trying to call her for the past four days, most likely wanting to know what happened to his truck and trailer. It's a happy accident that his handgun is tucked behind a wad of convenience store napkins in the glove box. To be fair, Lucy did leave him a note. *Borrowed your truck. There's something I have to take care of. Call you later.* Obviously, he wants further explanation.

A '70s rock station plays on the radio, the only one she can find that doesn't hum with static. The sun is dipping behind the mountains, tossing a kaleidoscope of orange and pink and blue into the sky. She hangs a sharp right, and the truck and horse trailer rocks down a pitted gravel road. Then she presses down on the accelerator. The rear tires fishtail on the loose stones, but Lucy cajoles the truck to go faster. The road disappears in a cloud of gray dust, making it impossible for her to see the path in front of her.

She's been driving aimlessly for hours trying to figure out her next steps and is hungry and tired and, if she is being honest, lonely. Time to find something to eat and drink, and if she's lucky maybe a handsome stranger. Lucy floors it, and the steering wheel rattles beneath her fingers. An ominous groaning noise comes from the engine, and the rusty frame shakes beneath her ass. She dares to take her hand off the wheel and cranks the radio as loud as it can go, filling the cab with an old song by The Kinks, a band her father loved. Something Lucy always thought was funny for a straight-arrow, no-nonsense tough guy. Go figure.

Ahead, Lucy spots a flash of yellow through the swirling dust and she lifts her foot from the accelerator and stomps on the brakes, but the truck's bald tires can't gain purchase on the road. It careens from one side of the road to the other, dipping into a ditch and then bouncing out, coming to a teeth-rattling stop. She squeezes her eyes shut and prepares for a collision, but nothing comes.

"Jesus," Lucy says, trying to catch her breath, her heart thumping in time to the music. She snaps off the radio and peers through the windshield. The dust starts to settle and an eerie quiet falls. There is nothing. No other cars, no homes, just the mountains and a wide expanse of shadowed field tucked behind barbed wire and the evening sky.

What had she seen? Clearly not another vehicle. An animal? Or maybe nothing at all. Then she sees it crouched among the overgrown grasses, its golden eyes, its shape clearly feline. A mountain lion. She gasps in surprise. Nearly laughs. When her pulse steadies, she cautiously makes a three-point turn and rolls slowly forward, the gravel crunching like popcorn beneath the tires. She finds her way back to the highway and heads west. She'll get a drink, and then she's going to finish some unsettled business.

Twenty minutes later, Lucy pulls into a small parking lot with weeds poking up through the cracked concrete. Rick's Tavern is a squat brick building that was once a filling station. Nobody bothered to remove the pumps and the price per gallon is frozen at thirty cents. Lucy parks in the half-filled lot, steps from the truck, and moves toward the bar, pushing through the door, momentarily blinded by the dim interior. Patsy Cline is on the jukebox.

Next to the jukebox, a woman hunched over a half-empty glass of whiskey snaps her head up and gives Lucy a searing look. Lucy ignores her and settles onto a stool at the bar.

The place is a dive, but Lucy likes the vibe. The low lights, the overly salted popcorn, the hoppy scent of cheap beer. She has even come to appreciate the herd of stuffed jackalopes mounted on the walls. She orders a shot from the sleepy-eyed bartender and downs it, the amber liquid burning her throat. She signals for a second round. The song ends and then begins again. "Really?" Lucy asks loudly. "This song again?" She throws back the shot—this one goes down much easier—and she waits for the limb-loosening effects she's come to appreciate. When it comes, Lucy switches to beer. Again, Patsy starts singing about being crazy. "For Christ's sake," Lucy calls out. "Someone take the quarters away from her."

"You know if you keep giving Maggie a hard time, you're going to get thrown out of here," a man says, sidling up next to her.

Lucy lifts the frosty mug the bartender slides across the bar and takes a drink before answering. She has to play it cool. She's been waiting patiently for him to approach her, and here he finally is. "I like Patsy as much as the next person, but I don't know, maybe Taylor would be a good change of pace."

The man laughs. "I didn't peg you for a Swiftie," he says, looking her up and down. Lucy may be wearing her old Levi's and a black tank top, her hair pulled back in a haphazard ponytail, but she knows she still looks pretty good.

"I'm still in my *Red* phase," she answers lightly. "2021 *Red,* not 2012."

"Obviously," the man says, signaling the bartender and pointing at Lucy's beer, indicating that he wants two more.

He is handsome. Tall and broad-shouldered with flinty gray eyes and a cowboy's swagger. Probably a little too young for her, Lucy guesses.

"I'm Trent," he says, sitting down beside her. She considers responding with a fake name but thinks better of it. It will be easier if she keeps to the truth as much as possible.

"Lucy," she says, raising her mug. "Nice to meet you, Trent."

Three beers later, Lucy and Trent are still at the bar, a basket of fried Rocky Mountain oysters between them. "I've seen you around," Trent says.

"Oh yeah?" Lucy says, taking a swing from her bottle of Peroni. Pricey for sure, but she wasn't buying. "And you're only saying something now?"

"I'm shy," Trent answers.

Normally, if a guy said this, Lucy would think he was bullshitting her, but Trent's ears are actually turning red. She finds it quite endearing and is tempted to reach out and touch the tip to see if his skin is hot. Instead, she signals the bartender for another round. The jukebox has mercifully stopped playing Patsy Cline, and the TV above the bar shows the ten o'clock news. A Breaking News chyron scrolls across the bottom of the screen.

"Boring!" Lucy calls out, not wanting Trent to become distracted by anything but her. "Isn't there a game on or something?"

The bartender sighs and reaches for the remote. He clicks through the channels until he finds a Minnesota Timberwolves–Utah Jazz game. "Much better," Lucy says.

"Aw, Jesus, I've got to work in the morning," Trent says, rubbing his eyes. "I'm going to be worthless."

"You don't look worthless," Lucy says, pushing his beer bottle toward him. Trent smiles and takes a drink. "You can always call in sick," she says after he sets the glass down.

"Nah, I'm lucky I got tonight off," he says.

But the thing is, the alcohol doesn't seem to be affecting Trent in the least. He's clear-eyed, not a slurred word to be heard. Well, shit, Lucy thinks. The man can hold his liquor.

"Maybe we should get out of here," Trent whispers in her ear.

"Oh yeah?" Lucy asks, arching an eyebrow. "Where do you want to go?"

"I don't live too far from here," Trent says. His enunciation still maddeningly precise. Damn, she has never met anyone who could hold his liquor quite like this.

He slides one hand up and down her arm, his calloused fingers rasping roughly against her skin. He is handsome, Lucy thinks.

Trent's grasp on Lucy's arm tightens, and beneath the bar his other hand slips between her legs. "Trent," she says, removing his hand from her crotch with what she hopes is a lighthearted laugh. "Buy a girl a drink first?"

"Been there, done that," he says, standing and spinning her barstool toward him. He nudges her legs apart and steps into the opening. Lucy glances around. The bartender has abandoned his spot behind the bar. She can see him through the windowpane, sucking on a cigarette out front. It is fully dark now, the parking lot illuminated only by the neon sign flashing *ick's*. Even Patsy Cline has given up her spot next to the jukebox and stumbled home. One other patron sits in a corner booth with his head tipped back and eyes closed. "Come on," he says and leans in, brushes his lips against her neck. "Let's go."

She's beginning to have second thoughts. She can hear her late stepmom's voice in her head warning her not to be so impulsive. Fair, she thinks. She hasn't always made the best decisions when it comes to men. Outside, the bartender is still smoking and staring at his phone. It's time to bug out now. Trent whispers a few fantastically dirty words in her ear, and Lucy feels she's going to end up having sex with this stranger. Be smart, she tells herself. Stay focused on the endgame.

She presses both hands against Trent's denim shirt and pushes. "That last beer went right through me," she says as he shuffles backward a few steps. "I'll be right back."

"Hey," Trent says, his eyes narrowing, frustration creeping into his voice. She gets up from the barstool and walks nonchalantly toward the bathroom.

She doesn't know this guy, and she's pretty much in the middle of nowhere with unreliable cell service. What if Trent doesn't take no for an answer? She came to Wyoming for a reason and has to keep her wits about her. She pushes through the door and into the musty-smelling, grimy bathroom, well aware that by stepping into this small, confined space, she is making it all the easier for Trent to come inside and corner her. Four block windows the size of tissue boxes sit a few feet above the hand dryer. There is no way Lucy can fit through one of the windows, let alone break through the glass.

She pauses to splash cold water on her face, knowing that she is going to have to go back to the bar and tell Trent thanks for the drinks, but she has no intention of sleeping with him. When she walks out of the bathroom, the bartender has once again taken his place behind the counter, and Trent is nowhere to be seen.

Seeing the surprise on her face, he hitches his thumb toward the door and says, "He left."

Huh, Lucy thinks, weirdly offended. She wants to be the one to slip out the door, to be the ditcher rather than the ditchee. She moves to the door and peers through the glass. The dark lot is now empty except for two vehicles, Lucy's truck and what must be the bartender's four-door parked in the far corner of the lot. She sees no sign of Trent or his vehicle.

"See you," Lucy calls over her shoulder and steps out into the night. There are no stars or moon, and the air has cooled like only May nights do. Lucy climbs into her truck and sits for a moment trying to decide her next move. Find a motel in Nightjar—what a stupid name for a town—or head toward her final destination? A motel sounds like the smart idea. She'll be sober and clearheaded by morning.

She starts the truck, cranks the radio, and pulls onto the road heading toward town. Lucy drives for about a mile when she feels the truck pull right, nearly sending her into a ditch. She swings the wheel to the left but can feel an unmistakable vibration coming from the undercarriage. She flips off the radio, and The Eagles are replaced with a rhythmic thumping. Fuck. She slows the truck and pulls off to the side of the deserted road. Pissed, Lucy leaps out and, using the light from her phone, stomps to the rear of the truck to assess the damage.

A flat tire. "Fuck," she says, her voice too loud in the quiet night. What to do? Lucy wonders. Lock herself in her truck, try to catch a few hours of sleep, and change the tire in the morning? Or wrestle the spare from beneath the truck's carriage in the pitch dark and do it now?

In the distance a set of headlights appear, pinning her into place with their brightness. "Oh shit," Lucy murmurs. It's never good to be alone on a deserted highway in the middle of the night, and her pocketknife suddenly seems entirely inadequate. The gun seems like overkill. Her only other weapon, the lug wrench, is snug in its spot beneath the front seat. She might not be able to reach it in time.

As the approaching vehicle slows and comes to a stop behind her, Lucy presses her phone to her ear, pretends to talk. Laughable, because Lucy no longer has anyone to call. She's burned all those bridges.

And lo and behold, it's Trent who steps from the truck.

"Looks like you've got a flat," Trent states the obvious.

"Mm-hmm," Lucy says, pointing to her phone, letting Trent know she is talking. "Yeah, I'm out on County Road 12." He crosses his arms, leans against her trailer. "I got this," she says. "You can head out." She keeps her voice calm, even. She doesn't want to give him the satisfaction of knowing that he's scaring her.

"I don't mind waiting," Trent says and smirks. "I'd hate for you to be out here all alone."

"Probably a nail or something," Lucy says into the phone giving Trent a dismissive wave. "Thanks, sweetie. See you in five."

Trent's hand shoots out and snags the phone from Lucy's grasp. "Actually, sweetie, you don't worry one bit," he says into the phone. "I'll take good care of Lucy. Hello? Hello?" His eyebrows rise in mock concern. "I think we lost the connection."

"Give me my phone," Lucy says, reaching into the truck for the lug wrench, her fingers snagging on the cool metal.

"Sure," Trent says. "But why don't you tell me what the hell you're up to first."

"I don't know what you're talking about," Lucy says. He is ballsy. Or a psychopath. Lucy is betting on the latter.

"The bar," Trent says. "You coming on to me? What were you planning on doing? Get me drunk and then rob me? I felt the knife in your pocket."

He takes a step toward her.

"Back the fuck up," Lucy says, raising the tire iron. She doesn't know what she'll do if he calls her bluff. Trent is bigger and stronger than she is and turning out to be as clever.

Another vehicle comes into view, its high beams spotlighting them both.

"Jesus," Trent breathes. "It's the sheriff. Put that thing away."

Lucy doesn't go as far as to put the wrench back in the truck but lowers it to her side.

The lightbar mounted to the top of the approaching SUV flashes as it pulls in behind them. It's quite the little caravan they've got going here.

The man inside the SUV kills the engine and steps from the vehicle. "Trent," he says, with a nod. He looks Lucy up and down. "You okay here?" he asks. He wears a brown sheriff's department uniform and a grave expression on his acne-pocked face.

The entire truth is out of the question, so Lucy decides to go with the abridged version. "Flat tire. He's giving me a hand." A small uptick of Trent's mouth lets Lucy know he thinks he's won this round.

The sheriff sweeps his flashlight across her truck, examines her mud-splattered license plate. "License and registration, please."

Lucy's stomach flips. She can only hope that her ex hasn't filed a police report about his stolen items.

"They're in my glove box," she says. "Can I grab them?" The sheriff gives a stiff nod, and he follows her as she walks back to her truck and climbs inside. She considers making a run for it but decides it will be useless. She leans across the seat, opens the glove box, pretends to riffle through the contents.

"Huh," Lucy says, sitting upright. "I can't seem to find them. It's a mess in there, and it's so dark."

Trent paces impatiently at the side of the road. "You know who I am," he grouses. "Can't I be on my way?" The sheriff shoots him a look that shuts him up.

"Keep looking," the sheriff says.

It's no use—she has to give him the paperwork. If she plays it cool, maybe everything will be okay. Lucy grabs the registration, slides from the truck, and pulls her driver's license from her back pocket.

"The truck is under my husband's name," she explains. Trent gives her a look that says *You're married?* Lucy ignores it.

The sheriff clicks on his flashlight, examines the paperwork, gives Lucy a quizzical look. She doesn't speak. The less she says, the better.

She waits for the sheriff to take her license back to his car. If he does, Lucy is done for, but he simply hands the card back. It can't be this easy, she thinks.

"You work yesterday?" the sheriff asks, turning to Trent.

"Me?" Trent is taken off guard. "Yeah, until about four. I put in about sixty hours this week, and they let me off. Why?"

"I'm guessing you haven't heard what happened earlier," the sheriff says, leveling his gaze on Trent.

Lucy's heart starts to thump. Confusion or maybe fear skitters across Trent's face. "No. What happened?" he asks cautiously.

"You definitely weren't there last night?" the sheriff asks.

"Dad," Trent says with exasperation, "what's going on?"

Dad? Lucy repeats to herself. *Dad?* The sheriff is this big lout's father?

The sheriff stares a long while at his son before speaking. "The Drakes went and blew themselves up with that damn gender reveal thing. Lots of injuries, at least one dead."

Lucy holds completely still. Her limbs have gone numb.

"Who died?" Trent asks, panic rising in his voice. "Who was it?"

The sheriff glances over at Lucy as if not wanting to say more. "Take care of this nice lady's tire and then you better head over there." Of course he can't tell them who died. Not in front of her anyway.

Lucy has to say something. Now. They would find out soon enough who she is, why she is a thousand miles away from where she is supposed to be. She has to say the right things, act the right way. "Did you say the Drakes?" Lucy manages to ask.

"That's right," the sheriff says, looking at Lucy with new interest. "You know them?"

"Yes," Lucy says, her voice shakes on the word. "Madeline Drake is my sister. Is she dead?"

CHAPTER 4

JAMIE

SUPERVISORY SPECIAL AGENT Jamie Saldano is hiding in the kitchen long after the microwave popcorn has popped and he's dumped it into a bowl. Funny, he thinks, in the past seventeen years, he's faced violent criminals, arms dealers, arsonists, and domestic terrorists, but the thought of being in the same room as his wife right now causes him to break into a cold sweat. Tess hadn't wanted to make the move from DC, has never lived in a city with a population less than a million, and now they are in Nowheresville, Wyoming, and it is all Jamie's fault.

The supervisory special agent opportunity with the Bureau of Alcohol, Tobacco, Firearms and Explosives, also known as the ATF, came just when the boutique business-strategy consulting firm that Tess worked for closed its doors. To her credit, Tess has tried to be happy in Cheyenne, but two months in, Tess is bored and lonely and no closer to finding a comparable position. Her friends and family—all miles away. Why Wyoming? she asked, tearfully. He had a bachelor degree in criminology from the University of Maryland, five years with DC Metro, twelve years as an ATF agent working on everything from gun trafficking to arson to the criminal use of firearms and explosives. Of all the places he could have transferred, why here?

It was a fair question. Jamie didn't have fond memories of

the state he lived in for six torturous months as a kid, but it was also the state he had the biggest connection to.

Last week, Jamie made the mistake of telling her that maybe she should find a hobby. It came out wrong, and Tess has barely spoken to him since then.

Somehow the chill has started to thaw, and they are in the midst of watching an old movie, but still their conversation is forced, stilted. Jamie hates this but truly doesn't know how to make it better. Blessedly his cell rings, and one glance at the screen tells him it's important. The special agent in charge, or SAC, doesn't call after eight o'clock on a Friday night on a whim.

"Saldano, we've got a possible bombing over in Woodson County," SAC Linton Sykes says brusquely. Sykes is responsible for ATF operations throughout Wyoming and three other states. The hair at Jamie's neck bristles at the mention of Woodson County. "At least one dead and multiple injuries at a gathering involving a high-profile family," Sykes continues. "We need a certified explosive specialist out there now."

"Yes, sir," Jamie says. "Right away."

"Good," Sykes says. "I'll send you the information. And keep me posted. The press is going to be all over this."

Jamie disconnects and looks up to find Tess standing in the doorway. Her dark hair is piled atop her head in a messy bun, and she's wearing a pair of plaid flannel pajama bottoms and one of Jamie's old ATF T-shirts. "You have to go?" she asks, and Jamie can't tell if he hears disappointment or accusation in her voice. She looks small and vulnerable. So unlike what he's used to. He doesn't like it.

"Yeah," he says. "Explosion west of here. Linton wants someone out there right away."

"Greta can't go?" Tess asks. Greta Martin is the intelligence research specialist in the Cheyenne office and has befriended Tess, though they have little in common. "I thought being the boss meant that you could delegate."

"Normally that's the case, but this time my boss is the one doing the delegating," Jamie says. This wasn't technically true. Linton hadn't expressly requested him, but Jamie was the most experienced CES in the Cheyenne office.

Tess nods in understanding. They've been married long enough for Tess to be used to Jamie having to leave at a moment's notice. "Want me to help pack your bag?" she asks.

"Nah," Jamie says. "I've got it. You watch the movie. Thanks, though." He brushes past her on the way to the closet in the extra bedroom where Jamie keeps his suitcase. Their modest, tidy house seems huge in comparison to their tiny one-bedroom apartment in DC. He's itching to get to his car and to read the email from Linton but is almost afraid to find out. Tess watches in silence as he changes his clothes, packs quickly, and retrieves his sidearm from the safe.

"I'm sorry," Jamie says once his suitcase is stowed in the trunk of his ATF-issued vehicle.

"I know," Tess says, but her voice is flat. He bends down to kiss her, but he can feel her tense beneath his touch. He's losing her, and he doesn't know how to stop it from happening. That's not quite right. He knows he needs to get Tess back to DC, back to a career she loved and to the people she loved, and he will eventually. But for now he has a job to do.

He lifts his bicycle onto the rack on the rear of his vehicle. He takes it with him whenever he travels for work. As a kid he logged hundreds of miles on his skateboard, but in college he swapped it out for a secondhand ten-speed. Jamie backs out of the garage and waves to Tess as he clears the driveway, but she's already turned away.

Once on the road, he checks his phone for the email from Linton. It's brief but gives him the basics. An explosion. One dead, at least two critical, and dozens of others with injuries. But it's the town where he's headed that causes him to nearly swerve off the road.

Nightjar.

Nightjar, Wyoming, population 1200. He hasn't stepped foot in the town—if you can call it that—in twenty-seven years. But isn't this why he took the job in Wyoming? Because he knew that one day he would be called back to the town that tore apart his family? To the town that took his sister.

Driving across Wyoming at night is a lonely trek. On moonless, starless, and misty nights such as this, and on certain stretches of highway, the mountains retreat into the blackness, and the earth and sky become one. With only his headlights to lead the way, Jamie feels as if he could drive off the end of the world. To pass the time, he listens to a podcast and takes swigs of Mountain Dew, cracks sunflower seeds between his teeth, and presses his foot down on the accelerator. The drive would normally take five hours, but he'll make it in four.

His headlights bring a sign into focus, and Jamie pulls over. *Welcome to Nightjar.* Nearly three decades earlier, when Jamie's mother first told them they were moving from San Antonio to some godforsaken town named Nightjar, a town name that brought to mind a mason jar filled with swirling black air, Jamie and Juneau both balked vehemently. Their mother was insistent, though. They had to go where the jobs were, and the opportunity to be the night manager and head of housekeeping at a motel in the mountains was too good to pass up. Especially when it came with free lodging.

Later, Jamie would learn that the nightjar is a rangy, speckled bird the size of a crow, and after a few months in the town, he became inured to the harried calls of the bird when the sun began to settle behind the mountains. He also learned that people used to believe that nightjars were the souls of unbaptized children fated to fly the night sky. After his sister disappeared, Jamie would search for her along dusty gravel roads and in weedy ditches, and the nightjars would follow along with him in graceful loops, their hollow knocklike calls chasing Jamie's own. *Juneau, Juneau, Juneau.*

Jamie gets back in his car and drives for about ten minutes when he passes an abandoned filling station. The Sip and Fuel. Jamie makes a wide U-turn, his tires squealing on the asphalt, pulls into the gas station, and gets out. It's shut down now, the gas pumps removed, and a large For Lease sign hangs from the eaves. Suddenly his mind goes back to that awful night.

He and Juneau had pooled their money to buy a half-gallon of milk, a box of cereal, and a bag of chips at the Sip and Fuel before heading back to the motel room where they were living with their mom. They had driven about half a mile when Juneau said something about wishing they had gone to the high school football game that night. Jamie remembered being surprised by this. He thought Juneau felt the way he did—that their new school was stupid, football was stupid, and they were biding their time here until they could go back home to San Antonio.

"I thought you already screwed your way through the football team," Jamie said, jokingly. "Who's left, the water boy?"

Juneau slammed on the brakes of the Lynx station wagon, and they came to a skidding stop in the middle of the gravel road. "What the hell?" Jamie said, the seat belt catching and punching the air from his chest.

"You are an ass," Juneau said. "Get out."

"Yeah, right," Jamie said. "Just drive."

"No, I mean it," Juneau said. "Get out of the car. You can walk home."

"I was kidding," Jamie said and laughed.

"You don't joke about those kinds of things, Jamie," Juneau said angrily. "It's hard enough being new without having your brother starting rumors about you."

"I didn't!" Jamie protested, but Juneau was having none of it.

"Get out!" she yelled, grabbing the black knit cap from his head and throwing it out the open window.

"Hey," Jamie cried, scuttling from the car to retrieve it, and watched as Juneau drove away, the taillights getting smaller and smaller until the car took a left onto the gravel road that led to home. Jamie never saw his sister again.

Get in your car and go, Juneau's voice whispers. *Don't think about it anymore. It wasn't your fault. It was never your fault. Get back in your car, and call your wife.*

Now Jamie trudges to his car and opens the driver's-side door. But instead of getting in, he reaches inside and grabs his jacket. A dusty pickup truck roars by and hangs a right onto the gravel road. In it are two teens, music blaring from the open windows. Jamie starts walking, following the fading taillights, slips on his jacket, and zips it up to his chin. It gets cold in the mountains at night.

He trudges along the gravel road, a cold mountain breeze pushing at his back. Nights in Wyoming are different than anywhere else. The sky is bigger, the air is cleaner, and the dark swallows you whole. It's muscle memory that pulls Jamie forward. As a kid he walked this route dozens of times. He liked the remoteness, liked turning up his secondhand iPod full blast while listening to Pearl Jam and Alice in Chains. He knew what the other kids in Nightjar thought of him, of Juneau, of his mother. They were just another loser family, down on their luck, looking for whatever work could be thrown their way. Most of his classmates were from families who were landowners or land developers or business owners. Sure, there were some kids whose parents catered to the wealthy ranchers, but they weren't interested in Jamie. Why would they invest any time getting to know someone who probably wouldn't last the winter?

Night sounds in the mountains are different too. The wind, the animals, the echoes all have an unearthly quality. Jamie peers intently into the dark, glancing left and right into the ditches that line the road. After walking for about twenty minutes he begins to think he may have made a mistake. He should be coming upon a bow in the road, a sharp turn that will take him toward Nightjar and the motel they once called home. It's also the spot where his sister disappeared. No, he tells himself. He's not mistaken. As wild as it sounds, the ground beneath his feet feels familiar.

He continues forward, the road curves again, gently at first and then sharply. Jamie stops and pulls his phone from his pocket, turns on the Flashlight function, and sweeps the light in a wide arc in front of him. Small animals, with blinking, glowing eyes, scurry into the brush. Off to the left is a forest of ponderosa pine hidden in the shadows, but he can smell the woodsy resin. This is the spot. He's sure of it. This is where the glare of the car's headlights blinded him. At first, Jamie thought Juneau had come back to pick him up. The night was cold, much colder than tonight, and even in her anger she wouldn't leave him outside in late-September temperatures that tended to tumble quickly.

Juneau hadn't driven toward him. She simply sat in the car, engine idling, high beams like lasers blinding him. Okay, Jamie thought at the time, she's still going to make him pay, make him come to her and beg to be let back into the car. What he had said to his sister had been mean, cruel, but he hated how Juneau was trying so hard to fit in here after they promised each other they wouldn't bother.

But something had shifted after only eight weeks in Nightjar. School started, and the snide comments they volleyed back and forth about their classmates, the disdain and the disgust, became one-sided. Juneau started coming home later and later in the evening, smelling of beer and weed. She seemed more secretive. Juneau was seeing someone—Jamie was sure of it. When he asked her about it, Juneau laughed and told him not to be stupid—she was doing school stuff, and it wouldn't hurt him one bit to try to get involved too. Maybe join the cross-country team or Future Farmers of America. At that, Jamie had told her to fuck off. Juneau would once again learn it did no good to try to make friends and fit in, because in a matter of months their mother would up and move them somewhere new anyway.

Blinded by the headlights, Jamie walked toward the car. He'd apologize. Juneau would let him in the car, they would go back home, make microwave popcorn, and drink sodas from the machine they'd figured out how to jimmy. Everything would be okay.

When he was about thirty yards away from the car, he heard the engine rev and then watched as it backed up a few yards before coming to a stop. He took a few more steps and raised his arm against the glare of the headlights as the car reversed again. So, Juneau was going to play *this* game with him. "Come on, I'm sorry," he called out. The car's engine gunned again, and Jamie shook his head. Fine, he thought. He would walk home. He was cold and tired and hungry. Let Juneau be mad. She'd get over it eventually.

He continued on, but this time, instead of the car moving in reverse, it gunned forward, tires spinning on the gravel. "Very funny," Jamie called out, but his words were drowned out by the scream of the engine. The car barreled toward him, and Jamie stood there frozen in disbelief. What was Juneau doing? The roar of the engine grew louder, and Jamie turned and started to run. His tennis shoes slipped on the slick gravel, and he nearly fell before righting himself. This wasn't funny anymore. He veered to the side of the road and, if he had to, would jump into the ditch, which he knew was filled with cheatgrass and thistle and probably poison oak, but all that was better than getting crushed.

Jamie dared a look over his shoulder. The car was getting

closer, and that was when he noticed the figure sitting behind the wheel. Juneau was small. She looked like a little old lady hunched over the steering wheel when she drove. This person was tall, big, and broad-shouldered. The person driving could not be his sister.

Jamie closed his eyes and began his leap when the car's bumper struck his right hip. A flash of pain exploded through his body, and he could feel himself taking flight. It felt as if he was airborne for minutes, though it could have only been a second or two. It was like riding the Super Shot at the fair when you are flung into the atmosphere, and you leave your stomach behind for a moment, and you feel sick and excited and terrified all at the same time.

He landed hard in the ditch and was swallowed up the weeds. The pain in his hip was unbearable, making it impossible to exhale or inhale, his breath lodged in his chest hard and heavy. Somehow, he was drowning in a dry ditch. Was this what it was like to die? Jamie wondered. If I close my eyes, he thought, I won't wake up. Panic spasmed through his body as he tried to sit up, but his body wasn't working.

Finally, his throat opened, allowing a thin thread of air into his lungs. He breathed it in greedily in long raspy breaths. Someone had tried to run him over. Someone had tried to kill him. Where was Juneau? She would never have handed over the keys to someone else, at least not willingly.

He tried to hold still, tried to quiet the jagged wheezing of his breath, hoping that the dark and long grass kept him well hidden. Seconds passed, then minutes. The air was still, the crickets and kissing bugs had grown quiet. Even the nightjars had stopped churring. The driver couldn't have been his sister, but maybe she was with a friend, a boyfriend. Maybe they were playing a stupid game of chicken, thinking they were being funny, and had accidently hit him. But Juneau wouldn't leave him all alone in the dark, hurt, would she? As annoying as he was, she never stayed angry at him for long.

The pain in Jamie's hip had dulled to a throbbing ache. If he could just sit up, maybe he could scoot his way out of the ditch, then use a fence post to pull himself to a standing position and wait for help. He knew this was wishful thinking. The gravel road was only used by locals, and that was typically during the day. He could be here all night, but surely his mother would get worried and come looking for him. Jamie took a deep breath and eased himself onto his elbows, wincing in pain with each shift in position. From his vantage, he still couldn't see the road, only the lattice of the dried grasses in front of him.

The sound of rustling grass came from somewhere behind him. An animal, maybe, curious about what had landed in its backyard. But then the sound took on a rhythmic quality. A soft *crunch, crunch,* then silence. *Crunch, crunch,* pause. Footsteps. Someone was wading their way through the ditch toward him.

"Juneau?" Jamie called out hopefully, his voice trembling. No response. "Juneau!" he said more loudly. Whoever was coming his way was not his sister. She would have answered him, and the steps were too heavy. *Crunch, crunch, crunch, crunch,* pause.

Fear sent a surge of adrenaline through him, and Jamie was able to flip over onto his stomach. The pain a white-hot poker stab to his hip, it didn't stop him from army-crawling away from the noise. He inched forward, his right leg dragging heavily behind. Though the night was cool, sweat slid down his face, stinging his eyes. Or were those tears? Jamie didn't know. His arms trembled with exertion, his skin tearing where it snagged on rough stems and brambles. He was getting nowhere and didn't have the strength to keep trying anyway. *Crunch, crunch, crunch, crunch, crunch, crunch,* pause. Then nothing. Only his heavy breathing, intermingled with someone else's.

Jamie didn't want to look up. He didn't want to see who

had done this to him, to see what was going to happen next, but he couldn't help himself. The shadow that loomed over him was preternaturally large with broad shoulders that rose and fell with each breath. A wet, musty odor rolled off the dark figure. Jamie wanted to say something, tell him he didn't have to hurt him, that Jamie wouldn't tell anyone, that he could keep a secret. He didn't get the chance. The shape raised one tree trunk of a leg and swung it back as if preparing to kick a soccer ball or a football.

At the last second, Jamie ducked his head in hopes that his attacker would miss, would lose his footing, giving him a chance to get away. The impact was dead-on, though, striking Jamie in the cheek. Jamie used his arms to cover his head, but the blows kept coming, unrelenting in finding flesh and bone until the pain had no beginning, no end, and that was all that remained. His throat filled with a thick coppery liquid, and Jamie thought he would choke on his own blood.

Hours later, he woke to a gentle shake of his shoulder and a voice. "Oh my God. Hey, buddy, hey," it said. "You okay?" It was a young man, his voice scared and uncertain. Jamie tried to open his eyes, but the sky was too bright, and sleep kept dragging him back into blissful unconsciousness. Every inch of his body hurt, but the electric pain in his mouth was the worst. He used his tongue to feel around and found the jagged edges of his broken right molars.

The sound of an approaching car filled Jamie with a panic, and he cried out. The cool morning air sent shock waves of pain into the space where his teeth used to be. The driver was coming back. He was going to finish what he'd started.

"Weston," a far-off voice said, a woman this time. "Good game last night. You'll get them next time." And then there was a change in her tone. "Everything okay here?"

"I don't know. It looks like he's hurt really bad," the young man said.

Jamie heard the same crunch of dry grass beneath feet that he'd heard the night before.

"Jesus, Mary, and Joseph," the woman said. "He's just a baby," she said. "Is he still alive?"

"I think so," the youth said. "But he's really hurt."

I am, Jamie wanted to say. *I am alive.* He wanted them to call for help, call the police, find his sister.

A shadow moved in front of the sun, and Jamie felt warm fingers press against the inside of his wrist. "He's got a good, strong pulse," the woman said. "I'm going to drive to the gas station up the road and call the police and for an ambulance. You okay to stay here with him, Weston?" she asked.

Jamie ran the name through his mind. *Weston.* The only one with anything close to that name was Wes Drake, an older kid. A senior whose family owned most of the land in the county.

"Yes, ma'am," Wes said. But he didn't sound okay. He sounded scared.

Maybe I could still die, Jamie thought. Tears filled his eyes, then spilled down his cheeks, the salty liquid setting the deep cuts in his face afire.

"Oh man," Wes said. "Don't cry, it's going to be okay. Mrs. O'Brien is going to get help. She's a teacher at the high school. I think your sister has her for English. That's her car down the road, right?"

How did Wes Drake know Juneau? No one knew them, especially the rich kids who lived in Woodson County their entire lives. Jamie thought of the car barreling toward him, then the hulking figure standing over him before a large foot stomped down on his face. Where was Juneau? What had happened to her? Icy panic flooded his chest, and Jamie tried to sit up, but the pain kept him pinned in place. "Juneau," he tried to say, but it came out as a garbled "Uno."

"Hold still, hold still," Wes urged, but Jamie couldn't. If

someone had tried to kill him, then what had happened to Juneau? Did that mean she was dead or lying in a ditch bleeding too?

"Uno, Uno," he cried out again. Fuck, Jamie thought, he sounded like he'd just won a kid's stupid card game.

"J. J., stop!" Wes ordered. "Hold still. You're going to make it worse."

Jamie knew this was true, could feel the pain migrating throughout his body, but couldn't stop screaming his sister's name. Wes pressed his hands against Jamie's shoulders, trying to keep him flat, and Jamie felt the other boy's fingers momentarily disappear into the shredded flesh below his collarbone, then touch bone. Wes withdrew his fingers as if electrocuted, and then they were both screaming. It wasn't until later, after Jamie was out of the hospital and emerging from the painkiller fog that he'd been in for weeks that he remembered Wes Drake calling him by name. Jamie was surprised and, if he was being honest, a little bit pleased to know that big-shot football star, Wes Drake, knew who he was.

Now Jamie kicks at the hard-packed dirt at the edge of the road. Over twenty-five years have passed. Why has he come back here? Jamie wonders. To stare at the spot where he nearly died and his sister disappeared? Seasons have come and gone, and the wind, rain, and snow have pounded this earth but revealed nothing. In all these years there have been no reliable sightings of Juneau. Not a scrap of clothing, not the silver ring she wore on her right thumb, no collection of bones or teeth.

Go home, Jamie, Juneau's voice scrapes across his skin. And this time, he's going to listen to his sister. Once he wraps up this case, he's leaving Nightjar and going home to his wife.

Jamie pulls back onto the road, and the navigation system directs him along a winding road that eventually straightens. Fifteen minutes later two pinpricks of light appear. As he comes closer, he sees that they originate from the headlights of a cruiser. The deputy inside is sipping coffee, making sure no one disturbs the scene. Jamie parks and steps from his car. The air is still heavy with the scent of smoke and wet wood. The barn is nothing but a sodden pile of lumber. Jamie hopes there is still some evidence beneath the rubble, but that will have to wait until sunrise. He likes to step into the debris field, amid the wreckage, and get an up close and personal perspective of the scene. He calls out to the deputy, who also steps from his car with his hand on his sidearm.

"Supervisory Special Agent Jamie Saldano," Jamie says, lifting his badge from the loop around his neck. He squints against the glare of the flashlight that the deputy centers on his face.

"Bill Ladd. I'm a Woodson County deputy," the officer says, lowering the light so that Jamie can get a better look at who he's talking to. Deputy Ladd is a short, powerfully built man, a few years older than Jamie. "The sheriff said you'd be showing up. Not much to see right now. Too dark, but you're welcome to walk the scene. We did put a tent over the explosion site as soon as the firefighters gave the all clear."

"It'll wait until the morning," Jamie says, agreeing that it's much too dark to get any kind of sense of the scene. "What're your initial thoughts? Accident? Arson?"

"I doubt it's arson," Ladd says. "I'm guessing the planned explosion went south. The fire marshal will be here after sunrise."

Are the homeowners available?" he asks.

"No, they're both at the hospital," Ladd says.

"And their names?" Jamie asks.

"Wes and Madeline Drake," Ladd says, wiping mist from his face. "They own this ranch, along with Wes's brother, Dix, though he doesn't have much to do with the day-to-day workings."

Jamie's heart starts pounding as anxiety winds itself around his throat. This would be the time to call SAC Sykes and tell him he needs to recuse himself from the case, but something stops him. He hasn't done any actual investigating yet. He doesn't even know what they are dealing with. "How many dead?" he manages to ask.

"Right now, one, but there are plenty of injured. I think there were no less than a dozen ambulances from area hospitals that showed up. If you want to talk to the Drakes, your best bet is to drive to the hospital in Jackson."

"I'll be back at first light, but call me if something comes up," Jamie says, handing Ladd his business card.

THE DRIVE FROM Lone Tree Ranch to the hospital takes him about thirty minutes. He tries not to think too hard as he travels down the winding country roads and long highways until lazily spinning wind turbines, ghostly giants, give way to more prehistoric landforms. Jamie knew he would find himself back in Nightjar again one day. Maybe he'd even wanted to be back here. Why else would he have taken this job? Why else would he have dragged his wife all the way here?

Jamie parks his car in the hospital lot. It's one thirty in the morning, but the sooner he can talk to any witnesses, the better. Jamie pulls his lanky frame from the SUV and stretches, his muscles tight from the long drive from home. He walks through the brightly lit parking lot to the hospital emergency entrance. Inside, the waiting area is nearly empty now, except for a few miserable-looking people, and he's welcomed by a weary woman sitting behind a desk with a plastic barrier. Jamie shows her his badge, and she guides him into the inner workings of the ER. The smell of latex gloves and antiseptic is strong.

A tall man, dressed in cowboy boots and a Western shirt, his face smudged with soot, is looming over a petite nurse who is not in the least intimidated. The two are shouting at each other, and a deputy is trying to wrench her way in between the man and the nurse, but neither is budging.

Jamie fights the urge to intervene. Over the years he's found it much more effective, when entering the fray of a new case, to linger on the periphery, to watch, to examine the dynamics before flashing his ATF credentials. Better to be seen as a resource rather than an interloper.

"If you'll come with me, Mr. Monaghan," the deputy urges. "We can go speak somewhere privately."

"I'm not going anywhere with you," the man shouts. "I want to see my wife. Now!" He glares at the nurse who calmly explains that there is no way she's letting him search the examination rooms for his wife.

A very pregnant woman wearing a hospital gown steps from an exam room. Eyes wide, she takes in the scene in front of her.

"Dalton," she says. No one appears to be listening, and the shouting continues. Jamie is ready to step in when the pregnant woman speaks again. "Dalton, I'm so, so sorry," she says, loudly. "She's gone."

Dalton turns to her. "What do you mean?" he asks, his voice filled with fear.

"Johanna's gone. She died," the woman says, tears streaming down her cheeks. "I'm so sorry."

"Died?" the man repeats, his eyes narrowing with confusion. "Johanna?"

"I'm so sorry," the pregnant woman says, rushing to the man and pulling him into an embrace. "I'm so sorry. I don't know what I'm going to do without her."

The man's face goes slack, and his hands hang limply at his sides. "Dalton, I'm so sorry. I don't understand what happened," the woman says. "I really don't."

"She's dead?" the man asks, looking to the deputy, who nods.

"I'm afraid so," the deputy says. "Sir, please, come with me, and I can tell you more." All the earlier bluster has leached from the man, and he allows himself to be led away.

The nurse gives the pregnant woman, who is openly crying now, a hard stare before returning to her spot behind the nurses' station.

The ER begins to hum again with beeps and alarms, nurses bustle through the hallways, and a maintenance worker pushes a large dust mop across the tiled floor. The pregnant woman looks helplessly around the hallway, then retreats into the room and shuts the door. Jamie approaches the counter, and the nurse looks at him expectantly.

"I'm Jamie Saldano with ATF. I'm here about the incident at Lone Tree Ranch, and when the deputy here is done with the gentleman she's talking to, I'll need to speak with her."

"Badge," the nurse orders, and Jamie lifts it from where it's hanging around neck. "All right," the nurse says. "But it could be a while. She's notifying the husband about his wife. What a mess. The things people do for attention. This is the most ridiculous thing I've heard of in a long time. I hope they get arrested for this nonsense. Are you sure you don't want to go back with the deputy?"

"No, I'll give them their privacy for now," Jamie says. "Do you have a name of the victim?"

"Not officially," the nurse says. "She was brought into the morgue DOA with no ID. He—" she points toward the room where the deputy took the distraught man "—is looking for his wife, Johanna Monaghan. I imagine the husband will go down and make a formal identification soon. Who knows? Maybe it isn't her."

Jamie hopes she's right. "How many other victims were brought into the ER tonight?" he asks.

"We had about thirty," the nurse explains. "That's about all we could handle. Some were sent to the hospital in Cody.

A few went other places. Most were minor injuries except for a heart attack and a young woman who came in with some burns. She's getting checked out right now. I don't see her being much help to you at the moment." She points to the exam room that Jamie saw the pregnant woman go into. "I suggest you start with her."

"Thanks." He glances at her name badge. "I appreciate your help, Kendra."

"Oh, and give her these," Kendra says, plopping a set of pink hospital scrubs atop the counter. "The sooner she gets out of here, the better."

Jamie scoops up the scrubs. The nurse is right. It is ridiculous. He had a similar case recently where an expecting couple accidently started a fire that destroyed over twenty thousand acres and killed a firefighter. All for what? To find out the kind of equipment their kid was coming into the world with.

Jamie raps gently on the closed door, and when he hears a soft voice inviting him in, he opens it and steps inside. On first glance, the room looks unoccupied, the narrow hospital bed empty except for a tangle of bed linens. "I'm here," the woman says.

Jamie peers around the door. The woman is sitting in a chair, her belly resting heavily on her lap. Her face is streaked with soot and tears, and she smells of smoke. She is staring down at her fingers, also dirty, and he can't help but notice the huge diamond on her left ring finger. She notices him noticing and covers it with her other hand. Wealthy, thinks Jamie, but not entirely comfortable with it.

"Jamie Saldano, ATF," he says, looking around the room for a place to sit. He lowers himself to the only other seat in the room, a round, squat stool on wheels. "And you are?"

"Madeline Drake, and I've already told that deputy everything I know," she says, helplessly. "Can you help me find my husband? His name is Weston. Wes Drake."

Jamie feels a little dizzy. Drakes are a dime a dozen in the area, Jamie knows. At least that's how it was when he lived here. Aunts, uncles, cousins, cousins' cousins. The Drake family owns a big slab of Wyoming. His fingers find their way to the jagged scar behind his left ear.

"Can you help me find my husband?" the woman repeats, pulling Jamie from his thoughts.

He blinks, looks down at his hands where the pink scrubs are now balled up tightly in his fist. "I'll see what I can find out," Jamie says, trying to smooth out the wrinkles before passing them to Madeline. "That really sweet nurse behind the desk asked me to give these to you."

When Madeline raises her eyebrows at him as if to say *Really?* Jamie can't help the tiny uptick of a smile that creeps onto his face, and he watches Madeline visibly relax. This is what he knows he's good at—making witnesses, victims, and suspects feel more at ease, more willing to open up to him. Jamie thinks of it as one of his greatest strengths. Tess, on the other hand, thinks it's duplicitous, manipulative. "Don't do that thing you do," she'd say when they went out with her colleagues. He tried to argue with her, explain that he was simply trying to let others know he was interested in what they have to say, learn about who they are. "Well, don't. It feels like you're interrogating them."

The hospital room door suddenly flies open, striking the arm of Madeline's chair with a loud thud. The figure of a man fills the doorway. His clothes are rumpled and soot-stained and smell of smoke. His eyes are wild, searching. They land on Jamie and then narrow as if trying to place a familiar face. Jamie immediately recognizes him. He could never forget Weston Drake, though Jamie hasn't seen him since he was twelve years old. Apparently, Jamie hasn't had the same effect on Wes, because that moment of recognition dissipates like a popped bubble.

"I'm looking for my wife. The nurse said she'd be in here," Wes croaks. His words come out harshly, as if it is painful to utter them. Which they probably are, Jamie thinks. This is the effect that smoke inhalation has on the throat, the voice box.

"I'm here," Madeline says, struggling to get to her feet. Wes whirls around and, upon seeing his wife, envelops her in a tight embrace. Madeline cries out in pain, and he steps back, still grasping her hands.

"I'm sorry, I'm sorry," Wes says over and over. "Where are you hurt?"

Jamie's heart is pounding so hard that he can barely hear their words above the thumping in his ears. He pretends to check his phone but watches as they embrace, more gently this time, and Madeline says that the doctors have had her on a fetal heart monitor for the past six hours. And assures her husband that the baby is fine, that she is fine. Wes insists that he is fine too. Everyone is fine. Except, Jamie thinks, he himself is not fine.

"Where were you?" Wes cries. "I couldn't find you. I told you to stay in that one spot, and when I came back you weren't there."

"I'm sorry," Madeline says. "I meant to, but I was bleeding, and then the EMTs were there telling me I needed to go with them."

"You should have told someone," Wes chides. "I was worried sick."

"I'm sorry," she repeats. "It all happened so fast." Madeline is crying hard now, telling Wes how Johanna is dead. Asking how this could have happened. It was supposed to be safe. Wes murmurs soft words of comfort. "It's going to be okay. You're going to be okay."

Wes must feel Jamie's eyes on them, because he turns, looks at Jamie hopefully. "She's really okay, right? And the baby?"

Wes must think he's the doctor. Jamie has been mistaken for worse.

"No, honey," Madeline says, sniffling. "He's with the police, right?" She directs this question to Jamie.

"That's right," Jamie says. "Agent Saldano. I'm with the ATF."

Wes stares more intently at him now, and Jamie waits for understanding, recognition, to wash over him. Over the years, Jamie has rarely allowed thoughts of his time in the tiny town of Nightjar, Wyoming, to creep in. He has worked so hard to forget, to put that summer out of his mind. But when his thoughts inch back twenty-seven years, it is always Weston Drake's face he sees. Younger, less lined, less hardened, but still his.

It's going to be okay.

The exact same words Wes said to his wife but directed at a twelve-year-old Jamie lying in a roadside ditch, broken arm, broken leg, broken eye socket, broken nose, broken jaw.

Of course, Weston Drake didn't recognize Jamie because when he found him, Jamie looked less than human. For a long time, Jamie had misplaced hate for Wes Drake. Why hadn't he come upon Jamie earlier when there was still a chance they would be able to find Juneau? Why hadn't Wes found his sister too? Wes saved Jamie's life that night, and over the years, Jamie had wondered what would happen if they ever met again. Would Jamie want to thank Wes for saving his life or punch him in the face for not letting him die?

CHAPTER 5

MADELINE

MADELINE LEANS INTO Wes, his solid frame the only thing holding her up now. Beneath the odor of his smoke-permeated clothes, she finds the woodsy tang of the cologne he wears. Her best friend is dead. Wes could have been killed too. In one fell swoop Madeline could have lost the two people who love her most in the world. And the baby. What would have happened if that jagged shard of metal had struck her just a few inches to the left or right? She can barely stand to think about it.

"ATF?" Wes asks. Madeline feels him tense. "But why? It was an accident."

"We're often called by local law enforcement to investigate explosions," the agent explains. "Someone died on your property. We need to know why." Madeline's stomach lurches, and she buries her face into Wes's shoulder. "I know this has been a traumatic night for you both," the agent says, "but the sooner we're able to talk to witnesses, the better."

"Sure, yes, of course," Wes says, nodding vigorously. "We'll do anything we can to help."

"Great. Thanks," the agent says. "Please sit."

Madeline gingerly returns to her chair, and Wes lowers himself onto the doctor's stool. He rolls it close to Madeline, slips his hand into hers, and rubs her cold knuckles. She's exhausted, any earlier adrenaline from the day has seeped from her body. All she wants to do is go home and crawl into bed. But that's not right, not when Johanna has died and so many others were injured. It's selfish. Madeline sits straighter, focuses her gaze on the agent.

He's tall and slim with dark hair, cut close at the sides, longer on top. Day-old stubble on his face can't hide the deep dimples in his cheeks. The agent isn't dressed as she expects. She thought federal agents only wore white shirts with dark suits and ties. Not this one. He's wearing khaki pants and a long-sleeve black high-performance T-shirt with a small circular ATF logo on his chest. On his feet are a pair of retro black-and-white Vans Sidestripes. Apparently, the man interviewing them was a skateboarder back in the day.

Agent Saldano pulls a small notebook from his back pocket but doesn't open it. He takes them through the timeline of the evening. He asks what they saw, what they heard, whether there was anything unusual or unexpected about the evening. Wes takes the lead.

"It was a great night, everything was perfect until . . ." Wes says, shaking his head. "Everyone was having a great time until that second explosion."

"So you definitely heard two separate explosions?" the agent asks.

It all happened so quickly, but Madeline is certain that there were two explosions: the truck one hundred yards in front of her, and then the barn behind them. "Yes," Madeline says. "Definitely two explosions."

"I agree," Wes says. "It doesn't make sense. There's no possible reason the barn would explode. It was nowhere near the truck."

"What was stored in the barn?" the agent asks. "Anything flammable?"

"Sure," Wes says, shrugging. "It's a storage barn. There were propane tanks, gas tanks, kerosene."

Madeline's stomach drops. "You think that the truck explosion might have somehow triggered the barn fire?" she asks. It's the only scenario that makes sense to her. So it was their fault.

"That's what we're trying to find out," the agent says mildly.

"No," Wes says, releasing Madeline's hand. "No way. We were careful. Tannerite is perfectly safe."

The agent gives a slight smile, his dimples making another appearance. "In many cases, yes. In others, no."

Madeline knows what the agent is referring to. She's seen the news stories: the grandmother who died when a piece of shrapnel from an old refrigerator stuffed with Tannerite and a can of diesel fuel blew up; the wildfire caused by Tannerite exploded in tandem with a firecracker; the gender reveal that caused a fire that destroyed over forty-five thousand acres of woodland, leaving only a jagged burn scar across the landscape.

"Who prepared the Tannerite?" the agent asks.

"No," Wes repeats, getting to his feet. "We didn't cause this to happen." Madeline knows he is avoiding mentioning his brother's name, because it was Dix who mixed the Tannerite with the pink chalky powder.

"Do we need a lawyer?" Wes asks. "We want to help, but I think we should call our attorney."

"I didn't mean to give you that impression," the agent says. "I simply wanted to get your initial thoughts. Once the sun comes up, we'll investigate the cause. Can you think of anyone who might hold a grudge? Would want to hurt you or any of your guests?"

"No," Wes says with finality. "No one."

"Sully Preston—" Madeline begins, but Wes gives a little shake of his head, and she claps her mouth shut. Wes isn't going to give this man anything. But why? Why wouldn't he want to know what caused Johanna's death?

If Wes's reluctance to share information is suspicious, the

agent doesn't show any indication but simply moves on. "How about security around the property? Any cameras?"

Wes takes a breath and lifts his eyes to the ceiling as if thinking. "We have cameras at the front and back of the house and around the stables and the equestrian barn. We also have alarm systems for the house and stables. If someone got on the property who wasn't supposed to, we'd know."

"How many acres?" the agent asks.

"Three thousand, give or take," Wes says, impatiently. "Listen, can we do this later? My wife needs to get home, and I still haven't found my brother."

"I understand," the agent says. "Please, go get some rest. I'll check in with you in the morning." He holds out his hand, his eyes intently examining Wes.

Madeline can't quite name the expression on the agent's face. A prickle of fear runs through her. Could this really have been all their fault? Could Wes really go to jail? Could she? Wes reluctantly shakes the agent's hand, then quickly releases his grip.

"Mrs. Drake," the agent turns to Madeline, grasps her hand. His fingers are strong and warm, reassuring. "Congratulations on the baby girl. I'm glad you're okay. I'll be in touch."

"What did he say his name was?" Wes asks once the agent steps from the hospital room and gently closes the door behind him.

"I can't remember," Madeline says, numbly. "Saldano, maybe? Please, can we go home now?" She can't hold it together much longer.

"Yeah," Wes says, distractedly as he scrolls through his phone.

Madeline doesn't have to ask what he's looking for. She knows he's searching his contacts for their attorney's number.

"Wes, please," she says, trying to keep the irritation from

her voice. It's been a terrible night for them all. "Can't you call him later? Besides, we don't even know what happened yet."

"It doesn't matter," Wes says, as he helps Madeline to her feet. "The fire was on our property, and whatever caused it, we'll be on the hook. We can be sued for all we have. And why do you have to question everything I do? I know what people are like. And why would you bring up the Prestons? The last thing we need is for people to think we're blaming them. It's only going to hurt our business. From now on, just let me talk."

"But how can you think about that right now?" Madeline asks, horrified. "Of all things, you're worried that someone is going to sue us? And that poor girl who got burned so badly. If it's our fault, of course we have to help her out." Her voice is shaking, and a tightness forms in her chest.

"What girl?" Wes asks.

"The waitress. Mellie something," Madeline says. "We shared an ambulance to the hospital. She's pregnant too." She looks down at her lap.

"I fucking don't care about some pregnant waitress, okay?" Wes says with a vehemence that surprises Madeline. "Can't you just stop talking right now? I have to think." The shock must show on her face, because Wes lowers his voice. "I'm sorry. All I want to focus on is you and our baby. That's all that matters to me."

Madeline looks down at the hospital scrubs she's still holding and doesn't know if she has the energy to put them on. With effort she shrugs out of the robe, and pain shoots through her lower back, and her breath hitches.

Instantly, Wes is at her side. "I'm sorry. You're right, let's not talk about that now. Here, let me help," he says. Madeline stays seated while Wes unties her hospital gown. She is self-conscious of her nakedness, of the strangeness of her pregnant body, but she is too sore, too tired to protest. Wes tosses aside the hospital gown, then gently pulls the scrubs over her head. He gets down on his knees in front of her, presses one large hand on her belly. "I can't believe I could have lost you," he says, looking up at her. His eyes are wet. "Both of you."

Madeline runs a hand across the top of his head. His hair smells of smoke and is dusty with ash. "We're okay," she says, and Wes wipes his eyes. He guides each of her legs into the scrubs and carefully pulls them up over her bandages.

"How are the horses? Pip?" Madeline asks with another surge of worry.

"I don't know," he says, voice grave. "That's why we have to get home. And I have no idea where my brother is. My phone's dead. Do you have yours?"

"No, I lost it," she says, looking down at her bare feet. She lost her shoes in the explosion too.

"Jesus, Madeline," Wes says. "You're always losing your phone. I'm going to check with the nurse to see if she knows anything about Dix," Wes says. "I'll only be a few minutes."

"Yeah, of course. Go ahead," Madeline says. "I'll meet you at the front doors."

"You can walk okay?" Wes asks.

"I'm fine," Madeline assures him, thinking of Mellie, possibly burned, somewhere in the hospital.

After a few minutes, Madeline gets painfully to her feet and limps from the room. Down a long hallway, she sees a hunched figure moving toward Wes. It's Dalton Monaghan. A sob escapes her throat. Poor, poor Dalton. Madeline expects Wes to embrace Dalton, to offer him some comfort. Instead, he just stands there, hands hanging helpless at his side. Voices rise, but the distance keep the words from reaching her. Are they arguing? But as quickly as the encounter began it is over.

Dalton moves down the hallway with the deputy while Wes storms off. That's when Madeline notices the ATF agent leaning against the nurses' station. He also witnessed the exchange between Dalton and Wes.

Could the explosion really be their fault? Madeline knows how conscientious Wes is about safety. With the horses and the equestrian center, they have to be. Yes, blowing up an old truck was over-the-top, but Wes had overseen nearly every aspect of the setup, except for placing the pink powder and the explosive inside the truck. That was left to Dix and one of their ranch hands. Could they have made a mistake?

Madeline makes a slow trek to the emergency room exit. She glances into an open doorway and catches sight of a familiar face. The young waitress from the party. Madeline hesitates, a little voice in her head telling her to not get involved—she has enough to worry about as it is—but they bonded in that ambulance ride. Both scared, injured, pregnant, and in that moment very much alone. What harm could come from peeking in and saying hello?

CHAPTER 6

MELLIE

I STARE UP at the ceiling. Despite the medication, the pain in my leg feels like a million wasps buzzing and stinging the nerves beneath my skin. The doctor told me I was lucky, that things could have been much worse. Funny, I don't feel lucky.

The shades are closed, and I have no concept of time. It could be midnight or noon for all I know.

There's a tap on the open door. "Come in," I say, my throat still scratchy from the smoke. I run a hand self-consciously through my hair, knowing that it's in need of a good wash, as a woman steps into the room. "Mrs. Drake," I say in surprise.

"No, call me Madeline, please," she says, as she limps to my bedside. She looks as bad as I feel. She's wearing hospital scrubs, her face is puffy, and the skin beneath her eyes is purple with exhaustion. She smells like a campfire. "I wanted to see how you are doing," she says, looking around the room nervously.

"I'm okay," I say, because what else am I supposed to say? I'm in the most fucking pain I've ever been in my life. The doctor says the burn on my leg is only surface-level, but it hurts like a son of a bitch. "How are you?" I ask because it seems like the polite thing to say. "Is the baby okay?"

"I'm fine. She's fine," Madeline says, with a relieved smile.

"A girl?" I ask, a knot forming in my stomach. "You found out what you're going to have?"

"Yeah," Madeline says with a smile. "A little girl." Then the smile drops. "How are you? How is your baby?"

The baby. One little lie has become so big. When I told Madeline and Johanna about the baby, it was a means to an end, a way to get my foot in the door. I did my homework. I scoured social media for insights and clues. Their personal accounts were locked down pretty tightly, but I saw an opening when I found Johanna's midwife page.

"She's fine too," I say, laying my hands across my midsection.

"We're both having girls!" Madeline says, and the happiness and warmth in her voice makes me like Madeline Drake even more, makes me more conflicted about what I've done, what I'm going to do.

Tears fill my eyes. Real tears.

"Mellie," Madeline says, sitting down next to me on the edge of the bed. "What's wrong? Do you want me to get a nurse?"

I sniff, wipe my eyes with the corner of my bedsheet. "No, I'm fine. The doctor says I can go home soon."

"That's a good thing," Madeline says, eyeing my wrapped leg with concern. "Do you have someone to help take care of you? Family?"

"No," I say in a small voice. "My family isn't from around here. But really, I'll be okay," I insist. "They wouldn't send me home if they didn't think it was safe."

"But who will get your groceries and fix you meals?" Madeline persists. "Don't you need someone to stay with you for a while?"

Why is this woman being so nice to me? In my experience, rich women have little time for underlings like me. Sure, they are polite, and if I do my job well and am attentive—but not too attentive—if I'm pretty—but not too pretty—I might get a good tip. But no one has ever been this interested in how I'm doing.

"No, it's okay," I sniffle. "I'll figure it out. And I'm really sorry to hear about your friend. Did they find out what happened yet?"

Madeline's own eyes rim with tears. "Thank you. No, they don't know or aren't telling us much. I can't believe she's gone."

She looks so lost, so sad. I lean forward in my bed and wrap my arms around her, and suddenly I'm the one doing the comforting. I thought she would be like all the others: snobby, fake, condescending. I had taken this particular job with the catering company for one reason: to show Wes Drake that I will not be fucked with. To let him know that though he may think he's done with me, I'm not going away. At least not quietly.

"I'm sorry," Madeline says, pulling away with an embarrassed laugh. "You've got enough going on without me crying on your shoulder. Now, listen," she insists. "I want you to get a hold of me if you need anything. Anything at all."

"Oh, no," I say. "That's okay, really . . ."

"I insist," Madeline says. "Do you have your phone?"

Confused, I nod to the bedside table. Somehow, during the entire fiasco at the ranch, I hadn't lost my phone. Madeline picks it up, hands it to me, then rattles off a phone number. "I don't know what happened to my cell," she says. "But you can reach me on our home phone." She must see the skepticism on my face as I key in the numbers. "I mean it, Mellie," she says forcefully. "I want to help. I don't have any of my own family around here either, except for Wes, and I know how hard it can be so far from home. How lonely. You can reach out to me, day or night. Understand?"

"Okay," I say, sinking back into my pillows, still suspicious of this unexpected kindness. Madeline leans in and gives me one more hug, gets to her feet, and moves as if in pain to the door.

Before she leaves, she turns, gives me a mock-stern look and shakes a finger at me. "I mean it, Mellie. Call me. Promise?"

"I promise," I say.

I fell in love with Wes Drake the first time I saw him. It was a year ago, and I was working some Horsemen Association luncheon. I served Wes an old-fashioned on the rocks, and he said something about how it was too bad that a nice young woman like me was stuck waiting on such a lecherous group of old men. I responded by saying they weren't *all* bad, just the ones that ordered whiskey with their lunch. He laughed, and I went about my business of pouring drinks. I'm used to men hitting on me, but there was something about Wes—he was different.

I saw him with his wife a month later at some fancy fundraiser. Madeline Drake wasn't just one of those pretty rich women I've come to know working these kinds of events, she was beautiful *and* nice. While the other wives looked right through me, Madeline made eye contact and thanked me every single time I brought her a drink or presented a tray of hors d'oeuvres. What Madeline Drake didn't seem to notice was how her husband was looking at me the entire night. But I noticed. I could feel the hot pull of his gaze, the way his eyes followed me around the room. And I watched him too. Wes Drake was funny, sweet, and, to my surprise, hot for a guy twice my age. We even talked for a while. Wes made me laugh, made me feel like the only woman in the room.

The third time I saw him, at an anniversary party, Wes completely ignored me. Didn't glance my way, didn't acknowledge my presence at all. My feelings were hurt, which was silly. He was rich, important, and married. But then I saw him at yet another event, and that night we ended up having sex in an empty hotel conference room. I can't even remember what the event was for—just a bunch of rich ranchers smoking cigars and drinking top-shelf booze. From then on, we couldn't get enough of each other and met up whenever possible. But Wes had rules. Lots of them. No phone calls, no texts, no emails, making it nearly impossible to coordinate times to be together until I suggested we have a standing date. Every Thursday afternoon we met at a hotel in Jackson. The reservation had to be in my name, and I had to pay for it, but Wes always gave me cash to cover the costs. It made me feel a little dirty, doing it that way. But I didn't take a dime more from him, even when he offered me gas money.

Then his wife got pregnant. I have to admit, that was a surprise. The way Wes made it sound, he and Madeline were on the outs. Obviously, at least for one night, that wasn't true. What does a fortysomething man and a twenty-one-year-old have in common? Lots, actually. We lie in bed and can talk about anything: music, movies, books, politics. Wes listens to me—really listens. And those few hours we have together are the highlight of my week. Maybe I'm being naive, but I really do think he loves me.

True, he's been more distant lately and has stood me up more than once, but he has a lot on his plate right now. So yes, I made sure I was going to work the gender reveal party. And yes, I concocted the story about being pregnant just to get close to his wife's best friend.

Then there was the explosion, and I ended up in the ambulance with his wife, and we bonded over being pregnant and motherless. My mom just happens to be alive and kicking in West Virginia, probably drinking a gin and tonic in front of the television right now.

As I sit in the dark all alone, it dawns on me that Wes is somewhere in this hospital right now. He most likely rushed over here as fast as he could to make sure his wife and baby were okay. I try not to let it bother me, but a little voice in my head keeps saying *What about me?*

I think of the invitation that Madeline so kindly offered. *You can reach out to me, day or night. Understand?*

An idea creeps into my mind. A terrifying, dangerous, exhilarating idea. I have a feeling I'll be calling on Madeline Drake very, very soon.

CHAPTER 7

JAMIE

JAMIE WAITS OUTSIDE the hospital morgue doors until Dalton Monaghan and the deputy step into the hallway. The deputy has her hand on Dalton's elbow as if she's afraid he's going to pass out.

"Excuse me," Jamie says. Identification at the ready, he introduces himself. "I'm sorry for your loss, Mr. Monaghan. Can we talk for a few minutes?" Red-eyed, the man nods, and Jamie leads him down the hallway until he finds an empty family lounge. A TV hanging from the wall is blaring an infomercial for cookware. Jamie finds the remote under a pile of magazines and presses the power button.

Dalton sits, and Jamie pulls a chair over so that he's sitting directly across from him. Like Madeline Drake, Dalton smells of smoke. His clothes are smudged with soot, and his dirty hands tremble in his lap.

"Again, Mr. Monaghan," Jamie says, "I'm so sorry. We're going to do everything we can to find out exactly what happened."

"Thank you," Dalton says, swiping at his eyes. "But I'm not sure why the ATF is here. Wasn't the explosion caused by the gender reveal?"

"That's why I'm here," Jamie explains. "When there are incidents like these, where there are deaths and injuries and major property damage, we come out, assess, and decide if further investigation is needed."

"I can tell you whose fault it is," Dalton says, his voice shaking with anger. "It's Wes's and Madeline's. If they hadn't planned this stupid stunt, Johanna would still be alive."

"When was the last time you saw Johanna last night?" Jamie asks. "How did she seem?"

"I didn't," Dalton says. "I didn't see her at the party at all. I came straight from work and got there just as people were moving to the field to watch the reveal. The last time I saw her was yesterday morning before I left for work. We were both in a hurry." He lowers his face into his hands.

Jamie gives him a moment before he asks his next question. "I saw you and Wes talking upstairs in the ER, and it looked like you were having words."

"Yeah, we had words," Dalton says, clearing his throat. "I told him blowing up a fucking truck wasn't safe and that my wife was dead because of him."

"How did he respond?" Jamie asks, though he saw the entire exchange.

Dalton shakes his head. "He wasn't happy that I called him out," Dalton says. "But you know what? It doesn't matter. There will be zero consequences for them."

"Why do you say that?" Jamie says.

"Because the Drakes are rich," Dalton says as if it's obvious. "They own half the county and can buy their way out of anything. Someone might go down for this, but I guarantee it's not going to be Wes Drake."

"That's not true, Mr. Monaghan," Jamie says. "We'll get to the bottom of what happened and hold those responsible accountable."

"Yeah, right," Dalton says, getting to his feet. "Is there anything else?"

"Nothing for now," Jamie says, also standing. "Let me drive

you home. You can try and get some rest, and we can talk more later."

"Nah," Dalton says. "I'm good. And just you wait. You're not from here, right?"

Startled by the question, it takes a beat for Jamie to answer. "No, I came over from Cheyenne."

"You'll see," Dalton says as he begins to walk away. "The Drakes and people like them own more than land around here. Just you wait."

JAMIE STEPS OUT of the hospital into the dark parking lot and jogs to his car. Once inside he glances at his watch. Almost six o'clock. He needs to call Greta, who he's banking on being in the office even though the sun isn't up yet.

"Jamie," she says, picking up on the first ring.

"Greta," he responds. "First one in the office?" As the intelligence research specialist, she is their go-to person for, among other things, digging through massive amounts of data and information in databases, public records, and open-source intelligence to assist in investigations.

"Always," Greta says. "I'm actually already on cup of coffee number two. What do you need?"

"Can you look up anything you can find on Dalton Monaghan of Nightjar?" Jamie asks as he presses the car's ignition and flips on the windshield wipers. "I'm specifically looking for any arrest records, employment records, anything that might indicate familiarity with explosive devices."

"That's a tall order for six in the morning." Greta chuckles, but already he can hear her fingers tapping the keyboard. "But I can tell you right now that your Dalton is forty years old and a wind turbine technician," Greta recites. "Grew up in Ohio, moved to Nightjar about nine years ago with his wife, Johanna. This is interesting. He's been arrested three times as an adult and once as a minor. All in the state of Ohio. The minor record is sealed, but it looks like he was arrested once for trespassing, once for drunk and disorderly, and once for assault."

"Who was the victim?" Jamie asks, snapping on his seat belt.

"Someone named Zeke Hollinger. Monaghan also pressed charges against him. Looks like it was a bar fight. Both sets of charges were eventually dropped," Greta explains.

"Well, it proves this guy has a temper," Jamie says. "Anything else?" There's more key tapping. Through the rain, Jamie sees a figure moving through the parking lot. Dalton Monaghan. He unlocks his car door and climbs inside.

"Looks like Monaghan was trained as a combat engineer in the army back in the early 2000s," Greta says.

"So he would have plenty of experience with explosives," Jamie muses, his eyes still on Dalton, who now has both hands on his steering wheel and drops his head.

"Not really. He never got much of a chance," Greta says. "He was injured in a training exercise and blew out his knee. Had surgery and ended up working as a recruiter in Cleveland for a few years."

"But he has the skills," Jamie says. "He would have learned how to use explosives to clear minefields and pathways, demolish buildings."

Jamie watches as Dalton lifts his head and abruptly slams the palm against the dashboard before putting his car into Drive and speeding from the parking lot.

"Looks like you have your first suspect," Greta says. "It really is always the husband, isn't it?"

CHAPTER 8

LUCY

LUCY LOOKS OUT the passenger-side window of Trent's pickup trying to see the craggy landscape through the rain-splattered glass. She can feel the heat of his gaze as it flicks back and forth from the road to her face. Lucy is grateful for the dark.

Trent is driving with one hand on the steering wheel while fumbling with his phone with the other, and a harsh trill fills the cab before Wes's voice interrupts the ringing. *"This is Wes. You know what to do."*

"Wes," Trent says, "I just heard what happened. I hope you and Madeline are okay. I'm on my way and will be at the ranch in about twenty minutes. Let me know what you need."

He disconnects and then makes another call. This time it goes straight to voicemail, and Lucy hears her sister's voice for the first time in a month. *"You've reached Madeline. I can't answer the phone right now. Please leave a message, and I'll return your call as soon as possible."*

"Hey, Madeline," Trent says, and Lucy is surprised at his shift in tone. From businesslike to—what?—gentler, more familiar? "I can't believe this. God, I hope you and the baby are okay. Give me a call, okay? And don't worry about the horses and Pip. I'll make sure they're taken care of." He disconnects.

Interesting, Lucy thinks. Perfect little Madeline and the

ranch hand. This could be much more fun than she thought, or maybe it would just complicate things.

"So you're Madeline's sister?" Trent finally says.

She could feign sleep, but he wouldn't buy it. Who could sleep after they've learned their pregnant sister may have been blown up in an explosion? Only a monster could do that.

"Stepsister," Lucy says. Her breath leaves a ghostly sheen of condensation across the window. "Her mom married my dad when we were kids. We grew up together."

"I guess I'm surprised you're here," Trent says. "Madeline said you had quite the falling-out last time she was home."

Lucy shrugs and drags one finger across the glass drawing a fat heart. "And I guess I'm surprised your sheriff dad didn't haul your ass off to jail for drunk driving tonight."

"I only drank the first shot, you idiot," Trent says with a laugh. "Then I told the bartender to switch to Coke. And besides, I could say the same about you. You matched me drink for drink."

"Maybe I can just hold my liquor," Lucy shoots back. And what the hell? Madeline was telling this guy about the last time they saw each other? "And from where I sit, it looks a lot like you were trying to get me drunk, and then my tire goes flat? Seems pretty coincidental, don't you think? I wonder what my sister would say about that?"

The screech of tires fills the truck's cab, and Lucy's seat belt snaps against her chest, preventing her head from striking the dashboard. For one interminable moment, the truck's wheels hydroplane across the wet pavement, sending them sliding toward the ditch before coming to an abrupt stop. "What the fuck?" Lucy gasps when air returns to her lungs.

"Get out," Trent says, reaching over to release her seat belt. "Get out of my truck."

Lucy surveys the surroundings outside the truck. Beyond the headlights lies a barren stretch of road that ends in blackness. It's raining harder now, and one glance down at her phone shows zero cell reception. Like usual, she's overplayed her hand. She hesitates a moment too long, and Trent reaches over her lap to open the passenger door. Cool air floods the cab, and rain pelts the side of her face.

"Jesus, sensitive much?" Lucy says, wrenching the truck door shut again. "What's your problem?"

"You know I didn't force any of those drinks down your throat. And when you looked like you weren't into it, I backed off," Trent snaps. "That's why I left. So don't you dare suggest anything different. If I was another kind of guy, I would have followed you into that bathroom."

"Fine," she concedes, wrenching the car door shut again. "Now, can we just go?"

"I have a few more questions first," Trent says. "Madeline and Wes never mentioned you were coming to visit. Why is that?"

"It was going to be a surprise," Lucy says.

"You were going to surprise your sister, but don't show up to her party?" Trent asks skeptically. "Right." He draws out the word for emphasis. "And you just so happen to run into me, the guy who works at the ranch that your sister owns, the sister who you haven't talked to in over a month? I don't buy it."

Wow, Lucy thinks. What else has Madeline told him about their relationship?

"You think I hit on you to get to Madeline?" Lucy can't believe the arrogance of this guy. "You approached me, re-member?" Trent just stares at her, eyebrows raised, waiting for further explanation. "It's complicated," Lucy finally says with a sigh. "We've had our disagreements, but I'm here now, right? And all I want to do is find out if my sister is okay. And for the record, I had no idea who you were."

"And how do I know if you're really Madeline's sister? How do I know you're not lying?" Trent asks.

Lucy sighs, shifts in her seat, and pulls a phone from her back pocket. She clicks through to Facebook, taps a few times, and turns the screen toward Trent showing him a picture of Madeline, Lucy, and an elderly man sitting in front of a cake emblazoned with candles. Then another of Madeline in her equestrian gear, a gold medal around her neck, sitting atop a horse, while Lucy stands below, smiling broadly. Then she shows him a picture of Madeline and Wes at their wedding. "I introduced Wes to Madeline," she says. In fact, Lucy and Wes dated for a time but figured out they were better off as friends. She swipes through several more photos. "See? Sisters." Trent stares at her a moment longer before putting the truck back into gear.

Lucy eases back into her seat in relief. Maybe she hasn't made a complete mess of things after all. Yes, she alienated Trent, but at least she didn't make the huge mistake of sleeping with him. Now he thinks he's smarter than she is, has a leg up. Well, let him think that. Yes, she'll have to be a little bit more careful, be more diligent, but in the end, Lucy'd bet that it wouldn't be hard to bring Trent around to her side.

THIRTY MINUTES LATER, the truck leaves the paved road and begins a rough trek down a long gravel lane. Lucy has never been to Lone Tree Ranch but knows from looking up the property on Google Earth that they are taking the back way in, the employee entrance for lack of a better term. From what she recalls, the unpaved road will lead to a cluster of ponderosa pine trees and three small cabins that she assumes serve as bunkhouses for the ranch hands. Beyond the pines is a creek, a meadow, the stables, barns, and finally the main house.

The truck comes to a bumpy stop in front of the cabins. All three are dark.

"Three of you live here?" Lucy asks. This put a hitch in her plan. One ranch hand she could handle. Three would be a problem.

"No. Only me," Trent says. "The part-timers crash here once in a while, but I figured they would stay here tonight because of the party. I'll drive up to the house, and we can see what's happening." Trent follows the path around the pines, the truck's headlights guiding their way. "Oh, fuck," Trent breathes out. Lucy peers through the windshield, but all she sees is the outline of a ridiculously big house and lower slung, but equally impressive, stables. Stables she would love to have back home.

"What?" Lucy asks as the interior light from within a car parked at the edge of the meadow pops on. A wide-set man exits the car and holds up his hand, ordering them to stop. Then she sees it. The ragged wreckage of the burned barn.

"Hey, hey!" the man shouts, and now Lucy sees he's wearing a sheriff deputy's uniform. "Hold up, now."

Trent stops the truck and rolls down his window. Immediately, Lucy's nose fills with a sodden, ashy smell. "Hey there, Coop," Trent calls back. "My dad told me I should head back this way."

The deputy's stance relaxes, but he still holds up his hand. "Stay there, Trent. Don't drive any closer. I don't want you tearing up the crime scene." For the first time, the deputy notices Lucy. "Who's that?" he asks sharply.

"You're not going to believe what I found on the side of the road," Trent says, and Lucy wants to smack him upside the head. "Madeline's sister."

"Sister?" the deputy says, coming up to the truck's window and ducking his head down to get a better look. He examines her closely, like most people do when they learn she is Madeline's sister. They look nothing alike. "She's never mentioned a sister."

"Stepsister," Lucy says by way of explanation. "I'm Lucy."

"Ahhh," the deputy says. "You must have come for the party."
Lucy doesn't correct him. "Wes and Madeline aren't back home
yet, but my understanding is they are both okay. Have you talked
to her?"

Lucy shakes her head.

"Hey, Trent," the deputy says, switching his focus, "can I
snag you for a minute?"

"Yeah, sure," Trent says, rolling up his window and then
stepping from the truck. "Be right back," he says before shut-
ting the door again with a heavy thunk.

Lucy watches as the two men move toward the burned-out
barn, heads tilted toward each other. She longs to go to the
stables to see Sonnet, one of the horses Madeline brought back
from Iowa. Lucy's horse. Instead, she grabs her backpack from
the floor and quietly slips from the truck. The rain has turned
to a spitting mist, and Lucy ducks her head, stuffs her hands
into her pockets and moves toward the darkened house, picking her way across the lawn littered with champagne glasses,
deflated balloons, and cracked china. She half expects the
deputy or Trent to come sprinting after her, but once at the
back terrace Lucy turns to see them still deep in conversation.
Lucy hesitates as she lifts her foot to climb the steps that lead
to the wall of windows and entrance to the house. Will the
backyard light up with security lights? It doesn't matter, Lucy
tells herself. Madeline is her sister. She belongs here. No lights
come on as she moves up the steps, and even more surprising,
the glass doors that lead inside the house are unlocked.

Lucy steps inside. The only glow is coming from the base-
boards, giving the room a cold, ghostly aura. Lucy moves to
the center of the large living room and looks up. Above her is a
monstrosity of a chandelier made of elk antlers that cast a sharp
tangle of shadows across the floor. Even in the dark, Lucy

knows that everything in this house is over-the-top expensive. Madeline did always expect the best.

From somewhere at the front of the house comes the soft jangle of keys and the indecipherable murmurs of a couple trying to argue quietly. Madeline and Wes are home. From behind her comes the clatter of footsteps. The sheriff and Trent finally realized Lucy wasn't in the truck any longer.

"Hey," the deputy says breathlessly just as the living room lights flick on. Madeline gasps and grabs Wes's arm.

Lucy almost doesn't recognize her sister. She is hugely pregnant and dressed in hospital scrubs. Her face is pale, her hair lank, and she smells like an ashtray. Lucy watches as Madeline tries to make sense of who is in front of her. Their last encounter included true but harsh words and hours of debate and ended with Madeline loading up Lucy's beloved Sonnet in a trailer and leaving without a backward glance. Madeline's appearance, only four weeks later, is alarming.

Wes appears equally stunned at seeing his sister-in-law standing in his living room but is the first to speak. "Lucy," he says, and there is no rancor in his voice. Lucy and Wes have always gotten along well. "Madeline didn't tell me you were coming."

"That's because I didn't know," Madeline says, her voice hard.

"I heard about the explosion," Lucy says. "Are you okay? Is the baby okay?" She opens her arms wide and first moves to Wes, embracing him, and then turns toward her sister, ready to draw her in close, ready to tell her that she's here now. That everything will be okay, though that's one colossal, bullshit lie.

The slap sounds like a firecracker, and heat explodes across Lucy's cheek.

"Madeline!" Wes says, rushing between the two women. "What are you doing?"

"Get out of my house," Madeline says, her voice even,

absolute. "How dare you come here." Without another word, Madeline turns and makes her way up the curved staircase to the second floor.

"Lucy, my God," Wes says. "Are you okay?"

"I'm okay," Lucy manages to say, the sting of Madeline's slap still radiating across her face.

"Do you want me to escort her off the property?" the deputy asks. "I'm sorry she got in the house. Trent brought her here, said she was Madeline's sister. I thought it would be okay."

Trent looks mortified, ready to jump in and drag Lucy from the house himself.

"No, no. It is okay," Wes says. "We've had a bad scare today. Of course Lucy can stay here. Madeline will feel better in the morning. We'll work it out then. Are you sure you're okay?" Wes asks again, concern in his dark blue eyes. "You know she didn't mean it. You're family, Luce. You're always welcome here."

Lucy cups her flaming cheek in her palm, covering the smile that has inched its way across her face.

CHAPTER 9

JAMIE

IN THE DIM morning light, Jamie pulls up to the only motel in town—the Grandview Mountain Lodge. When the sun rises, he knows the view will be pretty. He has to give the founders credit for truth in advertising. But the Grandview is no lodge. No pool, no hot tub, no mints on your pillow. It is still the grim, flat-roofed, two-story motor inn where twelve-year-old Jamie and sixteen-year-old Juneau lived with their mother when they moved to Nightjar. Jamie's mother was the night manager and cleaned for this motel. It wasn't easy work and paid poorly. That summer, he and Juneau spent a lot of time helping their mother clean up other people's shit, and Jamie prayed they could move on. A strong statement from a kid who only wanted to settle into the same town for more than a year or two. He didn't expect much—his own bedroom, a nearby skate park, and kids who'd rather play video games than castrate cattle after school. Then his sister disappeared, and he was left for dead. Ultimately, Jamie got his wish when he and his mother moved away from Nightjar. He got his skate park and gamer friends, but all he wanted was his sister back.

Jamie parks and walks to the unit where a dingy sign that says *Office* hangs in the window. He pulls open the creaky door, and a jingling bell announces his arrival. Same annoying bell, even, Jamie thinks. The space is stuffy and overwarm and smells of cigarette smoke. The clerk behind the counter is in her seventies with rheumy eyes and deep crevices around her lips. "Is room seventeen available?" he asks before he can stop himself.

"Ah, the presidential suite," the woman says with a small uptick of her mouth. "Good choice." She runs his credit card. "Returning customer?" she asks.

"Yeah, but it's been a while," Jamie says, accepting the key hanging from an orange plastic key tag adorned with the faded silhouette of the motel.

He goes back outside, grateful for the cool morning air, and takes the metal steps to the second level. He walks along the balcony until he finds himself standing in front of the door with a crooked number *17* affixed just above the peephole. Using the key the clerk gave him, Jamie opens the door, and a wave of nostalgia sweeps over him. That's not the right word. *Wistfulness*, maybe? *How about* a bad idea? comes Juneau's voice. *You know you can stay at a La Quinta over in Jackson, right?*

The layout of the room is the same: a small area with a pullout sofa and a coffee table with a scuffed laminate top. In the kitchenette there's a small table that sits two, a hot plate, a sink, and a dorm-size refrigerator. Behind two closed doors, Jamie knows he will find a bathroom with dingy tile and a small bedroom that only has room for a bed and a dresser. On the walls are the same tacky velvet paintings of a buffalo, a wolf, and a bear. He can't help smiling. Juneau had named them—Barney, Winston, and Bianca. He moves across the carpet, squishy beneath his feet, to the closed bedroom door. Inside is a queen-size bed and, thankfully, what looks like a relatively new comforter. He's not tired, though. His nerves are still jangling from coming back to Nightjar and seeing Wes Drake at the hospital.

He goes back outside and moves down the stairs, his footsteps making the iron vibrate. The sun has risen. The sky is watercolor-blue, and the grass is still wet with last night's rain. The morning sunshine softens the sharp edges of the mountains off in the distance. Jamie knows better, though. There is nothing soft or welcoming or gentle about the mountains. It's a hard life, living in this part of the world, especially if you don't have the money to pay others to do the work for you. He unhooks his bike from the rack and wheels it back up the steps and into his motel room. There will be no bike ride this morning.

Once in his car, Jamie pulls out his phone and calls Tess.

"Hello," she answers shortly, and Jamie winces.

"Hey, I made it to Nightjar. I'm getting ready to head to the scene now," Jamie says.

"Okay," Tess says, and Jamie can feel the chill over the line.

"What are you up to today?" Jamie asks, as he watches a mule deer and her fawn cross the asphalt parking lot.

"The same thing I've been doing for the last two months. Looking for a job. But wait, that's right. There are zero jobs in consulting right now. Especially in Wyoming," Tess says irritably. "But you knew that already because I told you this would happen."

"Tess," Jamie says wearily. "Come on . . ." His voice is loud in the morning quiet, and the sound startles the deer and fawn, and they scurry away.

"Yeah, got it," Tess says, her voice thick with tears. "You don't really want to know what I'm doing today, just want the credit for asking."

"I'll call you later," Jamie says. "We'll talk about it when I get back to my motel. I'm sorry."

"Yeah," Tess sniffs. "Me too."

Jamie disconnects. He knows it's been hard for Tess, but she agreed to move to Cheyenne. He didn't force her, and at the time she had some job leads. It wasn't his fault they fell through. He had wanted to tell Tess about seeing Wes Drake after all these years, wanted her take on things. They used to be able to do that, talk about everything.

As Jamie pulls out of the parking lot and drives toward the Drake ranch, he tells himself that things with Tess will sort themselves out. They'll work it out. They always do. But he can't help but kick himself for not identifying himself to the Drakes. His presence at the site of an explosion involving the man who once saved his life could easily and understandably be misconstrued. No matter how fastidiously he investigates, even the whiff of favoritism could blow a potential murder case and sully Jamie's reputation as an ATF agent. He has to make this right. He'll have to say he didn't make the connection at the hospital. It has been twenty-seven years after all, and the Drake name is common in the area.

Thirty minutes later, he turns onto the road that will take him to the ranch. In a recently mowed stretch of the meadow are a dozen vehicles. The guests and hired workers must have parked here for the party. Grimly, Jamie knows the remaining cars probably belong to the injured and dead.

Today Jamie is dressed for the crime scene. Lace-up waterproof boots, jeans, an ATF windbreaker, and service revolver at his hip. Using his cell phone, he pauses to snap photos of the vehicles and their license plates, hoping that local law enforcement will have already done so. Still, at some point he'll speak with the owners. He leaves his car parked on the side of the road and begins the trek toward the house and the explosion site. The guests would have made this same walk after parking their cars, or more likely, the Drakes would have had an ATV or golf cart handy to bring them the rest of the way to the house.

The Drake home, made of stone, lumber, and glass, looms large against the rugged landscape. Jamie guesses with its three thousand acres, the property has a price tag of upward of around twenty million.

The Drakes were well-known in Woodson County when Jamie was a kid. Wes's father was one of the biggest landowners in a county where the number of acres you own means everything. Jamie didn't meet him until after Juneau disappeared and Jamie was out of the ICU. Mr. Drake wanted to meet the young man his son had rescued and express his condolences. Jamie remembered Wes's dad as a large man, with a sun-craggy face and sharp blue eyes. He was warm and kind and said goodbye to Jamie's mom with a lingering hug.

After Jamie was released from the hospital, he and his mother tried to get on with life in Nightjar, but it was too hard. The sky was too big, their motel room strangely too small without Juneau. At night, after his mother passed out from the sleeping pills the doctor prescribed, Jamie would sneak out of the house and find himself limping along the gravel road where his sister disappeared, searching. Without fail, Deputy Colson would end up on the same stretch of road, flashing his truck's brights to let Jamie know it was him.

"Aren't you nervous being out here by yourself so late at night?" Colson asked one night after cajoling Jamie into his truck.

"Not really," Jamie said dully, looking out the passenger-side window. "Why would he bother killing me now? It's obvious I didn't see anything." Colson didn't have anything to say to this but tried to fill the silence with small talk while he drove Jamie home.

Juneau's case grew cold, and just before Christmas, his mother told them they were moving on. They argued bitterly, and Jamie vowed to stay behind. "How can you give up?" he would shout. "How can you leave, knowing she's out there somewhere?"

"Because she's not," his mother said, tossing their meager possessions into plastic tote boxes. "She's gone, Jamie." She paused to look at him, her eyes uncharacteristically clear. "She's dead and never coming back."

Now in the light of day, the ranch is abuzz with law enforcement. Crime-scene techs dressed in their protective gear sift through the rubble of the burnt-out barn. Another cluster of techs are standing around a large crater in the meadow just beyond the stables. It appears there are two explosion sites. Not unheard of, but they are so far apart with no apparent destruction in between.

"Thanks for coming," a voice behind him says. Jamie turns to find a man dressed in coveralls and a hard hat. "Dave Ostrenga, Wyoming State Fire Marshal," he says sticking out his hand. "Glad you could come out so quickly. This one's got us a little stumped."

"Jamie Saldano," Jamie says, taking the marshal's hand. It's cold and calloused. "Glad to be of help. I spoke briefly to the homeowners last night at the hospital. Sounds like a gender reveal gone rogue."

"Yeah, at first glance." Ostrenga starts walking toward the meadow, and Jamie falls into step next to him. "Apparently, Wes Drake got it in his head to pack an old Dodge with Tannerite and blow it up in front of a crowd of two hundred." The two walk through a meadow littered with chunks of metal and stop in front of a charred hole carved into the dirt. Tannerite is a mixture of ammonium nitrate and ammonium perchlorate— not explosive on their own, but when combined and ignited by a high-speed bullet, the result is a booming explosion. Mix it with pink or blue powder and you've got a gender reveal in a mushroom cloud. Mix it with gunpowder or gasoline and you get an IED.

"How much Tannerite did he use?" Jamie asks, surveying the crater.

"Wes says four pounds," Ostrenga says, shaking his head. "But from the looks of things, I'm guessing someone added something to the mixture."

"That would explain this mess," Jamie says. "But it doesn't look like the debris went any farther than over there." He points to a gnarled hubcap.

"Yeah," Ostrenga says, taking off his hat and running his hand across his balding head. "The witnesses I talked to say that the explosions happened almost simultaneously."

"Wes and Madeline Drake thought there was a second or two in between the blasts. Could one explosion have triggered the other?" Jamie asks.

Ostrenga shrugs. "Too early to tell, but I doubt it. There's a good football-field distance between the two blasts. The debris fields will tell us more. Weird coincidence, though, and the Drakes aren't exactly a low-profile outfit."

"Arson?" Jamie asks.

"I'd like to find out what caused the second blast before I start speculating," Ostrenga says.

"Any reason to believe the homeowners would be involved?" Jamie asks.

Ostrenga lets out a puff of air. "I've known the family for years, but who knows. People have done a lot more for less."

Jamie agrees. He's been around long enough to know that people are exceptionally good at hiding their dirty little secrets and, when desperate, will do about anything for money. "Do local law enforcement have any initial thoughts?" Jamie asks.

"We can ask Sheriff Colson right now," Ostrenga says, nodding toward a man who is talking intently with one of the crime-scene techs. "Hey, Jerry," Ostrenga calls out. "Got a minute?"

A shot of adrenaline shoots through Jamie. He knows Jerry Colson. The deputy was one of the first people Jamie saw when he woke up in the hospital. "I'm going to catch whoever did this, son," Colson had told him. He tried. Jamie had to give him that, but the case had gone cold, and then Jamie's mother wanted to leave Wyoming, wanted to forget. Colson tried to keep in touch, gave them updates, but they moved and then moved again.

"Jerry," Ostrenga shouts again.

Sheriff Colson looks up, raises a finger indicating he needs a minute.

"That's okay," Jamie says, clapping Ostrenga on the back. "We'll debrief later. I want to take a minute to look over the scene and get the lay of the land."

Jamie makes his way toward the burned-out barn and notices a man dressed in faded jeans, cowboy boots, and a Carhartt jacket standing at the edge of stand of pine trees, shifting nervously from foot to foot. Jamie slows his pace and watches the man carefully to see if he might bolt.

Up close, Jamie sees the Lone Tree Ranch insignia embroidered across the man's baseball cap. It's pulled low, but Jamie can still see his pale face and bloodshot eyes. Jamie lifts his hand in greeting. "Mornin'," he says and then introduces himself.

"Trent Colson," the man says.

"Any relation to—"

"Yeah, he's my dad," Trent says with a hint of resignation. "I'm one of the ranch hands."

Jamie remembers Madeline Drake saying that one of the hands helped pack the Tannerite. "You were here last night?" Jamie asks.

Trent shakes his head. "No, I only work with the horses. Once they were squared away for the day, I headed out. But when I heard about what happened, I came right back here."

"What time was that?"

"Around two, I think," Trent says, his face flushing red.

"You live on-site?"

"In the cabins, back there." Trent hooks a thumb over his shoulder.

"Were you here for the setup yesterday?"

"Yeah, I helped some. But like I said, I just take care of the horses. The Drakes hired people to help with the setup and made sure the stage was good to go for the entertainment."

"Reba McEntire, right?" Jamie says.

"Yes, but thankfully she wasn't here at the time of the explosion. Apparently, someone was able to catch her while she was still at her hotel in Jackson," Trent says. "Listen, I was there when Dix loaded the Tannerite into the old truck. He was very careful. Read the directions like ten times."

"Dix Drake?" Jamie asks. "Wes's brother?" Jamie never met Dix back when he lived in Nightjar. Dix was older, in his twenties and away at college.

"Yeah. It had to be some weird accident, right? Have they found him yet? Dix?" Trent asks.

Jamie still hasn't seen the list of injured or missing. "I'll check on that. So you haven't seen or heard anything suspicious as of late? Any threats to Wes or his wife? Any strangers hanging around?"

Hesitation flickers across Trent's face. Jamie waits him out. "No, no one, except Madeline's sister, Lucy. I met her at Rick's last night. It's a bar." Trent's face grows hot again. "Her car broke down, and I was helping her when my dad pulled up and said that something happened at the ranch. I brought her here."

"What time was that?"

Trent thinks a moment. "We met up at about eight at Rick's and headed this way around two. I'm not exactly sure."

"So what were you doing between six and eight?" Jamie asks.

Trent lifts his hat from his head and rubs and hand over his

hair. "I don't know. I wanted to get away from the ranch before all the people showed up, so I stopped at my folks' house,
but no one was there, so I grabbed a bite to eat at the Nightjar
Café. From there I went to Rick's."

"And how long of a drive is it to Rick's from the café?"
Jamie asks.

"Hey!" comes a shout. "We got something!"

Jamie moves quickly toward the wreckage. The crime-
scene techs are working in two-by-two-foot areas looking for
evidence by using screens to sift through the debris.

The tech points to a spot on the barn floor where debris
had been cleared away. The wooden planks are charred and
covered in large rolling blisters that resemble alligator skin.
The burn pattern along the wood floor indicates a rapid heat
buildup. Not a clear indication of arson, but it looks that way.
"Is this where the victim was found?" Jamie asks.

"No, she was found just outside the barn," Ostrenga says,
his mouth set in a grim line. "It looks like she tried to run but
barely made it past the door when the barn went up."

Using a gloved hand, the tech holds up a jag of metal.
"Looks like it used to be a double-head nail. We found a whole
bunch of them along with some ball bearings."

"An IED, then?" Jamie says, and the tech nods.

"And this," says another tech. "PVC piping and duct tape."

"So whoever did this would have a working knowledge of
explosives," Jamie says.

The first tech nods again. "But you can find out a hell of a
lot about bomb-making from a Google search."

"True," Jamie says. "Let me know the minute you find
anything else."

Jamie knows he has one of the best post-blast identification
teams here. In a matter of a few hours, they will be able to
determine the type of explosive and its components and come
up with a solid theory of what happened.

More evidence needs to be collected, and an autopsy has to be conducted. Cases involving improvised explosion devices can take days to process and months, even years, to investigate. All the evidence will be packed up and sent the ATF lab in Maryland. But at first glance, it appears that whatever killed Johanna Monaghan was no accident, and because of his experience in munitions and his arrest record, Dalton Monaghan is at the top of Jamie's list of suspects.

CHAPTER 10

MADELINE

MADELINE LOOKS THROUGH the wall of windows at what once was her beautiful backyard. A black hole sits in the middle of the meadow with the gnarled remains of the old Dodge strewn throughout the tall grass and soot-covered wildflowers. It's unbelievable, she thinks, that just yesterday, Johanna was here, reassuring Madeline that all would be well.

She presses her fingers to her mouth, trying to hold in the sobs that racked her body all the way home from the hospital. Then there was the shock of finding her sister standing in her living room. Madeline still can't believe she slapped Lucy. That was definitely out of character. If anyone was going to throw punches, it was Lucy. She still has a few scars from their childhood tiffs.

The lawn is littered with traces of yesterday's party, and there's little left of the old barn. Crime-scene technicians and law enforcement have descended across the property, and yellow crime tape is stretched tautly around the yard, a flimsy barrier but somehow more intimidating than any electric or barbwire fence. There is a sudden flurry of activity at the foundation of the burned-down barn. She watches as the ATF agent from yesterday and several others rush toward one of the investigators. They've found something. The cause of the fire? Another body? Madeline shudders, fights the bile that rises in her throat.

A strange whap-whap sound fills the air, like a thousand bird wings beating. Madeline presses her face to the glass trying to get a better look. A helicopter hovers high above the meadow, the rotor blades a blurry swirl against the blue sky. Emblazoned across the side of the helicopter is the logo for the news station out of Cheyenne. The media is here. Another spasm of panic runs through Madeline. Of course this would be big news—over-the-top gender reveal turns deadly. The media will have a field day, and Madeline knows that one helicopter is probably only the beginning. The Drake family is high-profile, and everyone likes to see the wealthy and privileged fall hard and spectacularly.

Madeline tries to push the thought aside. She thinks of the tense interaction Wes and Dalton had in the hospital last night, and she needs to talk to her husband about it today. Madeline feels like she should reach out to Dalton—he must be in agony—but Wes told her under no circumstances was she to call him. He also told her that she needed to rest, but she's too keyed-up, beyond exhausted. Instead, she passes quietly by the kitchen where Wes is still talking with the sheriff and into the mudroom where she keeps a barn jacket and a pair of tall rubber muck boots. The morning air is cool but holds the promise of a warm, pleasant day. Once outside, she registers her mistake. The news helicopter that has retreated to a far end of the property is returning and would get the money shots they were looking for. Her pregnant belly and the stitches in her lower back make it impossible to move quickly, but Madeline keeps her head down until she reaches the stables. Wes will be irritated with her for going outside, will say that it will be her own fault if her face ends up plastered all over the news.

Once inside, Madeline is met with the familiar scent of sweet hay, dust, leather, sweat, and the wet-dog smell of Pip who, tail wagging, comes to her side. Madeline pauses to rub her head and then moves directly to Blackjack's stall, where he snicks and stomps at her arrival. A twelve-year-old ebony Arabian with a white comma in the middle of his forehead, Blackjack is the horse that helped her win the gold in dressage at the Pan American Games before she gave up competition and married Wes.

"Hey, sweet boy," Madeline says, running a hand along Blackjack's muzzle and offering him a sugar cube.

"You know Dad would say you are spoiling him," comes Lucy's voice from behind.

Madeline's spine stiffens, but she keeps her gaze firmly on Blackjack. "I can't deal with you right now, Lucy," Madeline says, her voice shaking. "My best friend died, I could have lost the baby, and my yard is crawling with police. I thought we agreed the last time we were together that it was best if we didn't see each other for a while." Blackjack's muscles are tense beneath her fingertips. He can sense when she's stressed out, has always been able to read her.

"We need to talk," Lucy says. "You know we do."

Intent on ignoring her sister, Madeline makes her rounds in the stable, stopping at each stall, while Lucy lingers next to Mathilda, one of the dozen horses that Lucy's father left to Madeline when he died. He also left Madeline half his estate and put the other half in a trust for Lucy. Lucy wasn't known for her financial acumen and went ballistic when she learned that her stepsister held the purse strings and controlled the money.

Madeline didn't have to take the horses when she left after the funeral; she and Wes had plenty of their own. If she'd had access to the money, Lucy would have continued to expertly care for them all as she had throughout their father's illness, but if Madeline is being honest, at the time it felt good to take the herd from her sister. Lucy's father, who Madeline came to think of as her father too, was a practical man and must have understood that Lucy was in no position to care for them. Taking the horses was almost the only thing that seemed to crack a piece of Lucy's notoriously hard heart.

"This is just so like you," Lucy says, moving next to her stepsister and leaning her elbows atop the stable gate. "You'll do anything to avoid a fight."

"And you'll do anything to provoke one!" Madeline cries. "You shouldn't be here right now, and you know it."

"Mathilda is looking a little on the thin side," Lucy says, sidestepping Madeline's comment. "Is she eating okay?"

"She's fine," Madeline insists. She's about ready to tell Lucy to go home and say she can't deal with all this right now and maybe they can try again in a few months, when Trent opens the stable door.

"Just grabbing a rake," Trent mutters and moves off to the far end of the stables. Lucy raises an eyebrow but doesn't comment.

"And really?" Madeline says. "You really think I need your input on how to take care of horses?" She turns her back on her sister and returns her attention to Mathilda.

The horses do seem fine, if a little antsy to get out of their stalls and into the paddock where they can stretch their legs, but that won't happen until the sheriff says it's okay. Outside, the hum of the helicopter has disappeared, and Madeline thinks she can make the trek back to the house without being filmed. Her back hurts, and she's in desperate need of a shower or sponge bath, something to get the stink of smoke from her skin.

"You know why I'm here, Madeline," Lucy says crossing her arms and giving Madeline an infuriatingly serene smile.

"Lucy . . ." Madeline says, her voice a warning.

"Okay, okay," Lucy says and laughs. "I'll shut up. I wouldn't want another one of your right hooks."

"It was a slap, not a right hook, and I shouldn't have done

that," Madeline says, giving Mathilda one final pat and moving to the next stall.

"No, no, it's good," Lucy says, shadowing Madeline. "At least there's a little personality left in you."

"My best friend is dead, Lucy." Madeline is yelling now, and it unsettles the horses who begin stomping their feet. "I'm seven months pregnant, and I had a piece of shrapnel removed from my back. So, yes, it's fair to say I've had a rough twenty-four hours."

Lucy crosses her arms across her chest, her jaw set at a defiant angle. "I'm here because I'm trying to be a good sister."

"Hey," comes a voice. "Sorry to interrupt." Madeline whirls around. It's the ATF agent from the hospital. He's looking at them with concern. "Everything okay here?"

"Yes, we're fine," Madeline says. Pip gets up from her spot in the corner and comes over to sniff the new arrival. Today the agent has swapped out his Vans for a pair of sturdy boots.

Lucy steps forward and holds out her hand. "Lucy Quaid," she says. "Madeline's sister, and for the record, I did not blow up the barn."

"Stepsister," Madeline interrupts.

"My sister," Lucy says, casting a pointed look at Madeline, "still blames me for cutting the hair off her Barbie doll—and for the record I didn't do that either."

The corners of the agent's mouth go up. Damn Lucy. She somehow always finds a way to slither into people's good graces, and today she's putting on a good show. Typically, Lucy is the first one to point out how they are related or, to be more accurate, how they aren't.

"Jamie Saldano, ATF," the agent says, taking Lucy's hand and shaking it.

"Do you have any news?" Madeline asks. "Do you know what happened?"

"Not yet. We are still gathering information," Agent Saldano says, turning his attention to Sonnet, the Dutch Warmblood that Lucy raised. "She's a beauty. Can I touch her?"

"Of course," Madeline says, distractedly. "It had to be an accident, right? Johanna smoked once in a while. When she was stressed. Could she have dropped a cigarette and accidently started the fire?"

Agent Saldano runs a tentative hand over Sonnet's stormy gray flank, and the horse jerks her head away. "Whoa," he says, with a nervous laugh. "I guess it's obvious I'm not a horseman." He's not giving them anything. No information at all. But isn't that the way investigations go? They'll probably be the last ones to know what really happened, and until then they will be expected to answer all the questions and be patient. She tries to tamp down her frustration.

"She's a little skittish," Lucy says. "You need to rub her here, on her withers." Lucy demonstrates by stroking Sonnet firmly between her shoulder blades.

Agent Saldano follows Lucy's directions, and instead of flinching, the horse leans into his touch. Madeline bites her cheek, hating that Lucy is right.

"Good girl," Saldano murmurs. "Until we have definitive proof that the explosion was an accident, we have to explore all possibilities. I know we talked briefly about this last evening at the hospital, but can you think of anyone who might have wanted to target you or your property?"

"No, no one," Madeline says and then backtracks. "Our neighbor, Sully Preston. We were in business with him for a short time, and it ended badly. He and his wife crashed our party."

"Badly enough that you can see him blowing up your barn?" the agent asks.

Madeline thinks for a moment. Sully Preston is a shady businessman and could have destroyed their business, but arson? Murder? It was possible. "I don't know, but I saw Wes's brother, Dix, and Sully having words earlier in the evening."

"The partnership went south," he says. "Why?"

"Bute," Lucy says, and Madeline glares at her, willing her to shut up.

"Bute," the agent repeats. "What's that?"

"Phenylbutazone," Lucy says. "It's used as a pain reliever for horses. Sully Preston uses it to trick horse buyers into thinking a lame horse is healthy. And acepromazine can make a badly trained horse appear safe." The Prestons could have made a mint duping potential buyers into spending tens, even hundreds of thousands of dollars under the pretense that the horses they purchased were potential superstars. Luckily, Dix caught on and the partnership was quickly dissolved.

"I just have a hard time believing that Sully could kill someone over this," Madeline says, regretting having told Lucy about the whole mess. "We parted ways with the Prestons last fall. It's not an issue any longer."

"But they showed up at your party uninvited?" the agent asks. "Isn't that odd?"

It's very strange, Madeline thinks. Over the last eight months, she has been doing everything she can to avoid running into Sully and Mia Preston—not an easy feat considering how small Nightjar is. So far she has been mostly successful.

"Yes," Madeline admits. "There's no love lost between us." And hadn't Mia Preston acted like they were practically best friends at the party? It was almost like she was putting on a show. But for who?

"I'll talk to the Prestons," Agent Saldano says. "Is there anyone else you can think of?"

"You had those animal activists running around here, didn't you?" Lucy asks, and Madeline brushes the comment away with the shake of her head.

"What about Johanna Monaghan? How long have you known her?" Saldano asks.

"We've been best friends for nine years," Madeline says. "We met at the coffee shop in Nightjar and just clicked."

"Can you think of anyone who might want to do her harm?" he asks.

"Johanna?" she asks in surprise. "No, everyone loved her. All she ever did was help people and bring babies into the world. I can't imagine anyone hurting her." Lucy has grown bored with the conversation, and Madeline watches as she moves down the aisle, stopping in front of Blackjack again.

"And Johanna's marriage? All good on that front?"

Madeline hesitates. Like the Prestons, Madeline couldn't see Dalton killing his wife, but there were problems. "Johanna and Dalton had their issues," Madeline finally says.

"What kind of issues?" the agent presses.

"I don't know," Madeline says. "They argued. But what couple doesn't? Dalton has a temper, but I can't believe that he would do something like this." Even as she says this, there is a wisp of doubt. She loved Johanna like a sister, but Dalton? Not so much. And hadn't Johanna increasingly complained about how erratic Dalton could be?

"What do you mean by *temper*?" Saldano asks.

Madeline scans her memory for examples. "Johanna told me how, one time, one of their neighbors planted some trees just on the other side of the property line and in their back-yard. Dalton freaked out. He started yelling at them and ran over the seedlings with their John Deere mower."

"Seems over-the-top," Saldano agrees. "Anything else?"

"Dalton was, I don't know, overprotective of Johanna. Too much so. He didn't like that she had to go out at all hours of the day or night to assist with a birth. He didn't get that this went with the job. Johanna told me Dalton insisted on having

Location Services enabled on her phone, which makes sense, right?" Saldano nods. "But Dalton took it further, and Johanna found one of those little tags in her car."

"A GPS monitor?" the agent asks.

"Yes," Madeline says. "Johanna was so angry that Dalton didn't trust her."

"Any reason Dalton would have good reason not to trust her?"

Reluctantly, Madeline responds. "Johanna never right out told me she was involved with another man, but I think she might have been. She was secretive—even with me. And more than once asked me to tell Dalton that she was with me when she wasn't."

Saldano continues to stroke Sonnet's withers. "You have no idea who the other man might be?" Madeline shakes her head. "What about her other—would you call them *patients*? The women she helped give birth. Any issues with them?"

Madeline shakes her head. "Johanna didn't really talk about her other clients, not specifically anyway. She was careful about their privacy. But as far as I know, everyone was happy with her care. Everyone wanted Johanna to be their midwife."

Agent Saldano seems satisfied. "If you think of anything, no matter how small it seems, please let me know," he says.

"I will," Madeline says, then adds, "Wait, have you heard anything about Dix? No one seems to know where he is. We've called the area hospitals but haven't had any luck."

"No, but I'll be sure to check for you. Does he live nearby?"

"Down the road a few miles, but his truck is still here. We figured he was taken by ambulance to a hospital."

"I'll see what I can find out," Saldano assures her. "And how are you doing?"

"I'm fine," Madeline says automatically. That has always been her go-to response to that question. *I'm fine. Everything's fine.* But it isn't, hasn't been for a long time.

"Good," Agent Saldano says. "We'll figure out what's going on, and you focus on taking care of yourself and that baby."

Saldano turns away from Madeline. "Ms. Quaid," Agent Saldano calls out to Lucy and moves to the far end of the stable where she is grooming Sonnet. Madeline can't hear what they are saying, but Lucy seems relaxed, unfazed by the questions. But that's Lucy for you. On the outside she is calm. But inside, that's a different story.

When they were younger, Lucy always had an underlying current of discontent just below the surface of her skin. At first it would show itself in the most subtle of ways: a backhanded compliment, a stolen trinket, a biting pinch beneath the kitchen table. The anger would fester and boil until it no longer could be contained. The results were Barbie dolls with bald heads, stinging slaps, a loosened billet strap on Madeline's saddle. And always Lucy denied, denied, denied, looking at her father and Madeline's mother with her big doe eyes. Madeline's stepfather and Lucy's dad, who wasn't one to interfere in childhood spats, simply told the girls to get along. Madeline's mother and Lucy's stepmother tried to get Madeline to understand that Lucy was adjusting to having a new mom and sister, that she would come around. And she had. Despite their epic arguments, Madeline and Lucy became as close as two sisters could, at least until Lucy's dad died and he put Madeline in charge of the money.

Madeline watches as Lucy hands the grooming brush to Agent Saldano, guiding his hand across a spotted Appaloosa's flank. The timing is strange. The sisters haven't talked in a month, and suddenly Lucy appears in the aftermath of a tragedy that has taken the life of Madeline's best friend. The thought of Johanna pierces Madeline so sharply she nearly doubles. In Johanna, Madeline thought she found another sister, one very different than Lucy. Sisters of the soul—that's what they called one another.

Agent Saldano is smiling at something Lucy is saying, and she moves close to him. Too close. A cold finger of dread crawls across Madeline's belly, and she cradles it protectively. Lucy glances over at Madeline to make sure she is watching. Her small smile seems to say *Do you see? Do you see what I can do?*

Madeline does see. She feels the sudden urge to flee, to run away from this nightmare. But she knows she can't. This is her life now. There's no running. She has to face whatever is coming her way head-on. She has no other choice.

CHAPTER 11

JAMIE

DESPITE LIVING IN horse country for a brief time, Jamie has never actually touched a horse before. Give him a skateboard over one of these creatures any day. The Appaloosa's coat is silky, the tangled mane rough beneath his fingers. Lucy shows him the proper way to brush him. Jamie isn't surprised to learn that the two women aren't biologically related. They look nothing alike. Lucy is shorter than her sister, more angular, but seems to take up more space in a room while Madeline is taller, softer. It's clear there's a rift between the two of them, and he wonders if Lucy Quaid may have come to Nightjar for much more nefarious reasons.

Though Jamie doesn't say anything to the women yet, the second explosion is clearly the result of an IED. While the fire marshal and the crime-scene techs finish up their work, Jamie needs to use this time to try and gather as much information as possible about the Drakes, Johanna and Dalton Monaghan, and the people around them.

"You said something about animal rights activists?" Jamie says, running the curry comb along the Appaloosa's back.

"Yeah. Madeline told me about the emails last year," Lucy says, tucking a wayward strand of hair behind her ear. "Some zealots not happy that the ranch raises and trains horses for competitions."

"Have there been complaints about how the horses are treated?" Jamie asks. "They look like they're in good shape to me."

"Oh, they are. My sister knows how to care for horses. In her mind they are better company than most humans." Lucy shrugs. "Some activists see it as a moral issue."

"And this group believes so strongly in this they might commit arson? Murder?" Jamie asks.

"Possibly," Lucy says. "When I was racing, I'd get threats, had people protesting the competitions."

"You raced horses?" Jamie asks. "Like the Kentucky Derby?" He eyes Lucy with new interest.

Lucy laughs. "Not quite. I was marathoner. I used to ride in endurance competitions, sometimes up to a hundred miles a day."

"On a horse?" Jamie asks, impressed. "I've never heard of that before. Kind of like the Pony Express."

"Sort of," Lucy says. "The horses loved to race. It was when they felt most free. Me too," she adds.

"Why'd you stop?" Jamie asks.

Lucy gives him a sad smile. "My dad got sick a few years ago. I came home to take care of him. He died last month."

"I'm sorry to hear that," Jamie says. He waits, lets the moment pass before going on. "Do you know the name of this particular group that threatened your sister and her husband?" Jamie asks.

"I don't," Lucy says. "As you probably noticed, my sister and I are not particularly close. We had a falling-out at our dad's funeral. I know you have to ask me, but I did not blow up my sister's barn. As much as Madeline loves horses, I do too. Even if I was angry with my sister, I would never put her animals in danger." Lucy takes the curry comb from Jamie's hand and returns it to the hook on the stable wall.

"Good to know," Jamie says. "But if things are so tense with Madeline, why are you here?"

"I missed her," Lucy says simply. "My sister and I may have our differences, but I love her. It's been a hard year. Our dad died. Well, my dad, Madeline's stepdad. Madeline's mom died when she was sixteen. We're all that each other has left, and I was hoping we could get past it."

"And?" Jamie asks. "Have you gotten past it?"

He watches as hesitation flickers across Lucy's face. "Not yet. Madeline has made it perfectly clear she wants nothing to do with me."

"Why is that?" Jamie asks.

"It's a long story, and stupid really." Lucy shrugs. "At the funeral I said some things to Madeline I probably shouldn't have. She left angry, took my horses."

Jamie waits for Lucy to say more. Instead, she moves to the next stall.

"So where were you yesterday at around six o'clock?" Jamie finally asks.

"I was in a bar about thirty miles from here, drinking shots with Trent. He's a ranch hand here. I left around midnight and then got a flat. Trent came upon me, and that's when the sheriff showed up and told us what happened, and we drove right here."

This was the same story the ranch hand told him, though Trent's account made Lucy sound a little off. "You came from where?"

"Iowa. Got here three days ago," Lucy says.

Jamie raises his eyebrows. "And you didn't go to the party? You came all this way and didn't even show up to find out if your sister is going to have a boy or a girl?"

"I was trying to get my nerve up to see Madeline. We left things in a pretty bad way."

"So she had no idea you were coming?"

"None. Looking back, it probably wasn't wise that I showed up," Lucy admits, "but if Madeline knew I was coming, she would have made a point to avoid me."

"Are you sticking around for a few more days?" Jamie asks. He can't detain Lucy, has no reason to, at least not yet. If she decides to leave, he can only take her contact information and reach out if he has more questions.

"I can't leave until my truck gets fixed," she says. "But as soon as that happens, I'm pretty sure Madeline is going to send me on my way. But I'd like to stay. I can see how upset she is about her friend dying."

Jamie can't quite tell if Lucy is being sincere. He knows how complicated family relationships can be, how fraught with emotion and tainted by real and imagined slights. Could their rift be due to a few horses? Maybe, but Jamie is willing to bet there's a whole lot more to it than what Lucy is telling him.

He takes Lucy's cell number and hands her his card. "Give me a call if you think of anything." He walks away, pausing to slide his hand across the nape of Sonnet's neck one more time, aware of Lucy's eyes on his back, and exits the stables. He sends a quick text to Greta.

Get me a list of all the stores in a sixty-mile radius of Nightjar that sell PVC piping and double-headed nails. And run a FinCen report on Sully and Mia Preston, Wes and Madeline Drake, Lucy Quaid, and the Monaghans.

A FinCen report will give them an overview of someone's financial records. If there are any red flags, they can apply for a subpoena with the US Attorney's Office for more detailed records. Jamie needs to talk to Madeline again, alone. Suss out her relationship with Lucy. He's seen it before in his work—

sibling rivalry, jealousy simmering until it bubbles over into violence.

He thinks of his own sister. Jamie still has the puckered white scars on his arm where Juneau scratched him over some childhood disagreement. His sister had a temper but was quick to apologize and quick to forgive. That's why Jamie didn't get too worked-up on that warm September evening when she kicked him out of the car, telling him he had to walk the rest of the way home. He thought, at the time, he would walk a few hundred yards and Juneau would pull up behind him, tell him to get back in and then take him home, promising to make pizza rolls for supper. That never happened.

Jamie shakes away the memory as he moves toward the house. Now that it looks like an IED is what killed Johanna Monaghan, he'll talk to her husband again and set up an interview with the Prestons. Then he needs to get the guest list and the names of all the other attendees at the party, including the caterers and photographer. He also needs to get his hands on the security footage. If they are lucky, the perpetrator will be on video.

Wes and Madeline Drake are with Sheriff Colson on the back terrace when he approaches the house. A current of anticipation zips through him. It's the first time he'll come face-to-face with Jerry Colson in over two and a half decades, and a cold sweat erupts across his skin. He takes a few steps toward him, then stops.

"Sheriff," Jamie calls out, "can I borrow you for a second?"

The sheriff raises his hand to let Jamie know he heard him and finishes his conversation with the Drakes, and Jamie's heart skips a beat as Colson begins the slow walk across the yard toward him.

The sheriff narrows his eyes, peering hard at Jamie as he moves closer. It takes a second, but recognition floods the older man's face, followed by a broad smile. "J. J. Archer," he breathes out, using the name Jamie hasn't used in years.

"I go by Jamie Saldano now," Jamie says. "My mother's maiden name."

Once Jamie left home and went to college, Jamie ditched the initials and his father's last name and went with Saldano. Jamie didn't mind severing the tie to his dad, a man who had always been absent, but he did feel guilty severing this connection to his sister. He felt he had to do it to escape the scrutiny. Each year, around the anniversary of Juneau's disappearance, a renewed interest in the case would spark calls and ambushes from the press. His life has been much quieter since the name change, and Jamie is okay with that.

"Last I heard you moved back to San Antonio. My God, you've gotten tall," Colton says, looking up at Jamie. "I almost didn't recognize you."

"My wife and I moved back a few months ago. I'm at the Cheyenne office. Got the call about the explosion and here I am. And you look exactly the same," Jamie says, an unexpected lump rising in his throat. Sheriff Colson does look the same, a few pounds heavier, but Jamie will never forget the man's eyes. Sharp, watchful, but kind. "You're the sheriff now, Colson?" Jamie says. "Really moving up in the world!"

"Yeah." Colson laughs and claps him on the back. "So you're married? Any kids?"

"Nope, no kids," Jamie says. "But I met your son. Trent, right?"

"Yep, and I got two more just like him," Colson says and turns to look at Wes and Madeline on the terrace. "Does Wes know you're here?" he asks.

"No," Jamie admits. "I mean I saw him last night at the hospital, but he didn't recognize me. Can't blame him—he has a lot going on right now."

"And you didn't say anything?" the sheriff asks in disbelief. "Let me call him over. He'll be glad to see you."

"No, no," Jamie interrupts him. "I'd rather you didn't, at least not yet. I'm here to do a job, and I don't want our past to distract from it. And honestly, the whole incident is still a blur." *Incident*. Jamie knows his sister would be disgusted with that description of what happened. *Incident, really, Jamie?* she would have said. *I disappeared, and you were nearly killed. Incident is all you've got?*

Juneau came to Jamie like this every so often. He could hear the exact timbre of her voice. Low and husky for a sixteen-year-old. She came off as tough, when she was really a bookish girl who played the flute and learned to stand up for herself when she had to.

"You sure?" the sheriff asks doubtfully. "He's going to make the connection sooner or later."

"I am," Jamie says. "And in light of our past, I've called in another agent to take the lead." This is a lie, but he will make that call at some point. "Are you okay with not saying anything for now?"

"Not really," Colson says. "A woman is dead, and we have the press banging on our door. The fact that the lead investigator and the homeowner are connected isn't a good look. I don't want anything screwing up this case."

"I don't either," Jamie says. "I'm good at my job, Sheriff. Really good. That's why my boss sent me here. I'm not trying to hide my past, but honestly it's not relevant. Of course I'm grateful Wes found me, but I'd never jeopardize an investigation for anyone." Colson looks hard at Jamie, and he can't help feeling like that twelve-year-old kid again in a hospital bed. "Give me a few days," Jamie presses. "I'll get a lot more information from witnesses if they don't know my past. If it becomes an issue, I'll be the first one to say so."

"Listen, I just want to make sure your focus is going to be on this case and not your sister's," Colson says.

"I don't think that's going to be a problem," Jamie says. "There hasn't been any new information in Juneau's case for years." The sheriff lifts his eyebrows, and Jamie knows he hit a nerve. He knows that Colson worked hard to find out what happened to her, but it wasn't enough. There was no usable DNA, no hair or fibers, nothing that led to the person who took her.

"We haven't given up," the sheriff says.

"I know," Jamie says, "I get it." And he does. He knows that not all cases are solved, that sometimes, no matter the effort, the pieces of the puzzle don't always come together. He's got several open cases himself. But it's different when the victim is your sister. When it's you.

Are you really letting him off that easy? Juneau's voice says. *They didn't do shit. You know why? Because these small communities protect their own. Always have. Always will. Mom was a nobody cleaning lady who picked up their shit, and we were her nothing kids.*

Jamie tries to muscle his sister's face from his thoughts. "We know the explosion was due to arson. Now let's focus on figuring out who did it. What are you thinking?"

The sheriff shrugs. "I have no idea at this point. And who was the target? Johanna Monaghan? The Drakes? The techs found Johanna's phone in the wreckage, so that might tell us something or nothing. Who knows?"

"I hear Dalton Monaghan has a temper. Anything lead you to believe he might be involved?" Jamie asks.

"He has a temper, all right. Mostly a lot of bluster. We'll look through our records and see if anything jumps out," Colson says.

"Lucy, Madeline's sister, mentioned there were some animal rights activists making some noise. Anything to it?"

"Nah," the sheriff says, shaking his head. "I can't see them involved in something like this. It's just a ragtag group of college kids. Harmless, really. Here come Wes and Madeline," Colson says. "Maybe they have more ideas."

"Here's the guest list and the names of the photographer, event planner, and catering company," Madeline says, handing Jamie several sheets of printer paper. "I don't know the names of the employees they might have brought along, so you'd have to check with them."

"Thanks," Jamie says, looking at the list. There are well over two hundred names. A lot to sift through. The sheriff's phone buzzes, and he excuses himself to answer it. "I'd like to talk to each of you, individually, today." Jamie looks at his watch. "Say, three o'clock at the sheriff's office?"

"Sure thing," Wes says, "as long as our lawyer can make it."

Sheriff Colson lowers his phone and beckons to Jamie. "Excuse me," Jamie says to Wes and Madeline and follows the sheriff out of earshot of the couple.

"That was the hospital over in Jackson," the sheriff says. "The nurse says that the waitress who was injured in the explosion can talk to us now. We need to head over there and get her statement. Do you want to be the one to do that?"

"Yes, but you're welcome to come with me," Jamie offers. "Especially if you know her. It might make her feel more comfortable."

"I don't know her, actually," the sheriff says. "She's new to the area. What a welcome wagon." He shakes his head.

It's this place, Juneau whispers in his ear. Jamie brushes away the sensation as if waving away a gnat. *It's mean and ugly and spits out anyone who doesn't belong here. You don't belong here, Jamie. You should have learned that a long time ago. Go home. Go home to Tess.*

"You okay, Jamie?" He looks up to find the sheriff looking at him with concern.

"I'm fine," Jamie assures him, grateful the officer didn't call him by his old nickname. "I'll head over to the hospital to talk to the waitress. You okay holding down the fort here?"

"Yeah," the sheriff says. "And Jamie, it's great to see you again."

Jamie smiles. "I'm glad we could catch up," he tells the sheriff. "It's really good to be back."

You, Juneau says as Jamie heads to his car, *are a terrible liar. Always have been.*

CHAPTER 12
MADELINE

MADELINE WAITS UNTIL Agent Saldano and the sheriff have left before turning to Wes. "Did you know that Lucy was going to show up here?" she asks.

Wes pulls her into a hug. "I had no idea. But last night she told me she was worried about you. She said she felt bad about how you left things after your stepdad's funeral."

"I'm just surprised she'd come now," Madeline says, pulling back from his embrace. "She was awful to me. I can't help it that her dad put me in charge of his estate. She needs to grow up and take responsibility for her own actions." She had told Wes about her argument with Lucy but hadn't told him everything.

Wes tightens his arms around her. "Honestly, I'm surprised too. But maybe it's a good thing she's here. It's not healthy for you or the baby to have all that anger and resentment built up. This might be a chance for the two of you to make up. And besides, I'd feel a lot better having an extra pair of eyes looking out for anything out of the ordinary."

"Maybe," Madeline says noncommittedly.

"I love you so much, Madeline," he murmurs into her neck. "And the baby. I don't want anything bad to happen to either one of you." Wes is gripping her so tightly now that his fingers are digging into the tender area on her torso at the edge of her stitches. She gasps at the pressure, trying to pull away, but he holds on for a second longer. When Wes lets go, his eyes are damp.

Madeline reaches up, lays a palm on his cheek. "I love you too," she says, extracting herself from his grip.

"I'll go check on the horses," Wes says. "Maybe take Billy out for a ride. I need to wrap my head around all this. Will you be okay here?"

Madeline nods, not wanting to admit she's afraid. Afraid of whoever caused the explosion, afraid of the media circling like sharks around them, afraid of what her sister might do.

Out the window, Madeline sees Lucy making her way toward the house. Despite her small stature, she moves confidently and with purpose, as if she belongs here. Madeline can't deal with her sister right now and excuses herself to go upstairs and wash away the final remnants of ash and smoke.

She can't get her stitches wet, so a bath or a shower are out of the question. Instead, she stiffly lowers her head and washes her hair in the bathroom sink, then uses a washcloth to scrub her body, avoiding the strip of stitches on her back. She stands for a moment, staring at her pregnant body in the mirror. As her stomach expanded and her breasts swelled, Madeline thought that Wes might not find her as attractive, but until the last month it was the opposite. He couldn't get enough of her. His hands roaming, exploring the curves and valleys of her body. Then suddenly he stopped. Wes still hugged her and dropped perfunctory kisses on her cheek, but it wasn't the same. Secretly, Madeline was relieved. Her body felt like it wasn't her own any longer, and physical touch made her want to jump out of her skin. Madeline had spoken about it to Johanna, who assured her a change in sexual activity

"Okay," Mellie says. She sits up in bed, wincing at the movement.

"Here, let me," Jamie says, reaching for the remote-control dangling between the bedrails by its cord. He presses the button that will raise her head, watching to make sure he isn't causing her any more pain. She looks even younger than her twenty-one years. Her face is unmarred except for a small piercing in one nostril and her cranberry-colored hair is dusted with soot and smells smoky. Jamie pulls a chair next to her bedside but, before sitting, moves the breakfast tray with the offending smell to the far side of the room. "Does it hurt?" Jamie asks, finally settling into the chair.

"Some," she says, shrugging. "But the doctors said it could have been much worse. I'm more sore than anything. I can't wait to get out of here."

"Then, I won't keep you long," Jamie says, "but if you need a break or want me to get a nurse, let me know." Mellie nods. "You work for the catering company, correct?"

"Yeah," she says. "I started last summer. Mostly I walk around handing out appetizers during events, but I also help with setup and teardown."

"You live in Nightjar?" Jamie asks. Mellie nods. "And you've lived here how long?"

"For about a year. Thought it would be fun to live in the mountains." Mellie gives a little shrug of her shoulders. "It's beautiful, but it hasn't been much fun."

"That's understandable, given what you've been through," Jamie agrees. "But we're working hard to figure out what happened. Can you walk me through what happened yesterday?"

"Like from the beginning of the day?" Mellie asks wearily.

Jamie knows that even the smallest detail can be crucial in an investigation, how memories can dissipate, and despite Mellie's obvious exhaustion and pain, he needs answers. "Tell me everything you remember."

"Okay," Mellie says, shifting in her bed. "I worked an event that ended late the night before and slept in until about ten and hung around my apartment until about two, and then I ran a few errands before I headed to the caterer's and then rode with some of the other crew to the Drake ranch. We arrived there about four and got right to work helping to unload the catering vans and set up the food."

"Did you see anything out of the ordinary?" Jamie asks. "Anyone hanging around who looked out of place?"

"No. But I really wouldn't know who should be there or not. It was the first time I've ever been to the ranch," Mellie explains. "Once the guests started to arrive, I began handing out appetizers, then there was an announcement that the gender reveal was going to begin. So everyone started moving toward the field."

"And you headed that way too?" Jamie asks, thinking the waitress could be a dead end.

"No." Mellie shakes her head. "I went to the barn. I saw the midwife go in there earlier, and I was hoping to talk to her."

"You knew Johanna Monaghan?" Jamie asks, with surprise.

Mellie looks down. "It's a small town, and I'm not supposed to have personal conversations with the guests, but I'd heard what a great midwife she is. Was. And I had some questions."

"What kind of questions?" Jamie presses gently.

"You won't tell my boss, will you?" Mellie asks. "I just started this job, and I don't want to get fired."

"Fired for what?" Jamie asks, though he has an inkling as to what she's about to tell him.

"Being pregnant," Mellie says softly. "I heard that Johanna was this incredible midwife, and I was hoping she'd maybe be able to help me."

"You know you can't be fired for being pregnant, don't you?" Jamie says. "That's illegal."

Mellie looks at him like he's grown a second head. "Of course they won't say that's the reason why, but everyone knows it happens."

Jamie can't say that she's wrong. "I won't say anything," he promises. "You followed Johanna into the barn?"

"I was supposed to stay behind because once we saw the smoke, we were supposed to start pouring the champagne and top it with pink or blue cotton candy and hand it out to the guests. But it was kind of chaotic because they weren't planning to do the actual reveal until right before sunset, and it was only like six something."

"They went off-schedule?" Jamie asks. "Do you know who made the change?"

"The Drakes, I guess, but I don't know," Mellie says. "I heard it might rain later, so I figured it had something to do with the weather, but I'm not sure."

The change in schedule could be significant, Jamie thinks. He needs to find out who made the decision to push up the reveal and why.

"So, everyone is moving toward the meadow, and you hang back?"

"Yeah. I decided to peek inside the barn in case I could talk to the midwife for a minute. That's when I smelled smoke. At first I thought that my boss had moved the grills into the barn, which would have been weird. I was curious, so I opened the door, and I saw her, the midwife." Mellie takes a shaky breath. "She was smoking a cigarette and holding a gift. It looked like she'd been crying."

"She was holding a gift?" Jamie asks, his radar beginning to buzz. "Do you remember what it looked like?"

Mellie shrugs. "I'm not sure. It did have a big black bow on top, which I thought was a weird choice for a baby party." She reaches for the cup of water next to her bed, takes the straw between her lips, and takes a long drink.

"How big?" Jamie asks.

"The bow?" Mellie asks in confusion.

"No, the box," Jamie clarifies.

Mellie holds her hands about twelve inches apart to indicate how wide the package was. "I asked her what was wrong, but she yelled at me to leave her alone, to get out. I turned right around and left. Then she called out to me, said she was sorry, and started walking my way. That's when the barn exploded. I went flying, and when I hit the ground, I saw my legs were on fire." Tears fill Mellie's eyes. "It crawled right up my legs, and that's when I remembered I had spilled olive oil all over my pants earlier. Someone tackled me and put the flames out. The last thing I remember was how much it hurt."

Tears stream freely down Mellie's cheeks, and she wipes them away with the edge of the bedsheet. "I think I'm tired now," she says. Jamie can see that it's true. Her eyes are heavy with exhaustion, her face tight with pain. Their short conversation seems to have sapped any energy the young woman might have had in reserve.

Still, Jamie has more questions. "We're almost done here, Mellie, I promise. Did you see Johanna Monaghan carrying a gift earlier when you saw her?"

Mellie lifts her eyes to the ceiling, thinking. "No, I don't think so."

"And you don't know where Johanna got it from?" Jamie asks.

"I have no idea. It was so crowded and busy, I didn't even notice," Mellie says. "I'm sorry."

"Don't worry about it," Jamie says, though he's beginning to wonder if the package is what held the IED. "Did you see anything else unusual? Anything out of place?"

Mellie closes her eyes, as if thinking. After a moment she opens them and shakes her head. "No. Everyone looked like they were having a good time." She pauses, then adds, "Except for maybe Mrs. Drake. She looked kind of miserable."

Now that's interesting, Jamie thinks. A gender reveal party is supposed to be a happy, joyous occasion. And from what Jamie could gather, the party was one of a kind. An A-list country singer, hundreds of friends, great food and drink, finally learning the sex of her baby, all set against the beautiful backdrop of the mountains. Why wouldn't Madeline Drake be happy?

"Any idea as to why she was upset?" Jamie asks.

"I don't know," Mellie says. "And I wouldn't say she was upset, more like she didn't want to be there."

"Okay," Jamie says. "I will have more questions for you, but if you think of anything else, will you be sure to give me a call?" He sets a business card on the tray in front of her.

Once in the hallway, Jamie feels the buzz of his phone in his pocket and moves to a quiet corner and looks at the screen. It's his boss, Special Agent in Charge Sykes. Jamie lets out a breath before answering.

"Saldano," he says by way of greeting.

"Saldano," Sykes says. "What the hell do you have going on over there? It's all over the news, and my phone has been ringing off the hook."

"We found all the makings of an IED. Ball bearings, nails, PVC piping," Jamie explains. "The bomb techs from Jackson are packing everything up and sending the evidence off to the lab, and the deceased has been transported to the medical examiner's office for an autopsy."

"Anyone taking responsibility?" Sykes asks. "Is there any chance of terrorism? Domestic or otherwise?"

"It's too soon to tell, but my gut says no, that this is personal. I'm just not sure that the woman who was killed was the intended target. I'm in the process of interviewing witnesses."

"Keep me posted," Skyes says. "I'll handle the press for now, but you're going to have to talk to them sooner or later."

"Will do," Jamie assures him before disconnecting. Talking

to the press is Jamie's least favorite part of the job, but right now he has other matters to attend to, like interviewing the Drakes' neighbors, Sully and Mia Preston.

"Agent Saldano?" comes a voice from behind him. He turns to find a nurse dressed in yellow scrubs. "Mellie says she has to talk to you again."

"Great, thanks," Jamie says and quickly returns to the hospital room. Mellie is sitting in a chair now, dressed in the same kind of scrubs that Madeline Drake had been wearing the night before.

"I remembered something." Mellie's voice has a floating quality, her words are loose, unfinished. "I saw him."

"Who?" Jamie asks, trying not to sound too eager. "Who did you see?"

"Coming out of the barn. I saw him," Mellie says quietly. "I didn't think it was a big deal before, but now . . ."

"Every bit of information could be important, but you don't have to worry about that. I'll figure it out. Who did you see?" Jamie asks again. The nerve endings in his fingers jangle.

"Her husband," Mellie says. "I saw Johanna Monaghan's husband coming out of the barn before I went in, and then a few minutes later it exploded."

CHAPTER 14

JAMIE

JAMIE CALLS SHERIFF Colson and requests that a deputy brings Dalton Monaghan to the office for a formal interview, then keys Sully Preston's address into his GPS. As Jamie approaches the vast property, he sees a pair of eight-foot-tall horse sculptures flanking each side of the ranch gate. A metal sign affixed to the gate's arch reads *Long Horn Ranch* in loopy script. He turns onto the property and passes multiple pastures, each holding different livestock: horses, cattle, bison. As he draws closer to the house, he passes what looks like a pitch and putt golf course and a pickle ball court. Jamie does a double take when he sees a peacock with a plume of iridescent blue and green feathers staring at him curiously from behind a white picket fence.

"Who are these people?" Jamie asks himself as he parks in front of the massive, custom-made building constructed of honey-colored logs. Three stories high, it looks more like a luxury hotel retreat than a home. Equally impressive is the water feature, made up of large, smooth boulders and jagged rocks that form a meandering waterfall filled with brightly colored koi. As a kid, Jamie had had no idea that homes like this existed in Nightjar.

He presses the bell next to the front door, a twelve-foot monstrosity, and waits. He presses the button two more times.

Seconds tick by, then minutes, and he is about to give up when the door opens to reveal a small-statured man with close-cropped white hair and horn-rimmed glasses.

"Sully Preston?" Jamie asks.

"Who wants to know?" the man asks.

Jamie introduces himself, and reluctantly the man nods and moves aside to let Jamie enter.

"I'm Sully Preston," the man says. "I figured someone would be coming by. Let's talk in my office."

Sully leads him through the great room past an expanse of windows that look out over a lake and the mountains off in the distance and down a narrow hallway lined with black-and-white family photos. He opens a door and ushers Jamie inside. Hanging from the smoothly hewn logs walls are dozens of heads. Deer, moose, elk, bear, mountain goats, and what Jamie thinks is a warthog, their glassy eyes staring down at him. Apparently, Sully Preston is quite the hunter.

Sully takes a seat behind an executive-size mahogany desk that holds a computer, a stack of unopened mail, and a pile of file folders. Jamie takes the chair across from him.

"My wife insisted I keep my trophies in here," Sully says with a little laugh. "Says she doesn't like them looking at her."

"You must be a good shot," Jamie says.

"I am," Sully says. "So let me guess. Wes Drake told you that he thinks I'm the one who blew up his barn, right?" he asks, getting right to the point.

"What makes you think it was on purpose?" Jamie asks. "The cause of the explosion hasn't been released."

Sully gives Jamie a wry smile, as if to say *Come on.* "It's a small town. People talk. Why would the ATF come out to investigate if it was just an accident?"

"Why would Wes Drake think you had something to do with the explosion?" Jamie counters as he surreptitiously looks around the office.

"It's no secret that Wes and I had a falling-out. Some nonsense over a few horses. We were friends once, and Mia and I went to the party to try to put the past behind us. What kind of bomb was it?"

Sully is matching each of his questions with a question of his own, and Jamie doesn't like it. "And did you? Put the past behind you?"

"We really didn't get a chance to. Mia and I spoke briefly to Madeline, but there were lots of guests. She was busy. We hoped to catch up more with her and Wes later. I don't think I even saw Wes until they started the gender reveal. Then all hell broke out."

"Did you see anything strange or anyone acting suspiciously?" Jamie asks and then there's a tap on the office door.

"Sully, honey," comes a voice. "What's going on?"

Jamie turns around in his chair as a woman a good thirty years younger than Sully leans against the doorway. She's dressed in yoga pants and holds an arm in a bright pink cast close to her body.

"This is Agent Saldano with the ATF," Sully says. "And this is my wife, Mia."

"You were injured in the explosion?" Jamie asks.

"Yes," Mia says. "It was terrifying. One minute everyone was laughing and enjoying themselves, and the next I'm flat on my face with a broken wrist."

"That's too bad," Jamie says. "But I'm glad you weren't injured more seriously. Exactly where were you when the barn exploded?"

"Sully and I weren't next to each other," Mia explains, "but I was standing with a group of women off to the right of Wes and Madeline. The barn was behind me. Wes and Madeline were aiming the shotgun at the truck in the field. They pulled the trigger, and it exploded. A few seconds later I heard another big boom and was knocked to the ground."

"By the explosion?" Jamie asks.

"I don't think so," Mia says. "It happened so fast, but I think in the panic, someone knocked into me. A bunch of us went down like dominoes."

"How about you?" Jamie directs the question to Sully. "Where were you?"

"I was directly behind Wes and Madeline," Sully says. "It was like Mia said. Everything was fine one minute, and the next there were people bleeding all over the place."

"But you weren't injured?" Jamie asks, scanning.

"Miraculously, no," Sully says. "But Dix Drake wasn't so lucky. I tried to stop the bleeding, but he was in pretty bad shape by the time the EMTs arrived."

"Any idea what hospital they took Dix to?" Jamie asks, remembering that his family was looking for him.

"No. No idea," Sully says. "You mean you can't find him?"

Jamie ignores the question and instead says, "Tell me about bute." Mia and Sully exchange glances.

"So Wes did talk to you," Sully says flatly.

"He's lying," Mia breaks in. "We would never hurt a horse, and we would never put a rider in danger."

"It's a—what?—tranquilizer or something?" Jamie asks, feigning ignorance.

"It's like aspirin for horses," Mia explains. "But we aren't the ones who gave the horses any. We wouldn't do that."

Jamie knows that bute is much more than aspirin. It's used to ease the pain caused by musculoskeletal disorders, joint disease, arthritis. He recalls Lucy saying it can also temporarily mask any issues a lame horse may have, making them easier to sell. Jamie consults his notebook again. "What about acepromazine?"

"Absolutely not!" Mia says.

"But the horses were drugged," Jamie says. "Why? And who would do it?"

"You'd have to talk to Wes and Madeline about that. I sent them healthy horses. They should be looking at their own people, not me." Sully takes a deep breath. "Listen," he says, holding up his hands, "I buy and sell horses. I'm the matchmaker, the middleman. You're looking for a certain kind of horse—racing, dressage, an old nag for the kids to learn to ride on—I'll find you the perfect one. What I don't do is drug horses."

"I imagine these accusations aren't good for business," Jamie observes.

"I'm not worried," Sully says, getting to his feet and coming around his desk. "I've been in this business for a long time. People around here know me, trust me. Now, if there's nothing else, I've got a call in ten minutes."

"Just one more question. For now," Jamie says, remaining in his chair. "Have you ever been inside that barn?"

"The one that blew up?" Sully asks. "No, never. I've been in the Drake stables plenty of times, but not that barn, and if Wes tells you otherwise, he's lying."

Jamie stands and reaches across the desk to shake Sully's hand. "I'll be in touch if I have more questions."

"I'll walk him out, Sully," Mia says. "And I'll come back with an iced tea for you."

Once outside, Mia pauses in front of the koi pond. "Did you know koi can go all winter long without eating? Once the water temperature hits about fifty degrees, their metabolism comes to a stop, and they hang out at the bottom of the pond until spring. Wish my metabolism worked that way."

Jamie senses that Mia wants to talk about more than fish, so he waits her out. She examines her cast, flexes her fingers. "You know, it's not us you should be looking at," she finally says. "There are a lot of people who hate Wes Drake."

"Yeah?" Jamie says, keeping his eyes on the sleek, longbodied fish undulating through the water. "Why's that?"

"Wes is a big flirt," Mia says, and Jamie looks up. "Let's just say that not too many husbands would dare leave their wives alone with him," Mia says resolutely. "And the ones who have would like nothing more than to see Wes Drake blown to bits."

"Seems like a pretty extreme reaction to infidelity," Jamie says.

Mia shrugs and glances down at Jamie's ring finger. "How would you feel if your wife was screwing one of the richest, most handsome men in town?"

"I wouldn't like it," Jamie admits. "But I wouldn't resort to committing a federal crime and murder an innocent woman in the process. Do any of these husbands have names?"

Mia hesitates.

"Mrs. Preston, if you have any information that might help us solve a murder," Jamie says, "I suggest you tell me now."

"Rumor has it that Johanna Monaghan was having an affair." Mia looks toward the house anxiously. "And you didn't hear this from me, but lots of people think she was sleeping with Wes."

Jamie tries not to show his surprise. So the midwife was screwing her best friend's husband. "We'll look into it," Jamie promises. "So did Wes ever try and hit on you?"

Mia gives a half-smile and nods. "Of course he did. The man's shameless."

"But you didn't go for it?"

"Hell no, I'm not stupid," Mia says and laughs. "Wes might be one of the richest men in the county, but I'm married to the richest. I'd have too much to lose. Besides, if I had an affair with Wes Drake, that might be something Sully would kill over."

CHAPTER 15

MADELINE

MADELINE PULLS HERSELF away from the window and moves to their home office—a spacious area with large windows that provide plenty of natural light and another stunning view of the mountains. She takes a seat behind the desk made from reclaimed barn board and taps the mouse, bringing the computer to life. She logs into their business email account and is greeted with a flood of messages. Her stomach drops when she clicks the most recent email.

Dear Mr. and Mrs. Drake,

My name is Adrian Sheehan, and I'm a journalist with the *ABC World News Tonight*, and I would . . .

Madeline hits Delete. After seeing the news helicopters flying overhead, she should have known this was coming. She deletes several more interview requests from MSNBC, CNN, Reuters, and the Associated Press. Anxiety twists her gut with the realization that the story has gone national.

There are also emails from friends, business contacts, and the equestrian riders she helps train, asking what happened and whether they are okay. There's an email from Sully Preston letting them know that Mia has a broken wrist, and that he hopes that Wes, Madeline, and the baby are okay, that Dix turns up safe and sound. The words Sully chose, at first glance, seem innocuous, but Madeline can't help sensing an undercurrent of contempt. She shivers and wonders if Agent Saldano has spoken with Sully and Mia yet.

Absent-mindedly, she clicks on another email.

I'd like to be able to say I'm sorry for what happened to you, but I'm not. You got what you deserved, and I'm just sorry everything didn't burn to the ground right along with you and your baby.

Madeline pushes back from the desk as if slapped. It's from an email address she's not familiar with, and it's unsigned.

The house is quiet. Too quiet. She turns on the television and is met with a panel of women discussing a huge, blown-up photo from the gender reveal. In one hand Wes is holding his rifle in the air and the other is resting on Madeline's pregnant belly. They are both smiling broadly while the crowd behind them is clapping and cheering. The headline above the photo reads *Gender Reveal Celebration Turns Deadly.*

Before Madeline can change the channel, a video appears on the screen that shows Wes and Madeline both aiming the rifle at the old truck in the meadow and pulling the trigger, followed by two explosions, one after the other, the second knocking the videographer and his camera to the ground. Screams and cries fill the smoky air until the video blessedly fades to black but then is replayed, this time in slow motion. The video credit reads *Brady Lipton.* Brady works at their bank in Nightjar. She wonders how much money he got for the exclusive video. The panel discussion ping-pongs from the obsession with traditional gender norms to the wastefulness of the top two percent to a demand for accountability, including filing murder charges against the father- and mother-to-be.

Madeline frantically presses the Off button. Instant villains. That's all anyone is looking for anymore. What about the threatening email or Sully Preston? She has to tell Agent Saldano about the emails. She rushes to the kitchen and finds the business card he gave them. She stares at it a long time before deciding to wait for Wes to get home.

From below comes a dull pounding, and it takes a moment for Madeline to realize that someone is knocking on the back door. She hurries from the room and shuts the door tightly behind her, half expecting to find Lucy standing there, arms folded, but the hallway is empty. Madeline carefully navigates the steps, holding the railing with one hand and her belly with the other. Has the baby dropped? Johanna had explained that when this happens, it can mean the baby will be coming soon. A pang of grief so sharp nearly sweeps Madeline's legs out from beneath her. How will she get through the rest of this pregnancy, labor, and the birth without Johanna? Johanna was her only friend, her confidante, and she had come to rely on her so completely in the past several months. Of course she has Wes, but female friendship is different. There is a knowing, a comfort, and a connection that only sisters of the soul can have, and Johanna was that sister.

The knocking continues, and Madeline picks up her pace. Breathing heavily, she opens the door, and standing in front of her is Mellie Bauer, dressed in the same type of scrubs the hospital had given her. She tries to hold back her surprise, but it must be written all over her face because Mellie is instantly contrite.

"I'm so sorry," Mellie says in a rush. "The doctor discharged me, and I tried to call the number you gave me, but there was no answer. I can go." Mellie looks over her shoulder, and Madeline follows her gaze to a car idling in the drive. "It's an Uber, but I can have him take me home. I'm sorry." She turns to go.

"No, no!" Madeline says. "Please come in." Mellie bites her lip and looks back at the driver uncertain as to what to do. "It's okay, Mellie, really." Madeline says, waving her hand at the waiting car, signaling the driver that it's okay for them to go. "Come on in. You must be so tired," Madeline says, momentarily forgetting her own exhaustion.

Mellie steps over the threshold, and Madeline watches as she takes in her surroundings. It's not the first time that Madeline has been self-conscious about how much they have.

"You have such a beautiful home," Mellie says as Madeline leads her to the kitchen.

"Thank you," Madeline says. "Now, sit down. Can I get you something to eat or drink?"

"I'm not hungry, but a glass of water would be great." Mellie says as she sits gingerly on one of the leather stools next to the kitchen island.

"What did the doctors say?" Madeline asks, pulling a glass from one of the cupboards. She fills it with water from the sink, then sets the glass in front of Mellie.

"I'm okay," Mellie says. "Mostly stiff and sore."

"You were lucky," Madeline says, resisting the urge to give the poor girl a hug. She looks so small and sad. Yes, Madeline has lost her best friend, but she still has Wes and her home and her horses. But what does Mellie have?

"Were you able to get ahold of your family?" Madeline asks.

Mellie nods, taking sip of water. "Yeah. I talked to my grandma and my brother. They'd come if they could . . ."

"It's hard," Madeline says. "Being so far away from home." She remembers those first months away from home. She had just turned eighteen and wanted nothing more than to flee the home that seemed so empty since her mother died. But once gone, she'd desperately missed the drafty farmhouse and the bedroom she'd shared with Lucy.

Mellie nods in agreement but says nothing more, so Madeline presses on, trying to fill the silence. "Where is home?" she asks. "Is that a Southern accent I hear?"

"Uh-huh," Mellie says. "I know I shouldn't have shown up here out of the blue like this, but I couldn't stand the thought of going back to an empty apartment just yet. I tried calling," she says again apologetically, then begins to cry.

"No, no, it's okay," Madeline says. "I told you to let me know if you needed anything. I'm glad you came." Madeline pats Mellie on the hand. "Now, tell me what's wrong."

"It's hard to explain," Mellie says. "I tried to talk to my grandma about what happened, but I didn't want to make too big of a deal about it because she'd just worry. She's got enough going on, taking care of my little brother. I don't really have any friends here yet. I know some people from the catering company, but we're not really friends, and I can't really talk to them about it. You know what I mean?" Mellie looks up at Madeline. "Besides they're all freaked about not being able to work for a while. They have enough to worry about."

"What?" Madeline asks. "Why?"

"Katherine, the woman who owns the company, got hurt in the explosion, and her catering van was damaged. She had to cancel a bunch of events," Mellie explains.

"Oh no," Madeline says. "I didn't know about Katherine. Is she going to be okay?"

"Yeah, I think so," Mellie says. "But she hurt her shoulder and has to have surgery. She's not going to be able to work for a while." Madeline lets this sink in. The ramifications of what happened seem to go on and on. "And so we can't work. I can't pay my rent, and my landlord freaked out. Says I have to leave."

"That's awful! What about your boyfriend?" Madeline asks. "The baby's father. If you don't mind me asking."

"I don't mind," Mellie says. "He's not around anymore. Couldn't handle this." She taps her stomach.

"Oh, Mellie, I'm so sorry." Madeline says. Wes was so excited to find out Madeline was pregnant. So loving and attentive. "But it's better to find out now rather than later. It might be a blessing that he's out of the picture."

"Yeah, maybe," Mellie says, wiping her eyes. "I'm not feeling so good. Do you think I could use your bathroom?"

"Of course," Madeline says, getting to her feet and ushering Mellie to the nearest bathroom. Once the door is shut, Madeline can hear the retching. Morning sickness, she thinks, on top of everything else the poor girl is going through. Mellie emerges a few minutes later, pale-faced and red-eyed. "Why don't you lie down for a few minutes," Madeline offers.

"That's okay," Mellie says. "I need to figure out what I'm going to do now. I should go."

"I insist," Madeline says. "Morning sickness is the worst. Come on." Mellie continues to protest as Madeline leads her to one of the guest rooms, pulls back the covers of the bed. "Rest, Mellie. You'll feel better after a good nap." And before she can stop herself, she adds, "You can stay as long as you need."

Madeline forces herself to eat some toast, though the bread goes down like sandpaper. She gathers up their smoky clothes from the day before and considers tossing them in the washing machine but ends up taking them into the garage and throwing them into the garbage can. The minutes tick by at an excruciatingly slow pace. She presses her ear to the guest bedroom: all is quiet. Mellie must still be sleeping.

She goes upstairs to her room, lies down on the bed, and tries to read but can't concentrate. She gets up and wanders into the baby's nursery where everything is a pristine white—the walls, the flooring, the crib, and its bedding. On one of the walls is a huge art piece that Wes had commissioned for the space—an all-white mixed-media 3-D rendition of a Camarillo horse with flared nostrils and wild eyes, breaking through the canvas as if it's leaping into the room. It's meant to be dreamy, otherworldly, but doesn't quite hit the mark, but Madeline doesn't want to hurt Wes's feelings by complaining. Despite the decor choices, Madeline loves this space with its many windows and panoramic view of the property. She opens one window, and a soft, warm breeze dances across her skin. From here, she can see the front of the property and the road that leads to the house as well as the meadow that leads to the foot of the mountains.

She hears the crunch of tires on gravel. Someone is coming. The vehicle, a pickup truck, appears. It's approaching too fast, barely staying on the road before hanging a sharp right onto the lane leading to the house. It's probably the sheriff or even Agent Saldano coming back to talk with them. Or perhaps a concerned friend or neighbor. Madeline sighs. She's so tired, and talking to anyone right now seems like a herculean effort.

The truck slides to a screeching stop in front of the house, and the driver throws open the door. A man steps out, and from this distance, it takes Madeline a moment to recognize him. Dalton Monaghan, Johanna's husband. Again, she thinks of the tense encounter between Dalton and Wes in the hospital the night before.

"Wes! Madeline!" Dalton calls as he strides toward the front door, disappearing from Madeline's line of vision.

Madeline turns to head downstairs to let Dalton in but freezes in the doorway when she hears pounding on the front door, followed by a muffled "Open the goddamn door!"

Dalton is angry. She understands that. One moment his wife is at their home celebrating a happy occasion, the next she is dead. But how can he think that she or Wes are to blame? They loved Johanna, considered her part of the family. Or maybe the ATF agent told Dalton how Madeline described him as possessive and about the GPS tracker he put on Johanna's car. Had Wes remembered to set the alarm system before he left?

"Open the fucking door, Wes!" Dalton shouts. The banging on the door becomes more insistent and then is followed by rhythmic thuds, the sound echoing through the valley. He's kicking the door, Madeline realizes, trying to get into the house. She returns to the nursery windows.

From her vantage point, the ranch appears deserted. There is no sign of Wes, Lucy, or Trent, and a fingernail of fear drags itself down her spine. She prays that Mellie is okay and will call for help.

The pounding stops, and the sudden silence is somehow more unnerving. In the meadow at the edge of the mountain, a dark smudge appears. Wes and Lucy. They are moving at an interminably slow pace. "Hurry," she whispers, urging them to move more quickly. "Hurry." Lucy is a world-class distance rider, but today's the day she chooses to ride at a leisurely gait.

While Madeline remains at the window, trying to decide what to do, Dalton hurries back to his truck, and her shoulders sag with relief. He's leaving. But instead of climbing into the driver's seat, he moves around to the bed of the truck and opens the side-mount box, reaches inside, grabs something, and then returns to the front of the house. Next comes a sharp crack, and the sound of broken glass showering down. A scream escapes Madeline's throat, but she is frozen in place, paralyzed with indecision. She waits for the keening wail of the security system, but it doesn't come. She has no cell phone, and the landline is all the way downstairs. Madeline looks toward the meadow. Wes and Lucy are getting closer but are taking their time, still unaware of what's unfolding at the house. Hide, Madeline decides. It's the smartest, safest thing to do. The ranch has plenty of hiding spots, places to tuck herself away, places Dalton might not think of looking, like the unused storm cellar built into the floor of the stables, a remnant of the original structure on the property, or in the barn behind a stack of hay bales. But again, she will have to go down the steps to get past Dalton. She thinks of Mellie downstairs in the guest room and hopes she's safe, that she'll call the police.

Madeline hears the tinkle of more glass smashing and the sound of wood splintering. Wes and Lucy are close enough that Madeline could call out for help through the open window, and they might be able to hear her, but she doesn't want to alert Dalton. Instead, she lifts both arms and waves them above her head, big sweeping gestures in hopes they will see her in distress and hurry. They continue toward her at a maddeningly slow pace. Can they even see her through the window?

The hoarse scream of a red-tailed hawk fills the valley, and this is when Madeline realizes that the sounds coming from downstairs have stopped. Is Dalton finished with his rampage? Madeline strains to listen but can only hear the rustle of wind through the meadow and the continued shrill call of the hawk circling above. Wes and Lucy have veered off and are heading to the western part of the property with Pip on their heels. She's on her own.

Dalton has stopped yelling, and the house is quiet. Eerily so. Maybe he's given up and is going home. She peeks out the window, but Dalton doesn't emerge from the house, and the truck remains parked haphazardly in the driveway. Where has he gone? Madeline becomes aware of her breath, loud and rasping, and tries to quiet it.

Then comes the sound of footsteps and of something else scraping along the stairs. "Wes, come out and talk to me," calls a man's voice. It's Dalton, and now he's in the house. "Don't be such a damn coward." He is coming, and he is angry. She imagines he is carrying some kind of weapon—whatever he used to break into the house.

Madeline looks around the baby's nursery, so lovingly decorated and filled with the best that money could buy. The closet? That will be the first place he will look, and there is no way Madeline can sneak past him and down the stairs. There is nowhere to go, nowhere to hide.

CHAPTER 16

MELLIE

I SIT ON the edge of the bed not quite believing that I'm in the guest bedroom of the house belonging to my boyfriend. Maybe *boyfriend* isn't the right word. *Lover?* That doesn't quite fit either. I don't exactly know how to describe my relationship with Wes Drake, but I love him. I think he loves me too, but that could all change once he finds me in his home. With his pregnant wife. A little shiver of fear zips through me. All I want is the chance to talk to Wes. To ask him why he's been ignoring me, to tell him how much I love him. If I'm being honest, another reason I decided to come to the ranch was to see what his wife would do when I showed up on her doorstep. I wanted to find out if she meant it when she said I could call her if I needed anything, day or night. So far, Madeline is as good as her word.

The sound of breaking glass startles me to my feet. I go to the bedroom door and open it a crack. More glass shatters, and I hesitate before calling, "Mrs. Drake?" There's no response, so I step into the hallway and begin to move down the long corridor that leads to the great room. That's when I see a man carrying a crowbar and a gas tank, and I freeze. He keeps moving in and out of sight as if he hasn't seen me. Holding my breath, I scurry back to the bedroom and shut the door. The man is shouting now, and I don't know what to do. I open the closet door, crouch down in the corner, and begin to pull stacks of quilts over me.

I think of Madeline upstairs. Is he here to hurt her? To hurt me?

"Wes," the man calls in singsong. "Come out and talk to me. Don't be such a damn coward."

So he's after Wes. I wonder what he did to cause this kind of anger. Who could hate him so much? Through the ceiling above me, I hear Madeline screaming. If I'm going to act, I need to do it now. My phone is on the other side of the closet door. A little voice in my head tells me to stay put, that if I just wait it out, I won't have to worry about Wes's wife any longer. But if I don't, I will forever be known as the girl who hid in the closet. And what if Wes finds out I could have saved his unborn baby?

I'm damned if I do, damned if I don't.

CHAPTER 17

JAMIE

JAMIE DRIVES TOWARD the sheriff's office for the formal interview with Dalton Monaghan, his head filled with the onslaught of information he's learned so far, including Sully Preston's purported drugging of horses and Wes Drake's wandering eye. Mia Preston has already emailed him a list of three names of men besides Dalton Monaghan who may have a grudge against Wes because of indiscretions with their wives. He'll cross-check it with the party's guest list for any overlap.

He and Dalton Monaghan have a lot to talk about—the rumors about his relationship with Johanna, his military experience, and the waitress clocking him going into the barn just before the explosion. Funny how Dalton left that crucial bit of information out.

Granted, the timeline leading up to a blast can often be muddled for witnesses. After his own attack, when Jamie finally came out of his stupor, he had no idea what day or time it was and had blocked what had happened to him out on that gravel road. Over the coming days, weeks, and months it had come back to him in jagged snapshots. The fight with Juneau. The long, dark road. The headlights. The large man coming toward him.

At the memory, the yellow line down the center of the

road blurs, and the car leaves the pavement. "Shit!" Jamie
cries out and swings the steering wheel hard to the left, tires
squealing. Heart pounding, he pulls the car to an abrupt stop.
Breathing hard, he lays his head on the steering wheel. Focus,
he chastises himself. He nearly died on one of these roads
once, he's not about to do it again. There will be time to
think about what happened to him, what happened to Juneau,
but it isn't right now.

Slowly his heart rate steadies, and gradually his vision clears.
Jamie glances at the dashboard clock. Hopefully the pieces of
this convoluted puzzle will start to come together soon. Heart
rate out of the panic zone, he pulls back onto the road, and
his phone buzzes. He looks at the display. Speak of the devil.

Jamie taps Accept, and Sheriff Colson's voice fills the vehicle.
"Hey, Jamie, we just got a 9-1-1 from the Drake house. I'm
heading that way now, but I'm about twenty minutes away."

"What's going on?" Jamie asks.

"The dispatcher couldn't get much out of the caller. Said
she was whispering and couldn't make much sense out of it,"
Colson explains.

"I'm almost there. I'll let you know what I find." Jamie
ends the call and presses his foot on the gas, the speedometer
reaching eighty miles per hour.

When he turns into the long driveway that leads to the
Drake house, there's a white Ford truck sitting out front. Jamie
gets out of his car and scans the property, but it's quiet. No
sign of activity of any kind. He circles the truck, peeking
through the tinted windows. It's parked at an odd angle, and
the tailgate is down. He examines the truck bed. The saddle
box is open, and the contents are jumbled and spilling over the
side. He lets out a breath.

As Jamie crosses in front of the truck and approaches the
house, he spots the damaged front door and the spray of broken glass. Just inside, the home-security system panel has

been destroyed. His hand instantly goes to his sidearm, and he pulls his phone from his pocket and unclips his gun from its holster.

Jamie winces at the crunch of glass beneath his feet, aware that he may be alerting the intruder of his presence. He could be stepping into a hornet's nest, but the thought of Madeline Drake and her unborn baby in danger pulls him forward. Once inside the living room, he's faced with more damage. Though the home appears to be what many would describe as minimalist, with clean lines and no knickknacks or clutter, it's clear that what the Drakes do own is top-of-the-line. Or, at least, used to be. An oversize coffee table has a long, deep scratch down the center, the leather couches have been ripped, artwork on the wall has been destroyed, and the tempered glass covering the gas fireplace has been smashed.

Heart pounding, Jamie moves through the main level checking a large pantry in the kitchen, the mudroom, the bathroom, and the home office. Empty. He faces the steps leading to the second floor. They curve up and around, and he doesn't have a clear view as to what might greet him at the top. Someone with a weapon could be there, just out of sight, ready to pounce.

From behind him comes a gasp, and Jamie turns to find Mellie Bauer standing there. What the hell is the waitress from the party doing here? Mellie's eyes widen at the sight of Jamie pointing a gun at her. "Oh my God," she cries. "Oh my God."

"Were you the one who called 9-1-1?" Jamie asks. Mellie nods. "Go outside," Jamie says firmly. "Go outside, and wait for someone to tell you what to do." Without another word, she disappears, and he can hear her soft footfalls retreating.

Gritting his teeth, Jamie creeps up the stairs, head craning to see what's to come. When he rounds the corner, he breathes a bit easier. The landing is empty. He hears the murmur of voices and soft crying coming from down the hall.

Jamie hurries down the long corridor in search of the source of the weeping. He pushes open the first door—a bathroom, the second a guest room, the third is what looks like the master bedroom. All empty. The final door is ajar, and as he gets closer it's clear that this is where the sounds are coming from. He presses his back against the wall outside the door, gun in hand, pointed upward. He dares to peek around the doorjamb. Facing away from him, standing next to a crib is Madeline Drake, her hands slightly raised. From this angle, Jamie can't see the other person but knows someone is there. If startled, they could hurt Madeline. If he waits too long, they may do it anyway.

The destruction is frenzied. Whoever did this is angry. Angry enough to smash through the front door in broad daylight. Jamie runs through the possibilities: Sully Preston, Dalton Monaghan, Lucy Quaid, someone not yet on their radar.

Closing his eyes briefly before speaking, Jamie says, "Madeline, it's Agent Saldano. Is everything okay in there?"

"Don't come in," Madeline says in a rush. "I'm okay, but wait." Her voice is tight, filled with fear, but Jamie stays put. Madeline's voice drops, and though he can't understand what she's saying, from the low, earnest tone Jamie knows she's pleading with the intruder.

Jamie dares another peek around the door. Madeline is holding out her hands as if preparing to accept an offering. He edges in farther, and that's when he sees Dalton Monaghan sitting in a rocking chair, a gooseneck crowbar lain across his lap and a piece of paper in his hand. More concerning is that there's a red gas tank at his feet.

"Dalton, I'm staying out here for now," Jamie says, "but the sheriff is on his way, and things will be much easier if you lay down the crowbar and you let me come into the room. We can talk things over."

"There's nothing to talk about," Dalton says, with surprising calm. "Not with you, anyway. I'm here to talk to Wes."

"Let's take this outside, Dalton. You're scaring Madeline, and I know you don't want to do that," Jamie says, keeping his voice even, conversational.

"She's part of the problem," Dalton scoffs. "I told Johanna she was getting too involved with her. That Wes and Madeline don't really care about her—that she was nothing more than hired help to them."

"No!" Madeline says shakily. "Johanna was my best friend. I loved her."

"I bet you wouldn't say that if you knew your husband was screwing my wife," Dalton says, sending a scathing glance Madeline's way.

"That's not true," Madeline sputters. "Johanna would never do that to me."

"She would, and she did," Dalton says bitterly, holding up the piece of paper in his hand. "This proves it."

"Listen, Dalton, I'm putting my gun away," Jamie says already sliding his firearm into its holster. "I only want to talk." Where is the backup? Jamie wonders. He'd feel much better about this if he knew the cavalry was coming. With a steadying breath, Jamie steps into the doorway with his hands raised and empty. There's a strong smell of gasoline, and Jamie takes note of the wet ring of carpet encircling Dalton and Madeline. Dalton has risen from his seat in the rocking chair, the crowbar held in his hands like a baseball bat. One swing and Dalton could easily crack Madeline's skull.

"Whoa, now," Jamie says, his eyes fixed on Dalton's. "My gun is holstered, see?" Dalton's gaze flicks down to Jamie's waistband, then returns, but he doesn't lower the crowbar. "I know how painful this is. I do," Jamie says. "Why don't you let Madeline go, and we'll talk about it. Just the two of us."

"She's not going anywhere," Dalton shouts. He kicks at the plastic gas can at his feet and reaches into his pocket, pulling out a lighter, the piece of paper fluttering to the floor with the movement. Dalton turns to Madeline, the crowbar shaking slightly in one hand, the other worrying the lighter's spark wheel. He uses his shoulder to swipe at the sweat running down his face. "People like your husband act like they can get away with anything. He thinks he can have whatever he wants and blow up lives like it doesn't matter."

"You're wrong," Madeline says, as Jamie inches his way toward Dalton. "They wouldn't do this to us. They just wouldn't."

"Stay there," Dalton orders, and Jamie stops in place.

"Listen, Dalton," Jamie says. "Your wife just died. I know you're angry and sad, but this isn't the way to handle it. Let Madeline and her baby go."

Dalton barks out a laugh. "You think I'm sad about my wife's death? Johanna got what she deserved. Now I want to make sure Wes does too."

"Madeline?" comes a desperate cry from below. "Where are you?"

"Wes!" Madeline cries out.

Dalton's eyes widen, then a weary half-smile lifts the corner of his mouth. "Good, now you're both here," he says.

Damn, Jamie thinks. Wes showing up now is going to make things worse. "It's Agent Saldano," Jamie shouts. "I'm here. Wes, do not come up here. I repeat, do not come up here."

"No, come on up, Wes," Dalton calls out. "I insist!"

There's the thunder of feet pounding up the steps. Madeline looks to Jamie, and he can see the desperation in her eyes, the pleading for him to do something, anything. She's right. Jamie has to disarm Dalton now before Wes comes into this room.

"Dalton," Jamie says, more sternly this time, "it's time to stop this. Give me the crowbar and the lighter, and we'll go talk, just the two of us."

Dalton shakes his head. "You're no help to me," he says,

venom in his voice as Wes and Lucy appear in the doorway of
the nursery.

"Jesus, Dalton! What the fuck!" Wes cries.

"Oh my God," Lucy says, clapping a hand over her mouth.

"Stay back," Jamie orders, but Wes steps into the room
anyway.

"Yeah, what the fuck," Dalton repeats. "What did you do to
my wife, Wes?"

"Nothing. I did nothing, Dalton. Why would you think that?"

"I've been trying to tell him," Madeline says, her voice shaking, "but he doesn't believe me."

"Listen, I'm sorry about Johanna," Wes says, holding his
hands up in supplication. "We want to know what happened
as badly as you do, but we have to be patient while they do
their investigation." Wes looks to Jamie for confirmation.

"Yes," Jamie says, "we were just talking about that. Why
don't you all head downstairs while Dalton and I talk. We'll
get this figured out."

Dalton doesn't seem to hear him and keeps his eyes pinned
on Wes. "You fucked my wife." He takes a step toward Wes,
who doesn't back down but takes his own step toward Dalton.

"You're wrong," Wes says.

"I know you were screwing my wife, and I know what you
did," Dalton says in a low growl. "I know because Johanna
wrote it all down." He bends down to retrieve the rumpled
piece of paper from the floor. "What I don't understand is
why she would be with you, knowing what a monster you
are."

Confusion ripples across Wes's face.

"Don't act like you don't know what I'm talking about,
Wes," Dalton says.

"I don't know what the fuck you're talking about. Now, get
the hell out of my house before I take that crowbar away and
shove it down your throat," Wes shoots back.

"Enough," Jamie says, unholstering his gun. He had things under control until Wes came into the room. "Put down the crowbar," he orders. "Now." Dalton ignores him. Jamie doesn't want to use his weapon, he doesn't want to ignite a fire by firing a bullet anywhere near gasoline, but he may not have a choice. He lifts his gun, but the there's no way he can get a clean shot without hitting Wes.

"No more talking," Dalton says through gritted teeth and swings the bar like a baseball bat. Wes steps out of the way, sending Dalton off balance and briefly to his knee. Dalton pops back up and swings the bar again. This time he hits his mark with a sickening crack of metal on bone. Blood explodes from Wes's head, and he staggers and drops to his knees. Jamie sees an opening, finds Dalton's center mass, but before he can pull the trigger, Madeline steps into the fray, trying to pull the crowbar from Dalton's hands.

"Stop," she cries. "Please stop!" Dalton shoves Madeline aside, and she falls to her knees, knocking over the gas can, causing more of its contents to stream across the floor. From the corner of his eye, Jamie sees Lucy, who has returned from corralling the dog who is now barking furiously from another room, crawl to her sister's side.

Dalton hesitates as if deciding whether to use the lighter in his left hand or the crowbar in his right. After a moment, he raises the crowbar high over his head and strikes Wes again. Jamie knows that he won't stop. He won't stop swinging until Wes is dead, no matter who gets in the way.

Jamie takes aim, but before he can pull the trigger, a deafening bang fills the air, and Dalton drops to the ground, the crowbar clanging beside him. In the doorway stands Sheriff Colson, still in a shooter's stance, breathing heavily. Dalton lies on the floor, eyes staring at the ceiling unblinking, while his white shirt blooms red. Jamie kicks the crowbar away from Dalton's outstretched fingers, bends down, and feels for a pulse. He's dead. On the floor, hands clutching his bloody head, sits Wes Drake.

From the floor, Lucy scrambles to her feet and grabs an ivory baby blanket from the crib and hands it Madeline, who presses it gently to the wound on Wes's scalp. It quickly becomes sopped with blood.

Colson speaks into his radio, calling for an ambulance. "I'm fine," Wes insists, trying to get to his feet.

"Lie down," Jamie says, guiding him back to the floor. Wes's eyes become unfocused and flutter open and shut. "It's going to be okay," Jamie says, echoing the words that Wes had whispered to him in the ditch all those years ago. But alarm bells are clanging in Jamie's head. Had Dalton just confessed to blowing up the barn and killing his wife? Jamie replays Dalton's words in his head. *Johanna got what she deserved. Now I want to make sure Wes does too.*

The case is closed, Jamie thinks. Thank God. Now he can leave this godforsaken place.

Brother dear, Juneau whispers in his ear like a pesky gnat, *you know better than that. Nightjar won't let you go until it's good and ready to.*

CHAPTER 18

LUCY

LUCY WATCHES FROM the living room windows as the ambulance pulls away with Wes and Madeline inside. Lucy had offered to come with them to the hospital, but Madeline waved her off, saying they were fine without her. Upstairs is a bloody corpse and half a dozen law enforcement officers and crime-scene techs, and sitting on the bottom step is a young woman Lucy has never seen before.

"Who the hell are you?" Lucy asks, bluntly.

"Mellie. Who the hell are you?" the young woman shoots back.

"You doing okay?" a voice asks from behind her. Lucy turns around. Agent Saldano. His jacket and jeans are darkened with blood, and there's a streak of red across one cheek.

"I'm fine," Lucy and Mellie both say at the same time. Lucy crosses her arms across her chest.

"Just shaken up," Lucy says. "I don't understand what happened. Why did he do that?"

"Was it my fault?" the girl on the steps asks. "Did he find out I told you he was the one in the barn before the explosion? Was he after me?"

Agent Saldano shakes his head. "No one would have told him that." To Lucy he says, "You didn't know Dalton Monaghan, then?"

"No," Lucy says, examining the broken glass littering the floor. "I've never met him or his wife. And I think Wes was as shocked as I was to find him in the baby's room. He had nothing but nice things to say about the Monaghans. He feels terrible about Johanna's death." It's true. On their horse ride, Wes had said he couldn't believe what had happened, how badly he felt about Madeline losing her best friend. They had had a nice ride, a nice chat. "He was in the barn with Johanna? You think he did this, and he wasn't in custody?"

The agent holds up his hands. "We're investigating. But for now, you aren't going to be able to stay here until the crime scene is released," Agent Saldano says. "Do you and the Drakes have somewhere to go in the meantime?"

Lucy was sure that Madeline and Wes had plenty of options. They could stay at the most expensive hotel they wanted for as long as they needed to. Lucy, on the other hand, had fewer options. "Can I stay in one of the bunkhouses on the property?" she asks.

"That's fine," Saldano says. "It's not part of the crime scene."

Lucy tips her head, signaling to the agent that she wants to talk to him alone. Together they move to the hallway. She takes a step closer to the agent and lowers her voice. "Who is she?" she asks, waving a hand in the direction of Mellie.

"You don't know?" Saldano asks.

"I've never seen her before," Lucy says. "Why is she in my sister's house?"

"No idea, but apparently, she's the one who called 9-1-1," Saldano says. "She works for the caterer from your sister's party. She could very well have saved their lives."

Lucy eyes the girl suspiciously. "Can I talk to her?"

"Not now," Saldano says. "We need to get her statement first."

Agent Saldano walks Lucy through the house to the back door. In the kitchen, Sheriff Colson is sitting at a table talking to a deputy, explaining to her how she has to take his service weapon into evidence.

"I have to take care of the horses," Lucy says. "When we got to the house and saw the broken glass, we tied them out front. Is it okay for me to go into the stables?"

"Yeah," Jamie says. "But you won't be able to go inside the house until the scene is cleared. Do you need anything from inside?"

Lucy thinks of the handgun in her backpack, but she can't say anything to the agent about it since it doesn't belong to her. "How long will the house be off-limits?" she asks.

Agent Saldano looks toward the house and the parade of crime-scene techs that have descended once again on the property. "It won't take more than a day. You should be able to get full access by tomorrow at the latest." This is a surprise to Lucy. She would have thought that a man's death would have taken more time to document. The agent notices Lucy's disbelief. "This is a pretty straightforward case. There are plenty of witnesses."

Lucy nods. She saw the rage on Dalton Monaghan's face and wonders if what he said was true. Was Wes really having an affair with her sister's midwife?

Lucy crosses to the front to where Blackjack and Billy are tethered to a lacy dogwood tree. She takes a moment to speak to them in soothing, hushed tones before leading them back to the stables.

She checks her phone, hoping for an update from Madeline about how Wes is doing, but doesn't find one. Lucy's not surprised that Madeline is once again freezing her out, but in the end it's much better this way. It will make what has to happen later much easier. Pip, the big white dog that always seems to be underfoot, follows behind her. She could be a problem.

The thought of having to ask Trent for a key to one of the bunkhouses pisses her off. And the girl. Why would Madeline invite her to stay at the ranch? It makes no sense. She swears to God, if this girl gets in her way . . .

Lucy pushes open a door that leads to the office that is connected to the stables. The space is small and dim, with only one north-facing window, and she flips on the light switch. On the rough-hewn walls are photos of Lone Tree Ranch's champion horses and Madeline's students. There's also a picture of Madeline in her plum-colored riding jacket, tan breeches, and tall boots, her blond hair in a sleek bun beneath her helmet, standing next to Blackjack after winning the FEI World Cup in dressage. There was a time when Lucy's heart swelled with pride at her sister's accomplishments, but she gave it all up for—what?—marriage and motherhood? What a waste of talent. Had Madeline never heard that women can actually do many things at once? She thought about what she herself had given up to take care of their father, but that was different. Lucy gave up her dreams so Madeline didn't have to, and look how she'd repaid her for it.

Lucy's heart stutters when she sees the wooden desk tucked into the corner of the room. It's the desk her father made for them to share when they were kids. Six feet long and made of white pine, it had two drawers, one for each of them. It was long enough for both of them to use at one time, but they would inevitably end up bickering, so they had to use the desk in alternating shifts. When she was younger, Lucy always wondered why he hadn't built them each a desk of their own; the room she shared with Madeline was certainly large enough. Later she realized it was her father's way of trying to get them to share, to cooperate.

Lucy runs her hand along the top of the scarred pine top. She pulls on the drawer that was once hers, and it opens easily. Back in the day Lucy kept copies of *Young Rider* magazine and the Little Debbie snack cakes she liked so much in her drawer. Later, she hid her weed and birth control pills there.

Now Madeline uses the drawer to hold dozens of multicolored hanging files, each labeled with a horse's name in Madeline's loopy print. Their dad made the drawers extra deep, so Lucy explores the remaining space between the folders at the bottom of the drawer. She pulls out a rectangular box that holds blank checks with the Lone Tree Ranch logo printed in the upper corner, then returns them to their spot.

Lucy moves to the other end of the desk and tugs open Madeline's drawer. When they were young, Madeline stored her collection of *Misty of Chincoteague* books and her plastic horse figurines. Now there are more file folders, these labeled with decidedly human names—most likely Madeline's clients. Future world-champion equestrians, no doubt. Madeline always knew how to bring the best out of people. Most people.

Lucy snakes her hand between the file folders to explore the space beneath them and is surprised when her fingers hit wood more quickly than she thought they would. Strange, she thinks, because their dad had constructed both drawers exactly the same.

Lucy moves to the window to make sure no one is near the stables. The crime-scene techs are still filtering in and out of the house, and Agent Saldano is speaking with Trent who, as promised, has been keeping a close eye on her. She'd have to figure out a way to keep him busy, out of her way. The young woman, Mellie something, is talking to a deputy. Lucy has only a few minutes.

She returns to the desk and begins to lift the file folders and set them in a pile at her feet until the drawer is empty, revealing the wooden bottom. The wood panel is a darker shade than the rest of the desk and looks to be made from cheap plywood and definitely sits higher than it once did. Damn, Lucy thinks. Madeline went and put a false bottom in the drawer.

She runs her fingers along the perimeter of the plywood but can't find any kind of mechanism to get to what's underneath.

She scans the desktop for some kind of tool—a pair of scissors, a letter opener—but quickly realizes these will damage the wood. She finally slides a small paper clip from a stack of papers in one of the file folders and stretches it until it resembles a fishhook. Carefully, she works the thin clip in between the wall and the floor of the drawer, twists it, and pulls up gently. The panel lifts just enough so that Lucy can use her fingers to pull it free. In the narrow space is a sealed manila envelope.

Lucy glances over her shoulder. She doesn't know how much time she has. Someone could walk in at any moment, but curiosity gets the better of her. She lifts the envelope from its hiding spot. It's sealed and free of any kind of writing, and whatever it holds is unsubstantial. Lucy hesitates only a second before running her finger beneath the seal. She tries to be neat about it, but the envelope tears, making it impossible to cover up what she's done. Lucy tips the envelope and several photos slide out, and the images stare up at her. Her stomach tilts dangerously, then anger, hot and hard, roils through her chest. It's all she can do not to tear the photographs into a million bits, but she knows she can use them to her advantage. Dammit, Madeline, Lucy thinks as she returns the photos to their hiding place.

Lucy picks up the file folders from the floor and begins replacing them in their proper spots, but one file catches her eye. It's labeled with only one word: *Will*. Lucy opens the folder and finds a stapled set of papers titled "Last Will and Testament of Madeline Ann Drake." Stamped in bright red is the word *Copy*. She skims the contents. As expected, Wes is named as Madeline's main beneficiary. What's written near the bottom of the will, however, is more shocking than the photos in the hidden compartment. *I bequeath the entirety of my estate to my husband, Weston John Drake, as the primary beneficiary. If my husband is not alive at the time of my death, then the account shall be distributed to my sister, Lucy Marie Quaid, as contingent beneficiary.*

Madeline and Wes are worth millions. To say that Lucy is surprised by this turn of events is an understatement. She was sure that after all of Lucy's financial woes and their strained relationship, Madeline would have cut her from the will a long time ago. Maybe she needs to start being a little bit nicer to her sister. Nah, Lucy thinks. This is so much more fun.

CHAPTER 19

MADELINE

MADELINE SITS ON the hotel bed staring blankly at the television, waiting for Wes to come out of the shower. The doctors in the emergency room took X-rays and a CT scan of Wes's head, diagnosed a mild concussion and sent them on their way, advising plenty of rest. It could have been so much worse, the physician said. If Dalton had hit Wes with a fraction more force, he would have shattered his skull, given him a brain bleed, or even killed him.

Waiting in this Jackson hotel room for the last two days is making Madeline want to jump out of her skin. She's eager to get home, but Wes insists they stay in the hotel until the house is no longer a crime scene so they will be more comfortable. Madeline knows he's right. The cots in bunkhouses are a far cry from the temperature-controlled, king-size bed and Egyptian cotton sheets they slept in the last two nights.

Madeline still can't believe that Dalton broke into their house and came after them with a crowbar, accusing Wes of having affair with Johanna. At times, she does wonder if Wes has been faithful to her. Admittedly, he is a notorious flirt. His behavior with Lucy is a perfect example, but she always thought the flirtations were harmless. Madeline is confident Johanna would never have broken her trust. She might have been cheating on Dalton, but it wasn't with her husband.

The bathroom door opens and steam billows out as Wes steps into the room wrapped in a towel. His left shoulder is a nasty shade of purple, and his right eye is swollen shut. Madeline cringes at the sight. Wes is lucky, Madeline thinks for the hundredth time. He could be dead.

"Are you hungry?" she asks. "Do you want to order room service?"

Wes gives a little shake of his head and winces with pain. "No, I'm not hungry, but you order something. You have to eat."

"Okay," Madeline says but knows she won't. She has to get out of this room. Wes is getting short-tempered, and she is getting tired of sitting in this dark, silent space. "I'll get you more ice," she says.

"No, thanks," Wes says. "I'm going to call Trent. Will you grab my phone for me?" He sits on the bed next to Madeline.

"Here, why don't you lie down," Madeline says, reaching over him to adjust the pillows.

"Dammit, Madeline, I'm fine," he says, swatting away her hand.

"Wes," Madeline says, unable to keep the hurt from her voice.

He expels a long breath. "I'm sorry. I'm going stir-crazy here, and I'm worried about my brother. And those things Dalton said about Johanna and me . . . You know I would never cheat on you, right?" he says.

"I know," Madeline says, brushing the hair gently from his eyes, all the while wondering if he is lying to her. "Dalton wasn't making any sense. Why would he think such a thing?"

"How the fuck should I know?" Wes says, dropping his head into his hands. "And why wasn't the alarm set? I told you to make sure it's armed whenever I'm not home, and look what happened. Now we're the ones who have to clean up Dalton's brains from our baby's floor."

"Wes!" Madeline gasps, shocked.

"What?" Wes says. "It's true. And why the hell did you invite that waitress to stay with us? Seriously? Of all the times for a houseguest."

"Her name is Mellie, I told you that after the explosion we rode to the hospital in the same ambulance. She's scared and all alone. I was just trying to be nice," Madeline says, pulling a bottle of water from the wet bar. "I'm sure she'll leave soon. She just needs time to get her bearings." She unscrews the lid and offers it to Wes, but he waves it away.

On the dresser, Wes's phone begins to vibrate. They both stare at it.

"Will you grab that for me, please?" Wes finally says, his tone formal and clipped. Madeline picks up the phone, sneaking a look at the display. There's no name, just a string of numbers. She hands it to Wes and then lowers herself onto a chair covered in chintz. The sun is barely up, and any incoming calls at this time of morning can't bring good news.

"Hello?" he says cautiously into the phone. "This is Wes." He then falls silent while the person on the other end continues. He glances toward Madeline, who is holding her breath, and he holds up one finger as if to tell her hang on a second.

Dix, Madeline thinks. It has to be the hospital. Or maybe the police. Or the worst-case scenario—the coroner. "Uh-huh," Wes says, his face falling.

"Who is it?" Madeline asks. "What's happening?"

Shut up, Wes mouths and then returns to his call. "No, I understand . . . Keep me posted? . . . All right." Wes's voice breaks. "Thank you."

He sets the phone down on the bed beside him and covers his eyes with one hand.

"What?" Madeline asks, her heart thundering in her chest. "What happened?" Wes and Dix are as close as two brothers can be.

"That was the sheriff's office. They haven't found him yet," Wes says. "They've checked all the hospitals in the county. He's not at any of them."

"Oh my God, that's awful. He has to be somewhere," she says, dropping on the edge of the bed just as Wes is getting to his feet.

"What are you doing?" Madeline asks as he moves to the closet where the clothes he wore the other day hang, now laundered by hotel housekeeping.

"I'm going home. I can't take another minute just sitting here doing nothing."

"Home?" Madeline asks in surprise. "Do you think we can even get back into the house yet?"

"Not *we*, *me*," Wes says, getting to his feet with a groan. "And yes, they released the scene, but I want you to stay here."

"I don't want to be here without you, and you can't drive yourself," Madeline says in disbelief. "You have a concussion, and you can barely keep your eyes open."

"I'm not planning on driving," Wes says, tapping a text out on his phone. "I'm texting Trent for a ride. You stay here, get some rest."

"But I want to go home too," Madeline insists. "I don't want to stay here all by myself."

"You're staying," Wes says, removing the plastic cover from his laundered clothes. "Besides, I'm only stopping at home to grab a few things, and then I'm going to find Dix myself. Phone calls obviously aren't working."

"Wes," Madeline says in exasperation. "You were nearly killed. Be smart about this."

Wes shoots a dark look her way, and Madeline clamps her

mouth shut. "No," he says with finality. "I want to make sure the house is safe and secure before you come home, and I don't want you staying there without me."

Madeline knows better than to argue. Once Wes makes up his mind, there's no changing it.

He finishes dressing and sits in moody silence until there's a knock at the door. Wes's ride.

"I love you," Madeline says, kissing his lips gently before he goes to answer the door to let Trent in.

"I love you too," Wes says. "Get some rest. There's a credit card on file at the front desk, and I'll call the room with any news."

Wes opens the door, but it isn't Trent as Madeline expected. It's her sister. Lucy has her hands stuffed in her pockets and greets them with an innocent smile.

At the shocked look on Madeline's face, Wes says, "I texted Trent, but he said one of the mares is foaling. He has to be there, so Lucy was kind enough to come get me."

"It's my pleasure," Lucy says, hooking her arm through Wes's. "Don't worry, Mads. I promise to take excellent care of the patient and make sure he gets home safe and sound."

"I'm sure you will," Madeline says, working hard to keep the irritation from her voice. Lucy hasn't called her Mads, the family's pet name for her, in years.

Wes gives her one more peck on the cheek before stepping out into the hallway. "I'll call you with any news," he says and then shuts the door, leaving Madeline all alone.

CHAPTER 20

LUCY

ONE MILE OUT of Jackson, despite the glare of the bright morning sun, Wes falls asleep in the passenger seat of Madeline's Lexus. Why anyone needs a luxury car while living on a working ranch is beyond Lucy, but she's not going to complain. She has to admit it's a nice ride.

When Trent found Lucy in the stable's office, she was trying to figure out what to do with the information she just discovered. Luckily she had returned the envelope to its hiding place, but still, he seemed suspicious. And as much as she was looking forward to more time alone with Wes, she had been hoping to snoop around the ranch more, see what other dirty little secrets she could dig up before Madeline came home. It would have to wait.

Abruptly, Lucy pulls off Highway 191 in hopes that the sharp motion will wake Wes, but he's out cold, snoring softly, his head lolling against the passenger-side window. She pulls into a gas station, parks, and goes inside. It's one of those filling stations with an all-night café to feed all the truckers who come through. Lucy orders a chocolate shake for Wes and a sausage biscuit for herself. By the time she returns to the car, food in hand, Wes is awake.

He looks like crap, and Lucy tells him so. "Yeah, you get hit in the head with a crowbar and see how you look," Wes says, poking the straw through the lid and taking a long drink. "God, this tastes good. Thanks."

"No problem," Lucy says, clicking her seat belt into place. She and Wes have always had a good rapport. Back when they first met, Lucy thought that maybe the two of them could have been good together, but the timing was never quite right—they were too different, or maybe too much alike. Then Lucy introduced Wes to Madeline and the decision was made, for better or worse.

"So, your brother?" Lucy says, pulling the truck back onto the highway.

"Yeah, it's unbelievable. How does a man just disappear? Especially Dix—he's pretty unforgettable."

"Yeah?" Lucy says. "I remember him from your wedding. He was trying to get people to drink shots out of his cowboy boot."

"Yeah, Dix is a good guy, but he's a character," Wes says. "Madeline gets a kick out of him. I swear sometimes she thinks she married the wrong Drake brother."

Lucy raises her eyebrows and gives Wes a wry look. "You know Madeline is crazy about you. Always has been, always will be."

Wes shakes his head. "She's been different lately. You sure she hasn't told you what's been going on with her?"

"Me? Nooo," Lucy laughs. "I think you might have forgotten that my dad made Madeline my fucking banker. We don't talk much anymore, and I'm not thrilled about it, okay. But how would you feel if your brother was in charge of your finances?"

"I'd hate it," Wes admits. "Dix and I have had our fair share of knockdowns over money."

"It sucks," Lucy says. "Dad's funeral was hard, but it was good he wasn't suffering anymore. Before we read the will, Madeline and I genuinely had a nice time, laughing over memories, going out with some old friends."

"What old friends?" Wes asks. Lucy knows he's trying to keep his voice nonchalant, casual, but there's a sharpness that he can't hide.

"Just some old classmates. Lydia Dunne, Angela Walker, Marc Lee," Lucy says, ticking the names off on her fingers. "A few others. It was nice, kind of like a mini-reunion." Lucy sees Wes's face darken at the mention of Marc Lee, Madeline's high school boyfriend. Madeline and Marc fell hard for one another, were inseparable, and almost immediately started planning their life together: get married, have kids, raise horses. It lasted through the summer after graduation, but that's when Madeline got more serious about equestrian competitions and began winning on the international circuit. The romance fizzled, and a few years later, Lucy introduced Madeline to Wes. Still, Wes didn't like hearing about Madeline's first love.

"Everyone had a little too much to drink, I said a few things, Madeline said a few things." Lucy shrugs. "It got ugly."

"Madeline wouldn't have been drinking," Wes says, setting his shake in the cupholder. "She's pregnant."

"It was just a sip. A toast to old friends," Lucy clarifies. Wes grows quiet and turns to look out his window. Madeline is going to be pissed when she finds out Lucy told Wes about meeting up with Marc and possibly drinking while pregnant. And Wes will bring it up. Lucy is counting on it.

"So who is this Mellie person, staying at the house?" Lucy asks, as she slows the car and takes a right turn.

Next to her, Wes shakes his head. "You'll have to talk to Madeline about that one. There isn't a stray animal she won't take in. I just hope she doesn't stay long. I can't wait for things to go back to normal—whatever that means."

"I don't trust her," Lucy says.

"What? Why? Did she do something?" Wes asks.

"Not really," Lucy admits. "It's weird, though, right? She just shows up on your doorstep and doesn't leave?"

"Kind of like you, right?" Wes says, trying not to smile.

She smacks him lightly on the arm. "You were always a smartass. No, really, though. I don't trust her."

Wes turns thoughtful. "I'll try and get rid of her before Madeline gets back home, but in the meantime, will you keep an eye on her for me?"

"It would be my pleasure," Lucy says, meaning it, then changes the subject. "You know, I was thinking, the baby will be here in the next few weeks or so, and I'd love to be able to fix up the nursery. It's a mess after what happened, and the sooner it's cleaned up, the sooner you can put all of this behind you."

Wes looks skeptical. "Honestly, I don't know if Madeline will even want that as the baby's room anymore. I don't know if I want the baby to stay where a man died, where she could have died."

Lucy nods, in understanding. "I get that. But I also think of it as the place where her life was saved too. If you hadn't walked in when you did, who knows what he would have done to Madeline? You distracted him so that the sheriff could get a good shot in and stop him."

Wes laughs. "I distracted him with my head."

"You know what I mean," Lucy says, taking her eyes off the road to look at him. "I mean it could have been so much worse, and it wasn't. What do you say? Let me fix up the nursery."

"You really don't have to do that, especially with how things are going between you and Madeline. Trent can do it, or we can hire someone," Wes says.

"Yeah, but do you want to take Trent away from his other work? And do you really want a stranger in your house?" Lucy asks. "Some ghoul who will go home and start spreading gossip about you and Madeline?" Lucy knows she has Wes now. Despite his social nature, he's also a man who values his privacy.

"Come on, let me do this. It will be my gift to you both. And by *gift*, I mean I'll provide the physical labor. You're footing the bill for everything else."

Wes laughs, but Lucy can tell he's mulling it over. She needs to be indispensable to Wes and Madeline. For now. "Okay, then. Sure," he says, as she maneuvers the car through Lone Tree's front gate. "But let me talk to Madeline. She might need a little convincing."

"Trust me," Lucy says. "It will be spectacular, and Madeline deserves every bit of it."

"Thanks for coming to get me, Lucy," he says, reaching over and squeezing her hand. "I owe you one."

"My pleasure," she says, bringing the car to a stop in front of the house. It's quiet. There's no sign of Trent or Mellie or any of the other ranch hands. "Now, you need to go directly to bed," she orders.

"No," Wes says, with a shake of his head. "I'm going to go find my brother for myself."

"Today?" Lucy asks. "You think that's a good idea?"

"Probably not," Wes says. "But he's my brother."

"I get it," Lucy says. They sit there in silence for a moment, staring at the spot where the old barn used to be. "So Johanna Monaghan, huh?" she says, with a sly uptick of her mouth.

"No way," Wes says, holding up one hand as if in surrender. "Dalton was way off with that. I don't know who his wife was screwing, but it wasn't me."

"He seemed pretty sure of himself," Lucy says, snagging the cup from Wes's hand.

"I'm not cheating on my wife," Wes says, looking Lucy straight in the eye.

Lucy holds his gaze and slides the straw between her lips, taking a drink of the melted shake before speaking. "I believe you," she finally says. "But would you?" she whispers, leaning in close.

"Would I what? Cheat on Madeline? No way," Wes says, snatching at the cup, but Lucy pulls it out of reach. "Did you cheat on your husband? Is that why you got divorced?"

"Nah, it was nothing like that," Lucy says. "But that's not to say I wouldn't have, if the right man came along."

"Oh?" Wes says. "And who would the right man be?"

Lucy shrugs. "I think the bigger question right now is who is the right woman?" She slides the cup between Wes's legs, letting her fingers rest on his thigh.

Lucy watches as Mellie comes out of one of the bunkhouses and stops short when she sees who's in the car. Lucy leans in close to Wes and whispers in his ear. "She's staring at us. I wonder if she likes to watch."

"Lucy," Wes groans, lifting her hand from his leg but not releasing it. "What are you doing? I'm married. To your sister."

"True," Lucy says. "She is my sister, but you have to admit, she is kind of a bitch. And if you ask me, so is that one." She tips her head toward Mellie, who has bent down to busy herself with tying her shoe.

Wes shakes his head with a laugh, releases her hand, and pushes open the car door and heads to the stables while Lucy lets herself into the house. She brews coffee using Madeline's fancy espresso maker and pours some into Wes's stainless-steel travel mug, when he comes in from outside.

"They found Dix," he says, excitedly. "I'm going to grab a few things and head out."

"Oh wow!" Lucy says. "Is he okay? Where is he?"

"At a hospital in Salt Lake City," he responds. "The ambulance took him to Idaho Falls first, but he was in too bad shape, so they airlifted him there. He had to have emergency surgery. They removed his spleen."

"Do you want me to go with you?" Lucy asks. "I can drive." She hopes Wes says no. She really wants to be here in the house, but offering seems like the right thing to do.

"No," Wes says. "I'm going to stop and talk to the ATF agent first, but if you can stay and work on the nursery and keep an eye on things here, that would be great."

"I'm sure he'll be okay," Lucy says, laying a hand on Wes's arm, and he pulls her into a tight hug.

"Thanks for everything, Lucy," Wes says. "And I'm having Madeline's new phone delivered to the house today. Will you keep an eye out for it? And here's a card to buy the things you need to fix up the nursery." He slides the credit card into the front pocket of her jeans.

This could be fun, she thinks.

Lucy watches at the window as Wes walks to his truck. Mellie exits her cabin, and he tries to move past her, but she steps in his path. Lucy can't see their faces but can tell by their body language that there's tension between them. After a brief exchange, Wes skirts past Mellie who looks after him with a scowl on her face. "Now, what's that all about?" Lucy murmurs to herself as Wes speeds away in Madeline's car.

She waits thirty minutes to make sure Trent and Mellie are nowhere to be seen. She returns to the guest room, retrieves her backpack, and reaches into the inner pocket for the seven tiny surveillance cameras hidden inside. Each camera lens is only three-and-a-half millimeters wide, the entire device only as big as the top of her thumb. She would have brought more but thought she would be pushing it. She's put a lot of thought into where to place the cameras and finally settles on the kitchen, the living room, the home office, Wes and Madeline's bedroom, the stables, and the guest room where she'll be staying—she wants to make sure she knows if someone is snooping around her things, sparse as they are. Deciding where the seventh and final camera will go is trickier. She'd like to find a way to get it into Trent's bunkhouse so she can keep tabs on him, but doing so unnoticed will be tough. Instead, she'll hide it in Mellie's room.

Lucy is casual about it, keeping the cameras hidden in her pocket and nonchalantly situating them in spots where they won't be noticed. There's always the chance that Wes and Madeline have their own security devices hidden within the house, but Lucy doubts it. Because behind closed doors and all.

CHAPTER 21

MELLIE

I RUSH TO the bunkhouse and wait until I'm inside before allowing myself to cry. Wes totally brushed me off. He talked to me as if I was a nobody, like I was some random acquaintance of his wife. I know he was acting that way for the benefit of Lucy, who I know was watching us from the window. All I want is a few minutes. A few minutes to ask him what I did wrong. Why can't he even give me that?

I lie down on the lumpy cot and press my face into the pillow. Maybe it is time for me to leave. If I can't even get Wes to look at me, what's the point? I hear a soft tap on my door and groan. I ignore it. I do not want to see Trent or Madeline's creepy sister. The door creaks open, and Wes steps into the room. I sit up, prepared for the onslaught of anger I'm sure is coming my way.

"What are you doing, Mellie?" he asks, angrily. "What could you possibly think you would accomplish by coming here?"

I have a speech all prepared. I want to tell him that I am not disposable, that I can't be simply tossed aside, but I know that's not true. He already has. But that doesn't mean I have to go down without a fight. "Your sweet wife invited me," I say breezily.

"You stay the fuck away from her, do you understand?"
Wes growls. "I want you out of here."

"I guess that's up to Madeline," I say, examining my fingernails. "She told you, didn't she, how much we have in
common?" I lay a hand on my stomach.

A storm of emotion spreads across Wes's face. I search for
something that looks like happiness but don't find it. Wes
turns, and for a moment I think he's going to leave without a
word, but instead I hear the click of the dead bolt being turned
into place. "I don't believe you," he says, turning back to me.
I shrug, going for casual indifference, but my heart is ready to
pound right out of my chest. "You know this isn't the way to
get what you want," Wes says.

I give him my sweetest smile. "Oh yeah? Tell me the right
way," I say, getting to my feet and burying my face in his
chest. I breathe in the scent of him.

"Mellie," he murmurs into the top of my head. "Don't."
His hands grip my shoulders, and he takes a step back, creating
space between us.

I lift my chin to see his face, and there it is—the way I'm
used to having Wes look at me. "Don't worry," I say, moving
my fingers to his zipper. "I'm not going to say anything to her.
I just want to be close to you."

"We shouldn't," he says, but there's less conviction in his
voice. "I have to go talk to the police, and then I'm going to
my brother."

"Ten minutes," I whisper. "That's all I need."

CHAPTER 22

JAMIE

JAMIE WAKES UP on Monday morning with a start. He hates this, the disconcerting feeling of not knowing exactly where he is. Bleary-eyed, he takes in the bland surroundings, the drab curtains, the scratchy comforter that he kicked to the end of the bed during the night, the digital clock on the bedside table squawking obnoxiously at him. Six o'clock. Dread washes over him.

Not all the memories from his time in Nightjar are bad, but it's difficult to sift through the horrible ones to latch on to any of the good ones. There were the times, when their mother was crashed out on the pullout sofa, exhausted from cleaning rooms all day and working the front desk all night, when Jamie and Juneau would flip on a flashlight and pull bags of flour and sugar from the cupboards and eggs and lemons from their dorm-size refrigerator in the tiny kitchenette. It was nearly impossible to be quiet in such a small, cramped space, but that was half the fun. They would hunch together, heads bent over a faded, limp recipe card trying to decipher their grandmother's elegant handwriting, and toss together the ingredients for lemon squares without speaking. Inevitably, they would collapse into spluttering bursts of laughter and would present the overly browned, overly tart lemon squares to their mother when she awoke.

Jamie doesn't linger too long on memories like these because they always lead to the night that Juneau disappeared. Instead, he replays the events of two days earlier in his mind, and he wishes he could have done something to prevent Dalton Monaghan's death. Second-guessing himself is like playing a futile game of what-if. It does nothing but keep him from focusing on the case in front of him.

Wes and Madeline Drake, Dalton Monaghan, Sully Preston, Mellie Bauer—all pointing fingers at someone else. Then there is Lucy Quaid. The threads swirl around his head, none of them connecting, and leaving Jamie even more confused. He needs coffee.

He pushes himself up from the bed and checks his cell. A missed call from Tess. He should call her back, but Jamie can't stand another conversation about how she hates their new home, hated giving up her career, and hated that Jamie had talked her into moving. He wants Tess to be happy, he really does. And in the end, he knows they will most likely move back to DC. But first, he knows he has to come to terms with his sister's disappearance, to bury the ghosts that have been haunting him for twenty-seven years.

Today Jamie is going to visit the seven hardware stores in the area that carry the items found in the IED blast. It's a long shot, but he's hoping one of the clerks will remember someone purchasing double-headed nails, PVC piping, duct tape, and ball bearings in the weeks leading up to the explosion. He starts in Nightjar at the local hardware store. The clerk, who is also the owner, isn't much help and explains that this is ranch country and everyone buys these items at one time or another. He moves on to Jackson City, and while more successful, he runs into the same roadblocks—dozens of each of the items on his list have been sold the two weeks before the gender reveal party but none to the same person. He gets back in his car, disappointed but not surprised. They are going to have to widen their search.

He drives back to the sheriff's office, and the first thing Jamie does is cross-check the guest list with the names of possible men who might hold a grudge against Wes that Mia Preston sent him. They aren't listed. Apparently, they didn't get invited, or the husbands didn't want their wives anywhere near Wes. Still, this doesn't mean they didn't plant the bomb. He calls one of the deputies over and sends him on his way to question the men and find out where they were Friday night and the days leading up to the explosion. "Be discreet," he advises. "Just tell them we are interviewing everyone in the Drakes' orbit. Verify their alibis, and let me know what you find out."

Jamie turns his attention to the clear plastic evidence bag that holds the piece of paper with frayed edges that Dalton was holding when he was shot. Now it is black with dried blood, the writing nearly impossible to decipher. Dalton said that Johanna had written something down. Something that implicated Wes. But what did it say? Unfortunately, Dalton and Johanna Monaghan are both dead and can't answer these questions.

After they finished at the Drakes', the forensic team went directly to the Monaghan home and executed a search warrant. They found nothing related to the explosion—no double-headed nails, no ball bearings matching the ones left behind at the crime scene, though Dalton had an impressive cache of firearms in the gun safe. The Monaghan computers have been packed up and sent to experts who will do a digital inspection, looking for evidence that Dalton had researched how to make an IED. The techs did find a journal belonging to Johanna that looks like it could be the source of the now-bloody paper.

Jamie slips on a pair of gloves and begins thumbing through the journal and opens to a page that looks as if a sheet was roughly ripped out. He aligns the bagged paper with the journal's inner spine and finds that the ripped edges match like a puzzle piece. The entries before and after are about the clients she served as a midwife or the mundane details of an ordinary life. Johanna mostly wrote fondly of her husband and regarded Madeline Drake as her best friend. What Jamie doesn't find are notes documenting Johanna's deepest, darkest secrets or an affair with Wes Drake or anyone else. What had Dalton said? *"What I don't understand is why she would be with you, knowing what a monster you are."*

He checks the date of the torn entry. Two months ago. What was so important about this particular page? It's odd that Johanna was so careful not to mention an affair on any of the other pages but seemingly poured out her soul on this one. He has an appointment with Wes later this afternoon, and he'll ask him that very question. His phone vibrates, and he's relieved to see the caller isn't Tess but Greta. "Whatcha got for me?"

"Well, good morning to you too," Greta says. *"No, don't worry, Greta. I'm just fine after my near-death experience the other day."*

"I am fine. Now, tell me what you found out."

"A few interesting tidbits. Where do you want me to start?"

"How about with Dalton Monaghan?" Jamie says, reaching for a pen. "Anything new?"

"I was able to contact his supervisor at the wind turbine company he worked for, and he said he was an okay employee but a bit of a hothead. He wrote Monaghan up a few times for getting into it with a fellow coworker, but nothing too serious. Said he was more likely to punch a wall than a person. I also talked to his former lieutenant at the army recruitment center. Said he liked the guy well enough but mentioned that Monaghan was obsessed with firearms and munitions. And that *obsessed* is a direct quote," Greta says.

"That explains all the guns found in the home," Jamie says, rubbing his forehead.

"Are you thinking Monaghan planted the bomb?" Greta asks.

"He certainly was angry enough, but we need a lot more than that to close this case," Jamie says. "What else do you have for me?"

"How about another angry person?" she says, lightly. "Lucy Quaid, thirty-eight years old, owned a small horse farm in Lone Tree, Iowa, where she and her stepsister, Madeline Drake, were raised. Lucy is in the middle of a contentious divorce, no kids."

"No kidding?" Jamie says. "Lone Tree, huh? Madeline and Wes Drake named their ranch after the town where the sisters grew up. Interesting."

"No kidding," Greta repeats. "And she's broke. Not a little bit broke but had-to-sell-off-all-her-worldly-possessions broke. Lucy's father died last month, and in his will Madeline was named the executor. Lucy has to go through her stepsister to get a penny. To top it all off, he left all his horses to Madeline."

"So Lucy's dad made his stepdaughter in charge of his daughter's trust. That would be cause for hurt feelings. Maybe she's come to Wyoming to ask her sister for more money?" Jamie muses. "Or maybe she came all this way to blow Madeline up and Johanna stepped on the IED by accident. If Madeline dies, who does the money go to? Does it revert to Lucy or go to Wes?"

"I'm still waiting for the Drake financials to come in, but I'm on it," Greta says.

"Perfect," Jamie says. "Anything else?"

"This may be a coincidence, but nonetheless interesting," Greta says. "Before moving to Nightjar nine years ago, Johanna Monaghan née Mills moved around some. She lived in

Ohio, Mississippi, Minnesota, and West Virginia. And guess who else lived in West Virginia?"

Jamie sits up straighter in his seat. "Who?"

Greta pauses for dramatic effect. "Mellie Bauer."

"The waitress?" Jamie asks.

"Yeah. At one point, they lived only about twenty miles away from one another."

"You're kidding." His heart begins to thrum the way it does when he gets that one piece of information that might be the break in a case.

"Not kidding," Greta says.

"How long ago?" He needs to have another chat with Mellie. He hears the shuffle of papers.

"Johanna moved there twelve years ago. Stayed for just under one," Greta explains. "That's when she moved to Ohio."

"Twelve years," Jamie repeats, his excitement extinguishing. "Mellie Bauer would have only been about nine years old then. Any other connections between the two of them?"

"Not that I can find. Yet," Greta emphasizes. "But I'm still digging. I'll keep you posted."

"Anything on Sully and Mia Preston?" Jamie asks.

"I was saving the best for last," Greta says. "At first glance, they appear richer than God—the house, the ranch, their business, the family money. But looking closer, it's all one big facade."

Jamie perks up again. "What do you mean? The Prestons aren't rich?"

"They have a shitload of stuff, but none of it's theirs," Greta says. "The house is mortgaged to the hilt, the acres of ranching property actually belong to the Preston family estate, not specifically to Sully. The only thing that the Prestons own is their horse-brokering business, which is millions of dollars in debt."

Jamie lets this sink in. The huge house, the mini-golf

course, the peacocks, all one bad horse-deal away from disappearing? "Thanks, Greta. You are truly the best."

"I know. And call your wife," Greta says into the phone before disconnecting.

He turns his attention to his computer and begins the tedious process of scouring cell-phone video footage from the party gathered from the guests. The scene is festive, people are smiling, dressed in expensive Western wear—cowboy hats, rhinestones, boots. And guns. Jamie sucks in a breath. So many guns. Waiters and waitresses mill about, offering drinks and appetizers. He spots Mellie Bauer right away. She's hard to miss with her brightly dyed red hair. He sees Madeline Drake and Johanna and a fleeting glimpse of Wes. Jamie has to force himself to focus and takes a sip of the high-octane coffee that the office receptionist handed him when he came in this morning.

Sully and Mia Preston appear on-screen, and Jamie shifts in his chair to get a closer look. Mia is carrying a present wrapped in robin's-egg blue gift wrap and topped with a big black bow. The two approach Madeline, who doesn't look happy to see them. Mia hands the gift to Madeline, who hands it right back to Sully and then turns away from them. The ultimate brush-off. The video ends.

Jamie watches six more videos with nothing new until once again the package with the black satin bow appears in a clip of a rodeo clown milling through the crowd, snagging cowboy hats off heads. This time the present is tucked under the arm of Johanna Drake, a cell phone pressed against her ear. She veers to avoid a grab from the clown, and Jamie's pulse quickens with each step she takes. Off to the right is the table set up for the gifts, and off to the left is the storage barn. Johanna goes left and steps into the barn, carrying the package.

Jamie sits back in his chair. Could this be it? The smoking

gun? The present that Mellie Bauer said Johanna had in the barn with her just before the explosion was the package that the Prestons tried to give to Madeline Drake. By chance it ended up in the hands of Johanna, and a few minutes later she ended up dead. It makes sense. According to Wes and Madeline, the Prestons were buying lame horses for cheap, drugging them to make them appear healthier and more docile than they really were and then selling them at a much higher price point. The Prestons were in financial trouble, and the Drakes' accusations about drugging the horses threatened the one part of their lives that was lucrative. Maybe the Prestons wanted revenge.

But there's a lot more to figure out. He makes two calls. One to Sully Preston, ordering him to come into the sheriff's office right away or he'll send a deputy out to bring him over, and then one to a judge who grants Jamie the warrant he needs so they can search the Preston property.

"Agent Saldano," the sheriff's receptionist, Ruby, says from the doorway, "Wes Drake and his attorney are here to see you."

"Put them in the interview room. I'll be right there," Jamie says but doesn't get to his feet. Interesting that Wes felt the need to bring his lawyer along, especially since the Drakes are the probable targets of the IED. He spends the next ten minutes trying to read the blood-splattered journal entry and deciphers a few words or parts of words: *arm, hos, use, Mad.* He squints trying to read a section of the entry that isn't covered in blood. The paper had been crumpled in Dalton's hand before he was shot, his sweat causing the ink to bleed some. Jamie tries to smooth the creases through the plastic bag, and slowly a few more words come into focus. Words that in any context would be disturbing, but with Jamie's history, even more so.

From the lobby, Jamie hears an angry, insistent voice. "I don't care if he's busy," Wes says loudly. "I want an update on the case. Now."

"Hey, Wes," Jamie says, sliding the plastic bag holding the journal entry into a file folder and coming out of his office. He heads to the lobby where Ruby is trying to corral Wes and a man in an expensive Italian suit into the interview room. Wes's lawyer, Jamie presumes. "Thanks for coming in. Let's talk in here where we'll have some privacy."

"This is bullshit," Wes says, following Jamie into the small, cramped room. "We came here to be of help, and I don't appreciate being kept waiting."

"I understand, and I'm sorry for the inconvenience, Wes," Jamie says, then turns to the attorney and offers his hand. "Jamie Saldano, ATF."

"Franklin Stewart," the man says, shaking Jamie's hand with a strong grip. "I'm the Drake family attorney. I know Wes and Madeline want to help in any way they are able."

Jamie waits for the two men to sit in the hard-backed chairs and then takes a seat across the table from them. Wes, with his swollen black eye, looks exhausted.

"How are you doing, Wes?" Jamie begins.

"Just give me the update," Wes says impatiently. "They found my brother in a hospital in Salt Lake City, and once we're done here, I'm heading there."

"I'm glad to hear that," Jamie says. "First of all, the investigation into the explosion and Johanna Monaghan's death continue to be a top priority of our agency."

"But Dalton is the guy, right?" Wes asks. "He's the one who planted the bomb."

"We're still gathering evidence, but Dalton Monaghan is a suspect," Jamie says.

"A suspect?" Wes asks. "You mean he's *the* suspect, right? You saw him the other day, the way he was ranting. He tried to kill me. You can't think someone else is responsible for the bomb."

"Like I said," Jamie says, evenly, "we're still gathering evidence, and I have a few questions for you."

"Sure, whatever you need," Wes says. "But I don't know how much help I'll be. Half of what Dalton was saying was nonsense."

"Like you and Johanna having an affair? Was that nonsense?" Jamie asks.

"Of course," Wes scoffs.

"Tell me about the barn," Jamie says. "Do you keep it locked?"

"No. It's just an old storage barn," Wes explains. "It's mostly filled with junk my brother and I have collected over the years. There's nothing of value in there."

"But anyone could go in and out of it?" Jamie prods.

"Yes, but there's no reason anyone would want to."

"Except to plant an IED?"

"Apparently," Wes says.

Jamie opens the file folder and slides the bagged journal entry in front of Wes, who grimaces at the sight of the dried blood. "From Johanna Monaghan's journal," Jamie explains. "The section that Dalton ripped out and brought to your house in order to confront you. You can see Johanna wrote your name on the page a few times."

Wes scans the document and shakes his head. "You're going to have to help me out here. All I see is scrap of paper with blood all over it. What am I supposed to be seeing?" he asks, then looks to his attorney.

"Can we move things along here, Agent Saldano?" Stewart says. "Mr. Drake would like to get on the road and see his brother."

"Of course," Jamie says. "Right here." Jamie taps the bottom of the page. "It's a little hard to see, but if you look hard enough you can read what's written."

Wes squints down at the paper, then lifts the baggie, holding it up to the light. "Sorry, it's too faint." He pushes the bag back toward Jamie. "Why don't you just read it for me?"

"Sure," Jamie says. "You can clearly see your name written a few times on the page. Now, some of ink is smudged, but I think I get the gist of what Johanna wrote down here. *Scared . . . Wes . . . make me disap . . .*"

"What's that supposed to mean?" the attorney asks. "And what does it have to do with Wes?"

"We'll send the it to the lab for testing," Jamie says. "But to me it looks like Johanna wrote something to the effect of *I'm scared that Wes will make me disappear.*"

The attorney snorts. "You got all that? Sorry, I don't see it." Jamie glances over at Wes, who is staring back, his eyes hard.

"So, Wes, did you ever tell Johanna Monaghan that you were going to make her disappear?" Jamie asks, holding Wes's gaze.

"Of course not," Wes says at the same time his attorney says, "Don't answer that."

"Did you have an affair with her, and perhaps she felt guilty and was going to tell your wife?"

"No, no," Wes says. "I want to answer. I did not say anything like that to Johanna, just like I did not have an affair with her. Dalton went after *me*, remember—"

"Wes," the attorney says, "stop talking." To Jamie he says, "Agent, this interview is over. Any further communications go through me."

"Who's your supervisor?" Wes blusters. "I want to talk to him."

"You're looking at him, Mr. Drake," Jamie says. "We'll talk again soon."

Wes glares at Jamie but says nothing more, then turns and leaves the building, his attorney close at his heels. Jamie returns to his office, shuts the door. It's most likely a coincidence that the words in Johanna's journal echo what happened in his own life: Juneau disappearing. Still, Jamie remembers what Dalton had told him the first time they had talked. *The Drakes and people like them own more than land around here. Just you wait.* Jamie may owe Wes his life, but he's in charge of this investigation, no matter how powerful Wes thinks he is.

CHAPTER 23

MADELINE

MADELINE WAITED IN the hotel room as long as she could but finally couldn't stand it any longer. She wanted to go home, sleep in her own bed, see Pip and the horses.

When the Uber pulls up in front of the house, she steps from the back of the car and shivers. The night had snuffed away any remaining heat of the day, and the night air is cool against her skin. She rubs her arms to generate heat and hears a soft nicker and the shuffling of hooves. The moon is a milky yellow, casting an anemic glow over the ranch, and she squints, trying to see into the dark. Parked near the stables is a truck. More specifically, Lucy's truck. Wes must have arranged to have the tire fixed. And hooked to the back of it is a horse trailer.

"Son of a bitch," Madeline murmurs, shaking her head. Lucy really did plan on taking Sonnet with her when she left. A light burns in the stable. It's probably Wes checking in on the animals. She's nervous at what he's going to say at her sudden appearance.

Cautiously, she approaches the house, stopping at the bottom of the porch steps. It looks abandoned, forlorn against the shadow of the mountain, and Madeline can see that someone has swept away the broken glass and boarded up the broken windows, but already there is a brand-new door in place. She tests the knob and finds it locked and knows that the back door will most likely be locked too, so she'll have to go find Wes in the barn or bother Trent.

"Fancy meeting you here," comes a disembodied voice from the dark.

Fear clamps a tight fist around Madeline's heart. She nearly tumbles backward down the steps before grabbing onto the porch railing and steadying herself.

"Jesus," Madeline says, pressing shaking fingers against her chest. "What the hell are you doing out here in the dark?" In the weak moonlight, Madeline sees Lucy swaying gently on the porch swing. She's holding something in her right hand, dark and shiny in the moonlight. A gun, the barrel pointing straight up toward the porch ceiling. Madeline's legs are weak with fear as she watches Lucy lift the gun and tip it toward her lips.

Not a gun, Madeline realizes, relief flooding through her body. Lucy is holding a bottle of Sam Adams.

Lucy shrugs. "I couldn't sleep. It's a nice night."

"Where's Wes?" Madeline asks. She hates that she needs to ask her sister about the whereabouts of her own husband.

"Doing Wes things," Lucy says, taking a long pull on the beer. Once she swallows, she scoots over on the porch swing as if inviting Madeline to sit beside her. "Don't you want to guess what your dear husband is up to?"

Madeline does not. She does not want to play these stupid head games with her sister. "Listen, Lucy, I'm tired. Are you going to tell me where Wes is or not?" she asks, arms crossed.

"Fine," Lucy says, her voice thick. "They found Dix," she slurs. "Wes drove to Salt Lake City to see him. Isn't that a refreshing concept? Someone looking out for their sibling?" That's when Madeline spies the beer bottles at Lucy's feet. She'd been out here for a while. "Come sit down, Mads," Lucy says, patting the space beside her. Madeline fights the urge to settle next to her sister on the swing, to lay her head on Lucy's shoulder, like she did when she was little.

"Did Wes say when he was coming home?" Madeline asks, begrudgingly. "My phone got lost in the explosion," she adds by way of explanation as to why she hasn't gotten this information from Wes himself.

"He said tomorrow, if all goes well." Lucy adds another bottle to the pile at her feet. She checks the watch on her wrist. "Make that today."

"Christ," Madeline says, rubbing her forehead. "He has a head injury, Lucy. How could you let him go off on his own like that? He shouldn't be driving. He could hurt someone."

Lucy shrugs. "He insisted. And you, better than anyone, know how stubborn Wes can be. If it's any consolation, he seemed fine. But what do I know?"

"Listen," Madeline says, her voice taking on a resigned note, "I'm sorry. I'm sorry about everything that happened back home. I said some things I shouldn't have. Can't we just forget about it?"

Lucy opens her mouth to interrupt, but Madeline doesn't give her the chance. "You can have Sonnet back. And I'll talk to a lawyer, find a way to get you your share of the money. I know Dad left the money and horses to me"—Madeline can't help but get that dig in—"but I also know he wouldn't want this for us either."

Lucy shifts in her seat, planting her feet on the porch floor so that the swing stops swaying. She leans forward, elbows on knees, and looks up at Madeline. "You know that my dad's trust is rock solid. Do you think you can give me a horse, my horse for that matter, and I'll just go away? Uh-uh," Lucy says shaking her head. "You said things I'll never, ever be able to forget. And you know me. I can hold a grudge."

Madeline holds up a hand. "Come on, Lucy, I'm offering

you a way out. I'm giving you Sonnet, I'll get you the money. Why can't that be enough?"

"You know why," Lucy says, grabbing Madeline by the wrist, the slur in her voice replaced with steel. "And who the hell is this Mellie person? And why is she staying here?"

"Mellie?" Madeline says, shaking off her sister's hand. "Where is she?"

"I don't know, but she's around here somewhere," Lucy says. "Do you really think it's a good idea inviting a stranger into your house at a time like this?"

Madeline hates to admit that Lucy is right. Having Mellie here when things are so chaotic isn't helping her stress levels, but what else could she do? The poor girl is all alone and pregnant with nowhere to stay. "She'll only be here for a few days. Just until she finds a different apartment."

"Uh-huh," Lucy says, nodding her head. "Right. But my advice would be to send her on her way as soon as possible."

"Everything okay?" comes a voice from the dark. Madeline lets out a breath, relieved to see the silhouette of Trent standing a few yards away. Madeline has always liked Trent. He's a hard worker, is at once gentle but firm with the horses, always has their best interest in mind. She worries about him as a sister would a brother, as she has heard he can be reckless in his personal life—a hard drinker, messy relationships—but he always gets the job done. She also thinks Trent may have a bit of a crush on her.

Lucy gives Madeline's wrist a final squeeze before releasing her. Trent's eyes flick between the sisters. "Madeline?" Trent prompts.

"Everything's fine," she replies.

Lucy rises from the swing, her foot banging against the empty beer bottles, sending them scattering. "Yes, everything is fine. Everything is always fine with Madeline Drake," Lucy says, her voice sharp with sarcasm. "I'm going to bed."

Lucy brushes past her and moves down the porch steps, and Madeline can feel Trent's eyes on her. Her face burns with embarrassment.

"You okay?"

"I'm okay." Together they step from the porch and walk toward the rear of the house. Trent rests a hand lightly on Madeline's elbow, and she's grateful for his proximity. The last few days have left her reeling, bereft, bruised, and strangely alone. Madeline feels a surge of anger toward Wes. He should be here.

At night, even in mid-May, the smell of snow can drift down from the mountains, and Madeline breathes it in— the crisp, clean air that has replaced the sooty stink from the explosion. A wolf howls in the distance, and the spell is broken. Madeline rushes to the door.

She tugs on the sliding glass door, half expecting that Lucy has locked her out of her own home, but it slides open with ease. "Come on in," Madeline invites, and Trent follows her inside. She flips on the lights. Her house feels strange to her now, different. A man has died here. A woman has died just outside these windowpanes. "I'll be right back. I just want to grab a sweatshirt."

She moves to the stairs; the landing above is curtained in darkness. Madeline stops short as she puts one foot on the first step. Upstairs is where Dalton Monaghan died. Their baby's nursery is splashed with his blood.

"Madeline?" Trent says, watching her with concern.

She can't move. Her foot is glued in place. Madeline knows that Dalton can't hurt them any longer, that the danger has passed. But has it?

Madeline looks to Trent helplessly, and he seems to read her mind. "Come sit down for a minute." He reaches for her hand and guides her to the great room. His fingers are strong and warm, but Madeline is hesitant to enter that space, doesn't want to see the carnage Dalton left behind. But Trent gently pulls her along. "It's okay," he murmurs. And to her surprise, it is. There is a new door and all the broken glass and wrecked furniture is gone. The only remnants of the carnage are the boarded-up windows.

"You did all this?" Madeline asks.

"Yeah," Trent says, almost shyly. "I figured the last thing you needed to come home to is a family of raccoons."

"Yes, the door, but you cleaned up all of this," Madeline sweeps her hand over the space. "That was above and beyond. Thank you so much." Madeline settles onto the soft leather sofa, and the dull ache in her belly eases.

"The police released the scene earlier today, and that girl Mellie moved back into the house. Was that okay?" Madeline nods. "And your sister did too," Trent says, and from the stiffness in his voice Madeline knows that Lucy hasn't left much of an impression on him. "Want me to kick her out?" he asks, and Madeline can't help but smile.

It's tempting, but she's too tired to face more drama tonight. "No, thanks," Madeline says. "Lucy will be moving on in the next few days." She hopes this is true.

"I don't trust her," Trent says, sitting on the edge of a chair across from Madeline.

She gives a little laugh. "You've caught on early. You're smarter than most."

"I'm serious, Madeline," he says. "I caught her in the stable office earlier," he says.

At this Madeline sits up straight. "My office? What was she doing?"

"Just looking around, but it was weird. She was acting squirrelly," Trent says, resting his elbows on his knees and leaning forward. "I'm telling you, she's up to something."

Had Lucy been in her desk? She must have found the hidden compartment in the drawer. God, how embarrassing.

Trent is eyeing her with concern. "You all right?"

"The baby is kicking up a storm," Madeline says, trying to conceal her worry. "She must be hungry." *She.* They are having a little girl. The thought floods her with excitement, worry, fathomless love.

Trent hops up from the chair. "Want me grab you something to eat?"

"Oh, no," Madeline says, but it's half-hearted. She is hungry and thirsty and beyond exhausted. The baby gives another jab to her kidneys, and Madeline lets out a soft gasp. Standing above her, Trent looks so worried it's almost comical. "Want to feel?" Madeline asks. She doesn't wait for his answer, she pulls his hand, rough and calloused, toward her and lays it on her midsection. The baby rolls and swirls all elbows and knees in search of a comfortable position.

Trent's face lights up. "That's amazing," he breathes out. Their faces are so close that she can feel his breath on her cheek. It is, Madeline thinks. It is amazing. This little being floating beneath her rib cage, unaware of the turmoil happening outside her insulated world. Wes should be the one here with her right now, the one with his fingers splayed across her stomach. Trent must be thinking the same thing, because he pulls his hand back and stands upright as if burned.

"Your fingers are cold," he says.

"A little," she admits. She looks around the room for the chenille throw usually tossed over the arm of the sofa, but it's nowhere to be seen.

"Here," Trent says, slipping off the flannel shirt he's wearing over his T-shirt and wrapping it around her shoulders.

Madeline tries to murmur her thanks, but she's so very tired.

"Hey," comes a voice from the shadows.

"Mellie," Madeline says, jerking to attention. "How are you?"

"Well, you two look cozy," Mellie says, coming into the room. "And I should be asking you that."

"I'm good." Mellie looks much better than she had when she first arrived on Madeline's doorstep. The grime and soot have been washed away, and instead of the hospital scrubs she's dressed in Madeline's clothes—soft, wide-legged cotton pants and one of her old Iowa Hawkeyes sweatshirts.

Her surprise must be obvious, because Mellie blushes. "I grabbed them from the laundry room. I hope that was okay. I don't have any of my clothes."

"No, it's fine," Madeline says, but a new unease tugs at her. "Borrow what you need."

Mellie smiles her thanks. "I'm glad you're back. You look exhausted." Mellie's eyes flick toward Trent. "I bet you'll be glad to be in your own bed tonight."

"I am," Madeline says. "It's good to be home."

Trent gets to his feet. "It is getting late," he says. "Madeline, I'll talk to you tomorrow. Nell has a cut on her hind quarter that you'll want to take a look at." He gives a curt nod to Mellie and is gone.

"I should get to bed too," Mellie says, with a yawn, then pats her stomach. "This little guy saps all my energy. See you in the morning."

"See you in the morning," Madeline echoes and watches as Mellie retreats into the shadows and out of sight.

Madeline doesn't mind that Mellie borrowed some clean clothes to wear, but she hasn't worn that sweatshirt in weeks and hasn't fit into those pants since she was three months pregnant. Mellie didn't find them in the laundry room. They were both hanging in the back recess of Madeline's bedroom closet. So why is Mellie lying? And what was she doing in Madeline's bedroom?

CHAPTER 24

MELLIE

MORNING LIGHT STREAMS through the windows, and I scrunch my eyes shut, not wanting to wake up. It's so quiet it's almost unsettling. There are no next-door neighbors arguing through the thin walls, no heavy feet thumping above my head. The mattress is just the right amount of soft, and the sheets feel like silk against my skin. But I have to get up—I have work to do. I force my eyes open and stretch, kicking the bed linens aside. I've never been in a home as beautiful as the Drakes'. It's so different than the tiny two-bedroom I grew up in, and definitely different than the one-bedroom efficiency I've been renting in town. There it smells like whatever my neighbors cooked for dinner, and here it smells like mountain bluebells.

I crawl from bed and open the closet which is filled with more of Madeline's clothes and piles of thick comforters and linens. I look at myself in the full-length mirror hanging on the inside of door and have to admit I look good in Madeline's satin pajama shorts and camisole. I wonder what Madeline would think if I walked into the kitchen wearing only this. Wonder what Wes would think.

The surprised expression on Madeline's face when I showed up at her door isn't lost on me. I know that she hadn't really meant it when she told me to reach out if I needed anything.

Anything at all. But she did offer, and that should count for something. I don't like it when people say things they don't mean. And sadly, people do it all the time. *I'll see you on your birthday, munchkin. You can be anything you want to be if you work hard enough. Of course I love you, Mel.* Different people, different promises that turned out to be lies. It's unfair, wrong.

So, I probably should have let Madeline's words remain as they were intended—an empty promise—but I am so tired of being lied to for convenience or as a grand gesture. Not that I'm one to judge.

I dress in another outfit of Madeline's, this time a loose-fitting cashmere sweater and a pair of soft jeans that I happen to know cost more than a month's rent, the shoes probably two months', and step from the room. The house has a stillness about it. Madeline must be out in the stables, and God knows where Lucy is. I feel a sense of righteous satisfaction knowing that Madeline seems to prefer me over her own sister, and I try not to think too hard about what Wes will do when he finds out I'm still here.

One thing is for sure, I need to get rid of Lucy for good. It doesn't matter that the sisters seem to hate each other, Lucy doesn't trust me, and it's making things more complicated. I creep up the stairs, knowing what I'm planning will be risky, dangerous even. If I'm caught, Madeline will be so disappointed, and Lucy will kill me. I don't even want to think about what Wes will do.

At the top of the steps, I pause. What's the endgame here? I ask myself. Do I really think that Wes will leave his beautiful, smart, sweet, pregnant wife for a twenty-one-year-old waitress? Maybe not, but I don't plan on going down without a fight. I hurry down the long hallway and slip into the bedroom Madeline shares with Wes. My heart thumps, but I try to shake the unease away, reminding myself that I belong here. Madeline told me I was welcome to borrow anything I needed. If someone walks in on me, I'll just say I'm searching for a sweatshirt or something.

I peek out the window and see Trent in the paddock exercising the horses. There's no sign of Lucy or Madeline, and a zap of anxiety runs through me. I have to hurry. I step away from the window and move to the closet. Shoes are in a jumble on the floor along with a half a dozen outfits that look like they have been tried on and then tossed aside.

There's a heavy safe sitting in the corner of the closet but no way for me to crack the code. I need to choose something more readily available, something small, easy to transport. I step from the closet and see Madeline's purse sitting on a chaise lounge in the corner of the room and hesitate. Should I worry about fingerprints? Probably, but I decide it's worth the chance. Carefully, I lift Madeline's wallet from the purse, and right away I've hit the jackpot. I pull out three crisp hundred-dollar bills and tuck them into the pocket of my jeans and then move to the bathroom. I ease open one of the top drawers and find a men's razor, deodorant, Band-Aids. This must be Wes's side of the bathroom. Next, I go to the cabinet beneath his sink, crouch down, and find a wicker basket holding unopened tubes of toothpaste, a bottle of mouthwash, and an assortment of pill bottles.

I lift an orange bottle from the basket and peer at the label. Oxycontin, prescribed three years earlier. I give the bottle a little shake. This will do. I return to the master bedroom, roll the bills into a tight cylinder, and fit them into the prescription bottle. I slide the bottle into my back pocket and tiptoe down the hallway toward the guest room. I lean in toward the closed door, listening for any movement on the other side. Nothing. I tap on the wooden frame. "Lucy," I call softly and then once again more loudly. There's no response. With shaky fingers, I reach for the knob.

I open the door and to my relief find the room empty.

Once inside, I shut the door and scan the space. The bed is neatly made, and nothing seems out of place. I check the closet and find Lucy's Carhartt jacket hanging there. Riffling through the front pockets I find a lint-covered stick of gum and a few coins and move to add the pill bottle to the mix but then reconsider. No, chances are that Lucy would find it right away and figure out what I'm up to. I scan the room again and turn my attention to the guest bed, lift the comforter, and shove the pill bottle beneath the mattress. But this won't work either. What are the chances that Madeline will find the bottle quickly? I retrieve the bottle, spy a pair of Lucy's jeans crumpled in a corner of the room, and pick them up. I push the bottle into the back pocket of the jeans and will deposit them in the laundry room where Madeline will eventually find them. Lucy will deny it, will argue, throw an epic fit, and hopefully, Madeline and Wes will throw her ass out the door. Then I'll have just two remaining obstacles in my way—Trent and Madeline. Getting rid of Madeline will be more challenging, but I'm up to the task because, for once in my life, I'm going to get what I want.

CHAPTER 25

JAMIE

AT SEVEN IN the morning, Jamie is back at the sheriff's office, sitting at a battered metal desk pulled from storage, drinking his third cup of bad coffee. He is running on fumes and not thinking straight. Nothing is connected, yet everything is.

Mellie Bauer recalled seeing Dalton coming out of the barn a few minutes before the explosion, but after reading through the notes from the dozens of interviews with the other party-goers, he can find no other reference to this. The party was chaotic, loud, with lots going on, but Jamie is finding it hard to believe that not one other guest saw Dalton going into or out of the barn prior to the explosion. But why would Mellie lie?

Sheriff Colson comes out of his office, grabs a chair and drags it across the floor and sits down next to Jamie's desk. "Christ, what a cluster," he says wearily, dropping a stack of papers in front of Jamie. His shooting of Dalton Monaghan has been ruled justified, and he is back on the job. "A bomb and a shooting. This has been quite the week."

"Yeah," Jamie says. "How are you?"

"I'm okay," Colson says. "Though, I was hoping to get through my career without having to shoot someone."

"You most likely saved the Drakes' lives," Jamie reminds him. "But you're right, it's too bad Dalton put us in that situation."

"Hey, Jamie," Ruby says from the doorway. "Someone's here to see you."

"Who is it?"

"Laura Holt," the receptionist says. "She was the photographer at the party."

Jamie gets up and makes his way toward the reception area of the office.

Laura is standing in the lobby, staring at a bulletin board tacked with Wanted posters. Her chestnut hair hangs down her back in a loose braid, she's wearing shorts, a T-shirt, and running shoes. In her right hand she holds a large professional-looking camera, and in the other she holds a book.

"Ms. Holt," Jamie says, "what can I help you with?"

She turns, and Jamie winces. Her right eye is black-and-blue and swollen completely shut. "Call me Laura, please," she says. "And it looks a lot worse than it is."

"Come on back," Jamie says and leads her back to the smaller of the two interview rooms in the building.

Jamie waits until Laura takes a seat before he sits down across from her. She looks around the room curiously. Like all the rooms in the sheriff's office, this one is crammed with all sorts of extraneous equipment: binders, ammo, armor gear. Jamie knows the state of the sheriff's office isn't unusual. Departments across the country are bursting at the seams and being asked to do more with less funding. "You were injured in the explosion?" Jamie asks. "Not exactly what a photographer expects will happen on a shoot, right?"

"I'm okay. Just this shiner," she says. "And no, I never dreamed anything like this would happen. I'm sorry I'm just bringing this to you now." She sets her camera atop his desk. "I was taken to the hospital over in Cody, and I had to make arrangements for someone to watch my son. I haven't removed the SD card, but I don't think it was damaged when the camera hit the ground."

"I understand," Jamie says, lifting the camera and examining it. The lens is broken, and it's dented in a few spots. "I'm glad you weren't hurt badly. So the SD card is in here?" Jamie asks, tapping the camera.

"Yeah. Want me to pop it out?" Laura asks.

"Please," Jamie says and pulls an evidence bag and sticker from his drawer as Laura retrieves the memory card. "It holds the original pictures?" Jamie asks. "None have been deleted or edited in any way?"

"No, not at all," Laura says, dropping the card into the plastic bag. "I haven't even looked at any of them."

"That's good," Jamie says, but falters when he notices Laura searching his face closely.

"You don't remember me, do you?" she asks with a little smile.

Jamie nearly groans out loud. He knew that this time would come. It was one thing to have Sheriff Colson recognize him, but he was hoping that it wouldn't be so obvious for random townspeople. Does he play ignorant? Pretend he has no idea what she's talking about?

Laura doesn't give him the chance. She sets the book she's been holding on the conference room table. It's covered in black pebbled faux-leather and embossed with gold lettering. A yearbook. The room suddenly becomes even smaller, the walls closing in, the ceiling bearing down on him.

"It's from back when the middle school and high school were in the same building. Before we consolidated with Clayton and Red Creek," Laura says. "You were in seventh grade, and I was in sixth, and we rode the same bus. When I saw your photo in the newspaper, I recognized your face right away." Laura flips through the pages. "Look." She pokes her finger at a black-and-white photo. She looks up at him expectantly. "You're J. J. Archer, right?"

It's definitely a picture of Jamie. It was taken the second week at his new school, a month before Juneau disappeared.

He is eighty pounds lighter and a foot shorter, and his shaggy hair falls over his eyes, but it's him. He's wearing an oversize flannel shirt buttoned up to the neck, and even without seeing them he knows he's wearing a pair of baggy shorts with his battered Vans. The expression on his face is one of barely contained contempt mixed with utter boredom. He wasn't happy about being in Nightjar and wanted the entire world to know it.

"Wow, that's a blast from the past," Jamie says with a little laugh because he can't think of anything else to say.

"Tell me about," Laura says, then flips the page. "There I am." She points to a skinny mouse of a girl with glasses much too large for her face and a smattering of freckles across her nose.

Jamie lifts his eyes from the page. "You still have the freckles," he says.

"You don't remember me at all, do you?" Laura says, rubbing her nose self-consciously.

"I'm sorry," Jamie says. He has no recollection of this girl, no memory of riding the bus with her. It's no surprise, really. "I've been told I was quite self-absorbed during that era of my life. And actually, my wife might say I still am."

Laura smiles. "That's okay, I didn't think you would. My last name used to be Higgins. It's Holt now. You don't go by Archer anymore?"

Jamie shakes his head. "It's complicated."

He really doesn't want to get into this right now, and thankfully Laura doesn't push it. Instead she says, "I have to tell you, your sister was really nice to me."

A spark of electricity shoots through Jamie, and he sits up straighter. "You knew Juneau?"

"Not really," Laura says, regretfully. "But she took pity on me on the bus and kind of took me under her wing. She'd sit next to me and show me how to make cootie catchers, and when other kids would comment on my clothes or my hair, she'd tell them to shut the fuck up."

"That sounds like Juneau," Jamie says with a fond smile.

"When it happened . . ." Laura falters, then continues, her words thickening. "When she disappeared, I was so sad. I know it doesn't make a lot of sense, but I felt like I lost a friend. I can't imagine what you and your mom went through. She really was a special person."

"Thanks," Jamie says. He's forgotten how nice it is to talk to someone who knew his sister. There was his mom, of course, but she avoided speaking about Juneau at all costs. He dreads the conversation telling her about his return to Nightjar. "Do you remember my sister having any problems with anyone? Or hanging around with anyone in particular?"

"Not really," Laura says, "but I did hear she was dating an older boy but never heard who it might be."

Jamie doubted this was true. He would have known if his sister was dating someone, wouldn't he? "I know she took pictures for the school newspaper, but she never mentioned anyone specifically," Jamie says.

Laura's forehead furrows as she thinks. "No, no," she says after a moment. "I don't know anything about her dating someone from the school paper, but I did see her taking pictures at a football game a week or so before she disappeared."

This isn't the earth-shattering news that Jamie is hoping to hear, but it is something. "Anyone she interacted with that stands out?"

"Not really. She took action shots during the game, and afterward I saw her talking to a few boys on the team. Steve Hoffman, Mike Gentry, Wes Drake."

Jamie's head snaps up. "Wes Drake?"

"Yeah, but it didn't seem like a big deal," Laura says. "Was it?"

"Probably not," Jamie says. "But it's good to know, anyway. Did the police talk to you during the investigation?"

"Me?" Laura says, placing a hand to her chest. "No, no one talked to me. I didn't exactly run in those crowds."

"Yeah," Jamie says with little smile. "Me neither."

"I'm sorry," Laura says. "I wish I could remember more."

"Ah well, it was a long time ago." Jamie tries not to let his disappointment show.

"I'll keep thinking," Laura says. "Anyway, I thought I'd tell you how nice your sister was and how sorry I am for your loss."

"Thanks," Jamie says. "But while you're here, can I ask you a few questions about the explosion?"

"Sure," Laura says. "Whatever I can do to help."

"Did anything about the night jump out at you? Anyone acting suspiciously?"

"No. I've been racking my brain, trying to remember if anything seemed off, but most of what I saw was through a lens," Laura says, tapping the cracked camera lens. "Not exactly a panoramic view."

"I'm sure your photos will be very helpful," Jamie says. "How well do you know Madeline and Wes Drake?"

"I don't know them at all," Laura says. "I mean beyond talking on the phone with Madeline. I've met Wes's brother, Dix. I was the photographer at one of his weddings. But beyond that, I don't know them."

Dix Drake. Jamie received word that he had been found in a Salt Lake City hospital. He was questioned by a local ATF agent, but nothing in their conversation stood out.

"I did see Wes and Dix arguing just before the guests started arriving," Laura says. "It wasn't a knockdown fight or anything, but they both looked upset."

"Could you hear what they were arguing about?" Jamie asks.

"No, I was too far away," Laura says regretfully. "But it was intense. Wes was poking his brother in the chest and going on and on about something until Dix kind of just pushed him away. Not hard, more like to get Wes out of his face. Then it was over."

"How long did it last?" Jamie asks, making a note to ask both Wes and Dix about this confrontation.

"Not long," Laura says. "Maybe a minute or two, and then they went off in different directions."

Jamie questions Laura for several more minutes, but when it's clear she has nothing more to add, he hands her one of his business cards. "Thanks for coming in, Laura," he says. "If you think of anything else, please let me know."

"Sure thing," Laura says. "And it's good to see you again, J. J."

"You too," Jamie says, picking up the yearbook and extending it to Laura, but she gently pushes it toward him.

"Keep it," she says. "My sister has one I can look at. It's not like anyone signed that one."

"Thanks," Jamie says. "And, Laura, I'm hoping you won't say anything about my history here, about who I used to be." Laura looks up at him, confused. "The sheriff knows," he adds quickly. "It just complicates things."

"Of course," Laura says. "I won't say anything. And by the way, I know you won't remember this, but you were also very kind to me."

"Me?" Jamie asks with surprise. "Really? I always thought I was kind of an asshole back then."

Laura laughs, and Jamie finds that he likes the way her eyes crinkle when she smiles. *Still an asshole*, he hears Juneau's voice in his ear. *By the way, have you called your wife yet?*

"Jamie, we've got something," Sheriff Colson says, poking his head around the doorway.

"If I remember anything else, I'll call," Laura says as she moves toward the door.

THE PERFECT HOSTS 209

"Thanks," Jamie says and watches as she skirts past the sheriff and out of the room. He turns his attention back to Colson. "Whatcha got?" he asks.

Colson steps into the room and holds out an evidence bag filled with what appears to be white rice. "It's the phone that was found near where Johanna Monaghan died. It was soaked from the rain, but it looks like the rice might have worked. It's turned on again."

Jamie takes the bag and examines the contents. The cell phone has indeed turned on again and glows dimly through the rice. "Are you sure it's Johanna's?" he asks.

"Pretty sure," Colson says. "The screen saver is a picture of the Monaghans' dog."

"Well, let's see what we can find," Jamie says. "Do you have any gloves handy?" Colson leaves the room briefly and returns with a pair of latex gloves. Jamie slides them on and then opens the evidence bag, reaches inside, and pulls out the phone. It's an older iPhone, and surprisingly the screen wasn't shattered in the explosion. Jamie presses the Home button and not surprisingly gets the prompt to enter a four-digit code. "Any ideas?" he asks, and the deputy shakes his head. Without the code, opening the phone could take months. Cell phone carriers are known for being stubborn when it comes to providing cell phone data without a court order. "Did anyone find a list of passwords during the search of the Monaghan home?"

"No," Colson says. "Whatever their passwords were, they died with them."

"Let me spend a little time with it, and see what I can come up with," Jamie says, rubbing his eyes. If worse comes to worst, he can send the phone to Cellebrite, a company that law enforcement often contracts with to aid in extracting digital data from phones and computers.

"Sure thing," the sheriff says. "I'm heading to the courthouse now, but why don't you stop over tonight? I have something I've been meaning to give you, and we can catch up."

Jamie looks up from the phone and examines the weathered face of the man who brought just about the only semblance of comfort to him after Juneau disappeared. "Yeah, yeah, that sounds good," he says. "See you tonight."

Jamie returns his attention to the phone and tries the most common number combinations: 1234, 1111, 0000, 1212. Nothing. Next he finds Johanna's birthday in his notes, December 15, 1985, and tries a variety of combinations of those digits. It doesn't work, and the same goes for Dalton's birthdate. He has one more try before the phone will lock him out. He refers again to his notes, and his eyes snag on her home address, 3308 Mountain Creek Road. He types in 3308, and bingo, he's in.

The phone's battery life is in the red, so Jamie goes to the lobby and asks Ruby if there's a charger lying around that he can have. She hands him her own personal charger.

"Keep it as long as you need, hon," she says. "I've got another one in the car. Oh, and Wes Drake has been trying to get ahold of you. He wants you to stop at the ranch this afternoon."

"Did he say why?" Jamie says, absent-mindedly as he punches Johanna's code into the phone again.

"No. Just said he expects you at the ranch at three thirty," Ruby says. "It wasn't a request."

Jamie pulls his eyes from the device. "Oh yeah?"

"Yeah. He was adamant. Want me to tell him to come here?"

"Nah, it's fine. I'll meet him. I want another look at the scene, anyway. But let him know I'll be there at three."

"I'll let him know," Ruby says, and Jamie goes back to the contents of the phone. The first thing he notices are the thirty-two missed calls Johanna has after six thirty, the reported time of the explosion. Jamie counts twenty-five of those as coming from her husband. There are two from someone named Katherine Logan and another three from a string of numbers with no names attached. Jamie jots down the information in his notebook and then looks at the call log before six thirty.

At 6:12 p.m., Johanna received and answered a call from another number. The call lasted less than twenty seconds. Jamie compares the number to the ones received after the explosion. No match. He adds this number to his list, then navigates to her text messages. Again, there are several from Dalton asking Johanna to give him a call. There's one from Madeline sent just before the explosion asking where she is, saying that the reveal is about to begin.

Jamie scrolls back through the mundane communications between husband and wife.

> What time will you be home tonight? Will you grab a gallon of milk on your way home?

Interspersed with these are plenty of shared videos from TikTok and *I love you*s. There are also several texts from Dalton demanding to know where Johanna is.

> Where are you? You said you were going to be home at 7.
> I went by the hospital—your car's not there.

There are dozens and dozens more like them.

He thinks of what Madeline mentioned about the tracking device Dalton put in Johanna's car, and indeed, the crime-scene techs found one when they checked her vehicle. They were still looking for any direct evidence connecting Dalton to the IED. They found double-headed nails in the Monaghan garage and a copy of a biography of Ted Kaczynski, the Unabomber. Not near enough evidence. The computer techs are still scouring through Dalton's computer and his search history.

As Jamie skims through the texts, he sees nothing of interest until he hits a thread sent three days before the party. The messages are initiated from a number with no name.

555–0110: We need to talk.

JOHANNA: There's nothing left to say.

555–0110: I can explain. Just give me a chance.

JOHANNA: Nothing you say will change a damn thing.

555–0110: Have you talked to her?

JOHANNA: Stop! I'm not doing this anymore. Leave me alone.

555–0110: Johanna, come on. You know me.

555–0110: Please, 5 minutes, that's all I need.

555–0110: So you're going to ignore me?

555–0110: Fuck this and fuck you, Johanna.

JOHANNA: No, fuck you. I'm finished. No more secrets.

555–0110: I don't want you anywhere near me or my wife. Do you understand? You call her, come see her, go anywhere near her, you'll regret it.

That's where the conversation ends. He double-checks it against the calls to Johanna's number the day of the fire, and there it is. The call that came into Johanna's phone twenty minutes before the explosion. The one that lasted about twenty seconds.

Well, thinks Jamie, this is interesting. At first glance, the texts read like a possible romance gone wrong. Was Johanna involved with a married man? Had she threatened to go to the wife, and the man wanted to make sure that didn't happen? Now he has to find out who it is. He enters the number into a reverse-phone-number site, and the answer is immediate. The number is registered to Lone Tree Ranch LLC. Jamie flips through his notes. None of the three ranch hands at Lone Tree are married. It looks like Dalton was right. Wes Drake has officially become a suspect in the death of Johanna Monaghan.

CHAPTER 26

LUCY

"BITCH," LUCY SAYS, watching the video on her phone. At the harsh tone, Sonnet stamps her feet and shakes her mane. "Not you," Lucy says, rubbing her flank. "You're the best girl." She's in the stables, checking on the newest foal. Madeline is at the far end of the stable talking with Trent. Lucy rewinds the video and watches again as Mellie, carrying what looks like an orange plastic pill bottle, steps from the master bedroom and then reappears in Lucy's room. Watches as Mellie looks around, goes to the closet and pulls Lucy's Carhartt jacket from a hanger, then moves to her bed, and finally picks up a pair of Lucy's jeans. She watches as Mellie slides the pill bottle into an inner pocket, then returns the coat to the closet.

"Bitch," Lucy says again. Mellie is setting her up. Making her out to be a thief so she can get Madeline to throw her out of the house or, worse, get her arrested.

Lucy made a mistake leaving the ranch that morning. She went into Jackson to run a few personal errands and to buy paint and other supplies for the baby's room. While she was gone, Mellie was busy.

She has to hurry. Lucy retrieves her purchases from the back seat of the truck, looping the plastic bags filled with painting and cleaning supplies around her wrist, and lifting a gallon of

primer to cover the blood-stained walls in the nursery. Pip
follows, and Lucy shoos her away. When she enters the house
it's quiet, and there is no sign of Madeline or Mellie. Lucy goes
directly up the steps and stops outside the nursery. No one has
removed the X of crime-scene tape across the doorway yet,
though the space has been released to Wes and Madeline.

Lucy sets down the gallon of paint and rips down the yellow
plastic and wads it up in her fist. She opens the nursery door and
is met with a bloody mess, stark against the pristine white room.
A constellation of dried blood streaks the freaky white horse
that looks as if it's leaping through the wall. Drips of dry, flaky
blood dot the white oak floor, and a stiff dark stain mars the
center of the large white area rug in front of the crib, marking
the spot where Dalton Monaghan died and smells of gasoline.

Lucy goes into the guest room, goes straight for the right
side of the bed. She slides her hand between the mattress and
box spring to make sure Mellie hasn't left anything behind.
There's nothing there. She rushes back down the steps and
into the laundry room and finds her jeans buried beneath a
pile of damp towels. She slides her fingers into a back pocket,
and there she finds the bottle filled with pills and money, just
as she knew she would. So this is how Mellie wants to play
it, Lucy thinks. She must admit she's a little impressed. She
checks the security camera on her app and finds Madeline and
Trent in the stables. Good. There is no sign of Mellie.

Now, how to use this to her advantage?

Taking the pill bottle with her, Lucy steps outside. Trent's truck
is parked near the bunkhouse. There's a narrow chance that she'll
be able to get to his vehicle without being seen on the outdoor surveillance camera. She goes back inside and into the living room,
trying to decide what to do. Then she sees it lying in a puddle on
the floor—Trent's flannel shirt, the one he wore the night before.
She picks up the shirt and slides the pill bottle in the front pocket,

then drops it to the floor between the leather ottoman and the sofa. Out of sight, for now.

The house phone rings, but Lucy doesn't answer; instead, she unplugs the cord from the wall. On the way back up the steps, she checks her text messages and finds one from Wes.

> I've been trying to call the house phone but there's no answer. Is Madeline around? Did her phone show up yet?

Lucy taps out her response.

> No phone yet. She's out in the stables with Trent checking on the foal. She's a beauty. How's your brother doing? Are you coming home today?

Wes responds immediately.

> Yes, just stopping for gas. I should be home in about 3 hours. He's doing well. Should be able to come home in the next few days. Will you tell Madeline I'm on my way?

She replies, Sure thing. Drive safe.

But she has no intention of telling Madeline anything and isn't ready to hand over the new phone that was delivered the day before. It's tucked away in her backpack along with her gun. She really doesn't want to have to use the gun but will if she must. A flutter of nerves fills her stomach. Things are in motion now, but it isn't too late to put a stop to it. The thing is, Lucy doesn't want to stop. She's been planning and preparing for weeks. Not only will she get her inheritance but she'll be able to dole out some well-deserved karma. Now she just needs to wait until Wes gets home, and that's when all hell will break loose.

CHAPTER 27

JAMIE

JAMIE DRUMS HIS fingers on his desk and stares down at Johanna Monaghan's cell phone. It looks like Dalton's suspicions were warranted and Wes had a romantic relationship with Johanna that he needed to keep hidden from his wife.

Jamie glances around the bullpen. Deputies are coming in and out of the space, Ruby drops a stack of mail on a desk, Deputy Ladd is on the phone, feet propped on his desk, laughing. Everyone and everything in Nightjar is connected. It's not that Jamie doesn't trust local law enforcement, but if he lets it be known that Wes Drake is a viable suspect in Johanna Monaghan's death, chances are it will get back to Wes before Jamie even has the opportunity to interview him again. No, he needs to keep this information under wraps for as long as possible.

"Hey, Saldano," Ladd calls from across the room, "any luck with that phone?"

"Not yet," Jamie says, giving a regretful shake of his head. "I'll keep trying, but it's pretty much fried. We can send it in to one of our tech guys. See what they can make of it."

"Yeah, not my area of expertise. I'm heading out. Going to talk to more of the party guests," Ladd says. "Catch you later."

Jamie waits until Ruby and the other deputies drift from the room before covertly taking pictures of Johanna's text messages with his own phone. He unplugs the device from the borrowed charger and then secures it in the evidence locker which is just a converted janitor's closet.

He returns to his desk, pops the SD card into his computer, and clicks on the icon that pops up and then on the blue folder labeled *Drake Gender Reveal*. Within the folder are hundreds and hundreds of files. "Christ," Jamie murmurs, rubbing his forehead. The files are labeled by numbers, and Jamie decides it's safe to assume that the photos named with the lower numbers are the ones taken earlier on the evening of the explosion. It would make sense to start looking at the pictures taken closer to the time of the explosion, but he doesn't work that way. He knows that sometimes the most important clues can be found in some of the most innocuous pieces of evidence, and he doesn't want to get careless and miss something.

Jamie clicks on the first file and a photo of the Drake property fills the screen, and once again he is reminded of the nearly incomprehensible wealth of the Drake family. The late-afternoon sun illuminates the lavish home on green and gold fields, giving the landscape an almost magical, otherworldly feel. The now-destroyed barn is still standing but lists to the side. It's an old barn. Next to the barn is the canopied tent where dinner was to be served, and beyond the house and stables sits the old truck, waiting to be blown to pieces. Jamie clicks on the next file and the next, and the next, and it's more of the same. He resists the urge to jump ahead. Pay attention, he tells himself.

In the next series of images, the photographer captures the arrival of the guests red-carpet-style. Couples dressed in Western wear, pause arm in arm and beam widely at the camera. There are lots of cowboy hats and boots. The women wear long strings of pearls and expensive jewelry, while the men and some of the women pose brandishing their guns. Guns and alcohol, Jamie thinks, a perfect mix. There are so many faces in the crowd they begin to blend together after a while. As he goes through each photo, he pays attention to body language and facial expressions, looking for anyone who appears uneasy or out of place. Everyone seems to be having a good time, happy to be there.

That is until a photo of Madeline Drake and the victim, Johanna Monaghan, appears, arms around one another. Jamie expected the women to be joyous for the occasion, but Madeline isn't smiling. Her expression appears a little angry. He wonders if Madeline suspected a relationship between her husband and her midwife. Were Madeline's earlier grief and distress about Johanna's death all an act?

Jamie spends the next hour going through pictures of the guests mugging for the camera, of the beautiful flowers, of the exquisite place settings, and of the cake with both blue and pink icing cascading down its sides. There are several of Wes smiling with various partygoers, and one of Madeline midcringe as Mia Preston reaches out to touch her belly.

Jamie's about ready for a break when he clicks on a photo that shows the ill-fated barn. There's a flurry of activity around it with catering staff holding platters of appetizers and beverages and of the guests twirling their pearls and a rodeo clown swiping a cowboy hat and turning to dart through the crowd. The next several pictures show more of the same, and Jamie examines them carefully, looking for any sign that anyone is entering or exiting the barn. And then, there she is at the edge of the frame. Jamie brings his face closer to the computer screen. Even though her back is to the camera, he recognizes the long sleek braid and denim top. It's Johanna Monaghan, and she is reaching for the barn door. Under her arm is the gift from the Prestons. In the next photo, Johanna is glancing over her shoulder as if checking to see if anyone is watching, but no one appears to be paying attention to her. The next photo shows Johanna stepping into the black hole of the barn.

This is it, Jamie thinks. If someone else followed Johanna into the barn, it could be captured in one of the remaining photos. There are only about twenty pictures left in the file, meaning that the explosion is coming. Holding his breath, Jamie clicks on the next photo, then the next and the next. No one is entering the barn behind Johanna. He clicks until there are only five photos left. His finger hovers over the mouse.

Jamie opens the next photo, and a man has entered the frame. His head is down, and his cowboy hat is pulled low, but it's unmistakably Wes Drake. The next picture shows Wes midstride with Mellie Bauer close behind, her fingers outstretched as if trying to snag Wes's arm. She has a wistful, almost hopeful, expression on her face. Interesting, Jamie thinks.

Jamie clicks the next image, sits back in his chair, and interlaces his hands behind his head. In this photo, Wes and Mellie are standing close to one another, almost chest to chest, as he leans down, his lips to her ear. Jamie zooms in on the photo. In one hand Wes is holding a cell phone, while the other is resting low on Mellie's waist.

So Wes was involved not only with Johanna but with the waitress too. Mia Preston was right. Wes got around.

He opens the next photo, and there it is—Wes Drake opening the barn door and stepping inside, with Mellie Bauer looking on.

Then it dawns on him. Mellie is the one who told him that it was Dalton Monaghan she saw going into the barn just before the explosion. She lied. She lied to protect Wes.

Jamie clicks on the final photo. This one shows Wes exiting the barn, face grim and determined, his cell in his hand. Could Wes have detonated the IED via cell phone? Jamie picks up his phone and calls his contact at the crime lab.

"Nina," he says, "it's Jamie Saldano. Have you got anything for me on the Drake crime scene?"

"Come on, Saldano," Nina says, a hint of mock-injury in her voice. "It's been—what?—five days? You know better."

"Yeah, yeah," Jamie says. "But can you tell me anything about how it might have been detonated? What it was housed in?"

Nina sighs. "I can tell you it wasn't in that package with the big black bow you were wondering about. The crime-scene techs found that pretty much intact beneath one of the fallen roof trusses. All that gift held was a sterling silver picture frame from Tiffany worth about a thousand bucks."

Jamie gives a whistle. Rich people are something else. He wonders what the Prestons gave people who weren't their sworn enemies.

"It was a pretty simple setup," Nina goes on. "What the techs found at the scene pretty much sums it up. Nails, ball bearings, PVC pipe, duct tape. Looks like the victim stepped on a trip wire."

"So just about anyone with a computer could have looked up how to make an IED and cobbled it together," Jamie says. "Thanks, Nina. Give me a call if you learn anything else, will you?"

"Sure thing," she says, and they disconnect.

"Dammit," Jamie murmurs, the reality of what he's seeing is sinking in. It didn't look like the Prestons were behind the attack. But Nightjar's golden boy and hometown hero—Jamie's hero—was one of the last people to see Johanna Monaghan alive. Could it be that the boy who saved him from death all those years ago grew up to be a murderer?

CHAPTER 28

MADELINE

MADELINE COMES IN from the stables, puts water on the stove for tea, and moves into the office to check her emails. She dreads the thought of what she might find but knows she needs to keep on top of things. When she opens the app, the screen floods with emails. She quickly deletes the junk mail and anything that looks like they might be media inquiries. There are several more messages blaming her and Wes for the explosion, calling them *shameful* and *out of touch*, and mocking their gender reveal. She forwards the threatening ones to Agent Saldano.

From the kitchen comes the breathy whistle of the kettle, but Madeline sees an email with the subject line that reads *Naughty, naughty*. It sounds like porn, but she decides to open the message.

An image fills the screen, and it takes Madeline a moment to figure out what she's seeing. Her vision blurs, and the room spins. She clutches the desk to keep from falling out of the chair. It's a photo. A photo of Madeline and Trent on the sofa. Trent is wrapping Madeline in his flannel shirt, their faces nearly touching. They look as if they have just embraced or perhaps kissed. The circumstances around the image are completely innocent, but if anyone saw it, they would think the worst of her. The last thing Madeline needs now is word getting out that she's cheating on Wes. She's not. She would never do that.

Who would do this? There are only two options—Lucy or Mellie. It had to have been Lucy—payback because Madeline controlled her finances now? Or was she simply trying to stir the pot? She must have been hiding in the shadows and took the picture after they thought she'd gone off to bed. If Wes saw this, he would be furious and go ballistic on Trent, who would surely lose his job, no matter how innocent the actual scenario was. But that's the point of the photo, Madeline thinks. For Lucy to show Madeline exactly how much power she has over her, over everyone in this household.

Unless, Madeline thinks, looking over her shoulder, Mellie sent the photo. But why? There is no message, just the damning picture. She moves the email into a folder labeled *Recipes*, knowing that Wes will never look there, and then gets to her feet.

Lingering outside Mellie's bedroom, Madeline taps on the door. "Mellie," she calls through the door. "It's Madeline. Are you hungry?"

"Coming," comes a muffled voice. The door opens, and Mellie stands before her wearing yet another of Madeline's outfits. Madeline tries not to let it bother her. The poor girl came to the ranch with only the clothes on her back; of course she needs something to wear. Still . . .

"You should eat. Come out to the kitchen, and I can get you something," Madeline offers, and Mellie follows her to the kitchen.

"Are you in any pain?" Madeline asks, opening the refrigerator. Their Sub-Zero Pro is depressingly empty. With all the chaos, they haven't had the chance to go grocery shopping. Madeline opens the freezer and pulls out a container of homemade beef stew and transfers it to the microwave, then pulls a glass from the cupboard and fills it with water.

"I'm okay," Mellie says, sitting gingerly at the breakfast bar. "Just a little bit sore from hitting the ground so hard."

"I'm so glad your baby is okay," Madeline says. "When do you go back for a recheck?"

"Recheck?" Mellie asks. "Oh gosh, I don't know. The other night is such a blur. I'll call the doctor later today."

Madeline nods. "That's a good idea. Who's your obstetrician?" she asks.

Mellie frowns. "Actually, I don't have one yet. I was going to ask Johanna Monaghan if she would be my midwife but . . ."

"Well, you need an OB," Madeline says. "Do you have your phone?"

"Yeah. Why?" Mellie asks, pulling her phone from her back pocket.

"I'll give you my doctor's contact info," Madeline says.

"But I thought Johanna was yours," Mellie says with confusion.

"Johanna was my midwife, but I also have an OB. You need one even if you use a midwife," Madeline insists, holding out her hand for the phone.

"No, I can do it," Mellie says, keeping the phone close to her chest.

Madeline gives her the information and watches as Mellie keys it into her phone. "Oh shit," Madeline says, "I left the stove on. Can you grab it?" Mellie hops to her feet and hurries toward the copper kettle atop the bright red burner. "You are going to love Dr. Williamson, I promise."

"I'm sure I will. Do you want me to boil more water?" Mellie asks.

"Yes, please. The tea is in the pantry."

Mellie opens the pantry door and scans the shelves. "Green or chamomile?"

"There's some rooibos in there that's very good," Madeline

says, trying to figure out how to ask Mellie about the photo and decides the best way is to jump right in. "Mellie, I got a strange email today."

"Oh? What kind of email? I can't find the rooibos," Mellie says, stepping from the pantry. "Chamomile, okay?"

"Chamomile is great," Madeline says. "Someone sent a picture of me and Trent."

"That's weird." Mellie hands her a tea bag.

"It had to have been taken last night, while the two of us were sitting on the sofa."

"Whoa," Mellie says, "that's kind of scary."

"There were only two other people in the house last night, besides me and Trent," she says, watching Mellie's reaction closely. "So it had to have been you or Lucy."

"Well, it wasn't me, so it had to be Lucy," Mellie says, dropping her tea bag into a mug. "Why would she do that?"

"I'm not sure," Madeline says, not wanting to get into the details with this girl.

"I wasn't going to mention anything," Mellie says, dropping her voice to a whisper, "but I saw Lucy coming out of your bedroom."

"Oh?" Madeline says. She doesn't like the idea of Lucy snooping around the house, but she isn't surprised.

"Wes was with her," Mellie says as if uttering the words is painful. "It was before you came home from the hotel." Madeline doesn't respond, her brain is still trying to catch up with what Mellie is implying.

"But I didn't actually see them doing anything," Mellie says in a rush. "I'm sure it was nothing, but Lucy looked mad. Like I interrupted them."

Madeline thinks about the way Wes and Lucy stood close to another, the overfamiliar touches, the stolen glances. Would Lucy really try to sleep with her husband just to get back at her? Was this the reason Wes didn't want her to come home with him from the hotel? Was this all just some sick game? Madeline tries not to let the hurt show on her face.

"Hey there," comes a voice, and both Madeline and Mellie whirl around.

"Wes," Madeline says with surprise. "You're back."

"Yeah," Wes says, eyeing Mellie, who is sitting at their kitchen counter. The skin above his swollen eye is shiny and tight and the color of a rotten banana. He hasn't shaved in days, giving him a wild, grizzled look.

He pulls Madeline into a hug, and she tries not to go rigid beneath his embrace. "I've been trying to get ahold of you," she says. "Why didn't you call?"

"I did. Lots of times," he says shortly. "At the hotel. I thought you were staying there until I got back."

"I decided to come home," Madeline says. "You said we could come back in, and I didn't like being cooped up in the hotel room. You've met Mellie, right?"

"I have," Wes says, nodding at Mellie. "We met when I got back from the hospital. How long do you plan on staying with us?"

Though Wes's question is ungracious, Madeline would like an answer too.

Mellie looks as if she wants to disappear into the floor. "Just a few more days, if that's okay. I can move into my new place on Thursday. I can't thank you enough," Mellie says. "Really. You're lifesavers."

Lucy slinks into the room. "Wow," she says. "This place is turning into a real bed-and-breakfast. How's Dix doing?"

"Oh my God, yes," Madeline says, not believing she has forgotten about Dix. "How is he?" And how did Lucy know before she did?

"Dix is lucky," Wes says. "He's minus a spleen and has lots of bumps and bruises, but he's going to be okay."

"That's great news! Where is he?" Madeline asks.

"If you had answered the house phone, you'd know," Wes says shortly again. "But he's at a hospital in Salt Lake City. He's getting out in a few days and will need to come and stay with us until he's better."

"Of course," Madeline says. Wes is angry. She can see it in the tight line of his mouth, the way he holds his shoulders. "Look at all of us," she says, "the walking wounded."

Lucy laughs and holds out the flannel shirt. "I found this on the floor in the living room." Madeline's heart begins to thump in her chest. It's Trent's shirt. The one he wrapped around her last night to help her get warm. She's taunting her. Lucy had to have been the one to have sent the photo of Madeline and Trent. Lucy is trying to stir up trouble.

Wes's eyes narrow. "It's not mine."

"Oh, it must be Trent's," Madeline says lightly. "He's been working on cleaning up the mess in the living room. He must have gotten hot and taken it off. I'll give it to him."

She reaches for the shirt, but Lucy holds onto it for a second longer, a silent tug-of-war between them. When Lucy releases the shirt, Madeline hears a soft jangle. Something is in the pocket of his shirt. Madeline reaches inside and pulls out an orange-tinted pill bottle. She glances at the label and sees Wes's name. No, Madeline thinks. Not Trent. He wouldn't do this. He wouldn't steal from them. Covertly, she slides the bottle back into her back pocket trying to keep the worry from her face.

Wes excuses himself by saying that Agent Saldano is coming to the ranch, and Mellie returns to the guest room. When Madeline is alone with Lucy, she produces the pill bottle. "What the hell, Lucy?" she says. "Why would you do this?"

Lucy laughs. "I didn't. I mean, I did, but it was joke. I put them in Trent's shirt, but that was after Mellie hid them in my room first, along with some cash. By the way, I'm keeping that. Something's not right with her."

"Oh my God," Madeline says, rubbing her forehead. "What about the photo?"

"I have no idea what you're talking about."

"So now you're going to tell me you didn't send me this picture?" Madeline pulls out her phone, brings up the photo with Trent, and shows it Lucy.

"Wow, Mads," Lucy says. "Getting frisky with the hired help. I didn't know you had it in you."

"Dammit, Lucy, I'm serious. Did you take this picture and send it to me?"

"I kind of wish I had, but it wasn't me," Lucy says. "Trust me, it was her."

"Let me see your phone," Madeline says.

"What? Really?" Lucy asks.

"Yes, hand it over." Lucy unlocks her home screen, navigates to the photo app, and hands it to Madeline. First, Madeline flicks through the photos and then brings up the recently deleted pictures. It's not there.

"Do you believe me now?" Lucy asks. "I mean, what do you really know about her? You gotta get her out of your house. Seriously, there's something really off about that girl."

"Funny," Madeline says, slapping the phone back into Lucy's hand, "she says the same thing about you."

CHAPTER 29

JAMIE

JAMIE STARES AT the photograph on the computer screen of Wes stepping into the barn minutes before it exploded with Johanna inside. It wasn't Dalton Monaghan like Mellie Bauer reported. Had she been confused? Add in Johanna's journal entry and the text messages on her phone, things aren't looking good for Wes. Could the same person who saved him decades earlier also be capable of murder?

He knows he's fucked things up coming to Nightjar. And all for what? Because he couldn't let the past go? Because he couldn't let his missing sister—no, dead sister—rest in peace? Because she has to be dead.

Well, that's harsh, Juneau whispers in his ear, and he brushes away the tickle. Jamie needs to get out of this office, think about something else for a few minutes. He backtracks and grabs the yearbook that Laura Holt gave him.

"Ruby," he says, "I'm going to grab a bite to eat and then head over to the Drake ranch. Call if you need anything."

"Sure thing," she says.

Jamie hurries to his car, climbs inside, and pulls out his notebook to review what he knows about Mellie Bauer. Twenty-one years old, moved to Nightjar months ago, waitresses for a catering company that worked the Drake gender reveal. Mellie is pregnant and was intent on talking to Johanna about being her midwife, and both seem to have had an overly familiar relationship with Wes Drake. More coincidences? Maybe. His brain is so muddled, he's not thinking straight. Always a dangerous thing. He starts the car and peels out of the parking lot, narrowly missing a vehicle pulling in.

Jamie grabs a gas station hamburger and a pop and eats while he drives to the ranch. Jamie tries Tess again, and it goes straight to voicemail. He knows he's been an asshole, and now Tess is punishing him by freezing him out. *Do you blame her?* It's Juneau again, sitting in the passenger seat, arm out the open window trying to catch the breeze in her cupped hand. *Here you've been walking down memory lane, while your poor wife has been at home waiting for you to call.*

Jamie rolls up the window, cranks "Even Flow" by Pearl Jam, and tries to ignore his sister.

Once at the ranch, Jamie moves toward the stables and finds Wes saddling a sway-backed butterscotch-colored horse with soft, sleepy eyes. Another horse, this one black-and-white and all muscle, is already saddled and pawing at the ground as if itching to get moving.

"Agent Saldano," Wes says. "Madeline mentioned you haven't had the opportunity to ride a horse before, and I thought it would be a shame if you left Nightjar without getting the chance."

This is not what Jamie anticipated when he walked into the stables. Though the words are friendly enough, there's an edge to Wes's voice.

"After we talked the other day, I got the impression you were done speaking with me, especially without your lawyer. Did something change, Wes?" Jamie asks.

"I'm sorry about that. A bomb was planted in my barn, and my wife's best friend was killed," Wes says, looking appropriately contrite. "I want to find out what happened on our property more than anyone."

"That's why I'm here," Jamie explains. "Let's talk."

"But let's do it while we ride," Wes says. "And don't worry, Nell here is a big old softy," he says, tightening the saddle straps. "You won't have to do a thing but go along for the ride. What do you say?" He has a smile on his face, but his eyes are hard and locked on Jamie's face.

Jamie stares right back. He knows that going off into the mountains with a possible murder suspect is not advisable, especially since Jamie isn't familiar with the area and has never been on a horse before, but he finds that he wants to. He wants this time with Wes, to hear how he'll explain the photos of him entering the barn just before the explosion. And Wes doesn't know that Jamie has Johanna's phone, that he knows about the phone calls and texts between the two of them. Jamie has the chance to catch Wes in a lie, to dig a hole deeper than the one he's already in.

"Sure," Jamie says. "Sounds fun."

"Wes, you've got a call on the landline," Madeline says as she walks toward them. She's moving slowly, her hands cradling her belly as if holding it up. She looks uncomfortable and exhausted.

"Take a message," Wes says shortly. "I told you I didn't want to be interrupted."

"But it's Franklin," she says. "You always take calls from him. He's been trying your cell, but it's been going straight to voicemail."

So Wes has been avoiding his attorney's phone calls, Jamie thinks. Why? And why would Wes agree to talk to a member of law enforcement without his lawyer present?

"Hold on a sec," Wes says, and he walks Madeline back toward the house, one arm around her waist as he talks a steady stream into her ear. Jamie can't hear what he's saying, but Madeline seems to wilt with each step.

"You sure you don't want to take that call?" Jamie offers when Wes returns. "I'm happy to wait."

"Nah," Wes says. "I want you to have my undivided attention." He leads Jamie and the horses out to the paddock and gives him an abbreviated riding lesson, showing him how to approach Nell calmly, how to stand on her left side and use the mounting block to step into the stirrup and swing his leg over her back and settle into the saddle. "Make sure you sit up straight and hold the reins with a light grip," Wes says. "Relax. She won't take off on you. Now, to get her to walk, squeeze your legs together." Jamie presses his knees into Nell's side, but the horse doesn't move.

"She won't break," Wes laughs. "Harder. Show her who's in charge." Jamie tries again, and still Nell stays put. "Well, look who's acting like a little bitch," Wes says, and Jamie doesn't know if he's addressing the horse or Jamie. "Get," Wes orders, and using the palm of his hand strikes Nell on the rump, and the horse surges forward. Jamie's teeth clank together as the horse gallops from the paddock and toward the mountains. After what feels like an eternity, Wes catches up with him.

"Now, to get him to stop," Wes says, "pull back on the reins, and say *whoa*. Just like in the movies."

"Whoa," Jamie says, and to his relief Nell stops.

"You got it," Wes says. "I'll show you more as we ride."

They start off again, and Nell ambles along at a leisurely pace. They pass the charred remnants of the blown-up barn and the mangled entrails of the truck and head toward the mountains.

The afternoon is warm, and Jamie likes the feel of the sun on his head and the smooth four-beat rhythm of Nell's hooves striking the ground. The mountains cut jaggedly into the crystalline blue of the sky, and the air smells like pine needles. They cross a shallow creek where the horses dip their heads to drink, and Wes explains to Jamie how to maneuver his horse to the left and to the right and warns him to keep an eye out for rattlesnakes. Jamie turns his head sharply to Wes to see if he's serious. It appears he is. It's a good thirty minutes into their ride before Wes pulls back on his reins and brings his horse to a stop. It takes Jamie a few tries to get Nell to do the same, then another few moments to bring her back to where Wes is waiting.

"This is as good a place as any to talk about the case," Wes says. "Do you have an update?"

Jamie decides to jump right in. "I reviewed the pictures and video from the party, Wes. And you omitted one very important detail when we first talked. You followed Johanna into the barn a few minutes before the explosion. Why?" Jamie watches him closely for a reaction.

Wes removes his cowboy hat and scratches his head. "I'm sorry," he says, sounding like he means it. "At first, it honestly escaped my mind."

Jamie is skeptical. How can someone forget that they were in a structure that minutes later exploded, killing a woman and injuring dozens of others? But Jamie doesn't contradict Wes, just waits for him to go on. "When I did remember, I thought it would seem suspicious that I didn't tell you right away. And it didn't matter. I mean, I didn't think it mattered."

"Everything matters in a murder investigation," Jamie says sternly. "Why were you going into the barn?"

Jamie expects Wes to say that it's his barn. That he was just going inside to check on something or grab something, not to rendezvous with his wife's best friend. Instead Wes says, "To talk to Johanna." Jamie can't hide his surprise, and Wes rushes on to explain. "I asked her to meet me there."

"What for?"

"I was going to fire her," Wes says, shaking his head. "I didn't think she was good for Madeline. I did some checking up on her, and it turns out she wasn't really a midwife. She had all the education and accreditation, but she never applied for a license to practice in Wyoming. She'd been practicing here for nine years. I thought she was sketchy as hell, but Madeline loves her. *Loved* her. And I didn't want to hurt Madeline or embarrass Johanna. I told her I wanted her to resign from being Madeline's midwife and to stop practicing, and if she didn't I'd go to the sheriff about it."

Jamie thinks of the text messages he found between them on Johanna's phone. What had Johanna said? *Nothing you say will change a damn thing. Fuck you. I'm finished.* From what he can recall, in this new light, their texts match Wes's narrative—an angry husband trying to protect his wife from malpractice. Unfortunately, Johanna wasn't around to confirm this narrative. And what had Wes texted in return? *I don't want you anywhere near me or my wife . . . you'll regret it.*

"What did Johanna say when you confronted her in the barn?" Jamie asks. Wes clicks his tongue and his horse starts walking again, and Jamie taps his heels urging Nell to move forward too.

"She agreed," Wes says. "Well, she said she just hadn't gotten around to completing the Wyoming licensing paperwork, but she would."

"And . . ." Jamie prods.

"I said I didn't want her touching my wife until she did. She was fine when I left the barn."

"But a few minutes later she was dead. How do you think that happened?" Jamie asks.

"My bet is on her husband," Wes says. "You saw the way he was acting in the baby's room. His accusations were ridiculous. He attacked me. I thought you would have figured this all out by now."

"Listen, Wes, I'm here to get to the truth, so if there's anything else I need to know, it will be really helpful if you tell me now."

"I would if I could, Jamie," Wes says. "No one wants this figured out more than I do."

Jamie wants to believe him. He wants to believe that the boy who sat with him in the roadside ditch until help came is a good person, but Wes still hasn't fessed up to the text message exchange with Johanna. He decides to hold on to that information for the time being. "Tell me about Mellie Bauer," Jamie says.

"The waitress? Not much to tell. She worked the party."

"But she's staying at your house?"

"Yeah," Wes says. "That's sort of weird, but Madeline hasn't met a stray cat that she doesn't end up taking care of."

Interesting choice of words. A crass, dismissive way of referring to another human being. Jamie doesn't like it. "You didn't know her beforehand?"

"Me?" Wes asks. "No, not at all. Why? Do you think she had something to do with the explosion?"

"Just curious," Jamie responds. "What about Johanna's journal entry? Why would she mention you? Mention being scared and disappearing."

"She probably was scared. I knew about her licensing. We'd talked about it more than once. I had threatened to go to the authorities if she didn't stop practicing. And disappearing? Maybe she was planning on taking off. If she was found out, she could have been in big trouble."

Wes is slick, has an answer for everything.

They ride along in silence, Jamie noting that they were a good hour into the ride, and the well-worn trail that they had been on earlier has all but disappeared into the tall grass. He has no idea how to get back to the ranch on his own and can only hope that his cell phone still has reception if he needs it. They move upward, the air cooling slightly against his skin. They leave the meadow behind, and a rocky trail appears along with tall, slender lodgepole pines and white-bark aspens with their trembling leaves. A nagging ache gnaws at his lower back, and he holds tight to Nell's reins as she picks her way across the uneven path.

"It's starting to get late," Jamie says, looking around and noting how the earlier intensity of the sun has now eased, giving the meadow behind them a buttery glaze.

"We'll turn around in a few minutes," Wes says. "I just want to show you something first." They plug onward and are swallowed up by a wall of ponderosa pines that soar a hundred feet into the sky. The air around them darkens and cools, and shadows patch the forest floor beneath their feet. Alarm bells ring in Jamie's head. He's in the middle of a mountain forest with a man he suspects may have murdered someone, and no one knows where he is. The only things keeping him moving forward are the gun in his shoulder holster and the cell phone in his jacket pocket. "Almost there," Wes says, just as the pines abruptly end and Nell steps out into an open field filled with heavy-headed yellow flowers. Jamie hears the rumble of a vehicle and scans the horizon for its source and spots a black pickup truck kicking up a cloud of dust. The dizzying sensation of déjà vu nearly sends him tumbling from his saddle. "Come on," Wes says, digging his heels into his horse's ribs, "follow me."

Tentatively, Jamie prods Nell forward, and she takes off into a rolling canter that clacks his teeth together. Up ahead, Jamie sees that Wes has come to a stop at the edge of a gravel road, and realization washes over him. He yanks back on the reins, and Nell comes to a skidding stop, nearly sending him flying headfirst over the saddle horn.

"Whoa," Jamie says belatedly, trying to catch his breath. Wes has taken him to the same stretch of road he'd walked along just a few nights before, the same stretch of road where Wes had found him twenty-seven years before.

"J. J. Archer," Wes says, taking his cowboy hat off his head, and wiping the sweat from his forehead. "When were you going to tell me you were back in town?"

Jamie can't speak. How did Wes know? There was no way he would have recognized Jamie. He was nothing like the twelve-year-old boy he used to be, physically, anyway. Back then, he was a good twelve inches shorter and a good deal lighter, and his face was swollen as a rotten melon.

Wes looks Jamie up and down, a polite smile on his face. "It took me a while to figure it out. There was just something so familiar about you, but I couldn't quite place it. Then I did a little research. Why didn't you say anything the other night at the hospital?"

Wes reaches into his saddlebag and pulls out two bottles of water and extends one to Jamie. Jamie twists the lid and takes a long drink, draining half the bottle before speaking.

"I didn't think it was relevant." Even to his own ears the explanation sounds weak.

"Of course it's relevant, J. J.," Wes says. "We shared a very intense moment in our lives. I'm just glad I was there to help."

"It's Jamie," he replies. "And I'm grateful you found me that day."

"You know, I always wondered what happened to you," Wes says, taking a drink from his own bottle. "It's pretty cool to think that you were inspired to go into law enforcement after what happened to your sister. Police officer, ATF agent, and now a supervisor. You've had lots of accolades over the years. Impressive. And your wife. She's been pretty successful in her own right. Too bad she's had so much trouble finding work since you've moved here."

Jamie freezes. Wes has been researching his wife?

"You know, I could help with that," Wes says. "I could put in a good word. Tess could have her pick of jobs."

"That won't be necessary," Jamie snaps. "Tess is fine." He doesn't like that Wes has been digging into their lives, and his offer to help Tess get a job feels more like a transaction than an act of goodwill. He needs to take back control of the conversation. "I didn't realize you knew my sister, Juneau, Wes."

"Your sister?" Wes says. "No. I didn't know her."

"That's strange," Jamie says. "Lots of people I've talked to report that you and Juneau were quite friendly."

Wes shakes his head. "They must be mistaken. But after learning about her, I wish I did. It sounds like she was a great person."

"She was," Jamie says. "She was the best."

"And to think thirty years later, you're back in Nightjar and ended up saving my life," Wes says, shaking his head in disbelief.

"Technically, it was Sheriff Colson who saved your life," Jamie counters.

"No, it was you," Wes insists. "If you hadn't shown up at the house when you did, who knows what would have happened to me, to Madeline."

"I guess we can call it even now," Jamie says.

"I don't think it works like that," Wes says. "Do you? I owe you, Jamie. I will always owe you. You saved me, but more importantly, you saved my wife and baby, and that means I'll always be there for you, just like I know you'll be here for me."

"You don't owe me anything," Jamie says firmly.

"You met my dad, right, Jamie?" Wes asks, and Jamie is thrown by the shift in topic.

Jamie had met the elder Drake, but wants to keep the conversation on Johanna's death so he lies. "Your dad?" Jamie says. "No, I don't think so. We lived here for such a short time, I didn't get the chance to meet a lot of people."

"He visited you in the hospital. After. He wanted to see the boy his son found in a ditch."

"I don't remember," Jamie says. "I was really in no condition to remember much of anything."

"He was shocked by how you looked," Wes says. "The extent of your injuries. And he felt so sorry for your mom. He wanted to help you both."

"What do you mean?" Jamie is almost afraid of the answer.

"Your mom wanted to get out of Nightjar. Moving is expensive. My dad wanted to see you both have a fresh start after something so traumatic."

"Your dad paid for us to move?" Jamie says in disbelief. His mother never said anything.

"He did," Wes says. "He also created a little college scholarship fund. It went to a young man who lived in San Antonio who has gone on to a very successful career in law enforcement."

Jamie can't breathe. Wes Drake's father paid for his college tuition? He thought he had earned that scholarship fair and square.

"It appears my father and my wife had a lot in common," Wes says. "Taking care of strays and all. Now, come on," Wes says, patting Jamie on the back. He takes Jamie's empty water bottle and stows it in his saddlebag. "We need to go back now. It will be dark soon. Oh, and say hi to your boss for me. Linton Sykes and I go way back. In fact, I owe him a phone call, and I'll be sure to mention what a good job you're doing here, Jamie."

Wes heads back toward the ponderosa pines, and Jamie follows behind, his pulse pounding in his head. Though Wes said he only recently realized who Jamie is, Jamie is convinced that Wes has known all along. The more Jamie learns about Wes Drake, the more he's sure he's behind the barn explosion. Now he has to prove it.

CHAPTER 30

MADELINE

CARRYING THE FLANNEL shirt, Madeline stops by the stables to see Trent. She knew he would never steal from them, never betray them like that. She doesn't trust Lucy, and she doesn't trust Mellie, so Madeline needs to get him safely away from here, at least for the time being. She tells him that Wes wants him to drive over to Spearfish and deliver the gelding to a family there.

"Right now?" Trent asks. "I'm not leaving you here all alone with that lot." He nods toward the house.

"Please," Madeline says, unable to meet his eyes. "I've got it under control, and I really think it's for the best."

"No way," Trent says, shaking his head. "With all that's been going on, you need an extra pair of eyes around here. I'm staying. Just holler, and I'll come running. Got it?" Madeline gives a reluctant nod.

She returns to the house to find Mellie in the dining room and covertly watches as she runs her hand across the $25,000 walnut-and-resin dining room table, examining the artwork. Mellie, who earlier had been limping around with shoulders hunched as if in pain, has suddenly gotten the spring back in her step. She walks around the room, turning on and off the gas fireplace, then pauses at the built-in liquor cabinet. Mellie looks over her shoulder, and Madeline ducks out of sight before peeking around the doorjamb to see the girl picking up a bottle of Pappy Van Winkle bourbon—the expensive stuff. Mellie quickly grabs a shot glass, pours a finger and tosses it back, then pours another. After downing it, she wipes the rim of the glass with her shirt—Madeline's shirt—and returns it to the shelf.

Strange, Madeline thinks, for someone who is pregnant. She wants to confront her but doesn't. She's not afraid of Mellie, exactly, but the young woman unsettles her, and the uneasiness at having her in their house continues to grow, but Madeline doesn't quite know how to get rid of her. Whenever she broaches the subject, Mellie assures her she has something in the works and will be leaving soon.

Madeline quietly retreats to the home office and takes a seat in front of the computer. She tries all the major social media sites but finds nothing. She then types Mellie's name into Google, and an entry for a Millie Bauer appears. Not who she's looking for. Mellie could be short for Melanie so she tries it, and this time dozens of pages of results pop up. She clicks on the Images tab and begins to sort through the photos. Finally, she finds a picture that matches the Mellie she knows.

Madeline clicks on the link, and it takes her to a newspaper article from what looks like a small-town paper in West Virginia with the headline *Valedictorian to attend Dartmouth College*. So Mellie was the valedictorian of her class. But how did she end up in Nightjar rather than the hallowed halls of Dartmouth?

The article is brief and ends with a quote. "I'm so proud of my daughter, and I can't wait to see what the future holds for her." The quote is attributed to a Veronica Bauer. Madeline has to reread the sentence two more times. Is Veronica Bauer Mellie's mother? Hadn't Mellie told her in the ambulance that her mother died when she was little? Madeline examines the accompanying photo closely. It shows a woman with her arm around Mellie, and the caption reads "Mellie and Veronica

Bauer." The woman is a carbon copy of Mellie, though about thirty years older. This is Mellie's mother, Madeline is sure of it. So why did she lie?

"You are never going to believe this," Wes says, coming into the office. Madeline quickly clicks out of Google and turns in her chair.

"How was your ride with Agent Saldano? Everything okay?" she asks, watching him carefully, trying to gauge his mood. He's holding a large glass of bourbon.

He looks at Madeline and gives a bitter laugh. "This week has been anything but okay. Is that waitress still here?" he asks.

"Mellie?" Madeline asks. "Yeah, she's still here, but not for long," she says, unable to keep the edge out of her voice. Once she's done talking with Wes, she's going to confront Mellie and send her on her way, no matter the sob story she gives.

"Good," Wes says, taking a drink. "And guess who Agent Saldano turned out to be?"

"Agent Saldano?" Madeline asks. "Who?"

"Kid who lived here a long time ago," Wes says. Not a good sign, Madeline thinks. "His sister disappeared, and I found him in a ditch the next morning. Had the shit kicked out of him. It was fucking awful."

"You found him?" Madeline asks. "Did they find the sister?"

"They never did," Wes says. "And now the girl's brother is back, and he's a fucking ATF agent. Can you believe it?"

Madeline sits with this information for a moment. Wes has never told her this story before. Why? "No," she finally says. "It's hard to believe. Why didn't you mention it before?"

"It was a long time ago," Wes says dismissively, but Madeline can see by the look on his face that he is shaken. "I was a senior in high school."

"But it was a huge event, Wes," Madeline says, "I wish you had told me."

"I couldn't talk about it, not for a long time," he says. "And it's still hard. It was horrible. I was just riding my horse one morning and nearly stepped on this half-dead kid. His face was like something from a horror movie. His nose and jaw were broken, his eyes swollen shut, blood everywhere. I thought he was dead, and then suddenly he starts moaning. I nearly shit my pants. I had nightmares about it for years. I still do."

Madeline shivers at the image Wes has conjured. She knows he has nightmares. She's the one who pulls him close at night when he cries out in his sleep, sweaty and disoriented, unwilling to tell her what he's dreaming about. "Then, talk to me about it," Madeline urges gently. "It might make things better. You know you can tell me anything."

Wes's eyebrow rises, and the implication is clear. He doesn't trust her. Not quite. But why? She has only ever tried to make him happy, to be supportive and positive, even when she shouldn't. The ridiculous gender reveal party, for instance. Wes was the one who insisted on hiring the party planner—ostensibly to make it easier on Madeline—but she knew better. She would have ordered a cake that, when cut into, would be dyed either blue or pink. That would never have been enough of a spectacle for Wes, wouldn't have impressed their friends and neighbors.

"How did you figure out it was him?" she asks, tamping down her frustration.

"I did some checking. He goes by his mom's last name now, but it's definitely him," Wes says, draining the rest of his glass. "I'm going upstairs," he says abruptly. "I'm beat. And it looks like Dix will be released from the hospital tomorrow afternoon or maybe the next day. I'll have to head back to Salt Lake City to get him."

Madeline has so many questions for Wes about finding the agent, about finding his brother, but it seems Wes is done for the night. "I'll be up soon," Madeline says, getting to her feet and kissing him on the cheek. "I love you."

"Love you too," he says wearily and leaves the room.

Madeline sits back down at her desk, her mind buzzing. There is too much to process. Johanna and Dalton are dead. Wes saved Agent Saldano's life. Lucy arriving at the ranch. And if Mellie lied about her mother, what else has she been untruthful about?

Madeline rarely uses Wes's family connections to get what she wants, but this time it seems warranted. The Drake family are big donors to the hospital in Jackson, even have a wing named after them, and Madeline's hoping this might carry some influence. It's after seven, but Madeline dials the hospital's director of obstetrics.

"Hello," comes a female voice.

"Dr. Raymond," Madeline says, trying to keep the nervousness from her voice, "it's Madeline Drake."

"Madeline!" the doctor says. "Are you okay? Is everything all right with the baby?"

"Yes, yes," Madeline says in a rush. "I'm fine, and so is the baby. Thank you again for checking in with us the other night."

"Of course," she says. "What can I help you with?"

"I'm sorry to call you on your personal cell," Madeline begins, "but I have a favor to ask."

"Certainly," she says. "I'll help if I can."

"A young girl was injured in the explosion the other night," Madeline explains. "We came to the hospital in the same ambulance. She's pregnant too, and we really bonded over the whole terrible experience. I really want to do something nice for her. I got the sense that she doesn't have the means for adequate pre- and postnatal care, and Wes and I would like to make sure that isn't one of her worries."

"That's so kind of you," the doctor says. "I'm happy to set something up through the business office" if you'd like."

"Yes, thank you," Madeline says. "But there's one more

thing I'm hoping you can help with." Madeline knows that the chances of this working are slim, but she pushes as much confidence into her voice that she can. "I'd also like to order Mellie a crib and bedding and all sorts of nursery items so she's good to go once her baby comes."

"Okay," Dr. Raymond says, this time with some hesitation. "I'm not sure how I can help you with that."

"This is where it gets a bit delicate," Madeline says. "I want it to be a surprise for Mellie. I know if I told her, she would say not to go to any trouble. What I'm hoping to get from you is whether Mellie is having a girl or a boy."

There's silence on the other end.

"I've overstepped," Madeline says. "I'm sorry. I just feel so bad for her. She doesn't have any family here, and she was injured on our property, but I understand."

"You just want to know the sex of the baby?" the doctor asks.

"Yes, please. She told me they did an ultrasound at the hospital, and the baby looked healthy. I just didn't think to ask if she's having a boy or girl." Madeline holds her breath waiting for Dr. Raymond's reply. She hopes the director is running through all the items that the Drake money has garnered for the maternity ward at the hospital over the years and what it still might procure.

"As luck will have it, I'm at the hospital right now," Dr. Raymond says after a beat. "Hold on while I pull up her records. What's her name again?"

Madeline tells her and waits.

"Hmmm," Dr. Raymond says. "Are you sure that's the correct spelling?"

"I think so," Madeline says, remembering the news article she found. "B-a-u-e-r."

"I've found a medical record for a Melanie Bauer, but I'm afraid she's not pregnant."

Madeline's stomach sinks. "So that means she lost the baby in the explosion? How awful."

"No," Dr. Raymond says. "She made no mention to the medical staff that she was pregnant. In fact on the form, the box that asks the question was left blank, and the blood tests and urine sample taken that night indicate no pregnancy."

"Are you sure?" Madeline asks, not wanting it to be true.

"I'm sorry, Madeline," Dr. Raymond says. "It appears your friend was mistaken or perhaps was not being honest with you. I'd think twice before giving her any money or gifts."

Madeline doesn't know what to say, but finally lands on a rote reply, "Thank you, I appreciate your help," and disconnects. She sits at her desk trying to figure out what to do with the information and bites back angry tears at the thought of being duped. Mellie lied. Lied about everything.

"What was that all about?" comes a voice from behind her. Madeline whirls around in her chair to find Mellie in the doorway, blocking her path. In her hand is a heavy ceramic mug filled with something hot, wisps of steam rising from its rim. It's as if a completely different person is standing in front of her. Gone is the sweet girl who was down on her luck, now replaced by someone jaded and venomous. "Is there something you want to ask me about, Madeline?" Mellie asks. "Madeline?" she repeats, taking a step toward her, her eyes narrowed, her voice hard. "Do you have something you want to say?"

CHAPTER 31

JAMIE

JAMIE DRIVES SLOWLY down the deserted backroads outside of Nightjar, trying to decide what to do next. His horse ride with Wes has left him unbalanced, his head swimming with more questions than answers. Still, he's come away certain that Wes is more complicit in Johanna's death than he first thought possible. He pulls up Colson's number and hits the Call button. It rings twice before Colson answers. "Hallo," he says in that gruff manner Jamie remembers from when he was a kid.

"Sheriff, it's J. J.," Jamie says. "Are you still up for me coming over tonight? I want to get your take on a few things. About the case."

"Everything okay?" Colson asks.

"Yeah, but I've learned a few things and just had the most bizarre conversation with Wes Drake."

"About the barn? I thought he clammed up. Would only talk through his lawyer."

"About the barn, about what I found on his phone. And about . . ." Does he really want to muddy the waters and bring up his sister's case right now?

"Juneau?" Colson finishes for him. "It's okay, J. J. I've been waiting for this conversation. I live on Killdeer Road, thirteen-oh-nine. It's the green house. Come on over."

"Okay," Jamie says, his stomach fluttering with nerves. "I'm on my way."

Colson's home is on a quiet cul-de-sac not far from the sheriff's office, where all the houses are built in the same craftsman style with their low-pitched gables, tapered columns, and covered front porches. Jamie easily finds the Colson house, painted green with a tidy lawn and surrounded by juniper. He parks on the street and steps from his vehicle to find Colson waiting for him on the porch, two bottles of beer in his hand.

With heavy legs, Jamie climbs the steps. "J. J.," Colson says, handing him a bottle, sweaty with condensation. "Thought you might need one of these."

"Thanks," Jamie says, accepting the offering. Colson takes a seat on a patio chair and waves his hand, inviting Jamie to sit. Jamie chooses the chair next to the sheriff so that he doesn't have to look him directly in the eye, picks up a plaid pillow from the seat, and sits. He takes a swig from the beer bottle, feeling only a little bit guilty for drinking while on duty.

"Nice place," Jamie says, looking appreciatively at the quiet green street in front of him. "I remember your wife made me homemade soup and brought it to the motel when I got out of the hospital. I couldn't eat much with my jaw wired shut. It was good. Is she home?"

"No, she's running some errands, meeting a friend for dinner. I know she'd love to see you, though. Maybe you can stop by again later," Colson says.

"Maybe," Jamie says noncommittally.

"So where would you like to start, J. J.?" Colson asks, picking at the label on his beer bottle. "With the Drake case or with Juneau?" This is when Jamie notices it. The thick binder sitting on the glass-topped side table between them. Jamie has seen hundreds of these binders. Has himself filled many of them with police reports, autopsy reports, witness statements, and photos. Juneau's binder.

"It's bigger than I thought it would be," Jamie says.

"We worked hard," Colson says. "I told you we would."

A knot forms in Jamie's throat. "Yeah, but my sister is still gone."

"That she is. But not for lack of effort," Colson says. "And I haven't stopped looking."

Jamie meets his gaze. "But the case file is here, not back at the station. We both know what that means."

"It's cold. But I haven't given up," Colson says.

Jamie wants to believe him, but the fact that Juneau's binder is at Colson's house and not on the sheriff's desk or even the desk of one of the deputies means that they aren't actually looking into Juneau's disappearance. Any work on the case is being done by Colson on his own time.

"Let's talk about the Drake case," Jamie says abruptly. "Tell me more about Wes. What's his story?"

"You're not going to tell me about your visit with him?" Colson asks.

"I'd like your take on things first," Jamie says. "Then I'll fill you in."

Colson releases a breath. "Where to start," he laughs. "His dad was one of the wealthiest landowners in the county, and when he died, he passed the fortune on to his two sons."

"Wes and Dix," Jamie adds.

"That's right. They own the land together. Rent a good deal of it out to smaller ranchers, run the equestrian center with Madeline, buy and sell horses."

"Wes is well thought of around here?" Jamie asks and almost misses the shadow that dims Colson's eyes for a moment. But it was there, however briefly.

"Wes and Dix do a lot of good for the community," Colson says. "They're very generous."

"But . . ." Jamie prompts.

"But just that," Colson says and takes a drink from his

bottle. "The Drakes give to a lot of important causes. They make a point to keep their money local, and most people appreciate that."

"But some people don't?" Jamie asks. He finds himself growing impatient with the sheriff and his caginess. Why is he being so evasive?

"When people have as much money as the Drakes, they want favors and are willing to offer some in exchange. Sometimes lines are crossed."

There it is, Jamie thinks. Not that what Colson is saying is some profound revelation.

"Did you know that Wes might have been having an affair with Johanna?"

"I did not," Colson says, rubbing a hand over his face. "But I'm not surprised. Wes has always had a wandering eye. Even as a teen."

Jamie hands Colson his phone. "These texts were found on Johanna Monaghan's cell. They're from Wes." Jamie watches as Colson reads through the messages.

"Well, this doesn't look good," the sheriff says, handing the phone back. "But it doesn't mean he murdered her."

"I also think he's having a relationship with Mellie Bauer."

"That young waitress?" Colson asks. "The one staying with the Drakes right now?"

"That's right," Jamie says. "And when I tried to ask Wes about this, about the explosion, instead of trying to help you know what he said?" Before Colson can respond, Jamie continues. "He told me that he knew who I was. Told me he had done some checking up on me. My wife. Pretty much told me he could talk to the right people and get Tess a job."

Colson lets out a long breath. "That's what Wes does," he says. "That's what makes him a good businessman, but not necessarily a very good person. He does his homework."

"He also said that after Juneau disappeared and I was hurt so badly, his father paid for me and my mom to move back to San Antonio. And that he created the scholarship that sent me to college. Did you know that?"

"I did not," Colson says quietly.

"The only reason I can think of for Wes telling me all this is that he is trying to leverage me somehow. He doesn't want me digging any deeper and is calling in that favor his dad did for me years ago. He has something to hide. What doesn't Wes want coming out?"

"You've got to understand," Colson says, "the Drake boys have never been held accountable for anything in their lives. Their father was always there to clean up things. Now Wes does his own cleaning up."

Jamie waits for him to continue, watching as the older man peels the label off the bottle and rolls the damp paper between his fingers. "The sheriff's office has gotten some calls over the years asking for one of us to do a wellness check on Madeline Drake. They always called the nonemergency number, but I sent a deputy out to see what was going on. Even went out there once myself."

"What did you find?" Jamie asks.

"Nothing," Colson says. "Nothing that we could act on. Each time Madeline said she was fine, that someone must have been playing a mean-spirited prank. There was nothing we could do." He sets his bottle aside, gets to his feet, and steps inside the house leaving Jamie on the porch alone. A few minutes later, he returns with two more beers and offers one to Jamie, who waves it away.

"You found nothing you could act on, but you found something. What was it?" Jamie asks.

"Madeline Drake bruised up and moving around like she got kicked in the head by one of her horses," Colson says. "Of course, that's exactly what she said. Blamed herself and said that she got careless and got knocked off a horse, and it stepped on her head. Nothing we could do about it."

"You still could have arrested him, brought him in for questioning. Something," Jamie insists. "Especially if there's a clear pattern of abuse."

"In a perfect world, yes, J. J., that's what we would do," Colson says, a spark of irritation in his voice. "But you have to know that even if you do all those things, if you don't have a prosecutor with the balls to do anything about it, your hands are tied."

"So what you're telling me is Wes Drake is capable of blowing up his own barn and killing a woman, but there's nothing we can do about it because he has deep pockets?" Jamie says with disgust.

"I'm not saying that at all, J. J." Colson says, matching his tone. "I'm just saying get the rock-solid, undeniable evidence and prove it. You're the feds, you have the resources. Do your thing. I'll do whatever I can on my end to help, but you gotta have the proof."

Jamie lets Colson's words sink in. He's right.

"I talked to someone who says that she saw Wes and Juneau talking before she disappeared. Did you know that?" Jamie asks.

Colson lifts his eyebrows. "They went to the same high school. I'm guessing Juneau talked to a lot of people."

"But did you ask Wes if he knew her? If he had any interactions with her?" Jamie presses.

Colson sets his beer aside and leans forward. "Of course we did. Wes was the one who found you, which was a miracle on its own. That stretch of ditch was so overgrown with grass it's a wonder he saw you at all. We questioned him several times, and he said he really didn't know your sister."

"But . . ." Jamie prompts.

"But . . ." Colson tilts his head from side to side. "Others did see them together now and again—at school, in town, all very innocent."

"Like they were dating?" Jamie asks. He can't believe it. How was he the last to know?

"No," Colson says. "No one said they were dating. They simply talked to one another now and then. They were *friends*."

"He has an alibi for that night?" Jamie manages to ask, his frustration building.

"He had a football game and then went home," the sheriff says, his voice tight. "His brother, Dixon, vouched for him. So did his parents. It's all in the binder, J. J. And to be honest, I'm getting a little worried about you. Are you sure you're not conflating Juneau's case with the Drakes'?"

"I'm just trying to be thorough, and I think we both know that Wes isn't quite the nice guy that so many people believe him to be. His affairs, the way he treats his wife, the text messages to Johanna prove at least that."

"Yes, but it doesn't prove he's a murderer," Colson says gently.

"Anything farther back?" Jamie asks. "You said Wes's dad got him and his brother out of a lot of scrapes. What kinds of trouble did they get into?"

"Mostly kid stuff. Underage drinking, speeding, general mischief," Colson recalls. "But there was something else. I was just a deputy at the time, so I wasn't privy to any of the details. It was all very hush-hush." He pauses as if debating whether to go on with the story. Jamie waits him out.

"A man came into the sheriff's office. He was distraught. Said his daughter was beat-up really bad—had a broken arm, a few broken ribs. She was just a wisp of a thing. Maybe thirteen, fourteen years old. The dad said her boyfriend did it. But then nothing came of it. Not one more word was said. When I asked the sheriff, he said it was all a big misunderstanding, that I should forget about it. A few weeks later I heard that the dad was laid off from his job at the meat-packing plant, but he landed a different job in Texas. The family moved away."

"The boyfriend was Wes Drake," Jamie says. "And Drake Sr. made it all disappear."

"That's what I heard. But again, J. J., if the victims don't follow through, there's not a whole lot to be done."

"When was this?" Jamie asks.

"What do you mean?"

"Before or after? Was this before or after Juneau?"

"Before," Colson says, looking down at the floor, unable to meet Jamie's eyes.

"I should go," Jamie says, getting to his feet. "Thanks for the beer."

Colson follows suit. "What are you going to do?"

"Get that proof," Jamie says.

"I'll do anything I can to help, J. J. You know that, don't you?"

"I do," Jamie says.

"And feel free to take that with you," Colson says, glancing down at the glass tabletop.

Jamie follows his gaze to the black binder that holds all the important information in his sister's case. He knows that if he picks it up, there's no going back. He'll be diving into a rabbit hole that he may never escape. "Thanks," Jamie says, picking up the binder. It has some heft to it, and that's a comfort.

Sheriff Colson walks with Jamie to his car and waits as Jamie places the binder carefully in the back seat. "It's good to see you doing so well, J. J.," he says. "You'll have to come over to dinner before you head back home. I know Janet would love to see you."

They say their goodbyes, and Jamie climbs into his car and pulls from the curb. In the rearview mirror he sees Colson, hands stuffed in his front pockets, staring after him. The sheriff was being kind, Jamie knows. Without Colson checking in on Jamie and his mom in the aftermath of Juneau's disappearance, Jamie could have gone down a very different path. He is the reason Jamie went into law enforcement.

He meanders through the streets of Nightjar for a few minutes, trying to get his bearings. The binder feels like having Juneau's body in the back seat and opening the case file will feel like witnessing his sister's autopsy. *Grim!* Juneau exclaims.

Jamie rolls down the car window, grateful for the warm spring wind that sweeps across his face, and turns his car toward the motel. He's got a long night in front of him.

CHAPTER 32

MADELINE

MADELINE STARES AT Mellie standing in the doorway. The nerve of this girl, she thinks, slithering her way into their home, lying about being pregnant, about losing her mother as a young child. Why is she here? What is her endgame?

She's about ready to let loose on Mellie and order her from the house when she hears Wes's voice. "Madeline, can you come up here?" he calls.

Madeline hesitates, considers pretending not to hear him, but knows if she doesn't answer, he'll come down looking for her.

"Wes is calling you," Mellie says. "Better shake your ass. He likes that."

Anger rises in her chest, but Madeline holds her temper in check.

"Madeline!" Wes yells.

She brushes past Mellie and makes the trek up the stairs, and although the doors are closed, she notices the lights are off in both the nursery and Lucy's room. Breathless, Madeline pushes open their bedroom door and finds Wes sitting back on the bed, still fully dressed.

"What took you so long?" Wes asks. "Didn't you hear me?"

Madeline goes to the bed and sits down beside him. "I

heard you. I just don't move as fast as I used to," she says. "Is everything okay?"

"I'm going to get Dix tomorrow," he says. "We need one of the guest rooms for him. You have to ask the waitress to go. She's been here long enough." Madeline debates whether or not to tell Wes about what she's learned about Mellie, about all her lies, but figures it will make him even more on edge. No, she'll calmly and reasonably tell Mellie she needs to go and hope that will be enough.

"You're right," Madeline says. "She'll be gone by tomorrow."

"You're too nice for your own good," Wes says.

"What did you and the agent talk about on your ride?" Madeline asks. "Is there anything new in the case?"

Wes gets to his feet so quickly that Madeline is nearly bounced from the edge of the bed to the floor. "Wes!" Madeline exclaims. "Be careful!" She immediately regrets the outburst. She didn't mean to speak so loudly.

"Shhh," he says, grabbing her arm and placing his face so close to hers she can smell the bourbon on his breath. He looks at her with such hate that Madeline feels as if she might combust beneath his stare. "Lucy and that damn girl you brought into the house will hear."

"I'm sorry," Madeline says quickly, trying to ease from his grasp, but this only makes him squeeze more tightly.

"You want me to tell you what's going on, Madeline?" Wes asks mockingly. "Well, sometimes it's none of your fucking business," he says, his voice rising until the final word is a shout.

"You're right," Madeline says as calmly as possible. She knows by now that nine out of ten times, the key to de-escalation is to agree with Wes. "I'm sorry."

With his free hand he grabs her by the face, his fingers pressing into her cheeks, the pain like a white-hot poker.

"That's what you always say," he says with disgust. "Can't you ever just shut up? Can't you ever just leave me alone?" Madeline fights the urge to claw at his hand—it will only make him angrier. "Do you have any idea what I'm going through?" he asks. "My brother nearly died, I've got Sully Preston talking crap about us, buyers are backing out of horse sales, and now I have to fucking deal with you too?"

Madeline is trying to follow his words, but panic is settling in. "The baby," she manages to squeak out. "Wes, please, you'll hurt the baby."

He drops his hand, but his anger is still palpable.

"The baby," he says mockingly. "I'm so fucking sick of you saying that. Yes, Madeline, we all know you're pregnant. We all know you have to be the center of attention."

"Wes," Madeline says, "I don't. I don't meant to—"

"I can't wait until you have her. Jesus, maybe you'll start acting like yourself again." He looks her up and down, revulsion on his face. "Or at least maybe you'll go back to looking like yourself."

Madeline goes very still. He's waiting for a reaction. He loves it when she fights back, speaks her mind. It gives him an excuse to put her in her place. She won't give it to him; she refuses. Not this time.

He glowers down at her, and she can still feel the spots on her cheeks where he grabbed her face. From experience, she knows that the bruises are already blossoming. She stares back at him, hoping he sees what he's done.

"I'm sorry. Oh God, Madeline," he says, his eyes beginning to clear. "I'm so sorry." He lowers himself to his knees and drops his head into her lap.

They stay that way for a while, Wes apologizing, his tears dampening her shirt, Madeline trying to sit as still as possible, not wanting to give him another reason to lash out again.

When he finally gets to his feet, he can't even look at her. "I'm sorry," he repeats. "I'll be better. I promise."

"It's okay," she soothes, knowing that's what he wants to hear. "I know how stressful it's been."

He nods. "I need to get some fresh air. Maybe go for a drive." Then he's out the door. Gone. Madeline knows not to expect him back tonight. He'll go drive into the mountains or crash in one of the bunkhouses, but he will leave her alone, at least for now.

She waits until she hears the slam of the door before she dares to move. She rubs her elbow, bends and extends it a few times. It's not broken, but angry, plum-colored bruises already dot her skin. She imagines her face is bruised too. That will be difficult to explain to others. He's usually so much more conscientious about where he leaves his marks.

For the first six months of her pregnancy things were peaceful. Madeline believed Wes had changed, that the fact that they were going to have a baby had smoothed and soothed the angry, jagged edges of her husband.

And for a long while he held it together, kept his composure. Not that Wes ever truly lost control. No, that was the whole point of the carefully placed smacks, pinches, and slaps, wasn't it? To keep Madeline in her place without the world discovering that their golden boy has a mean streak. *Mean streak* is an understatement, as Madeline knows she tends to do, but it's so much easier, less embarrassing, and less exhausting to face than the man she married is a monster. The fact that they live on a horse ranch is the perfect cover for the bumps and bruises and broken bones that Madeline has endured over the course of their ten-year marriage. Though a world-class equestrian, she gladly blames clumsiness or a particularly spirited horse for her injuries.

But a month ago, when she insisted that she go home for

her stepfather's funeral, the old Wes reared his ugly head. In the end, Madeline held her ground. She went home to say goodbye to the man who raised her. She just brought along a black-and-blue torso, a wrenched shoulder, and a ring of bruises around her throat. She wore turtlenecks the entire week she was home.

Madeline wipes the remaining tears from her face and gets to her feet and stares out the window at the mountains. When did she become so weak? Look at her—a smart, champion equestrian, letting herself get knocked around by a man. Her mother would be so sad, and her stepfather would be furious. But deep down Madeline knows spousal abuse has little to do with the victim's strength, smarts, or anything else for that matter. She knows that Wes is masterful at getting people to do what he wants them to, to think that his temper tantrums are their fault.

Many times Madeline thought about leaving. Just walking away. She has some money tucked away, left to her by her stepfather, but she knows it won't be enough to keep her hidden from her husband, who has endless resources.

New tears gather in her eyes, and she angrily swipes them away. She has to hold it together. Her eyes land on the top shelf and the box where Wes keeps his revolver. He'll come after her, she knows it, and how will Madeline protect the baby and herself? She drags the chair sitting in front of her vanity mirror to beneath the shelf and carefully climbs onto it. Her legs wobble beneath her, and she grabs the closet bar to steady herself, knocking a few of Wes's shirts to the floor.

Slow down, Madeline tells herself. Take your time. She reaches above her head for the wooden box and pulls it down, her elbow protesting with the motion. She eases herself down from the chair and, even without opening it, knows the box feels too light. Wes has taken the gun. Why? For protection? He has several more in his gun safe that would serve that purpose just as well. This particular gun holds sentimental value. It belonged to his father and grandfather before him. Madeline knew this day would come but hadn't thought this would be the day. She doesn't bother returning the box to the shelf and instead shoves it beneath the bed.

Johanna was the first one to see what was happening between Madeline and Wes behind closed doors. They had been friends for nearly three years when they were out riding horses and Johanna had broached the topic that nearly ended their friendship. *"I know what Wes has been doing to you, Madeline. You don't deserve that. No one does."* Madeline had denied it, of course, but Johanna was persistent in her kind way. Madeline thought she had been so careful, hiding the bruises, but it wasn't long before she was telling Johanna everything: the fights, the slaps, the kicks, the punches, the gaslighting.

Leave, Johanna had urged, but Madeline made all the usual excuses: *It's not so bad. He's always sorry. I shouldn't have . . .* But there was one thing that Johanna insisted upon— the photographs. So one morning, after a particularly rough argument with Wes, Madeline had driven to Johanna's and posed for the most heartbreaking photo shoot she could have imagined. Those were the pictures that Lucy had found in their secret hiding place, and Madeline could feel the disdain, the disgust, that must have rolled off her sister as she held them in her fist. *Really, Madeline?* she would have said. *Really? This is what you've become?*

Yes, it was. But never again.

First, though, she needs to get rid of Mellie. Madeline holds tightly to the banister as she goes down the steps, her anger and hurt making her unsteady on her feet. Once outside Mellie's door she pauses, fearful of how she's going to react. Just as Madeline's getting ready to knock, the door opens, and she comes face-to-face with Mellie.

She immediately notices Madeline's tear-stained face. "Are

you okay?" Mellie asks with what at first sounds like genuine concern.

"No," Madeline bites out. "I am not okay. Mellie, it's time for you to leave."

"I'm going to, I swear. I just need a few more days—" Mellie begins, her big eyes filling with tears, but Madeline cuts her off.

"You lied to me, and I just can't have you in my home anymore," Madeline says.

Mellie looks like she's going to argue, but Madeline stops her. "Your mother is not dead. She lives in West Virginia, and the hospital told me there is no way you are pregnant. I don't know what you think you were going to accomplish by coming here, but it's over. Done."

Mellie's face goes stony, her eyes snap with hate. "What I was going to accomplish?" she repeats. "I was coming to take what's mine."

"And what might that be?" Madeline asks. "The clothes you're wearing? The perfume? The bed you're sleeping in? Tell me, Mellie. What exactly is yours to take?"

Mellie smirks. "That's a question you're going to have to ask your husband."

Madeline freezes, trying to digest what Mellie has just said. "My husband?"

"Yes, your husband." Mellie rolls her eyes as if it is obvious. "Think about it. Why would he be interested in a cow like you?"

Though she doesn't want to believe Mellie, she does. If Wes would hit and berate his wife, he could certainly cheat on her. Still, Madeline doesn't want to give Mellie the satisfaction of knowing how this hurts her. "You have twenty seconds to get out of my house, or I'm going to call the police," Madeline says.

Mellie stands her ground. "I saved your life," she says. "If I hadn't called 9-1-1, Dalton probably would have killed you."

"You're down to ten seconds, Mellie," she says. When Mellie still doesn't move, she starts toward the home office, wishing for the hundredth time she had her new cell phone. Why hadn't it arrived yet?

Mellie trails behind her shouting all sorts of nonsense. "He loves me! He does. We've been together for months now. And you know what? He tells me how much he hates you. You disgust him."

In the office, Madeline picks up the landline and lifts it to her ear.

"Fine," Mellie says. "I'm going. But I'm not the one you should be talking to. It's your husband."

Madeline follows Mellie to the door. "You can call for a ride, or I can order you an Uber. You decide." She bites the inside of her cheeks to keep from crying, opens the door, and waits for Mellie to step outside.

Mellie turns to Madeline, her face filled with faux pity. "I feel sorry for you. I really do." Her eyes linger on the bruises that are beginning to form on Madeline's cheeks. "He's never touched me like that before. He must really hate you." With that, Mellie steps outside, and Madeline slams the door behind her. Through the closed door, she hears Mellie's voice. "In the end, he'll pick me. This isn't over, Madeline!"

Shaking with anger, Madeline retreats upstairs. How has her world come to this? she wonders. And she knows it's going to get much, much worse. The thought of bringing a child into this kind of chaos breaks her heart, but she also knows she'll do anything to protect her daughter. Anything.

From the bedroom window, Madeline sees Mellie trudging up the dark lane toward the road. She wants to hate her but knows the young woman is misguided and foolish. Now all she can do is hope that she will stay far, far away and get on with her own life.

The creak of floorboards causes Madeline to startle.

Standing in the doorway is her sister.

"Lucy." The word is no more than a murmur. Her eyes go to Lucy's hands. She's wearing a pair of Wes's work gloves.

"Let's get this over with, shall we?" Lucy says and takes a step toward her sister.

CHAPTER 33

JAMIE

BACK AT THE motel Jamie paces the room. His ride with Wes Drake rankles him. He had truly hoped that he would have been able to navigate Nightjar without anyone knowing who he was. How wrong he'd been about that.

For years, Jamie regarded Wes as some sort of mythical hero for saving him, but in the end, he is just some arrogant rich guy who thinks Jamie owes him something. And he is a possible murderer. The photos from the party don't lie. Wes went into the barn just after Johanna and just before the explosion, and Jamie doesn't buy what he said about wanting to fire Johanna for not having her midwife credentials up-to-date. That will be easy enough to check. He shoots off a text to Greta, asking her to check on Johanna's licensing and to dig more deeply into her past.

Will do. And check your email.

Jamie navigates to his email and opens the message from Greta.

I widened my search, and there's a mom-and-pop hardware store in Snowcap, ID, and they have record of double-headed nails, duct tape, ball bearings, zinc wire, and PVC piping being purchased within a month by the same individual, but not on the same day. Bad news is we don't know who bought them—they were paid for with cash. Working on getting a search warrant so we have access to surveillance.

Snowcap, Idaho, is less than two hours from Nightjar. Smart, Jamie thinks. If this is the guy, he purchased the bomb-making material out of state using cash, which makes things a bit more difficult to suss out. Too bad the perpetrator didn't realize that most stores keep track of the exact items sold and when. Now they need that surveillance footage.

He is restless but can't make a move until he has that arrest warrant in hand. He pops a few aspirin and stares down at the school yearbook and the black binder that holds Juneau's case file that he brought in from the car. Which one to open first? Both will release a Pandora's box of memories, all unwelcome. He hears Juneau sigh in his ear. *What's the point?* she asks. *It's been too long. Aren't you tired, J. J.?*

He is. But he also needs to know what happened to his sister.

Jamie takes a seat at the small Formica table and opens the black binder. On the first page is a plastic sleeve that holds a large photo of Juneau. Her final school photo. She's looking into the camera with her large dark eyes, a slight smile on her face that shows her dimple. *Ugh!* Juneau says. *I hate that picture!*

Jamie smiles, showing his own dimple. Juneau hated every single photo taken of her. He thinks this one is a good one. He flips the page and is thrust into a familiar world of police reports and interview transcripts, and there are hundreds. Sheriff Colson and the other officers were thorough, this much is clear. They interviewed teachers, classmates, business owners, guests who stayed in the hotel—no one remembered anything of note. Then came the interview with his mother. The notes were nearly incoherent; his mother was so grief-stricken, so scared, that she

was little help to the investigation. There are photos of the blue
Lynx station wagon sitting abandoned on the gravel road. Jamie
reads through the forensic report: Jamie's fingerprints and his
mother's were found in the car. He had forgotten about that,
getting his fingerprints taken for comparison purposes. There
were two other sets of partial prints also found in the car, one set
thought to be Juneau's, the other unknown. The same goes for
the DNA found, but to date there have been no matches.

Jamie turns the page and is met with the image of his swollen, disfigured face. He winces at the memory, runs his tongue
over his dental implants, put into place when he was eighteen
and his jaw had fully developed. Up until then he wore a re-
movable retainer with prosthetic teeth that never quite fit his
mouth. He doesn't linger long on the photo and flips the page
to his interviews. There were at least a dozen of them, most
conducted by Sheriff Colson who was a deputy at the time,
but in each he said the same things: He didn't know who took
Juneau; he didn't know who beat him up; he didn't see or hear
anything. The exception was in the final interviews he gave
before he and his mother moved away—a last-ditch effort to
squeeze any additional information out of him. It took place in
their motel room, and Sheriff Colson sat across from Jamie at this
same table, his mother sat on the sofa, looking anxiously at them
both, willing Jamie to remember something, anything.

And then, miraculously, Jamie did remember something.
He was lying in the ditch, pain radiating through his hip, his
heart nearly pounding out of his chest, listening to the crunching of feet coming toward him through the grass. There was a
bright light, a flashlight maybe, making it impossible to see the
face of who was coming toward him—he was big, monstrously
tall, and broad-shouldered—all of which he mentioned before.
Then he remembers the flashlight catching a glint of silver.
The silver tip of a fawn-colored cowboy boot with elaborate
stitching. Of what? Jamie remembers his twelve-year-old self

squeezing his eyes tightly shut trying to picture the design. *"An owl?"* Jamie said it as a question.

"An owl?" Colson repeated.

"Yes, an owl. It had wings and eyes, but it didn't look like a real owl, more like . . ." Jamie hadn't been able to quite put it into words.

"More like the suggestion of an owl?" Colson had asked, and he had agreed.

Jamie looks up from the binder. He had all but forgotten about this detail. After he told Colson about the boots, he and his mother moved away, and he'd never heard another word about it. But Colson clearly had not forgotten. He had printed off pages and pages of pictures of boots that might have matched Jamie's description. Now, he examines each, but none of them are quite right.

The rest of the binder chronicles tips that have come in over the years and the follow-up conversations that Colson and other deputies had; nothing came from any of it.

Jamie closes the binder and sets it aside, and a dark cloud of melancholy settles over him. It's his own fault. He knew stepping back into this world would be painful. He reaches for the yearbook and skims through the pages until he finds Juneau's school photo, the same one that's at the front of the binder, then finds his own and shakes his head. He thought he was so tough, so much better than his classmates. He wonders what could have happened if he'd tried a little harder.

He finds the photo of Laura Holt with her smattering of freckles and wishes he remembered her. He flips through the pages until he comes across the spread dedicated to the football team. There's a group photo of the team together, decked out in their gear, standing in rows shoulder to shoulder, but there is also another photo that causes Jamie to sit up in his seat. It's a picture of Wes Drake with seven other boys. They are dressed in their football jerseys but are wearing jeans and cowboy hats and holding—unbelievably—shotguns. That sure wouldn't fly in this day and age. The caption reads "Senior gridders take aim at a state title." The photo credit is listed as Juneau Archer. Jamie pulls the book close to his face to get a better look at Wes who is a head taller than and twice as broad as his teammates. He's certainly slimmed down over the years, Jamie thinks, and that's when he notices what Wes is wearing on his feet: metal-tipped cowboy boots.

But everyone else on the team is wearing boots too. Every single person in Nightjar probably has at least two pairs in their closet. His cell buzzes, and Jamie looks at the clock. It's nearly ten thirty. He considers letting the call go to voicemail but thinks twice. It might be Greta or one of the deputies with some info for him. He flips the phone over, and it's a number he doesn't recognize. "Hello," he says cautiously.

"Agent Saldano, this is Laura Holt. I'm sorry I'm calling so late, but I just wanted to tell you I remembered something. About Juneau. It's probably nothing . . ."

"No, no, that's okay. What is it?" Jamie asks, trying not to get his hopes up.

"I completely forgot about it, and I never mentioned it to the police, but I did see Juneau about a month or two before she disappeared. It was at the Dairy Ranch. She was behind the building, eating an ice cream cone."

"Was she with anyone?" Jamie asks, his pulse quickening.

"Not at first," Laura says. "Like I said, it probably doesn't mean anything, but she was behind the building, and then someone came up to her." Laura pauses, as if hesitant to continue. Jamie wants to hurry her along, tell her to just say it, but doesn't want to scare her away.

She takes a deep breath, then continues. "They talked for a minute, and then they started kissing. I think it was Wes," Laura says. "Wes Drake."

CHAPTER 34

LUCY

MADELINE TAKES A step backward and eyes the doorway behind Lucy.

"I knew this was coming but . . ." Madeline says shakily. Lucy can hear the fear in her sister's voice, and this gives her a little thrill. Not normal, she tells herself, but then again, Lucy has never been normal. She gently shuts the door, and it closes with a soft click.

It was hard growing up with such a beautiful, accomplished sister. Stepsister, Lucy reminds herself. Though they weren't related by blood, they were undeniably connected to one another. Lucy's father forced Madeline and Madeline's mother on her, and that was just the way it was. No one asked how Lucy felt about their new domestic situation; there was no consultation, no discussion, but eventually the kid grew on her.

And now she's going to be a mother. She has all the things that Lucy wants—or thought she wanted. When Madeline came home last month, Lucy saw the bruises. She saw firsthand what Wes was doing to her little sister. Then she saw the pictures hidden in Madeline's file drawer, the horrid bruises, the dead look in Madeline's eyes as she stared into the camera. Lucy would never let a man do to her what Wes has done to her sister.

"Let's do this, Madeline," Lucy says, reaching into her pocket and pulling out Madeline's new cell phone. "First of all, is Mellie gone? I need to know how quiet we need to be. Madeline, is she gone?"

Her sister nods. "Do you want to send him the text, or should I?" Lucy asks. When Madeline doesn't say anything, Lucy presses the phone toward her. "It's really best if you do it. Type this." With shaking hands, Madeline takes the phone. "*It's over, you fucking asshole. Do not come home tonight, or I'll call the police,*" Lucy dictates. "Now hit Send." Madeline doesn't. She just stands there, trembling. Lucy sighs, pulls the phone roughly from Madeline's hands, sends the message, and tosses it onto the bed. She crosses the room and steps into the closet. "Wow, Mads, you have a lot of shoes."

"Lucy, please," Madeline says, her voice pleading.

Lucy can hear the fear in her voice. She knows she should feel sorry for her sister, but the only thing she feels right now is disgust. How is it that Lucy is flat broke, divorced, and practically disinherited by her own father? Life isn't fair. She plucks one of Madeline's cowboy hats from a shelf and places it on her head. It's a ridiculous-looking thing—pink and embellished with crystals arranged in the shape of stars. She turns her attention to Wes's side of the closet and his array of leather belts. She lifts one from its hook. "Nice," Lucy says. "Is this mother-of-pearl?" she asks, rubbing the belt buckle. "Oooh, and amethyst?" She lifts it to her nose and breathes deeply. The scent of leather reminds Lucy of her father, and a sudden bullet of regret pierces her, but she tries to pocket it. There will be time for regret later—but only if she doesn't get away with this.

Lucy steps from the closet, the belt dangling from her gloved hand, passes Madeline, and moves to the window. It's fully dark out now, the mountains a mere smudge.

"Now we wait," Lucy says. Minutes pass, and Lucy occasionally looks over her shoulder to see if Madeline decides to try to make a run for it. She doesn't. Finally, two headlights puncture the night, and Lucy watches as a truck pulls onto the property. Wes is back. She closes the curtains, the only light in the room coming from the closet, then turns to face her sister.

"Lucy," Madeline says fearfully, eyeing the swaying belt in Lucy's hand and backing toward the door.

"You knew this was coming, Madeline," Lucy says, surprised at the calm in her voice. She watches as her stepsister looks wildly around the room. For what? An escape route? It's too late for that now.

Madeline shakes her head, her pretty eyes filling with tears.

"Now, hush," Lucy soothes, drawing the belt tight with her gloved hands and moving toward her sister. "It will all be over soon."

CHAPTER 35

MELLIE

I PULL UP the Uber app and fight back tears as I walk toward the road. There's no way I'm going to stand in the driveway and wait for my ride to show up. I still don't know why I lied to Madeline about my mom being dead when we were in the ambulance. I was so scared, and there was Wes's wife holding my hand and being so nice to me—it just kind of came out of my mouth.

I'm even more surprised that she found out I wasn't really pregnant. I guess having that kind of money means you can get anything you want, even private medical information. That lie was planned. Wes had been freezing me out, and I thought that by getting close to his wife, it would force him to make a decision—Madeline or me. Desperate, I know, but I really think he loves me. I wish I had Wes's phone number. I know he'd come for me.

Moonlight guides my way, but the night is cold, and Madeline's T-shirt does little to keep me warm. By the time I reach the road I'm shivering, and the Uber driver is still fifteen minutes away. I have to figure out what I'm going to do next. I'll have to find another job since the catering business really is on hold. That part wasn't a lie. I'm running out of money, fast.

The minutes feel like hours, and finally headlights appear

in the distance. I lift my hand and wave, so he doesn't pass me by. As he gets closer, I realize it's not the Uber driver's car but a pickup truck. Wes's truck. He swings into the lane and slams on the brakes, and I stumble backward to avoid getting hit.

Through the windshield, Wes's face is a mask of anger, and my initial happiness at seeing him turns to dread. I cautiously approach the driver's-side window as it lowers.

"Mellie," Wes says. "You're still here. I told you, enough is enough."

I begin to cry, even though I know that Wes has no patience for tears. I can't tell him about the way I talked to Madeline, the things I said. "Can you give me a ride?" I ask. "Please?"

"You know I can't," he says impatiently. "Call an Uber."

"But I need you." I'm crying openly now, snot running down my nose. "Wes, please." He shakes his head. I see the indifference in his eyes. He's ready to leave me behind. Panic floods my bloodstream, and I wrench open his door. "Please," I say. "Don't do this. Please . . ." I grab his sleeve.

"Whoa," he says, pulling back. "Mellie, I never promised you anything. You know that. Now, come on, be a grown-up about this."

"I'll tell," I say, sounding like anything but a grown-up. "I'll tell everyone about us. How will that look? I'll tell everyone you had sex with me in your bunkhouse while your poor pregnant wife was crying about her best friend dying."

"Who would believe you?" he laughs meanly. "You're nothing. A nobody."

"I lied for you!" I cry. "I told the police that Johanna's husband went into the barn before it blew up. I protected you."

"What do you want, Mellie?" Wes asks. "You want me to leave my pregnant wife? Did you think that was really ever going to happen? That I was going to marry you and move you onto the ranch? Come on, you're delusional."

"Don't say that," I sob. "I love you." I grab onto his shirt again, only wanting him to hold me, to tell me he loves me too. "Please, I'll do anything."

"Jesus, Mellie," Wes says, roughly pushing me away so that I tumble backward and land on my ass. My breath is knocked from my chest, and pain radiates through my body. "Grow up and stay the fuck away from my family," he says, pulling the truck door shut with a slam.

Before I can get to my feet he's already driving down the lane to his home, to his wife. I scrape away the pebbles embedded in my palms and brush away the dirt from my jeans. Madeline's jeans. In spite of the cool evening, my face burns with shame as another set of headlights appear in the distance. Finally, my ride is here. I climb inside, and as he drives off, all I can think is, This isn't over yet. I will not be treated this way. Wes and Madeline are going to pay—one way or another.

CHAPTER 36

MADELINE

MADELINE IS FROZEN in place. She can't believe this is really happening. But then again, hadn't her sister told her just one month ago that she was capable of murder? Where is Wes? Lucy grabs a framed picture from the bedside table and throws it in Madeline's direction. It smashes against the wall.

"You can throw harder than that, can't you?" Madeline says, a smile stretching across her face. She reaches for a vase of flowers on the same table, one of the only bouquets that survived the explosion, and throws it, sending it whizzing past Lucy's head. It explodes in a spray of glass and water.

"Good one," Lucy says. And for the first time since Lucy showed up, they laugh. It's time. Finally. All of Madeline's earlier fear has seeped away. "Now come here," she says, grabbing Madeline by her sore elbow, and she cries out in pain. "God, I'm sorry," Lucy says, dropping her arm, her face stricken. "But you know this is going to hurt, right? It has to hurt."

"I know," Madeline says. "It's okay. It can't hurt any more than what he's done to me before."

When Madeline came back for her stepfather's funeral, Lucy walked in on Madeline while she was changing and saw the jewel-toned contusions that spread across her sister's back in an ugly constellation of bruises. At first, Madeline lied.

"I fell off one of our new Morgans. He can be temperamental," Madeline had said, her voice unnaturally flat, her eyes unable to meet Lucy's.

"Bullshit," Lucy had responded, stepping closer to see the damage Wes had done. What had he used as his weapon? His fists? The metal toes of his boots? His belt? "I'll kill him," Lucy declared. "I'll fucking kill him."

"Lucy, no!" Madeline had said, quickly pulling a sweater over her head. "It looks worse than it is. I've got it handled."

The entire week of the funeral, Lucy had begged and pleaded with Madeline to leave Wyoming and come back home for good. But Madeline had every excuse in the book— *It could be so much worse. He loves me. I love him . . .* It went on and on until their conversations devolved into bitterness and ended in their cold estrangement. But Lucy wasn't done. She wasn't going to let her sister be killed by this sadistic monster. Over the coming days, Lucy was relentless until finally Madeline agreed. That night, after hours of arguing and pleading and crying, a plan was formed.

"We'll do it just like we planned," Lucy says now, guiding Madeline into the closet and down to her knees. "Tell me if it's too much." Madeline nods, and Lucy presses a knee to her back. "You know this is the only way."

"I know," Madeline grunts. "Just be careful! Please don't hurt the baby." Hot tears roll down her face. She fights the urge to get back to her feet, but like Lucy said, this is the only way to get Wes out of her life for good.

Madeline feels the stiff leather press against her skin as Lucy loops the belt around her neck. "Oh God," Madeline says, scrabbling at her neck, trying to pull it away, but Lucy is too strong.

"Just relax," Lucy orders, and Madeline feels the belt tighten, feels her windpipe constrict so that only the tiniest sip of air gets through. Fireflies dance in front of her eyes, and for a moment she's five again and back home in Iowa chasing lightning bugs with Lucy. It's a nice, warm memory.

Then the belt loosens, just a fraction of an inch, but it's enough. Madeline coughs and gasps and tries to fill her lungs. "Are you okay?" Lucy asks. And Madeline knows her sister is crying too. She doesn't want to do this either.

"I'm good. It's okay, Goosey," she croaks, somehow latching onto Lucy's childhood nickname. *Lucy Goosey.* The term of endearment that Lucy pretended to hate but everyone knew she secretly loved. "Goosey," Madeline pleads. "Be careful. The baby."

"It's okay, it's almost over. It has to look real," Lucy whispers in her ear, and once again the belt goes taut. Madeline's throat closes, and instinctively she claws at Lucy's gloved hands. She's on the verge of losing consciousness when the belt loosens again. "I'm so sorry, I'm so sorry," Lucy cries over and over. Madeline's starved lungs scream for air, and she greedily sucks in jagged breaths, but all she can think about is her baby. Again the belt tightens.

Somehow through the roaring in her ears, Madeline hears a voice coming from the floor below. It's Wes, calling her name. He sounds angry. Of course he is. She sent him a text she would never have dared to before.

It's over, you fucking asshole. Do not come home tonight.

She tries to cry out, but the sound is caught in her chest.

Suddenly, the knee in her back is gone, and the belt is on the floor at her side. The closet light is off, and the door is shut. She hears a knock at the bedroom door.

"Madeline," Wes calls, "unlock the door." He sounds pissed. She tries to answer him, but she's still trying to gather air into her lungs. "Madeline," Wes shouts, "open the goddamn door!" He's not done fighting. He's come back to—what?—finish their earlier argument? Madeline tries to crawl from the closet so she can unlock the door for Wes, but she's too weak. Instead, she curls up in a ball, her arms wrapped protectively around her belly. She doesn't feel the baby move. There are no kicks or somersaults, no tiny fists pummeling her bladder. A moan escapes her lips. This has all gone very wrong. They'll die together, Madeline thinks. She and the baby will take one final breath together and then go to sleep.

She begins to drift off, but the sound of splintering wood startles her awake. Wes is breaking through the locked bedroom door. "Madeline!" he calls, and she can hear his heavy footsteps as he bursts into the room. "Where the fuck are you?" From outside the closed closet door, a thin line of light appears. "I'm so sick of your games. You think you can tell me to stay out of my own house? This is my home, my ranch . . ." His voice has taken on an echoey quality. He must be checking the bathroom. And where is Lucy? A terrible thought creeps into Madeline's head. Maybe Lucy got scared and has abandoned her.

From her spot on the floor, Madeline sees a dark shadow pass in front of the closet door and then stop. There's the soft snick of a doorknob being turned. The door opens, and Madeline is momentarily blinded by the sudden light, and she puts a hand in front of her eyes.

"What the fuck?" Wes asks, staring down at her. "You're hiding from me?" He sounds incredulous. "Fuck you, Madeline. Fuck you. This is my house," he snarls. "Get up," he orders. He is in such a state that he doesn't even realize she's hurt.

She tries to speak but can only manage a raspy "I can't," but he's not listening.

"I've given you everything, *everything*." She watches his feet as he paces in front of the closet, the metal tip of his cowboy boot coming dangerously close to her head. A wave of nausea sweeps over her. She wants to close her eyes, wants this all to be over. The baby gives a resounding kick to her ribs, and with the jolt Madeline gives a small cry. Not a cry of pain, though, a small yip of delight. Her baby is still alive. She's not going to let her baby die in this closet.

She reaches out one hand and clamps it around Wes's ankle, nearly causing him to topple backward. "Wes," she croaks. Finally, finally he takes a good look at her face. She can imagine what she looks like.

"Jesus," Wes says, dropping to his knees and running a hand over her hair. "What happened to you? Who did this?" He touches her neck. His fingers are cool against the skin of her raw, hot neck. She tries to answer him, but words feel like glass in her throat.

"Madeline, tell me," Wes insists. "Who did this? Was it Mellie?"

"No, you did," Madeline manages to rasp, the words fighting their way out of her damaged throat.

"Madeline, no," he says. "I didn't. I would never do this to you. You're confused."

Her eyes dart around the darkened room. "Lucy?" she asks. Where did she go? It doesn't matter, Madeline thinks. She'll come back—she has to. Madeline lifts the belt from the ground beside her and pushes it into Wes's hands.

"She's gone. She must have run," Wes says, running the strap of leather through his fingers. "You're safe now. I'll call the police." He bends over to help Madeline to her feet. She feels light-headed, and her breath comes in ragged hitches. "But about what happened earlier," Wes says. "Our argument. You're not going to say anything, are you?"

Madeline looks up at her husband in disbelief. An argument? That's what he's calling it? That's what he's worried about? She's too weary, in too much pain to press the issue. She shakes her head, and he pulls her into a tight embrace, but there is no comfort in his touch.

The curtains sway slightly, and Lucy appears from behind the fabric and puts one finger to her lips, ordering Madeline to stay quiet. In the other hand she's holding a gun. Wes's gun. The one that was supposed to be in the closet. She gives Lucy an imperceptible nod.

"Don't worry, I'll take care of you. I won't let her hurt you again. I promise," Wes says into her ear. "God, she must really hate you, Madeline."

"Not quite," Lucy says from her spot in the shadows.

Wes spins around, placing his body in front of Madeline's. "Lucy," he says. "What the fuck? What have you done?"

"What does it look like?" Lucy asks playfully.

"Lucy, come on, now," Wes says, his voice suddenly calm, placating. "I know you and Madeline have had a complicated relationship, but you don't have to do this."

"Oh, but I do," Lucy says. "I most definitely must do this. Now, step aside, Wes." Madeline's blood curdles in her veins. This is really happening.

"I'll give you whatever you want," Wes says. "You want the horses? Take them. You want money? You can have it. Turn around and go, Lucy. We won't call the police. You have my word."

"Oh, come on, Wes," Lucy says. "We both know your word means shit. Now, step aside. I want to talk to my sister."

"No," Wes says. "No fucking way." A sudden bang fills the air, and the wall above Wes's right shoulder explodes in a cloud of plaster and dust. Madeline screams and covers her head with her arms.

"Lucy," Wes pleads.

"Step aside, Wes," Lucy orders. "This is the last time I'm going to say it."

Wes hesitates, and Lucy begins the countdown. "Five, four—"

"Lucy—"

"Three, two—"

Wes steps aside. Of course he does. He has no weapons. All he has is a belt in his hand that will do no good here. Nor will his fists. Madeline feels naked, exposed. Skin, sinew, and bone is no match for a bullet, but she knows the bullet isn't for her. Madeline pulls herself upright and steps forward. Now she's the one standing in front of her husband, as if protecting him, though he doesn't deserve it, not one bit. Madeline keeps her gaze firmly fixed on her sister's face. The gun is aimed squarely at Madeline's chest.

"Step aside, Madeline," Lucy says.

"Do you really want to do this?" Madeline manages to say, her throat still painfully raw. There's a flicker of hesitation in Lucy's eyes.

Lucy stares straight into Madeline's eyes, and years of hurt and whispered secrets, skinned knees and broken hearts, mothers and fathers lost and found, and laughter and tears and love and hate cross between them. Madeline braces herself for what comes next. "Duck," Lucy orders.

CHAPTER 37

LUCY

THE SHOT IS wide, and instead of hitting center mass, like Lucy's father taught her when they went deer hunting, the bullet grazes Wes's shoulder. Madeline is on her knees, arms covering her head, trying to cocoon her baby beneath her. Thank God her sister listened to her for once. If Madeline hadn't dropped to the floor when Lucy yelled *duck*, her sister would be dead. But for now, Lucy has Wes right where she wants him. He's clutching at his wounded shoulder, blood seeping between his fingers and dripping over Madeline.

"What? Why?" Wes asks, eyes wide. Lucy almost giggles at his absolute confusion. Her sister's husband has always been a narcissistic son of a bitch, so of course he wouldn't be self-aware enough to understand why she has just put a bullet in him.

"Hmmm, where to begin?" Lucy says, keeping the gun pinned on him. "How about, you are an abusive fuck?"

"No, no," Wes says. "That's not true. Madeline, tell her that it's not true. I never hurt you. I would never . . ." He begins to sidle toward the door.

"Shut up, Wes. Stay the fuck still. And Madeline, stay down," Lucy orders when she catches her lifting her head.

"I saw the marks when Madeline came home for our dad's funeral. She told me everything. You think you're a big man, Wes? Beating up your wife? Does it make you feel strong and powerful?"

"She's lying," Wes insists. "Tell her, Madeline. Tell her you were lying." He reaches down and grabs her shoulder, gives it a shake.

"Don't touch her," Lucy says icily, and Wes rears back. "And she's not lying," she adds. She keeps her gaze pinned on the man in front of her.

"Lucy," Wes says through his pain. "You'll never be able to prove it. No one around here will believe that I could hurt my wife. Everyone loves me. The sheriff will never believe it. And I've got friends—lawyers, doctors, judges—who will say whatever I want them to say."

"I've seen the pictures, Wes," Lucy says, losing patience.

"Pictures?" He glares down at Madeline.

"Yeah, pictures," Lucy says to him, using her teeth to pull the gloves off her hands. "There's plenty of proof."

"Tell me what you want," Wes says, his eyes wild with fear. "Money? I can give you money. Lots of it. I'll say it was an accident. We don't even have to report it. Fifty, sixty thousand?" he offers, and she looks at him incredulously. "Okay, a hundred, and your pick of the horses."

"Two hundred thousand, and Madeline gets the ranch in the divorce," Lucy counters.

"Five hundred thousand, in cash," Wes shoots back. "And Madeline and I will go our separate ways. But I want joint custody of the baby. She's mine too."

And this is when Lucy knows for certain that this nightmare will never end for her sister and the child who hasn't even formally met her father yet. Wes won't change. One day, Lucy will get the call that her sister is dead or has disappeared.

It will all be so tragic and sad, and Wes will play the part of Grieving Husband perfectly. He will get away with murder and will raise his daughter in a house filled with fear and anger and violence.

"Take off your belt," she tells Wes.

"What?" he asks, pain and confusion on his face.

"Take off your belt. And throw it over here. Do it."

"Come on, Lucy," Wes says, unbuckling his belt with his good arm and pulling it from his pants loops. "I can get you the money by morning. What do you say? Deal?"

"Hmmm," Lucy says and looks down at her sister still trembling on the floor below him. "What do you think, Madeline? Is that enough?"

"It's not near enough," Madeline whispers.

"What?" Wes asks, looking down at his wife. "What did you say?"

"I said it's not near enough," Madeline says more loudly. "No amount of money is worth what you've done to me over the years." She is sobbing now, but Lucy can hear the steel in her voice. Finally.

"You know, Lucy tried to sleep with me," Wes says, desperation strangling his voice. "From the minute she got here, she came on to me."

"I was just messing with you, Wes," Lucy says. "I was laughing at you. We were both laughing at you."

"You're in this together?" he says in disbelief. "Madeline? I love you. You know that, don't you? And I'm so, so sorry about how I've hurt you. I'll get help. I will. Our baby needs a father. She needs me."

Madeline's eyes are locked on Wes's. Her crying has stopped, her face has softened. She's looking at Wes like the adoring wife she's been for so long. Lucy can see her resolve wavering.

"Mads," Lucy says, trying to get her sister to focus. "Stick with me here."

Lucy looks over at her sister, her eyes filled with almost unfathomable sadness. Madeline struggles to her feet and stands directly in front of Wes, blocking the shot.

"You can't do this, Lucy," Madeline says. "I won't let you."

CHAPTER 38

MADELINE

MADELINE IS LIGHT-HEADED, and it's all she can do to stay on her feet, but she holds her ground.

"Get out of my way," Lucy orders.

"No, Lucy," Madeline says. "I can't ask you to do this. Give me the gun."

Lucy holds the gun tightly in her hand. "No," she says. "It has to stop. This ends now." She closes one eye and takes aim. "Move."

Madeline steps forward and gently pulls the gun from her grasp. "You're right. It does have to end, but not this way."

"Madeline, no," Lucy says, but she silences her with one look.

"Thank you," Wes cries from behind her. "Oh my God, thank you, Madeline."

Madeline turns and looks at her husband. Blood oozes from his shoulder, and he looks nothing like the big, larger-than-life personality she's known for the last eleven years. She holds out her hand, and Wes takes it, and somehow he's able to get to his feet. His shoulders slump in relief. Using his good arm, he pulls her into an embrace, and this time she doesn't fight it. She leans into him, and for a moment they are holding each other up. She smells the familiar scent of his aftershave inter-mixed with the stink of sweat and fear. "Give me the gun,

Madeline," he whispers. "It's going to be okay now. I'll take good care of you."

Madeline feels the cool metal of the gun pressed between them and tips the barrel upward, feels it settle into the soft spot just below Wes's sternum, and pulls the trigger.

CHAPTER 39

JAMIE

JAMIE FINDS HIMSELF speeding toward the Drake house. While he doesn't have enough for an arrest warrant yet, he knows it's just a matter of time. But tonight he's going to talk to Wes as a brother. He's going to ask him why he lied about knowing his sister, about why he was kissing her, why he was seen with her just a few days before she disappeared. Was Wes the one who knocked Jamie into the ditch? Had he simply come back to the gravel road to make sure Jamie was dead? Was he planning on finishing the job but was interrupted by the woman who came upon them driving down the road? And he wants to ask him if Wes's dad used his influence to cover up the crime. He just needs fifteen minutes with him. He'll get his answers.

He pulls down the lane leading to the Drake house, parks next to Wes's truck, and steps from his car.

Suddenly, the unmistakable sound of a gunshot rings out from above. Instinctively, Jamie reaches for his sidearm and takes cover behind Wes's truck. He makes a call for backup and, knowing that it could take a while for them to arrive, decides to go inside the house.

The newly fixed front door is unlocked, and Jamie cautiously pushes it open. The house is dark. He has no idea who is in the house with him but is confident that the shots came from the upper level.

He takes the steps two at a time, and at the top of the stairs he pauses. The acrid smell of gunpowder bites at his nose, and dull light from the master bedroom seeps into the hallway. Over the pounding of his heartbeat, Jamie hears crying. Harsh, hiccupping sobs. "ATF," he announces. "Come out of the room, hands up."

There's no response, no movement, only the sound of weeping and murmuring. Are there two voices? He moves down the hallway, pressed as close to the wall as possible, and pauses outside the bedroom door. "It's okay, it's okay," comes a female voice. "It's over now."

Dammit, Jamie thinks. He has no idea what he's going to walk into. He peeks around the corner, then pulls back, fearful that he might find a gun in his face. Breathing hard, he reviews what he saw in that split second. Not a shotgun. Three figures all on the floor. And blood. Lots of blood. He takes a deep breath, grips his service revolver tightly, and steps into the room.

"Let me see your hands," he barks. Instantly two pairs of hands go up in the air. From the light of the closet, he sees Lucy Quaid and Madeline Drake huddled together. Madeline is crying, and she's covered in blood. Lucy is dry-eyed, but her face is pale. Next to them is Wes with a hole the size of a fist in his chest, blood pouring from the wound.

"It's right there," Lucy says, voice shaking and nodding toward the revolver lying on the floor next to them. "She had to do it," Lucy says. "He was killing her."

"Don't move," Jamie says, watching the two women carefully. "An ambulance is on its way," he says. "Who else is in the house?" he asks.

"No one," Lucy says.

"How about the ranch hand? Trent?" Jamie says, peering down at Madeline.

"No," Lucy says, trying to wipe the blood from her sister's face, just as Trent appears in the doorway.

He takes in the bloody scene in front of him, and his face goes white. "Oh my God," Trent says.

"Go wait for the ambulance," Jamie orders. "Now!"

Jamie tries to get a good look at Madeline's injuries, and through the blood he sees an angry red welt encircling her neck and a leather belt lying on the ground next to her. "Wes did this?" he asks, addressing Lucy, who nods, her eyes wild with fear. "And she shot him?"

"We both did," Lucy says.

"You both shot him?" Jamie asks in surprise. "Where's the other gun?"

"There's just the one," Lucy says. "It happened so fast."

"Okay, lie down on the floor, and put your hands behind your back."

"But why?" Lucy asks, still clutching to Madeline. "He was choking her. I kept trying to pull him off, but he was too strong."

"We'll sort through it, but for now lie facedown. Do it!"

Lucy complies but continues to talk. "He wouldn't stop. He was so angry. I grabbed his gun. I told him to stop, but he wouldn't listen."

"Stop talking," Jamie says. He snaps a pair of handcuffs around Lucy's wrists, then rattles off her Miranda rights and asks if she understands.

"Yes," Lucy says, her words muffled by the floor. "Madeline? Madeline? Are you okay? Is she okay?"

Madeline is still crying, gasping for air and unable to speak, and Jamie takes a closer look at the injuries around her neck. Her trachea and face are swollen, and small crescent-shaped abrasions line her neck where he imagines her fingernails dug into her skin hoping to loosen the belt. "Madeline," Jamie says, "the ambulance is on its way. It's going to be okay. Is that what happened? Did Wes try to kill you?"

Madeline looks up at him. Her gaze is unfocused, and small

red pinpoints dot her eyes and lids. Broken blood vessels from
the attempted strangulation.

She gives a slight nod. "Johanna," she rasps. She winces as
if she just swallowed broken glass. "She knew," Madeline says
hoarsely, each word an effort. "I think he did it. I think he
killed Johanna. There are pictures of what Wes was doing to
me. Johanna was the one who took them."

Jamie runs the scenario through his mind. Initially, he
thought that Wes and Johanna were having an affair, but this
makes sense. What had Wes texted Johanna? Johanna, come
on. You know me. And Johanna had responded, No more secrets.
The secret wasn't an affair, it was domestic abuse.

"The baby," Madeline rasps through her damaged vocal
cords. "I think it's coming."

"No!" Lucy cries, struggling against her restraints. "No!
You have to help her. It's too early." Jamie helps Lucy to her
feet and leads her to a corner of the bedroom.

The sound of approaching sirens fills the air, and within
minutes EMTs flood the room. They are loading Wes and
Madeline onto stretchers when Lucy asks, "Is he dead?" Her
words are lost in the chaos of the scene. Jamie knows Wes
is probably dead, and if he isn't, he'll never be able to open
his eyes or speak again. He also knows that whatever secrets
Wes Drake had, he has taken them to the grave.

HOURS LATER, BACK in his motel room, Jamie lies on the bed,
staring up at the ceiling. He and Sheriff Colson spent the last
several hours interviewing Lucy Quaid, who repeated everything she had said to him earlier. She entered the room to find
Wes choking Madeline, she tried to stop him, and when he
wouldn't she was able to grab his handgun and use it against
him. Though the bullet struck him in the shoulder, Wes kept
coming, turning his rage on Lucy and knocking the firearm

from her hand. There was a struggle, with Madeline coming up with the gun and firing the final bullet.

Colson asked Lucy if Wes was so intent on killing his wife, why didn't he just shoot her with the gun he had with him? Why slip off his belt and try to strangle her? Jamie thought he knew the answer—domestic abusers liked to inflict pain, liked the control they had over their victims, and besides, strangling was quieter than a gunshot. In the end, they let Lucy leave the station. Her story made sense given the evidence. They found the pictures documenting Madeline's abuse in the desk drawer in the stable office and the originals on Johanna Monaghan's home computer. From where they sat, the shooting was justified.

And for now, in Jamie's mind at least, Wes is still the main suspect in the murder of Johanna. Between the photos of him entering the barn behind her just before the explosion, the threatening text messages, and the fact that she knew about the domestic abuse, it's their best bet, though there are some loose ends he needs to tidy up.

And then there's the second murder now linked to Wes, though Jamie hasn't voiced this suspicion aloud. He got there too late. Wes Drake was brain-dead before Jamie had the chance to ask him about Juneau, before he could beat the truth out of him, and now he'll never know what happened to his sister. The thought makes him want to break every piece of furniture in this hellhole of a room.

He reaches for his phone. He expects the call to go to voicemail, but Tess picks up on the third ring.

"Jamie?" she asks groggily. He glances at the alarm clock on the bureau. Five in the morning. He finds he can't speak. Grief has coiled itself around his vocal cords. "Jamie?" Tess repeats, this time on high alert. "What's going on? Are you okay?"

"I just wanted to hear your voice," he manages to say finally.

"Well, you picked quite the time to hear it," Tess says, not meanly, but her words aren't filled with the warmth he'd hoped.

He wants to tell Tess about Nightjar, about walking down the dark mountain roads, about the man who took Juneau, but all he can say is "I'm almost done here. Just a few more days and I'll be able to head home. I've got a lot to tell you."

"Good," Tess says. "That's good." Silence stretches between them, and Jamie wants to lie here with his phone pressed against his ear listening to Tess's breathing until he falls asleep. "But don't wait until you get home," Tess says. "Call me tonight. I want to hear all about it."

CHAPTER 40

JAMIE

ONE WEEK LATER, Jamie once again wakes up in his room at the Grandview. Something still isn't sitting right with him about the case. Tess says she understands, but Jamie isn't so sure. Their late-night phone conversations are becoming more and more stilted, and it feels like they're right back where they started.

Jamie crawls from the bed and slips on his shoes and a sweatshirt. He wheels his bike from the room and down the metal steps and begins to ride toward the mountains.

In the dark his head begins to clear, and he thinks about the three women in Wes's life he was determined to silence—Johanna, Madeline, and Juneau. Wes is now a proven domestic abuser. Madeline had the injuries to prove that. The latest update is that she is still in serious condition, and the doctors are doing their best to stop her labor. Juneau, though her remains have never been found, most likely faced a similar ordeal at the hands of Wes. Jamie was beaten so badly by the person who had taken Juneau that he had been unrecognizable.

It's Johanna's death that doesn't fit the pattern. Wes was a hothead who used his fists and his feet to get his point across, so why had he planted an IED? Wasn't Wes more likely to isolate Johanna and make her disappear as he did Juneau?

By the time he finds himself back at the sheriff's office, he's no closer to answering those questions. He should feel good at being able to close two cases at once, and probably a third, but something doesn't quite fit. He begins to read through Wes's financials that Greta sent.

After two hours, the numbers are blurring, and all Jamie knows is that that the Drakes are obscenely wealthy. Tucked within the documents is one sheet of paper with the letterhead of the Woodson County Courthouse at the top. It's a quit-claim deed that shows the transfer of property from an LLC called Mustang River Ridge to Lone Tree Ranch. He finds the signatures at the bottom of the deed. For some reason, Dix Drake has deeded millions of dollars of land to his brother.

For the last week, he's been spending hours each day reviewing security-camera footage from the hardware store in Snowcap where the PVC piping, duct tape, and double-headed nails were purchased. Today's no different, and for the next six hours he watches the footage until he thinks his eyes are going to start bleeding. Finally an image appears on the screen. The video isn't the best quality, but it clearly shows the items being purchased and who is buying them.

Bingo. Jamie makes a call to Greta and asks her once again to contact the US assistant attorney to arrange for another search warrant ASAP. Fifteen minutes later, Greta faxes him a copy of the signed warrant.

He makes another call. All he can do now is wait.

An hour passes, then two. Jamie grows antsy, wondering if by triggering the warrant he's tipped his hand. But it can't be helped. They have to do things by the book.

"Agent Saldano."

Jamie looks up to see Ruby standing in the doorway. "Dix Drake is here. He wants to know when his brother's remains will be released from the medical examiner's office. They told him to call you."

Wes's brother. Jamie takes a deep breath. "Can you take him to one of the interview rooms?" he asks. "I'll meet him in there."

He stops in the restroom to splash cold water on his face in hopes of clearing the cobwebs from his head.

Carrying his laptop and a file folder, Jamie steps into the interview room and finds a large man sitting behind the table. He is hunched over the cup of coffee that Ruby has given him.

"Mr. Drake, I'm Agent Saldano, and I'm sorry about your loss," Jamie says, pulling back a chair and taking a seat in front of Dix.

Dix looks at him, his face awash with grief. He looks like his brother, handsome but not as lean. He's broad-shouldered and thick-necked and has the physique of a man who does manual labor but drinks a lot of beer. He gingerly shifts in his seat. Of course he must be in pain, Jamie thinks, remembering the man had to have his spleen removed because of the explosion.

"I just don't understand," Dix says helplessly. "The bomb and coming after Madeline like that. It doesn't make any sense."

"These things rarely do," Jamie offers. "You didn't know about the troubles Wes and Madeline had?"

"Not at all," Dix says, shaking his head. "I mean, I knew Wes had a temper—he was my brother, I grew up with him—but he loved Madeline, and I can't imagine him hurting her that way." Tears fill Dix's eyes, and he wipes them roughly away. "Did they really have to kill him?" he asks.

"All the evidence points that way," Jamie says. "If they hadn't stopped Wes, he would have killed Madeline and their baby."

"God, the baby," Dix says, as if just remembering his sister-in-law was pregnant. "Is the baby okay?"

"I don't know," Jamie says honestly. "I hope so."

Dix clears his throat and runs a hand across his wide face. "So what do I do now? What are the next steps?"

"I just have a few follow-up questions for you about the explosion," Jamie says.

"Certainly," he says. "Whatever you need."

"Since I'm questioning you, I need to read you your rights," Jamie says.

"Why?" Dix asks, confused. "Wes did this. I didn't have anything to do with what happened. I'm not under arrest, am I?"

"No, no," Jamie says. "Nothing like that. It's standard when we interview witnesses. It's for your protection. If you'd rather have your attorney present . . ."

"That's okay," Dix says with the wave of his hand. "I want to help."

Jamie reads Dix his rights and then slides the land deed he discovered earlier in front of him. "Tell me about this."

Dix stares at the paper for a long moment before speaking. "I deeded my brother a chunk of land. That's all."

"But why?" Jamie asks. "I looked but couldn't find any actual bill of sale. You just gave your brother the land? It's worth—what?—three hundred thousand per acre?"

Dix shifts uncomfortably in his chair. "I've got plenty of land left from my father's estate, and Wes wanted to expand the horse-brokering business. I was happy to help."

"That's very generous," Jamie says.

"I loved my brother," Dix says, his voice cracking. "Now, is there anything else? I really need to make arrangements for Wes's funeral."

"Just one more thing," Jamie says, turning his laptop screen so Dix can see it. "Can you tell me what you were purchasing PVC piping, duct tape, and nails for?" Jamie presses Play and watches Dix's face as he sees himself on the screen placing PVC piping and two rolls of duct tape on the counter.

"Wes asked me to buy those things. I didn't have any idea what he was going to use them for."

"Okay," Jamie says, laying a piece of paper in front of Dix. "Could be. But right now your property is crawling with federal agents looking for anything that could have been used to make the bomb that killed Johanna Monaghan."

Dix's face turns stony. "I had nothing to do with that."

"I don't think Johanna was the target," Jamie says. "Your brother was, but Johanna went into the barn and accidently triggered the trip wire." Dix shakes his head but stays silent.

Jamie's phone dings, and he lifts it to check his messages.

Found it. PVC, nails, duct tape, plus a notebook filled with notes. We got him.

Jamie smiles at Dix. "Dix Drake, you're under arrest for the murder of Johanna Monaghan."

"No," Dix says, getting abruptly to his feet. "I didn't do anything."

"Turn around, and put your hands behind your back," Jamie says.

"I didn't do it," Dix says, face taut and hands clenched. He tries to charge past Jamie, and the two go down to the floor in a heap. The interview room door opens, and Sheriff Colson and Deputy Ladd appear. While he and Dix are the same height, Dix weighs a good fifty pounds more, but Jamie is lither and faster and quickly pins his legs while Colson and Ladd hold down his shoulders.

Jamie's eyes lock on Dix's fawn-colored, metal-tipped cowboy boots. His blood freezes in his veins as he sees the face of an owl staring back at him. Not an owl, Jamie decides. The engraving and stitching on the boots give the impression of a winged animal with black eyes. He's seen these boots before.

Twenty-seven years ago, when Jamie lay broken and battered in a roadside ditch. He saw these boots approach him, illuminated by the beam of his assailant's flashlight, then pause before drawing back and striking him over and over and over in the head. He feels the blood pooling in his head, his heart hammering in his chest.

They flip Dix over onto his back, handcuff him, and bring him to his feet. He is at least six-four with shoulders as wide as a linebacker's, and Jamie feels as small and vulnerable as the twelve-year-old he was nearly three decades ago. Everyone is breathing hard, sweating.

"Nice boots," Jamie says when he catches his breath. "Is that a bird on your boots?" He looks down at the metal tips. "An owl?"

"A nightjar," Dix says, glaring at him. "I get them custom-made."

Wes Drake wasn't his attacker. It was Dix Drake, his older brother. Jamie feels it viscerally. His once-broken jaw aches, and his skull radiates with pain. He clutches the tabletop in front of him to keep from swaying but steps toward Dix. "I know what you did," Jamie says, staring into the man's flat, emotionless eyes. "You killed her."

They both know Jamie isn't talking about Johanna Monaghan.

"Prove it," Dix says with a smirk as Colson and Ladd lead him from the room.

Jamie knows it will be nearly impossible to prove, but he won't stop trying. It had to be blackmail. Wes must have known that Dix killed Juneau and nearly killed Jamie. How else would Wes have found Jamie half-dead in the overgrown ditch all those years ago?

He'll reinterview everyone who was in town at the time of Juneau's disappearance, he'll test every bit of evidence in search of a forensic connection, and he'll find a way to search the Drake property until his sister's body is discovered. At least, Jamie thinks, they'll get Dix for the murder of Johanna and he'll go to prison for the rest of his life.

Took you long enough. He feels Juneau at his elbow.

"You could have just told me, you know," Jamie says, and he can almost hear his sister's laugh.

CHAPTER 41

MADELINE

One year later . . .

A LATE-AFTERNOON WARM wind sweeps down from the mountains, lifting the hair from Madeline's neck. It has been a long, frigid winter, and summer's arrival is a welcome balm after so many months cooped up inside. For months, Madeline was afraid that there would be a knock on her door and the sheriff would be there to arrest them for the death of her husband. The knock hasn't come. Yet. Blackjack whinnies and dips his head into the tender new grass in the meadow and chews it with his large yellow teeth. Pip runs ahead, then backtracks as if urging them forward. Chubby fingers are interlaced within Blackjack's coarse dark mane, but he pays no mind. Sitting on the saddle in front of Madeline, tethered to her chest, is Isla, now a year old.

In the front-facing carrier, Isla begins to squirm and fuss, so Madeline brings Blackjack to a stop and carefully throws a leg over the saddle and eases to the ground. She releases her daughter from the harness and sets her down in the meadow carpeted with thousands of yellow bells that have replaced the crater that the gender reveal gouged into the earth. Isla gathers up fistfuls of the flowers in her pudgy hands and squeals with delight, Blackjack bends his sleek neck to the ground and nibbles on green needlegrass, and Pip chases a grasshopper from clover to clover.

"Madeline!" comes a voice across the meadow. "It's almost time!" Madeline shades her eyes against the sun to see Lucy waving them toward her. They are dressed exactly the same: tan breeches, knee-high black leather riding boots, and long-sleeved T-shirts embroidered with a small dogwood tree above the heart.

The ranch is, once again, decorated for a party. There are balloons and flowers, but instead of champagne and fancy appetizers and people yelling about pistols and pearls, there is lemonade and cake and bouncy houses. And Reba agreed to come back and sing. The party is in celebration of the grand opening of the Lone Tree Equine Retreat Center—paid for through the trust created from Madeline's inheritance from Wes.

Madeline decided to use the same caterer they had for the gender reveal, but there is no Mellie. Last Madeline heard, Mellie left Nightjar. She tries not to have any ill will toward the young woman who had an affair with her husband and manipulated her way into their home. She was one of Wes's victims too, and Madeline knows all too well how good her husband was at controlling and manipulating the women in his life. Admittedly, Madeline was under his spell for a long time but finally came to the realization that one day he would kill her and leave their child motherless.

She's learned to think for herself, to follow her instincts, to be a hand up for those who feel like they are in those impossible situations with seemingly no way out. This is her life's mission now.

After Lucy and Madeline shot Wes and the ambulance arrived, Madeline rode with him to the hospital in Jackson. The EMTs had worked on Wes during the drive, his blood pooling over the side of the stretcher and onto the floor. Madeline kept expecting Wes to push them aside and lunge at her, but he hadn't. Twenty minutes after they arrived at the hospital, he was declared dead. And though she once loved her husband beyond reason, when Madeline heard the news, all she felt was profound relief.

Though the injuries to Madeline were necessary in order to make the entire scene look authentic, she and Lucy had gone a step too far. Both Madeline and the baby were in distress, their heart rates dipping dangerously low. Madeline was convinced this was her punishment for murdering Wes. She had been trying to protect her child from a man who was controlling and violent, but what if she had, instead, been the one to put her daughter in danger? It was touch-and-go, and Madeline spent a week in the hospital under close supervision. A week later, she gave birth to Isla—beautiful, healthy Isla.

Madeline bends down and picks Isla up from the grass. She lifts her to her shoulder and moves toward her sister, while Blackjack and Pip follow behind at a leisurely pace.

Was what she and Lucy had done murder? Madeline still lies awake at night for hours on end, wondering. Lucy, on the other hand, sleeps like a baby. When Madeline went back home for her stepfather's funeral, they'd had tense words about the inheritance. But then Lucy saw her bruises and figured out what was going on. Lucy had urged her to go to the police, but Madeline knew that would never work—Wes had resources beyond what they could imagine. He would weasel his way out of the allegations or kill Madeline, whichever came first. "He has to die," Lucy had finally said. "We have to kill him." They brainstormed and planned for hours until it all came together. What Madeline didn't expect was for Lucy to show up the night of the gender reveal party. Their original plan was to wait until after the baby was born, but unknown to Madeline, Johanna had reached out to Lucy.

Dalton had been wrong, as had Madeline. Johanna wasn't having an affair. But she had been covertly in contact with Lucy giving her updates and letting her know that she thought the abuse was escalating. Johanna hadn't known about Madeline and Lucy's plan to kill Wes but, like them, believed that Madeline was in grave danger.

The stepsisters are careful not to talk about any of that now. Who knows if they are being monitored by law enforcement?

Madeline, for her part, tried to lie low for the past six months, a nearly impossible feat after Wes's death and the arrest of his brother. Those headlines have been replaced with new ones, positive ones about Lone Tree Ranch.

"Are you ready to go?" Lucy asks, squeezing Isla's chubby foot. "Trent has everyone in their seats, ready to go."

Madeline nods, and together they walk toward the outdoor equestrian ring, the bleachers filled with over two hundred people, all waiting for Madeline to speak. They pass a newly constructed gazebo and garden, filled with flowers and plants and bird feeders, named in honor of Johanna.

Madeline passes Isla to Lucy and walks to the dais erected in the middle of the ring. She climbs the steps, her heart fluttering as she approaches the microphone.

"Welcome to Lone Tree Equine Retreat Center," she says. "My sister Lucy and I revamped and renovated this space for our nonprofit, offering adaptive riding classes for those with developmental and physical challenges and hippotherapy for those who have experienced trauma due to domestic abuse. We even have special programming for veterans, created especially for their unique needs. In addition to the state-of-the-art facilities, we have world-class equestrian trainers, counselors, nutritionists, physical therapists, and more."

Madeline looks around the arena. Lucy gives her a thumbs-up, and Trent, now holding Isla, smiles at her broadly. She recognizes a senator and a congresswoman as well as some of the wealthiest and most powerful members of the community. But what makes Madeline's heart soar are all the children and families here to help celebrate.

"I got the idea for the retreat center," Madeline goes on,

"from something Lucy said when we were teenagers. *Horses make everything better. You cannot not be happy when you're riding them. If every sad, broken person could come ride a horse, things would instantly get better.*'

"My sister was right. I have always turned to horses when things got hard—when friendships and boyfriends came and went, when our mother died, when our father died." Madeline scans the audience, and she can tell they are moved by her words. She notices a woman in the third-row bleachers who looks vaguely familiar. She's holding an infant and staring intently at Madeline.

Madeline clears her throat. These final few sentences are the hardest to say. "After what happened here at the ranch a year ago, after I nearly died . . . after my daughter Isla nearly died . . . one of the first things I did when I was able was take Blackjack for a ride."

Madeline's eyes keep flicking back to the woman holding the infant, and she loses her place in her speech, fumbles and then continues. "The thing about horses here at Lone Tree Ranch is their unique ability to instantly know what their rider needs. With their gentle eyes, their calming presence. I know better than anyone how lucky, how privileged, I am to still be here, and I want to share this sacred, special place with others who need time to heal."

The arena explodes with applause, and Madeline invites everyone to eat, drink, and tour the facility. She's just about to step down from the dais when realization hits her like a lightning bolt. The hair is now shoulder-length and no longer red, but the woman is unmistakably Mellie Bauer, holding a child who looks to be at least three months old.

With Isla back in her arms, Lucy approaches full of smiles and compliments for Madeline's speech, but Madeline is frozen in place. "What's wrong?" Lucy asks and follows her gaze toward the third row of the stands where Mellie still sits, as the crowd of people step past her down the bleachers. "Oh my God," Lucy says. "Is that Mellie?" Madeline nods. "Do you think that's his baby?" Lucy asks.

"I don't know," Madeline says. The timing could fit. Mellie may not have been pregnant when she first came to the ranch after the explosion, but that doesn't mean she wasn't pregnant when she left.

Mellie gets to her feet and shifts the baby to her other shoulder.

"What are you going to do?" Lucy asks.

"If the baby is Wes's, I'll do what's right," Madeline says. "That baby deserves to be taken care of, just like Isla. I'll pay her, and then hopefully she'll just go away." Madeline knows she sounds confident but can't help remembering Mellie's final words to her.

Madeline watches as Mellie straightens her spine and gives Madeline a little wave and a sly smile, her eyes hard.

This is not over.